William Eleazar Barton

A Hero in Homespun

A Tale of the Loyal South

William Eleazar Barton

A Hero in Homespun
A Tale of the Loyal South

ISBN/EAN: 9783337078317

Printed in Europe, USA, Canada, Australia, Japan

Cover: Foto ©Andreas Hilbeck / pixelio.de

More available books at **www.hansebooks.com**

A

Hero in Homespun

A Tale of the Loyal South

By

William E. Barton

Author of *Life in the Hills of Kentucky*, etc.

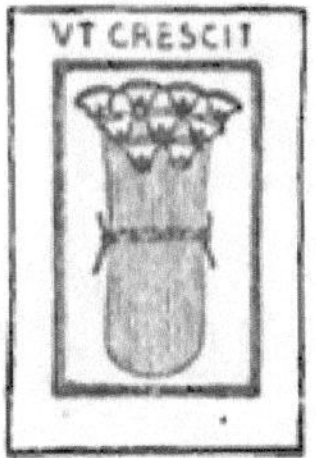

Lamson, Wolffe and Company

Boston, New York and London

MDCCCXCVII

Norwood Press
J. S. Cushing & Co.—Berwick & Smith
Norwood Mass. U.S.A.

To Her

*Who spent the First Years of our Married Life
with Me in the Mountains of Kentucky
and Tennessee
And whose Presence and Inspiration
abide to this Day*

Preface

How much of this book is history and how much is fiction will be apparent to readers familiar with the history. To extend popular knowledge of the Civil War as it affected a large but almost unrecognized body of our people, this volume has been written. The form of fiction has been employed to permit a larger use of incident and personal experience, and to allow greater freedom of treatment, but the historical background is believed to be true to fact. I have thought well not to locate too definitely the home of my principal characters. The name and some of the characteristics of Roundstone Creek, in Rockcastle County, Kentucky, have been borrowed and removed to a valley some fifty miles remote. With this exception, the geography of the book is correct.

I have had to allow my characters freedom of speech, even though they sometimes speak unwisely or too harshly. They lived in a day when men's passions ran high, and it would misrepresent them to tone down their utterances to the more temperate spirit of our time. I need not explain that I do not in every case share the views expressed. I should feel grieved if any word herein contained should seem to breathe a present spirit of bitterness. Seven years of residence in the South taught me how great is the need of charity in our judgments upon those to whom the war involved such momentous choices as it did the people of the South. The South to-day is loyal, and a considerable part of it has always been so.

I desire to thank the friends — too many to be named — who during the last twelve years have aided me in the securing of incidents for this under-taking. For aid in gathering historical material, I am especially indebted to Mr. Arthur M. Knapp of the Boston Public Library. I wish also to acknowledge the courtesy of the railroads passing to and through the region described, — the Big Four; the Southern ; the Queen and Crescent; the Nashville, Chattanooga, and St. Louis ; the Louis-ville and Nashville; and the Knoxville, Cumberland Gap, and Louisville. These, on our recent tour of three thousand miles, placed all possible facilities at the disposal of author and artist for the careful study of the field.

Thrice in the history of our country, at King's Mountain, at the battle of New Orleans, and in the Civil War, the homespun hero of the southern Appalachians has emerged from his obscurity and turned the tide of battle. Thrice he has returned to his mountain fastnesses and been forgotten. I have called him forth again, and am sending him out in hope that he may be better known to his countrymen. I have seen him in his home, and have great respect for his whole-souled hospitality. I have followed his track where he stained with patriotic blood a score of battlefields. I have confidence that he will be loved the more as he comes to be known the better, and that his great work will not forever fail of cordial recognition. And so to my Hero in Homespun, as he enters somewhat bashfully a world that is mostly new to him, I bid a hearty Godspeed and farewell.

W. E. B.

Boston, Sept. 1, 1897.

Contents

List of Illustrations

A Hero in Homespun

I

The Frolic at Hanson's

"GOIN' acrost to Hanson's, Jack?"

"Bimeby. Ma's goin' atter while to help with the supper. I'll wait an' pack some dishes over for her. You're goin' early."

"Yes. I allers 'low to be on time to a frolic. I'm fust to git thar an' the last to leave, or cal'*late* to be. That was the way with Washington, I've heerd: he was fust for war, an' the last fur peace, an' allers ready fur a hoedown."

"You got yer fiddle, Steph, I see. Goin' to be any dancin'?"

"Wall, not so awful much, I reckon. The Hansons is professors, but not right strict about sech like. Hank ast me to bring the fiddle over, an' sorter see wich way the cat jumped. Ef Mis' Hanson don't say nothin' agin it, an' they ain't no reason wy not, wy mebby I'll see how rosin sounds on catgut. But they didn't want to say nothin' 'bout it, fur Preacher Tate don't like it, an' they belong to his church."

"Yes, I knowed they was Babtis'. But they ain't quite so strict as the Methodis'."

"The *Reg'lar* Babtis' hain't, but Preacher Tate is Hardshell. He hates a fiddle wus'n pizen. Wall, I mus' be goin'. They hain't goin' to be no fun till I git thar, as the feller said wen he was goin' ter be hung." Steph Crowell patted his fiddle with the end of his fingers, and picked a little at the strings. "By the way, Jack, have you seen them kinfolks o' the Hansons' that's visitin' from Kaintuck?"

"Yes, I ben over two or three times sence they come. Hank ast me to come acrost an' visit with his cousin Eph."

"With Eph, hey? I 'lowed hit war the gal. They say she's a main scorcher. Sam Marshall told me he seed her at church the secon' Sunday, wen they was preachin' at Liberty Hill, — ole Preacher Post preaches thar the secon' Sunday, — an' he 'lowed she was purty as a picter. He means to shine up to her to-night. Ef I didn't hev to fiddle, I'd give him the wust possum hunt fur her ever *he* seed. But hit's the penalty o' bein' vartuous, an' makin' fun for the res', to hev to set by an' see hit, an' not have none theirselves. Say, Jack, *is* she purty?"

"I didn't notice p'tic'lar," said Jack, coloring. "She's good lookin' enough, I reckon."

"You didn't notice, ha, ha! You *kin* lie, Jack, cyain't ye? You didn't notice, hey? Well, you bes' ter look to-night, an' look sharp ef ye mean ter keep in with her."

Jack was evidently interested, but he changed the subject. "How's politics?" he asked.

"Sho 'nuff," said Steph. "I come by to ast ye,

an' plumb forgot huccum I ter come. I hain't seen ye sence the Greenville Convention. You was one o' the delegates, warn't ye? You'd best be a leetle mite keerful. What d'ye 'low ter do?"

"We 'low to have an election the first Thursday in August," said Jack, "an' see whether East Tennessy has got to go out o' the Union against her will."

"She won't go ef she don' hatter, that's plain enough. But I don't reckon hit's wuth wile to raise no dirt about hit. Hit's a groundhog case, as the feller said."

"I don't see why East Tennessy should go out o' the Union when she voted at two elections eighteen thousand clean majority against it."

"But ye see, Jack, the hull State voted agin separation in Febuary, an' changed its mind come June."

"East Tennessy didn't change its mind."

"No, my boy. But the vote didn't hold up to the vote in the winter."

"No, but that's easy 'nuff to account for. Still, it was three to one against separation. They was about as many votes cast for the Union as in the winter, but they counted more votes for separation."

"They voted a hull raft o' Jeff Davis' sojers, an' counted them in East Tennessy's vote. Hit didn't seem har'ly square, did hit?"

"Hit was a plumb shame!" cried Jack.

Steph threw one leg over the horn of his saddle, and leaned his elbow on his knee, holding his sandy chin whiskers in his hand. This was his attitude of seriousness.   The bobbing of Steph's chin when he laughed, and the twisting of it when he made his grimaces, always seemed to indicate with the sharp end of his beard the point of his joke.   There was often vaguely discernible an undercurrent of seriousness in his joking, but when he became thoughtfully sober, he held fast to his chin as the unruly member.

"You best be keerful, Jack," he said.   "I'm ten year an' better older'n you, an' I hain't tangled up with no fambly.   Ef I was in your place, I'd go slow.   Public sentiment's changin'.   In the winter the hull State wanted to stay in the Union, but the Governor and the Legislater passed an audience of secession, an' Fort Sumpter was fired on an' tuck, an' the people seed that the South was goin' to the devil an' the State was goin' with hit, an' they jes' 'lowed they mought as well git in out o' the wet. Now, you look at this here county.   Granger voted sixteen hundred to a hundred an' fifty-eight for the Union.   That was in Febuary.   In June, when Guv'nor Harris had passed that audience of secession, the vote stood about six hundred for the South to fifteen hundred for the Union.   That's a big difference."

"How did you vote?" asked Jack.

"Wall, that would be tellin'.   But hit was this way.   I've alers ben unfortunit."   Here Steph let go of his chin for a moment.   "You know that's wy I never got married.   I couldn't sorter seem to make up my mind.   I'd think I liked a gal, an' then in would come another, an' atwixt 'em I'd git all hesitated up.   I'm sorter lack the mule, you know, that starved to death halfway betwixt two haystacks. Well, now, when the fust election come, I voted for the Union, sho 'nuff. But when the June election come, I seed them Johnny Rebs at the polls, votin' theirselves an' watchin' how others voted, an' I says, says I, I'll split the difference. So I voted 'For Separation,' but 'Agin Representation,' in the secesh convention."

"You'll have a chance to vote agin come the first Thursday in next month," said Jack. "The Convention at Greenville adopted resolutions protesting against the action of the Governor and Legislature, and calling this election to make East Tennessy a separate State. We'll have our rights in a new, free commonwealth."

"I hope so, Jack. When you fellers git your new State, I'll come in an' run fur office. But don't say so too loud till ye git it done, or the rebs will arrest ye, an' then ye know yer got yer choice o' three things, — take the oath to defend the South, jine the rebs, or go to jail. Wall, this is pleasant, as the gal said about sparkin', but hit won't pay the preacher. I mus' go on. Look out for Sam Marshall. He's as sure to git that gal as ten cents is to buy ginger cake o' county cote day. Ef you let him git her, I'll fiddle fur him same's fur you. The fiddle's no respecter of persons, as the preacher says."

Jack stood at the fence for a few moments as Steph rode on. He was six feet tall, with brown hair that had just a touch of red, blue eyes whose pupils dilated at times till they seemed almost black, a fine brow, and a moustache that had survived the uncertain color of its first attempt and grown to a reddish brown. He was dressed up for the party now, in gray jeans trousers and unstarched white shirt. His coat was omitted till the last minute, but that also was of gray homespun jeans. Elizabeth Casey, who came to the door to say that she was almost ready to start, saw her son standing by the rail fence, the descending July sun lighting up his hair, and thought there was no boy in the neighborhood to compare with him.

"I'll come in a minute, mother," said Jack. "I'll go 'round to the barn a minute an' see to Jerry."

The horse whinnied as he came in sight, and Jack pulled a handful of unthrashed oats from a bundle and fed him from his hand.

"Want more, do ye? Well, ye shan't have another head. I've done fed ye a'ready. Well, yer a mighty fine boy, anyhow. I'll give ye just another handful."

He tossed the bundle back into the bay and sat down on an upturned bucket.

"Take the oath, jine the rebs, or go to jail, is it," he said to himself. "That's mighty slim pickin' fur choice. An' I don't reckon I could git into the Union army so fur away, an' I don't want to leave ma, nohow. I wonder ef Steph is as big a coward as he lets on." Then suddenly changing the subject, he said to himself, "She is pretty, sure enough. Sam Marshall wants her, does he? Well, we'll see ef Sam Marshall gits her."

The mountaineer mingles a clannish regard for family connections with an inconsistent disregard of ancestry. Who a man's brother is, is a matter of importance ; but who was his grandfather, few men care. But the Caseys possessed some family records, supplemented by tradition, which told the main events of their family life for several generations. It was in 1837 that James Casey, Jack's father, married Elizabeth Sevier, whose name told of her descent from the old hero of King's Mountain and the free state of Franklin, and moved from his father's house near Elizabethtown, down the Holston River to the home where Jack was born. There the young couple began life in a pole cabin, at first unchinked, and with a stick chimney, and "made their first crap o' corn" in the little deadening chopped by his axe. When he died, Elizabeth held the home and trained up her son in the way he should go.

James Casey was born near the close of the War of 1812, whose earlier engagements had been almost unknown in the mountains of East Tennessee. But the closing events gave to the region and to Alpheus Casey, James' father, a full share of struggle and of unrecorded glory; for the battle of New Orleans, when Old Hickory held the city with his cotton-bale fort, was won largely by Tennesseeans, and was fought with powder made in East Tennessee, of saltpetre leached from the earth in its caves, and of charcoal burned in its forests. In this patriotic work, superintended by Samuel McSpadden, of Jefferson County, Alpheus Casey, his kinsman by marriage, had his share, as well as in the actual fighting. Alpheus' father, Isaac Casey, was a young man of twenty when the Revolution broke out; and in that war, side by side with his father, the old Scotch-Irish Presbyterian immigrant, Alexander Casey, he did valiant service for the colonies against King George. Together they stood at Cowpens under Marion. Together they fought with Shelby and Robertson and Sevier at King's Mountain.

But this was not their first fighting. Before King's Mountain and Cowpens, before Monmouth or Bunker Hill, before even Lexington and Concord, the father and son had stood together, the son then only a lad of sixteen, and had faced the British troops at Alamance.

Who knows the real beginning of the American Revolution? For before as yet any blood had been shed, save that which a few months earlier had reddened the stones of King Street with the life-blood of the five victims of the Boston Massacre, a hundred men laid down their lives for American liberty at the Alamance Creek in western North Carolina. There, on the 16th of May, 1771, two thousand "Regulators" faced the royal governor, Tryon, with his regulars and the militia from the counties along the coast, in bloody protest against the right of the crown to tax the colonies. They fought till their powder and ball gave out, and then retreated, leaving of the slain of both armies two hundred on the field.

Tryon captured many of the Regulators, and executed six for high treason, and the rest fled to the mountains, or bought their lives with an oath of allegiance to the British crown. Among the many who refused to take the oath was Alexander Casey. He left behind his home in North Carolina, and, with his family on horseback, made his way across the mountains to the new and free commonwealth of Watauga in East Tennessee. His wife and the younger children rode, and carried a few domestic treasures with them; but Alexander and Alpheus trudged on foot, with axe and gun, sometimes chopping a trail through the wilderness to the new commonwealth where men were free.

The first battle of the Revolution was the battle of the Alamance, May 16, 1771. The first Declaration of Independence was that of the Scotch-Irish mountaineers at Mecklenburg, May 31, 1755. The first free commonwealth ever formed by American-born freemen was the Watauga Association in East Tennessee in 1772. For several years it exercised all the functions of statehood, and later its founders, Sevier and Robertson, had a share in the so-called state of Franklin, of which John Sevier was Governor. The love of liberty which was manifested in all these events was transmitted from father to son; and in the veins of Jack Casey there flowed, from his father, the blood of the heroes of Mecklenburg and the Alamance, of King's Mountain and New Orleans; and on his mother's side he was descended from the old pioneer and patriot, John Sevier.

Elizabeth Casey knew only the bare outlines of these great historic events. Her life had been one of hardship and privation. She had toiled long and hard to bring up to manhood her only son, left fatherless at the age of fourteen. Seven long years she had labored for him and he for her, and she had seen him grow from boyhood into the tall and strong young man he now was.

She was waiting for Jack when he came in from the barn.

"Put on yer coat, Jack, and pack them dishes fur me. I'm ready now, an' they'll be a-wantin' me to help git supper. I didn't know whar ye'd gone."

"I'm ready, ma. I jes' went out to the barn."

Together they walked along the path that led over the low ridge to the Hansons', the son ahead, and the mother following. She looked up at him with pride, he was so tall and strong. What a man he was! How much he knew! How brave and true he was! She had borrowed books and read them with him, increasing her own knowledge, beyond her previous ambition, to keep up with Jack. They had not read many, to be sure, but the Bible, "Pilgrim's Progress," "Robinson Crusoe," a school history, and a half dozen other books they had pored over till they knew them by heart. Now he was a man, and no young man on the creek was stronger, wiser, cleaner, or had more qualities to gladden a mother's heart than Jack. All this, and much more, she said to herself, and it was not the first time she had said it, as they walked over to Hanson's.

"Howdy, 'Liz'beth. Howdy, Jack," said Jacob Hanson, as they entered the yard. "Come over to help us out to-night, hev ye? Wall, I'm glad to see ye. These is my kinfolks, Mr. Eph Whitley and his sister Miss Jennie. This is Mis' Casey. You know her boy Jack, a'ready. These young folks has come over to sorter visit us an' goin' back nex' week to Roundstone, over in Kaintuck. We sorter thought we'd invite in the neighbor young folks, — that's you an' me, Mis' Casey, — an' give 'em a good time afore they go. Here comes some more. Howdy, Sam. Glad ye come. Didn't know whether ye'd be able to leave yer patients, ha! ha! I reckon a doctor has a power on 'em wen he fus' starts out. A heap o' doctors has more then than they ever git atterwuds, — they kill 'em off so fas'."

"Ah, you're always jokin' 'bout the doctors," returned the young Dr. Marshall. "You just wait till I git you where I can give you some med'cine I've got fur you in my pill bags! I'll show you what doctors are good for!"

"You won't git me. Not ef I kin help hit. Wen I die, I wanter die a nateral death, as the feller said wen he shot hisself to keep from gittin' hung. Here's Harry, now. Harry, take Doctor Sam over an' introduce him to yer cousins. I reckon hit's time fur me to git my coat on."

Jacob Hanson was a stout, jolly man in middle life, happy and hospitable, fond of a joke, and true to his friends. He soon reappeared with his coat on, and manifestly the less comfortable both in body and mind for the change.

"They keep a-comin'," said Jacob. "Wall, the more the merrier. Howdy, Bill. Howdy, Mary. Mighty proud to see ye. Bill, I didn't har'ly look fur ye. I thought you'd married a wife and therefore could not come. Glad you brought him, Mary. Go right in. Mother, here's Bill an' Mary Gossett."

There was a hum of welcome as they crossed the threshold. They had been married but a few weeks, and the story of their romance was known to all the neighborhood.

"They hain't but mighty few as pretty gals as Mary here to-night," said Henry Hanson to Jack. "Look at that head o' hair. Looks like flax off'n the swingling board."

"Fresh hetchelled," said Jack. "I never seen such hair. Bill deserves her."

"Sartin. He waited nine year fur her. Her paw didn't like Bill 'counter a furse he'd had 'ith Bill's dad, and Bill an' Mary 'lowed they'd wait till the ole man gin in or died, one."

"They didn't need to count on him a-givin' in."

"Well, they hain't nobody mournin' his death, as I've heerd. He had his good pints, but he was a main buster when hit come to hatin'."

Bill and Mary had married as soon after the death of her father as was counted proper, and their joy in each other showed itself in every act. There was something that was almost terrible in the love that shone from Bill's eye as he looked upon his flaxen-haired bride. There was the joy of the lover, but also the triumph that was almost that of a panther watching his prey. There was the memory of years of waiting, and of an affection that had been ever near the border line of hate.

"Tell us about the Convention, Jack," said Jacob, as the men gathered outside in the twilight.

"I reckon you know all about it," said Jack. "Judge Nelson presided and made a speech for the Union. The Convention was as strong for the Union as the one at Knoxville, first of June. Andy Johnson was at home, and he made a great speech. They say it was the biggest speech of his life. Judge Trigg spoke, and he called on loyal men to tear down the telegraph lines and pull up the rails of the track through Knoxville, to keep the rebels from crossing East Tennessy."

"A crowd of young fellers in Knoxville set out to do it t'other night," said Henry. "Parson Brownlow found it out an' persuaded them to not do it. But I heerd to-day that half them same fellers has jined the rebel army sence then."

"Sentiment is changin' fast towards the South," said Dave Hensie. "I kin see it among folks that's got kinfolks in ole V'ginny. Some that was strong for the Union a month ago, remembers their kinfolks that's got lots o' niggers an' is goin' with the South, an' they're a-goin' thataway, too."

"They warn't no sign o' that at the Greenville Convention," said Jack. "You ought to a-heerd Parson Brownlow talk."

"Oh, Brownlow is for the Union, everybody knows that."

"He ain't the only one. John Netherland spoke, and John Flemming and Temple of Knoxville and Judge Baxter and Captain Tom Arnold. They was delegates from every county in East Tennessy, and the hull Convention was strong for the Union."

"They ain't no doubt East Tennessy's thataway ef she kin have her way. Here comes Sam Marshall. What do you think about it, Doc?"

Sam Marshall entered the group, a tall, dark, slender young man with heavy black eyebrows. He had recently returned from Knoxville, where he had been studying medicine, and had begun to practise near his old home.

"I reckon we'll do what the State has voted to do," he said.

"I don't see," said Jack, "ef the country hain't got no right to coerce a State, what right West Tennessy has to coerce East Tennessy."

"And I don't see," said Sam, "if a State has no right to secede, what right East Tennessy has to secede from the rest of the State."

"Well, you kin burn my part o' Jeff Davis, anyhow," said Henry.

"An' mine o' Abe Lincoln," said Sam.

"You'd best not say that," said Jack.

"I'll say what I please. I'm for the South, an' I don't care who knows it."

"You'll have a chance to go South ef ye want to atter the August election. East Tennessy is goin' to cut out of the furrow an' stay in the Union."

"Here, boys," said Jacob. "This won't do. The ladies in thar is a-gittin' lonesome. No more politics, now."

But several times during the evening the question came up again.

The first part of the evening passed with mirth and song. The reigning queen of the frolic beyond a doubt was Jennie Whitley, the visiting cousin. Beside all the charm which novelty lends, she was truly a pretty girl. Her eyes were a dark brown. Her hair was heavy and rich. She was plump and rosy, and had a merry twinkle in her eye; and when she laughed, there was a dimple in her cheek that would have tempted any son of Adam to admiration, if nothing more. She was unused to so much attention as she here received. She was loved and admired at her home on Roundstone, but there she had grown up, and people saw her with the eyes that had known her from a child; and while every one admired her face and loved her sweet womanly way, no one had thought of her as a beauty. To-night she was the centre of an admiring group. The young men buzzed about her "like bees around a gum," as Steph Crowell said. Her brother Eph, who was with her, noted with admiration, and just a tinge of jealousy, the popularity of his sister. Yet he found a good measure of compensation with the young women of the party, among whom he found none more fair than his kinswoman, Martha Hanson.

After supper there was an awkward pause. No one knew just what to do. Everybody knew what all wanted to do, but it would never have done to go to dancing deliberately.

"Less play something," suggested some one.

"What shall we play?"

"Roll the platter."

That was the way it always began. The game was such a harmless one, and no one was supposed to think at first about the forfeits. They soon had enough of that, and tried "Weavilly Wheat." That is one shade worse, for it is played to music, and the players move about while they sing. Still, it is not dancing.

Then they played "Skip t'-m'-loo." The only worse thing about that was that some one proposed that Steph should play the air on his violin. The very next thing in this rapidly increasing descent was a Virginia reel, and that was dancing, certainly.

But it came about so gradually and so naturally, and withal so unexpectedly, that even a tender conscience had hardly a chance to slip in a protest edgewise before the dance was on.

But it was before the reel, and while they were playing " Skip t'-m'-loo," that the trouble came. Sam Marshall had bad luck. He was "it" twice in succession. Twice he stood in the middle of the ring, while the others marched about him in couples, singing admiringly, each of his lady,

> " Pretty as a red-bird, skip t'-m'-loo !
> Pretty as a red-bird, skip t'-m'-loo !
> Pretty as a red-bird, skip t'-m'-loo !
> Skip t'-m'-loo, my darling ! "

It was his duty to stand there until the song changed, and then snatch a partner for himself, while they sang,

> " Gone again !   Skip t'-m'-loo,
> Skip t'-m'-loo, my darling ! "

But when the time came, he missed his chance, being confused for the moment, and looking about for Jennie, whom just then he did not see ; and all the girls were snatched, and he was still in the ring, while they circled round him, singing,

> " I'll get another, skip t'-m'-loo !
> I'll get another one, prettier, too !
> I'll get another one, skip t'-m'-loo !
> Skip t'-m'-loo, my darling ! "

To be "it" once is no disgrace, though it always subjects a man to some pity and a few jokes.   But to be "it" twice makes a man the butt of the company through all the next threefold song.

Sam Marshall did not enjoy being ridiculed. He thought that among those who taunted him as he stood there the second time, Jack Casey's little joke was especially biting. It may have been. At any rate, Jack found himself in that round, just behind Jennie Whitley, and he was determined that the next time they were "gone again," the "other one" for himself should be Jennie, or he would know the reason why. Sam Marshall had a similar thought, and, flushed and angry, he stood in the middle of the ring, which was as large as the cleared-out room would allow, turning on his heel as the company moved, so as to face Jennie. This drew the attention of all, and he saw that his plan was detected. He also saw that Jennie noticed it, and was annoyed that he should be so constantly following her with his eyes, and attracting the attention of all to her; for all were now eager to see whether, having set his heart on one girl, Sam was again to fail, as a man is more likely to, who, being in the middle, risks all his chance upon one attempt. Seeing that he was annoying her, Sam turned away, yet timed the moving of the circle and the progress of the song, so as to be ready for a spring at the moment it should be time for Jennie to be "gone again." At the end of the next "skip t'-m'-loo, my darling," he turned suddenly, and attempted to seize Jennie, but, in his haste and his turning, slipped and fell sprawling on the floor amid shouts of derisive laughter, and when he picked himself up, red as a beet, and angry as a bull, he was again too late. Every man

c

had a partner. Jack Casey had Jennie's arm and was singing with the rest, and laughing as he sang,

"Pretty as a red-bird, skip t'-m'-loo!"

It was more than Sam Marshall could bear. His race was a hot-blooded one, and he was hottest of all. He regained his feet with an oath, and struck a savage blow at Jack, who caught him as he struck, and backing him against the wall, exclaimed,

"You git right out o' here, you coward, an' don't you never hit at me again or I'll thrash you, sure!"

With that, still holding Sam Marshall's hands, he backed him out of the door, and returned to the play. The game, after a moment of interruption, went on through that set, but then by unanimous consent they changed it, as people like to change from things that have involved unpleasantness, and they turned to the Virginia reel, and Jack danced in that with Jennie.

Jack had many compliments from the young men, when the party was breaking up, upon his agility, his courage, and his forbearance. To have so skilfully defended himself, to have humiliated his assailant in the presence of the whole company, and yet to have gone no step beyond what they counted the strictest propriety, and to have won for the rest of the evening the belle of the party, — all that was surely occasion for felicitation. But there were also reports of dire threats of the vengeance sworn by Sam Marshall. What he could do, Jack had no idea. He would hardly shoot him from ambush, — Sam Marshall was no coward, — and he did not fear any open assault. But he had a slight misgiving when he remembered how strongly he had spoken for the Union, and how pronounced Sam had been on the other side. Sam had acquaintances in Knoxville, too, among the officers there. He began to think it possible that Sam's vengeance might make itself felt in that way.

The young men and women did not allude to the sudden departure of Marshall until they separated to prepare for departure. Then the men talked about it outside, and the women within.

"Wasn't he brave, Jen? Wasn't you proud of him?" asked Jennie's cousin Martha.

Jennie did not attempt to conceal her admiration for Jack and the way he had behaved.

"He's a brave fellow," she said, "and treated me real nice."

"He is nice," said Martha. "I've knowed him sence he was a boy, and they hain't no nicer feller in all Granger County than Jack Casey."

Outside the men soon returned to the great question of absorbing interest. A few were for the South. A somewhat larger number were wavering, and disposed to go now with the State. But a considerable majority were for the Union, first, last, and all the time.

"By cracky, Jack!" said Steph Crowell, "you was the king bee to-night, sure! I'd a ben willin' to a broke my fiddle to a ben in your shoes. I would a broke a string, sure, so's to have an excuse to quit playin', ef I'd a stood any show. But you arnt it, Jack, you arnt it! But look out fur Sam Marshall!"

They were standing in the yard in the last stages of departure when a horseman drew rein at the fence.

"They's ben a battle," he cried. "They's ben an awful battle at Bull Run. The Yankees are defeated. Washington is about to be captured. The rebs is marching north, and the hull North is in terror. They's bonfires in all the cities of the South, an' they say the war will be over in three months, an' the South will be free."

They crowded to the fence and plied him with questions, and every detail brought fresh horror. The messenger soon rode on, and the people returned to their homes in the silence of a heart-breaking sorrow.

Later reports confirmed the news and added to the probability of the speedy triumph of the Confederate cause. It settled over East Tennessee like a pall. The election called for the first Thursday in August was never held, and when the Union cause rose from the ashes of that overwhelming disappointment, it was in another form, with no immediate thought of an independent commonwealth. Had East Tennessee adjoined Mason and Dixon's line, the attempt would not thus have failed. It was far from its friends, and in possession of hostile armies. But had Bull Run resulted in a Union victory, East Tennessee would have come into the Union, as West Virginia later did, an independent, loyal State.

II

The Soldier's Farewell

HENRY HANSON reined in his horse, wet with sweat, before the Casey cabin, one afternoon early in September.

"Good evenin', Mis' Casey.   Is Jack about?"

"Howdy, Henry.   Been ridin' hard, hain't you? Jack's still hidin' out, but I'll call him."

Elizabeth stepped across the rude porch, inside the door of the rough little cabin, and brought out a cow's horn, on which she blew three long blasts, then after an interval, three more.

She returned the horn to its place, and took up her sunbonnet, which, however, she did not wear, and came to the fence, her golden brown hair, that had been much admired in her girlhood, showing now and then a streak of gray in the sunlight.

"What's the news?" she asked, returning to the fence, and laying her sunbonnet upon it.

"Mighty bad news.   They're arrestin' Union men more than ever, and there ain't no prospect that them that's had to hide out kin come back. The rebs is a-goin' to invade Kaintuck.   Zollicoffer is a-goin' to push out from Knoxville, take Cumberland Gap, and move on north to the Ohio River."

"Law, law!   It don't seem possible.   But I'll be glad to have 'em go anywhere, so's we git shet on 'em, an' men don't have to hide out, an' women kin go about their work.   Here comes Jack, now."

Cautiously Jack entered the clearing, and, seeing his friend, came forward.

"Howdy, Jack.   How d'ye like sleepin' out?"

"Wall," returned Jack, with a faint attempt at humor, "they hain't no bugs in the beds a feller finds out in the woods."

"Been sleepin' right ou'door?"

"Slep' in the cave, mos'ly.   When it's clear and not too cold, I sleep out.   Where do you sleep?"

"Under the big rock whar it hangs over, fornent the barn, acrost the branch.   We're sorter whar we kin watch things, an' be out o' sight."

"Got yer horse yit, I see?"

"Yes, but had to hide him in the ravine furder up the branch from us, to keep the rebs from findin' him.   They ben atter him twicet."

"Mine's gone."

"Stole?"

"Yep.   Come an' got him night afore las'.   It was rainin' that night an' I had come in.   I heerd them ride up, an' I got out the back way, but it warn't Marshall an' his crowd that time.   It warn't me they wanted but the horse.   I fired at them as they was a-leavin', but I reckon I didn't git no game."

"I wisht you had!"

"So do I."

"I'm glad he didn't," said Mrs. Casey.   "I feel mighty bad about the horse, for I liked to ride him as well as Jack does.   An' I don' know how we'll ever make another crap without him.   But ef Jack had a-shot one o' them rebs, I don' know what we'd had to suffer. We're puttin' up with enough as it is."

"Do you reckon, Jack, that Marshall is at the bottom of all this?"

"Not all of it, I reckon, but he's got a finger in it, shore. Ever sence he jined the rebs las' month, he's ben a-ridin' round, huntin' down Union men, an' makin' 'em take the oath."

"I don't reckon he'll kill more men as a sojer than he would as a doctor," said Mrs. Casey, with scorn.

"Did Steph Crowell take the oath?"

"No; they brought him up, but he proved that he voted for separation, and they let him off."

"Dave Travers took hit, didn't he?"

"Yes, but he says he tuck it 'from the teeth out.' He had to do it or leave home, one, an' his pap is dyin' of a cancer, an' his ma is mighty triflin', you know, sence that time she got throwed off a horse goin' to mill."

"Hit was a mighty hard place to put Dave. I won't jedge him. But I hain't got nary tooth in my head that'll take an oath to support Jeff Davis. I wonder how much more o' this we gotter stand?"

"Well, I know how much more I'm goin' to stand. I hain't a-goin' to stand *no* more."

"What you goin' to do, Hank?"

"I'm goin' to enlist."

"Not with the rebs?"

"Not much!"

"How you goin' to git to the Union army?"

"I'm goin' to Kaintuck."

"Kin you enlist thar?   I heerd Gov'nor McGoffin' was for the rebs, an' is keepin' the State in an armed neutrality, as he calls hit."

"Gov'nor McGoffin's for the rebs.   An' so is the State Guard.   But the Legislatur is for the Union."

"Ef ourn had a ben we'd a had a different sort o' things round here now."

"Yes, they sold us out, the skunks!   Atter we'd voted the hull State, twenty thousand majority for the Union, too!"

"I'd like to make them hide out the way we hatter!   But how about Kaintuck?"

"Wall, the Blue Grass thar is secesh, same as West Tennessy is.   But the mountings is fur the Union, same's here.   An' they're goin' to raise troops, an' let the Gov'nor go to grass."

"How'd you hear?"

"I heerd at Rutledge to-day.   I heerd a heap more.   Zollicoffer's goin' to invade Kaintuck, as I was jes' tellin' your ma afore you come up; an' ef ary Union man wants to git through Cumberland Gap, he's got to make tracks right off."

"Well, I'd be mighty glad to hev him invade Kaintuck, or any other place, so's to git shet of him here," said Mrs. Casey.   "'Pears like we've hed our sheer o' the rebs."

"He hain't a-goin' to leave hyur fur good 'n' all, they say.   He's a-goin' to hold Knoxville, but push on an' git the Gap, an' then sorter look the ground over, an' ef all's well, he's a-goin' to move over into Kaintuck."

"How'd you hear tell o' all this?"

" Parson Brownlow, he sent word to Judge Green in Rutledge that ef ary Union man round here wanted to git inter Kaintuck he'd hev to hustle."

" They hain't killed Brownlow yit ?"

" No, he's alive an' a-kickin', an' a-printin' the *Whig*, same's ever."

" I didn't 'low Zollicoffer'd let him print it atter he tuck Knoxville."

" Wall, Zollicoffer's a Whig himself, they say, an' he used to be a printer, an' sot type in Knoxville, 'fore he got to be a reb an' a gin'ral. They say he's ben right good to Parson Brownlow, an' protected his office. But they can't bell that ole cat so's but wut he'll spit an' show his claws at the rebs."

" I didn't reckon Zollicoffer would protect nobody," interposed Mrs. Casey.

" Wall, he hain't hurt hisself a-protectin' Union folks out in the mountains, that's a fack."

" I shouldn't think he hed. He lets his sojers overrun the kentry, robbin' smoke-houses, stealin' chickens, arrestin' Union men, skeerin' women to death, destroyin' craps, an' stealin' hosses. I hain't hardly knowed how a bed felt sence he got to Knoxville," said Jack.

" Wall, 's fur's the arrestin's concerned, an' makin' folks take the oath, it's him's a-doin' hit, matter o' cose. An' they hain't no lack o' men like Marshall to sick him on to men they hate. But the fellers was a-sayin' to-day that a heap o' the stealin' he don't know about."

" He'd orter know."

" Wall, I ain't a-sayin' as how he don't. But the fellers was a-sayin' as how Brownlow wrote that

Zollicoffer hisself hain't so bad a feller, but he's on a bad side. But 'tain't wise fur us to stay hyur. I gotter git on. Like's not some Johnny'll be a-sneakin' up on us hyur. I'm goin' to Kaintuck an' 'list. The day atter the August election the Union men from Kaintuck commenced a-getherin' at Camp Dick Robinson, in Garrard County, an' a heap o' fellers from East Tennessy is a-getherin' at Camp Nelson, clost by on the Kaintuck River. I'm a-goin' to start to-night."

"Foot or hossback?"

"Hossback. Don' you want ter go 'long?"

"I hain't got no horse, an' I didn't 'low ter leave mother."

"'Tis too bad 'bout you a-losin' of yer horse."

"Say, Hank. Is yer pap a-goin'?" asked Jack.

"He's mighty anxious to, but ma teases him notter. I don't 'low he will jes' yit. You heerd tell, didn't you, 'bout arrestin' Preacher Tate?"

"No, I didn't. Wut's thet fur?"

"Wy, Sunday week he was holdin' meetin' at the Barren Forks, an' he prayed fur the Union. They've tuck him to jail to Knoxville!"

"The infernal hounds!" cried Jack. "An' he a' ole man, too."

"Yes, an' they've 'rested another ole Babtist preacher over in Campbell. They was some fellers goin' by to git into Kaintuck an' 'list. An' wen they went pas' the ole man's door, one o' the fellers pulled a flag out from under his shirt, were he'd ben a-hidin' hit, feelin' sorter safe 'caze he was gittin' nigh the Gap, an' they knowed the ole man was Union, an' they shuck the flag towards the house.

The ole man was a-settin' on his porch, a-readin' his Bible, an' wen he seed the flag, he jumped up an' cheered. That's ole man Post. They tuck him ter Knoxville, too."

"I hain't but mighty little use fur the Babtists," said Mrs. Casey; "but to put a minister o' the Gospel in jail, an' fur cheerin' the flag! Wicked men is waxin' wuss an' wuss, 'cordin' to Scriptur."

"Wall, Jack, I gotter go. I don' know's I'll ever see you agin."

"Hole on, Hank. Hit 'tain't right to hang onter yer. But I want to ast you a little more. Do you reckon ef I should go yer pap cud sorter look atter mother?"

"Wy, sartin he could, ef he kin look atter his own folks."

"O Jack!" cried Mrs. Casey, "you hain't a-goin'? Don' leave me here alone amongst the rebs!"

"I hate to do it, ma. I hate it powerful. But what *kin* I do? I hain't a-goin' to hide out furever."

"The rebs is a-goin' inter Kaintuck, didn't Henry say?"

"Yes, but that won't do us no good. They'll leave some on 'em here, an' they won't be no peace fur no man that kin fight till he gits out er hyur."

"But I'm all alone, Jack, an' a-gittin' old."

"Hank," said Jack, suddenly, "this here is somethin' ma an' me has gotter fight out alone. Ef I kin go, I wanter go with you. Wut time'll yer start?"

"Soon's it gits good 'n' dark. Ef you kin come,

we'll ride an' tie, an' 'twon't take us many days to
git thar."

"Wall, don' wait fur me. Ef I kin come, I'll
be thar. Goin' to take shootin' arms?"

"No. We hain't got but the rifle gun, an' pa
mought need hit. Besides, ef we should be ketched,
hit 'tain't pleasant for Union men to be found under
arms."

"I reckon ef I go I'd best leave my rifle fur ma,"
said Jack.

"Like's not she mought need hit, an' ef we git
through, the gov'maint'll furnish us with guns.
Good-by. Hope you kin go."

"Good-by. Ef I kin, I'll be thar soon atter
dark."

"Oh, say, Jack! Wy, ef you *don't* go, you know.
Wy, hit's sorter unsartin you know about me. An'
ef I shouldn't git back, wy, you know, you'll sorter
look atter pap, won't you? You know he's sorter
outspoken, an' hain't allers prudent. An' thar's
ma and the gals, too. But ef you do go, wy pap'll
do all he kin fur your ma."

"Good-by, Hank. But I've sorter got an idy
I'll mebby be with yer."

"Good-by, Jack; I hope so."

Jack Casey stood watching his friend out of sight,
while his mother stood beside him, leaning her head
upon the top rail of the low fence. It was a long
time before Jack turned and faced his mother.
They were simple people, with little sense of the
dramatic, and no thought of the heroic as related
to their poor, obscure lives. There was little that
to outward gaze seemed picturesque or interesting.

They were both roughly clad in homespun, he in jeans, and his mother in a tow dress of her own weaving, colored an uncertain shade with native dyes. It hung loosely upon her, and was made with regard to economy of material. She wore a checked apron, and carried in her hand a collapsible sunbonnet, which, with regard to conventionalities, she had taken with her to the road, but which now lay beside her on the fence. Even in her weeping she had thought to move it a little to protect it from her tears, and had buried her face in her apron. She now raised her head, gave her eyes a final wiping, twisted up her back hair, which had fallen down, and secured it in place with a horn comb.

"You're goin', be ye, Jack?"

"I reckon so, ma. I didn't want ter say so squar out 'fore Hank. I 'lowed mebby you'd sorter ruther lemme say hit fus' to you wen we's by ourselves."

"I knowed that was why, Jack. You're a good boy. Boys don' know how much their mothers keers fur 'em, Jack. Not allers, thet is. I reckon you know more'n a heap o' boys. They hain't no use in takin' on about it. Ef yer gotter go, wy yer gotter go, an' I'll see to things the bes' I kin. They hain't no stock to look atter like they used to be."

"Darn the rebs fur stealin' on 'em!" interpolated Jack.

"Don' swear, Jack. Hit don' do no good. But I reckon, Jack, you're goin' to be with me sech a leetle wile, — you needn't hide out the res' o' the

evenin' till dark, need yer?   I'd sorter like to have
yer 'round while I *kin* hev yer."

"No, ma.   I'll resk it.   Hit's a-gittin' sorter
late'n the day now.   The sun's gittin' sorter low.
They'll be some little things to do."

"Less do 'em together, Jack."

"Wall, I 'lowed to go through the corn an' see
ef they hain't a ear here 'n' thar thet I kin pick an'
hide back in the cave.   An' I did 'low ter grabble
the 'taters, an' take the biggest ones an' hide thar, too.
They's one ham an' a side o' bacon an' some squashes
thar aready.   I jis' wanter leave whatever they is
whar you kin git it, an' not no one else."

"They hain't time to grabble the 'taters, Jack.
But we mought look through the corn.   We kin
take it row 'n' row together, an' hit won't take long,
an' we kin sorter visit wile we *kin* visit, an' you
won't be much in sight in the corn."

It was all too short a task, and finished before the
sun was down.   The corn was just beginning to
ripen, and the ears that might be picked were few and
small; but these they gathered, and laid at the end
of the rows, and later Jack carried them to the cave,
while his mother cooked for him a few — a very
few — of the slices of the precious bacon, and baked
for his use four hard corn pones.   It was all she
could spare, and more than Jack would consent to
take.   But she insisted, and he took them.

They talked little, and what they said was mostly
about commonplace matters.   As fast as potatoes
got large enough, she would grabble them, and take
them to the cave.   As fast as corn ripened, she
would pick it and hide it there.   She would also

take there the blankets from Jack's bed, lest her apparent surplus should tempt some soldier beyond what he was able to bear. Indeed, she would take there a number of articles counted superfluities, and hold the cave in readiness for a dwelling and a fort if she should have need. The gun they hid under the floor of the house, carefully wrapped to preserve it from dampness; and Jack charged Elizabeth not to surrender it, but if need were, to hide that also in the cave. There, on a pinch, she could live for a time, if the house should be burned. But this was deemed improbable, especially after Jack was gone.

"I reckon I'm safer without you, Jack, sorter," she said. "They won't hurt a pore ole woman, an' they don' bear no gredge agin me."

"You'll be all right, ma. An' in about a month we'll come a-marchin' down through the Gap, an' we'll drive Zollicoffer back a heap faster'n he come. An' some day you'll be a-lookin' down the road, an' you'll see a cloud o' dust, an' you'll say, 'I wonder wut on airth is a-comin',' an' atter a wile you'll see it's somethin' blue. An' then you'll see it's sojers. An' then we'll come by, with the drum a-playin' 'Yankee Doodle,' an' the flag a-flyin', an' you'll come down to the fence whar you cried to-day, an' you'll see me an' you'll see the flag, an' you'll wave yer sunbonnet an' cheer. 'Pears like I kin 'mos' hear you now, ma, the way you'll do when you see us a-comin' back, the rebs a-runnin', full hickory, an' we chasin' 'em down the road, an' you out thar a-cheerin' me an' the flag, an' nary reb a-darin' to sass you."

"I reckon so, Jack.　Be ye right sure you'll come back?"

"Why, matter o' cose we'll come back.　The hull mountains is fur Lincoln an' the Union.　Wen we git out thar into the open, an' git our guns an' uniforms an' things, you better b'lieve we'll come back!"

This ought to have encouraged Mrs. Casey, but someway the uncertainty about the return was the thought that was uppermost in her mind.　She had borne it like a Spartan mother, ever since her first breakdown, but now she burst into tears again.

"O Jack!　My pore boy!　My only child! Mus' ye go?　My baby, Jack, ye don' seem to me har'ly bigger'n you was wen I useter sing you to sleep, an' you was roun' the floor an' under my feet.　I hater rub my eyes an' look twicet at you to make hit seem like you're a man.　O Jack, I know I'm a pore, foolish ole woman, an' I hadn't orter cry.　Hit hain't thet I'm skeered to be left alone, though it hain't real pleasant with them rebs all round a-plunderin' an' a-burnin'.　But, O Jack, O my boy!　'Pears jes' lack I wanter take yer right in my arms an' hole you like I useter, an' say I cyan't let yer go."

"Don' take on, ma, now don't.　I got jes' about all I kin stan' up under now.　I'm a-grittin' my teeth to keep from sayin' how I hate to leave you alone.　But they hain't no way to stay an' be at peace, only jes' to take the oath.　A heap is a-takin' hit 'from the teeth out,' but I hain't a-goin' to swar to no lies."

"No, Jack, ye hain't.　An' I hain't a-goin' to

hev you a-hidin' out forever, nuther, an' ketchin' yer death wen the cold nights come. Hit's bad enough in summer. They'll hev dry places fur the sojers to sleep, I reckon, won't they, Jack?"

"Oh, sartin. An' then hit hain't a-goin' to las' long. All we gotter do is to git up thar an' tell 'em how East Tennessy is loyal, an' the people jes' waitin' fur the ole flag, and they'll send us right back with a heap more, an' we'll hold East Tennessy in the Union."

"I reckon so, Jack. I hain't a-goin' to hang onter yer. Go an' do yer duty, lack your pa would a done."

"Hit's gittin' dark mighty fast, ma."

"Yes. 'Pears lack I never seed dark come on so quick atter the sun went down. You don' reckon hit's time to go?"

"I reckon it is, ma. I'd best be a-goin'. You bes' keep some o' them pones."

"No, Jack. You take 'em. Mus' yer be a-goin'? Good-by, Jack. An', Jack, wen you git away off, an' you lay down at night to sleep, you wanter think, Jack, says you, 'Ma's a-prayin' fur me,' says you. An' wen yer git inter battle, an' hit 'pears lack yer cyan't do wut the gin'r'l hollers out fur yer ter do, jus' says you to yerself, 'Ma's a-prayin' fur me,' says you, an' you go ahead an' do yer duty. An' ef there's ary rough fellers in the Lincoln army, like a heap o' the rebs, that's drinkin' an' swearin' an' gittin' inter devilmaint, an' they want yer ter go with 'em, you jes' says, 'No,' says you, an' ef they keep sorter urgin' you, an' a-pesterin' you so's you sorter feel lack doin' on it with 'em, says you to yourself, ' Ma's a-prayin' fur me,' says you.   An' hit'll be so.   Fur they won't be no wakin' hour, day nor night, that God a-lookin' down inter my heart, an' a-listenin' to hear ef I've got somethin' er other ter ast him, won't hear me a-prayin' fur you, ter help yer to be brave and clean an' true, an' spar yer life, an' fetch yer back.   Good-by, Jack."

"Good-by, ma.   I won't do nothin' that I wouldn't do ef you was thar or God."

" I know you won't, Jack.   Good-by.   Now you'll hatter hurry, cause hit's gittin' mighty dark, an' Henry won't wait."

He slipped out of the back door and pushed the latch-string in.   She stood with her head bowed against the door until the sound of his feet had died out, and then pushed the leather string through the hole again, and, raising the latch, crept out after him.   She was too late to overtake him, but she slipped along the path that he had trodden in his leaving, hoping to come near enough to hear the sound of his footsteps again without being heard. But he had gone rapidly, and she went slowly and quietly lest he should know that she had done so foolish a thing.   She followed him nearly to the house of Henry Hanson, and saw, as she came in sight of it, the light of the fire shine out for a moment as the door swung and some one entered. She waited, and after a time saw it open again, and two or three figures, she was not sure which, slipped out.   She wanted to go nearer, but feared to be seen, and felt sure that Jack would be ashamed if she should be detected in such an act of folly. Sadly she took her way back home, and, lifting the latch, entered the house that was left unto her desolate, and pulled in the latch-string. And then she dropped into a chair in the chimney corner, and her face sank between her knees, and she poured out a mother's grief and loneliness in prayers and tears for her boy who had left her to fight for the Union.

III

To Fight for the Flag

IT was a clear night, when summer was just sobering into autumn, that Henry Hanson and Jack Casey started on their lonely journey through the wilderness into Kentucky. Jacob slipped out with them, and went a mile on the way.

He gave them many directions, which were almost superfluous, for they were accustomed to finding their way through the woods, and knew well the first twenty miles of the road.

"You'll know Powell's River," said he. "Hit runs along the ridge-pole o' the rocks, sorter lack the rocks had fell down, an' stood up like the roof o' the house, an' the water runs down the ridge-pole, stidder down the shingles. Hit's a mighty quare trick the water plays thar. Wen you come to that, you're right under the shadder of the big Cumberland Mounting. The three States corners right in the Gap. You bar up stream to the right inter the pint o' V'ginny, whar it comes in like a smoothin' iron, and work up round the hill. Soon's you're through the Gap, you're safe in Kaintuck."

"We won't hev no trouble thet fur," said Jack. " I've ben to the Gap myself twicet, but it was by Rutledge an' Tasewell."

"You mus'n't go thataway to-night, ye know. 'Tain't safe. But hit'll give ye the gin'r'l *i*dy, to have went. Wen ye git to Kaintuck ye can't miss it. Yaller Creek heads up at the Gap. Foller hit down. They hain't no trouble to foller down stream. Then cross the Log Mounting an' go by Cumberland Ford, Barboursville, Mount Vernon, an' Crab Orchard to the Kaintuck River. Camp Nelson is on the river."

"What ef Zollicoffer has scouts ahead, an' we can't go by the Ford?"

"Then you gotter bar to the right, around through Harlan an' Clay, an' keep on till you come to the head waters of the Kaintuck River, an' foller them down. That's a long way 'round. But ef ye hatter go thataway, you mought find hit easy to go by Roundstone, an' see yer kinfolks."

"We'll git thar all right."

"Wall, keep together. Don't try no ride an' tie bus'ness. You'll git your horse stole, shore's you're a foot high. Jes' let Bill jog 'long, single footed, one o' you ridin' an' t'other holdin' to the stirrup leather, an' change wunct in a while. You hain't got no high water to ford except the Cumberland, an' that hain't high now."

"I wisht we could tote our guns along," said Jack.

"No ye don't nuther. You'd git yourselves inter trouble fust thing. Guns sorter encourages fellers to run their head inter trouble. Keep outer trouble till you git to whar you kin 'list, an' then make all the trouble you kin. Ef you meet any rebs, and they hold ye up, ye kin swar you're goin' to visit kinfolks on Roundstone, an' then go. Don't fail to go ef ye say you're goin' ter."

Even in such a time Jacob Hanson had his

standard of ethics, which, however it might be judged by moralists, was sacred to him.

"Wall, good-by, boys. I wisht I cud go, too. Mebby I'll hatter go. I'm above the age, but ef things keeps on as they're goin' hyur, I may be with you yet. Be brave, an' do yer duty, an' ef ever you gitter whar you kin see the flag again, don't never turn yer back on hit, or ye hain't no boys o' mine."

They promised and were gone. The old man choked a little as he bade them good-by, and the boys were silent after he had turned back. For half the night they rode across the hills through a rough and sparsely peopled region. At first one rode and the other walked, but their progress was so slow, and the horse already so tired from his long ride to Rutledge and return, that much of the time they both walked. About midnight they passed a corn field, and with the first suggestion of lawlessness born of their new position as guardians of the law, they crossed the fence and secured a feed for Bill, and while he ate, they picked a dozen additional ears, which they tied together by the husks, and laid across the saddle.

"Thar's two more feeds," said Henry, "case we should need 'em."

"Yes," said Jack; "but Hank, hain't this steal-in'?"

"No, Jack. Hit makes a feller feel sorter ef it was. But they's another name fur it wen you git to fightin' fur yer country. Hit's con-somethin'. Confist— confisticate. Oh, now I got it! Hit's confisticatin'!"

"Wall, I'm mighty glad ef it ain't stealin', but I'll be hanged ef it seems much diff'rent."

" Wall, that's because you don't own the horse. A marciful man is marciful to his beastis. An' ef the rebs hadn't a stole from us, we mought a brought more with us."

As it grew light, they saw plainly that they were not out of danger. The roads gave evidence of the passing of large numbers of men. It began to look as if their start toward Kentucky had been too tardy.

They came to a forest, and turned aside into the woods to rest and reconnoitre. They removed the saddle and bridle from Bill, and fed him half of the precious corn which they had confiscated, probably from a Union man like themselves. Bill ate the corn and husks, and contentedly nibbled the grass. They replaced the bridle, with the bit out, and fastened Bill to a swinging limb, where he had a radius of several yards grazing at his will, and, after nibbling a little of their corn pone, lay down with their heads upon the saddle for a pillow and their feet pointing in opposite directions, and fell asleep.

" Surrender ! "

Jack and Henry awoke with a start, and rose to a sitting posture. Over them stood a Confederate soldier in butternut, with bayonet on his gun.

" S'render ? " he asked.

" We hain't got no call ter surrender," said Jack. " We hain't sojers."

" No, nur you hain't a-goin' ter be, nuther. I know wut sorter fellows you be, I do. You think you're goin' over inter Kaintuck ter 'list, don't yer ? "

They were both silent. Then Henry said,

"We 'lowed to go inter Kaintuck ter visit some kinfolks we got over thar."

"Yas, I reckon so. Did ye 'low ter go foot or hossback?"

"We both 'lowed to ride, off 'n' on."

"Wall, ye won't be on so much as off from now on. Putt the saddle on that critter. I reckon *I'll* ride now. You fellers got ary shootin' arn?"

"Nary one."

"Wall, slip the bits inter that critter's mouth, an' putt the saddle on him, an' I'll see wut fur beast he ister ride."

There was no help for it, and they sorrowfully prepared Bill for a new master.

"Got some corn, too, hain't ye? Stole hit, I reckon? Wall, I hain't p'tic'lar, seein' 'twarn't me as did hit. I've got a sorter tender conscience myself, an' never steal nothin' smaller 'n a hoss. Lead him up hyur. Now stan off that, wile I git up."

He mounted, and tested the length of the stirrups.

"Too short," he said. "Don't you fellers come no nearer. Move off a little."

They started slowly away, and seeing him dismount without keeping his eye on them, they were seized with a sudden impulse.

"Less git, Hank!"

"Go ahead!" They made a wild break for freedom, rushing through the bushes, and down into a ravine. They had gone a matter of six rods before the Confederate noticed their departure.

"Hole on thar!" he called, but not very loudly.

"Halt, or I'll shoot," he called, seeing that they did not stop.

"Keep on, Hank!" called Jack.

"I'm a-comin' atter you!" called the soldier, and started on the horse down the ravine.

They redoubled their speed. They ran, breathless and panting, over rocks and through streams. They tore their clothes in the bushes. They fell and rose and pressed on. They had gone a full mile before they stopped. Jack was ahead, and he gradually slowed up and let Henry overtake him. Then they both stopped.

They looked about them, gasping for breath, and listening to the pounding of their hearts against their ribs.

"I reckon we're safe," said Jack.

"Less stop an' rest," said Henry. "We kin hide here."

They threw themselves upon the ground in a clump of bushes hard by, and waited to get their breath and think.

After a while Jack said,

"Hank."

"Wall?"

"We're two fools for runnin' so."

"Wall, I'm mighty willin' to run to git away."

"That feller jes' wanted us to git away. He wanted Bill, that's all he wanted."

"Do you reckon so, Jack?"

"Sartin. Ef we'd ben in uniform he'd arrested us. Or ef we hadn't a had no horse, he'd ast us more about whar we was goin'. But he wanted the horse, and didn't want to take no one inter camp that mought hev a claim on him. So he captured us, an' let on like he was a-takin' us inter camp, an' then let us git away."

"Wall, I believe you're right! An' he's got the horse!"

"Yes, but he hain't got us. It's mighty evident the rebs is ahead of us. Shall we go back?"

"Not a foot!"

"So I say. Less take our bearin's, an' start sorter easy like towards the Gap. Which way did we come?"

"Thataway."

"Yes, that's so. Wall, that's up stream. We mus' go thataway. Wut time do ye reckon hit is?"

"'Bout noon, I should think. The sun is high."

"I reckon you're right. The bark grows thicker on the other side of these big trees. That mus' be north."

Thus they got their bearings, and kept as nearly as possible in a northeasterly course parallel with the river, and avoiding the road. Their progress was slow, but as the sun was near its setting, they discerned in the Cumberland range that towered on the other side of the river, a saddle-like depression, which they knew at once for the Gap. Toward it they hastened with all speed.

In the twilight they came to a ford of the river.

"I wisht we hadn't a lost Bill before we got acrost," said Jack.

"I wisht we hadn't a lost him at all," replied Bill's sometime owner.

"I do, too, but they hain't no use cryin' over that. I hate to git wet afore night. Ef it was day, and we was goin' to walk, hit wouldn't matter. But I hate to lay down in the woods in wet clothes."

"I don't reckon we'll lay down much."

"Wall, less not git wet 'less we have to. Less strip an' wade."

The suggestion was eminently proper. They removed their clothing, rolled it into two wads which they could hold high and dry, and waded through. The river was not deep, however, and they were only wet to the waist. On the other side they replaced their clothing, and, following a road that showed little sign of recent travel, they pushed toward the Gap.

It was well past midnight when they arrived at the foot of the mountain. They attempted to ascend on the Tennessee side, but not far up the road they were stopped by the challenge of a sentinel. They beat a precipitate retreat, followed at a safe distance by the sentry's bullet.

They felt that they must make the Gap before morning, and there were few hours left. Departing from the road, they climbed the steep face of the mountain to the Virginia road, which they struck, as they rightly judged, well within the sentry lines, and cautiously made their way around the mountain toward the depression.

"We mus' keep the road fur's we kin," said Jack, "an' then when we hatter leave hit, take to the woods and cross above the Gap. We can't git through hit."

The mountain above was so steep that any distance saved in the almost perpendicular climb was worth some risk. So they cautiously pressed toward the Gap itself, though knowing that it must be held by the Confederates, and that erelong they must leave the road for a wide and steep detour that should leave the Gap below them. The dawn was just beginning to streak the east, when, cautiously turning a bend in the road, they found themselves face to face with a picket. He was more surprised than they, for there must have been guards below who should have stopped any approach along the line of the Virginia road. They had turned to run before he had time to challenge them, and hard on the heels of his challenge rang the report of his gun. A little way they ran down the road, and debated each in his own mind as they ran, whether they should turn to the right and down the hill, where their better progress would secure more quick seclusion, or up the face of the mountain, in the direction of their journey. Henry would have taken the downhill course had he been in the lead, but Jack chose the more perilous way. Suddenly turning to the left across a narrow level place covered with bushes, he fell into the mouth of a pitfall, barely saving himself as he fell, by catching at a stick that stood up in the hole. A moment he clung in hesitation. Henry was hard behind him, and not far back some soldiers were following.

"Go on down, Jack!" whispered Henry, "an' I'll foller!"

Jack let go his hold and descended the pole, hand over hand, finding crotches at convenient intervals. Henry was so close behind him that he trod on Jack's hands. They were soon at the bottom, and, looking up, could see in the dawn four faces that looked hideous in that place and light, peering after them.

Jack hastily seized the pole and drew it down. It was the trunk of a cedar tree that had been made into a rude ladder by the chopping off of the branches. Evidently the cave was sometimes visited by the people of the neighborhood, — boys, probably, — but unknown to the Confederate soldiers, who were themselves but newly arrived at the Gap.

It was pitch dark where Jack and Henry found themselves, at the bottom of a nearly circular and quite perpendicular hole some twenty feet in depth. They could hear the falling of water not far away, and they hardly dared to stir, lest they should step into some pitfall in the cave itself; but they groped their way to a place against the wall on one side none too soon, for their pursuers above, not daring to descend after them, began to amuse themselves by shooting down the hole. They were quite out of range, however, and had little fear that they would be attacked. After waiting until the voices above were heard no more, they made cautious explorations, and found no other way out than that by which they had entered. The sound of water came to them from a stream of considerable size, with a mighty fall, not far back from the mouth. They could go no farther, and if the cave had other avenues they failed to find them.

As the day wore on, the young men came to the place where the pole had stood, and looked up through the skylight above. There was a draft of air there that made their teeth chatter, but they

both remembered that in the single instant they
had stood above it on the ground the ascending air
had seemed warm. Back from the mouth it was
comfortable, though somewhat damp. After waiting a good while, and seeing no one above, they
carefully replaced the pole, and Jack ascended,
while Henry stood at the foot. Slowly he raised
his head above the opening, and then drew himself
up and sat on the ground with his legs in the cave.
After a careful reconnoitre he descended and reported. The mouth of the cave was not guarded.
Probably the detachment of troops that had held
the Gap the night before had moved on, and a new
body held it to-day. There was a sound of troops
and wagons moving up the road. Evidently Zollicoffer's army was marching through the Gap. The
road was too near to make any attempt at escape
safe at present, but they might easily get out later
and move on.

There are many tales that gather about that cave
near the Virginia road. They tell of men who hid
there, and shot their pursuers as they entered; of
dark tales of murder and of secreted bodies; of
moonshining, facilitated by the nearness of the
mouth to the road, making the bringing of corn
an easy matter, and the stream of pure water need-
ful for the still; of the interment there of men who
fell in the war, who found a speedy burial in the
waters of the cave. How many beside Jack and
Henry hid there in the days of the war, no man
can tell. What threatened to be a fatal accident
became to them a marked deliverance.

In the dusk of the evening they again replaced

the pole, and climbed to the top. They debated for a moment whether to leave the pole standing, and decided to do so. Then they began climbing the steep side of the mountain, leaving the Gap far below, and crossing the ridge halfway to the summit of the pinnacle, on which later stood the famous gun, "Long Tom." The crossing was made without incident, and before the darkness had fully set in they stood on the ridge, and looked back over the Powell's valley, and far over toward the Great Smoky Mountains, and then ahead, where there was nothing but an unbroken succession of wooded hills, without a human habitation in sight. But, thank God, this was Kentucky!

They pressed on that night and the next day. They hardly stopped to eat or sleep. They avoided all roads, knowing that Zollicoffer's men must hold them all the way to Cumberland Ford, and probably to Barboursville and beyond. They crossed by the headwaters of the Poor Fork of the Cumberland, and over the great and lonely Pine Mountain. They ate the last of their pone and pork. They gnawed corn from the cob as occasionally they passed a field. They lost count of the days, but later they found that since leaving home they had spent eight days in their wanderings, hardly seeing, and ever shunning, the face of man. They came to the divide, beyond which the waters ran the other way, and knew that these must be the tributaries of the Kentucky. Here they inquired for Roundstone, and found that they had left it one side, and it was now far out of their way. They followed the falling water, and kept on toward Camp Nelson. From this time on they had an unfailing guide. Through four counties they followed the tributaries of the Kentucky's South Fork. It was a long and roundabout way. On the morning of the ninth day they came suddenly upon a fence, just beyond which stood a girl, leaning over beside a cow, and holding a cup in one hand while she milked with the other. It was more than mortal man could endure.

"Howdy, miss," said Jack. "D'ye reckon you could give two pore fellers a drink o' warm milk?"

She brought the full cup to Jack, who handed it to Henry.

"No, you, Jack. I kin wait."

"Go ahead! I cain't stand this much longer!" said Jack. In the moment that he smelled that warm milk, he knew how a wolf might feel in winter at the smell of blood.

Henry drank the milk and handed back the empty cup. The girl turned to milk it full again.

"Say, miss," said Jack, "I hope you won't think wrong, but ef you stop to milk that cup full, I'll jes' go crazy. Dip me some out o' the bucket."

She dipped the cup in the tin bucket and brought it up level full, and Jack gulped it down as though famished.

"Thank you," said he. "I never tasted nothin' before that was so good."

"You're right welcome," said the girl. "Goin' to the army?"

"Yes, but you won't tell?"

"You don' need to be skeered. They won't

nobody hurt ye. That is, ef it's the Union army," she added, with an afterthought.

"That's jes' whar we're goin'. Kin you tell us whar we are at?"

"You're in Estill County now. You're gittin' near the blue grass. A lot of you Tennessee fellers has come up and is enlisting at Camp Nelson. The folks there is mostly secesh. But here we're mostly Union. But a heap o' folks here has got kinfolks below that's secesh, an' some on 'em don' know what to do. But they won't nobody hurt you. They're goin' to raise some sojers here, an' we women are goin' to make a flag an' give 'em."

"Say, miss," said Henry, "do you reckon ary person would keer ef we was to go inter the barn an' go to sleep on the hay? We've ben so long without a good night's sleep, 'pears like ef we're safe now, I cyan't go nary 'nother step without a little nap o' sleep."

"You kin come to the house an' sleep," she said. "Pa's name's Murray. The Murrays are all for the Union. Pa won't let no man that's goin' to be a Union sojer sleep in the barn."

They protested, but she insisted; and finally she went to the house for her father, who came to the fence and invited the young men in.

"You'll hev some breakfast fust, I reckon, an' then you'll go to bed."

They did not long object, and gladly ate the hoecake and bacon that were set before them, and then, ascending to the loft, slept until dinner was ready. They insisted on going on then, but their hospitable host refused his consent. They must rest that day

and night, and next day he would take them a step
on their journey and show them a nearer route.
They did so, and bathed and rested their sore and
weary feet and mended their well-worn shoes. They
enjoyed that night such sweet, refreshing slumber as
they remembered all their lives. While they slept,
the mother and daughter sewed up the rents in
their clothing.

Mr. Murray borrowed a horse from a neighbor,
and brought his own two horses to the door sad-
dled, just as the sun was rising. They were just
finishing their liberal breakfast when three men
stopped at the fence and asked for a drink.

"Come in an' se' down on the porch," said
Mr. Murray, "an' I'll send for some water to the
spring. Becky, fetch me some cheers here, an'
fetch the gentlemen some water from the spring.
Goin' below, gentlemen?"

"Yes; we're goin' to Camp Dick Robinson."

"I declar! Wall, here's some men'll like to go
with ye, ef ye kin keep up with 'em. They're a-goin'
to Camp Nelson. You're from Kaintucky?"

"Yes; we're from Roundstone."

Jack heard the name and stepped out.

"Why, Eph Whitley! Is this you?"

"Howdy, Jack! What you doin' here? Ain't
you lost?"

"Well, if I be, Hank's los', too. Here he is."

"Hank, what in creation are you doin' here?
These is my brothers. Bill, this is our cousin,
Henry Hanson; an' this is my brother Joe. An'
this is his friend, Mr. Jack Casey."

"Friends, be ye?" asked the host. "Well,

this is lucky. Becky, get these men somethin' to eat, right off, an' we'll start."

"We've had our breakfast, thank ye," said Joe, "an' we've got provisions to last us through. We've only walked one day. Pa fetched us day before yistiddy to some friends fornent Boneville, an' tuck the horses back from there. We stayed there night afore las' an' walked acrost the hills to save follerin' the river yistiddy. We stayed back here a mile, an' took a soon start this mornin' to git on as fur's we kin to-day."

"Well, you go right on with us. Your friends here has been trampin' more'n a week, an' their feet is sorter sore. You'll have to let them ride most o' the way. But they'll spell ye once in a while, so's you kin keep along. Where everything is plain sailin', we'll ride and tie, and where the road is unsartin, we'll keep along together."

Jack and Henry bade their new friends a hearty good-by, and all the young men bowed to Becky and her mother, who came out to wish them a prosperous journey and a short and pleasant experience in camp. The Whitleys had some provisions, but their hosts insisted that they should take some more corn pone and another fried chicken, which would be prepared for them in half an hour. Not to delay the entire party, all started on except Joe Whitley, for whom one horse was left, as he knew the road. The other five moved ahead, Henry and Mr. Murray riding, and Jack, who was more thoroughly rested than Henry, walking with the other boys.

As soon as they were gone, Joe and Becky set

themselves to catch the chicken. Becky scattered the feed, and called,

"Chick, chick!"

Joe stood by her side, and, when the chickens gathered, caught, after one or two futile attempts, the plump young rooster which she designated for decapitation, and the two picked it together. Mrs. Murray was making the corn pones. It was rather a long half hour, and the boys told Joe afterward that they did not believe that he had been in any haste to get away, but he affirmed that picking chickens was an important part of a soldier's duty, and by no means the least pleasant if one had good company. George Washington overstayed his time when first he met Martha Custis. If Joe tarried a matter of fifteen unnecessary minutes, all told, his own conscience, and not this history, must accuse him.

It is rather small business in the historian at the present day to search out and record such trivial incidents, but they were among those that the soldiers were glad to remember afterward, and it is rather pleasant to turn from the more sombre subjects which must form so great a part of our narrative. Besides, it is important to note even such trifling occurrences, for sometimes they had a future. It may be that it would not have made a classic picture, but one of the scenes which stands out with somewhat unusual clearness is that of Joe and Becky standing beside the smoke house that September morning, plucking the chicken together. Socrates plucked a cock for Plato's edification: this reduction of a biped to a featherless condition was quite as dignified a process, and, like that, sub-served at least one useful end.

Joe overtook his companions two hours after they had gone, and they punished him, as he deserved, by not allowing him to ride again for many a mile. The mountains were now left behind, and the beautiful blue-grass region, with its large fields of ripening corn, of tall hemp, and of broad-leaved tobacco, its rolling plains, and its pastures with fine cattle and horses, was about them. They paused for dinner, and rode another hour, and Mr. Murray stopped to turn back, riding one horse and leading two.

"Now this is the road to Richmond," he said, "the county seat o' Madison. I wouldn't go through thar jes' now. There's a good bit of excitement thar jes' at present. I don't reckon anybody would pester you, but you needn't give 'em no chance. Keep west an' a little north, an' you don't need to be skeered to ast the way."

They bade him a hearty farewell, and pressed forward with good courage. They slept that night in a barn only five miles from the Kentucky River. Before it was light they were up, and ate the remains of their food, and then took their way on in the direction indicated to Camp Nelson. It was still early in the morning that they stood upon a high bluff, with the river far below, and looking to the other side Jack saw something waving in the air.

" Boys, look there!" he called.

They looked, and Eph cast his hat high in the air with a glad shout, in which they all joined, " Hurrah! Hurrah! It's the flag!"

IV

Toward the Promised Land

THE Kentucky River runs between high bluffs at Camp Nelson, and the conformation of the land makes fortification easy and effective. General Nelson intended that if a battle was fought in central Kentucky it should be there; but the battle came a year later on other ground. Here, amid scenery of surpassing beauty, two thousand East Tennesseeans were enrolled for the deliverance of their own State. Jack and Henry entered Company A of the First Tennessee Infantry. Their captain, for a short time, was Joseph A. Cooper, a brave East Tennessee farmer, who was soon made a colonel and then a general. Their colonel was Robert K. Byrd, who had been prominent in the Greenville Convention; and the commander of the East Tennessee brigade was Colonel Samuel Powhatan Carter, of Carter County.

The six Kentucky regiments which gathered at Camp Dick Robinson were all officered by Kentucky men. After a brief service in another regiment, the Whitley boys were transferred to the Eighth Kentucky Infantry, where they served under Captain John Wilson. His company, recruited mainly in Estill County, carried the flag — the flag of which Becky Murray had told them, and which she had a share in making. Bill Whitley was chosen color-sergeant, and was jealously proud of his position until he saw the hungry look in the eyes of his brother Joe.

"Joe, whatcher lookin' that flag over fur, so?" he asked, as he entered the tent, and found Joe inspecting the stitches.

"Nothin'," said Joe, sheepishly, rolling up the flag.

"That's a lie," said Bill. "You was a-lookin' to see ef ye could tell what *she* sewed."

"I wasn't nuther," declared Joe, coloring.

"You was, too. An' you're wantin' to pack that flag yourself. Cyain't ye be satisfied with havin' the gal, an' let other folks have some sheer?"

"I hain't a-keerin' to pack the flag, Bill. I—"

"I know better," said Bill, bolting out of the tent. For several days the boys were near to quarrelling at every mention of the flag. Bill was ever the aggressor, taunting Joe with coveting his position, and drawing from him emphatic denials that were almost admissions. One evening Bill entered the tent, and found Joe alone.

"Lookyhere, Joe," he said. "This thing hain't a-goin' on no longer. You git up here an' take off yer coat, an' the best man gits the flag an' gal, too."

Joe started to his feet in surprise.

"Bill—Bill," he stammered, "do you keer for Becky?"

"Take off yer coat!" shouted Bill.

Joe wonderingly began fingering at the buttons. "I'll take off my coat, ef ye say so; but I won't fight ye. Bill—I didn't know—"

"Now put on that one," said Bill, extending his own. "I've ben to see Captain Wilson, an' you're to be color-sergeant stidder me."

"I won't do it, Bill," cried Joe, with tears starting from his eyes.

"You have obleeged to do it," said Bill. "An' I don't want none o' yer fool talk about it. You keer for the gal, an' I don't — much; an' you'll keer more for the flag than me for her sake. So we'll swap coats to save rippin' off an' sewin' on braid. Shet up! Ef ye don't keep still, I'll lick ye."

Thus far in the war Kentucky had preserved "an armed neutrality." The country at large ridiculed the idea, but President Lincoln was disposed to humor it. He knew that vain as was her attempt to be neutral, Kentucky could be trusted, and that it was better for the national government not to invade the State till the South had done so. Thus, when Governor McGoffin complained of the organization of troops at Nelson and Dick Robinson as an invasion, President Lincoln replied that these were Kentucky soldiers, officered by Kentuckians, who, with the refugees from East Tennessee, were organized to prevent invasion. So, without sending a soldier from the North, Kentucky was held by armed Union men until the South had invaded the State, when the Legislature, backed by a Union sentiment that had grown under Lincoln's tolerant treatment, declared for the Union, and passed its acts over the Governor's veto.

One day, early in October, the force at Camp Dick Robinson was augmented by the arrival of the

East Tennessee brigade from Camp Nelson. It was the beginning of a forward movement toward East Tennessee. There the Whitley boys were joined by Jack and Henry, and enjoyed their first visit since enlistment, nearly a month before.

"Well, Jack, how do you like sojerin'?" asked Eph.

"I'll like it when we git to doin' somethin'. How do you like it?"

"I don' like the drillin' wuth a continental. This 'Left! Left!' and 'Hayfoot! Strawfoot!' don' suit me a mite."

"Nor me. But I'm willin' ef we ever git anywhar."

"I hope we'll move now. Did you hear that General Nelson's been removed?"

"No; what's he removed for?"

"Well, he's got a mighty quick temper, an' he's arrested rebs about as brash as Zollicoffer did the Union men. A heap o' the sojers was mad at him, too. Did you hear about his fight with a teamster?"

"No; what was it?"

"Nelson had a sojer actin' as his clerk, an' he was a good writer, but tipped his elbow tol'able often. An' he knowed a teamster that kep' a jug under his wagon seat. T'other day the teamster was mighty nigh full, an' was tryin' to hitch up his mules, an' this clerk seen him, an' says, says he, 'Wy don' you git the horsler over thar to hitch up?' 'I didn't know as they war no horsler,' says the teamster. 'Yes,' says the clerk, 'a big feller over thar in yon tent.' 'Does he hitch up for teamsters?' asts the teamster. 'Yes,' says the feller, 'that's what he's paid to do, but he's lazy. I shouldn't wonder ef he's asleep, stidder doin' wut he's paid to do, an' lettin' hard-workin' teamsters do the work.' 'I'll raise him,' says the teamster. 'You best look out,' says the feller. 'He's a big feller, a main big one,' says he, 'an' he's cross as old Scratch.' The teamster was about as big as Nelson, an' he starts off to wake him, an' the clerk he gits inter the wagon an' gits the jug. Then the big teamster he comes to Nelson's tent an' breaks right in, and Nelson was sleepin' sure enough. An' the feller says, 'Git up here, ye lazy lout,' says he, 'an' hitch up my mules!' General Nelson, he jumps up an' draws his sword an' makes a lunge for the feller, madder'n a she bar that's lost her cubs; an' the teamster he hauls back with his whip, and they went in for each other like two painters. But some officers hears the racket and knows they's some one goin' to git killed, an' in they comes runnin' and separates them. Then they went to find the feller that kicked up the dirt, an' found him drunk in the wagon, an' the jug empty."

"I reckon he ketched it from Nelson."

"You're mighty right. Nelson sent him home acrost lots."

"Was that what Nelson left for?"

"No; but they's ben a heap o' trouble, an' he cyan't git on rightly with no one."

"Who's comin' atter him?"

"Gin'ral Thomas."

"Do you reckon he'll be as keen to invade East Tennessy as Nelson?"

"Oh, I reckon so. He's a Southern man, and

knows about it. I don' know about Sherman, though. He's over Thomas."

"Well, they dassent give up East Tennessy. We've enlisted for that. Our officers are commissioned ' For the East Tennessee Expedition.' "

"They say Zollicoffer's got to Barboursville."

"Did you hear that they had a little scrimmage there yistiddy ? "

"No ; how was it ? "

"Some Home Guards thar met his army, and they was a fight, but the Home Guards didn't make out much. They're sendin' word for us to come right off and help 'em lick Zolly."

"They're goin' to do it, hain't they ? "

"Yes. Cun'l Garrard's gone ahead a'ready, an' he cal'lates to stop Zollicoffer till the rest on us git thar."

"What for guns is your'n ? "

"Same as your'n. They call 'em Belgian rifles. They say that the Gov'nor of Pennsylvania refused 'em, an' they sent 'em on to Ohio, an' the Gov'nor of Ohio said he wouldn't take no sech guns for Ohio sojers, an' they sent 'em down here."

"I reckon we're as good as them fellers."

"Yes, but our fellers is mighty glad to git anything that'll shoot."

"I heerd that some of the men had got guns they was afeard to shoot off."

"Well, hit's so, mighty nigh. The breech is the dangerous eend. I seed two or three fellers kicked over with 'em."

The drums here began to beat. The young men did not know the different signals, but went to their respective regiments, where they were ordered to prepare for an advance against Zollicoffer.

It was a glad morning to Jack and Henry, when, turning their backs upon the blue grass, they marched toward the mountains again.

"Hurrah, Hank! ain't this fine?"

"You'd better believe it! Won't we drive ole Zollicoffer back, though?"

"Well, now, I reckon we will! Two thousand of us, all from East Tennessy, and six Kaintuck reg'maints! We'll drive him back through the Gap a heap quicker'n he come!"

"An' he won't have long to stop in East Tennessy, nuther."

"Not much, he won't. We'll send him out of the mountains a-flyin'. We'll go to Knoxville an' smash open the jail, an' we'll stop in front of old Parson Brownlow's house and cheer, and the old man'll come out an' make us a speech, an' call us the deliverers of East Tennessy!"

"Which way do you reckon we'll go from the Gap?"

"The way we come, like as not, an' down the Holston valley. Jes' think o' marchin' down the road past home, with the fellers a-comin' out o' the woods whar they ben a-hidin' out, an' the gals a-wavin' their sunbonnets and their handkerchers!"

Conversations like this were repeated among groups of friends all through the Tennessee brigade. They were men who had braved dangers to join the army. They had enlisted without draft or bounty, and for conscience' sake. They had resisted bribes, threats, and offers of protection, and

had left homes and friends unprotected, with the fond
hope of returning soon to fight for their own hearth-
stones.   Never did a band of men march forth with
better heart than that raw-boned but stalwart company of East Tennesseeans, as they shouldered their
clumsy old Belgian rifles and trudged toward
home.

The pike extends as far as Crab Orchard, and then
there is a " dirt road " of uncertain quality.   From
there the way leads across the hills of Rockcastle
County to the Rockcastle River.   There is a pre-
cipitous descent to the ford at Livingston, and then
comes the long ascent of Wild Cat Mountain.

It was fortunate that Carter's brigade had small
need of baggage wagons, for what wagons there
were, and these were hired, had a hard time of it.
No man who has not experienced them can fitly picture to himself the manifold adventures of a ride
in a wagon through the Rockcastle River and up
Wild Cat.

The ordinary army wagon on this expedition had
four mules and a negro driver, who sat on one mule
and guided the whole four with a single rein.   As
he had one rein, so he had but one word of command ; but it was marvellously flexible and effective.
When he wished to go to the right he would say,
" Yea-a-a-a ! " and manipulate the rein.   When he
wished to go to the left, he would say the same
word and appear to use the rein in precisely the
same way.   When going down the bank into the
stream, and he wished the mules to proceed with
caution, he would say, in an admonitory tone,
" Yea-a-a-a, now ! "   When he wished to urge them

up the bank on the other side, he would jerk the rein and call sharply, "Yea! Yea! Yea!"

It would not be fitting to speak of the swearing, but the army in Flanders never could have sworn as did the drivers of those mule teams. They swore at the mules, and at the roads, and at the loads, and at the broken harnesses, and at the collar galls, and at the officer, far back in authority, who was supposed to be responsible for this unreasonable exertion, and last, but not least, at Jeff Davis and the Southern Confederacy. It is two and one-half miles to the top, and the profanity grew denser as the climb grew more steep. Persons who stand to-day on the other side of the river, and see toward the summit of Wild Cat a streak of blue haze, which is sometimes visible there, are told that it has something to do with the profanity of teamsters, during and since the war, who "swore a blue streak."

But the Tennesseeans did not swear, or, if they did, it was not for disapproval of the expedition. The fording of the Rockcastle, the climbing of Wild Cat, were to them but the passing through the Red Sea and the beginning of a short wilderness wandering, before their entrance into their own land of promise, poor and barren, but full of all the meaning which speaks to the heart in the tender name of home. There were their firesides and their altars. There were their wives and children. There, in not a few cases, were their imprisoned relatives. There were their own plundered fields and barns, defenceless before the destroyer. A few weeks ago it had been imprisonment to cheer the flag. Now, they carried it aloft with shouts of joy, and pictured to themselves the scene that would appear when they marched, each man into his native town or past his own door, with the flag waving above him. They were not much given to gay music. They mostly sang the weird, minor tunes that belonged to their worship, with a few wild, odd, but equally solemn songs that might be sung on secular occasions. But there was one song that was popular in the army, and which, both for its tune and its sentiment, they enjoyed. They had learned it from the rebels, but it suited them equally well. The tune is martial, and is said to date back to the time of the Crusades. It is minor also, and has a touch of solemnity in it. They hummed it as Cromwell's Ironsides hummed their surly hymn, that had in it the conquest of all the enemies of the Lord. They hummed it as they marched, and the legs that had resisted all attempts of the drill sergeant in the few days during which they had had his painful instruction, now began to swing in something like rhythm. And there were times when the air broke out in one squad and was caught up in antiphone by another, and echoed up the hill and down, on this side of the river and the other.

"When Johnny comes marching home again, Hurrah! Hurrah!
  We'll give him a hearty welcome then, Hurrah! Hurrah!
    The girls will sing, the boys will shout :
    The ladies they will all turn out :
    And we'll all feel gay
  When Johnny comes marching home!"

Whether there were more stanzas or not, or other songs like it, few of the men knew, and none

of them cared.   To some, the sublime thing about
the war was the onward march of a mighty providential purpose; and for them there came the "Battle
Hymn of the Republic."   To others the impressive
thing was the leap of the nation's blood and the
answering rush of the thousands; and these might
sing, "We are coming, Father Abraham, three
hundred thousand more."   These were features not
wholly lost upon the mountaineer.   But the prime
thing in his thought at this stage of the contest was
his own return to defend his shrines and loved ones,
and the song that suited him, both as to its words
and its music, was "When Johnny comes marching
home!"   Alas! what a march it was!

V

The Battle of Wild Cat Mountain

MOLLIE CAMERON had a hard time of it after Joe died, but it couldn't be helped, as she said a hundred times to her comforters, and so that was the end of it. She seemed to the neighbors to have grown hard and cold, and some doubted if she really mourned for Joe, she "took it" so strangely. She was not seen to weep. She did not hide her face, but looked straight before her out of tearless eyes, with a countenance that was white and set. It was when they woke little Jim to see his father die that she seemed to change. She had watched Joe's breath growing shorter and shorter in the hours that he lay unconscious, and had given no sign that the neighbors recognized as that of grief. She had heard them say that he was dying, and had shed no tear. But when they held little Jim, whom she seemed until that moment to have forgotten, up beside the pillow to look into the face of his dying father, she gave a look that was first wild and then full of a grief that was awful to see. It was only for a moment. There was a short death-rattle in Joe's throat, a brief convulsive shudder, and the breathing ceased. One of the neighbors rose and stopped the little wooden clock upon the mantel, and turned to the wall the room's one picture, and they all knew that the end had come. Then Mollie clutched little Jim to her breast and wailed in passionate sorrow. Little Jim had stared about him bewildered, but now took fright, and added his cries to his mother's ; and the neighbor women at first wept beside her, but soon dried their tears that they, if possible, might comfort her.

The tempest of Mollie's weeping soon spent itself ; but when she ceased to weep, the hard look that was like a flint came back, and they wished that she would weep again. But she did not, or if she did, they did not know it. They "sat up with Joe," as in duty bound, she neither objecting nor expressing gratitude. They prepared his body for the burial, and she watched the preparations unmoved. They laid him away under the pine tree in the edge of the clearing, — for she refused to have his body taken to the cemetery, — and she witnessed his burial without tears. The funeral, which they held in the summer following, found her present, with sunbonnet of black drawn over her face ; but the face, when they saw it, was the same face of flint, and she led little Jim away and up the road from Hazel Patch church house to her home on the southeast slope of Wild Cat Mountain, and took up her lonely life, with little Jim and her sorrow for her only companions.

Yet the neighbors, who told of her conduct with awe, added strange and inconsistent rumors. It was reported that no day went by which did not see some token of affection laid upon the grave of Joe, and that at least once she had gotten little Jim to sleep at night, rocking him back and forth in a hard chair that had no rockers, and then, laying him on the bed, had gone out into the storm and spent the night upon Joe's grave.

There was no reasoning with her; and when she declared that she would live there just the same, and tend the little farm the best she could, the neighbors knew better than to try to dissuade her, and did their best to help her along. Several times she found a dressed chicken or a sack of meal at her door, and it was understood that before the end of October the neighbors would gather in and husk her corn. But it was in October that the fight came, and that changed many plans about Wild Cat.

Back from the road, and little concerned with the world outside, Mollie knew not of the approach of the two armies; of Zollicoffer on the east, and Garrard with his Kentuckians, and Carter with his Tennesseeans on the west. On the day that the battle came — which was the twenty-first, as they remembered so well afterward — she had gotten Jim to sleep, and had gone far down the branch to a neighbor's to see if they would market for her her little surplus of beans. She chose the time when Jim was asleep, because she had the beans to " pack," and the way was rough and hard for little Jim, who himself needed to be " packed " at intervals. She had rarely left him, and, as she went, she hurried with the sack upon her back. Just as she neared the neighbor's house, she was stopped by a soldier in gray, who ordered her to return; and, looking past him, she saw that the road was full of soldiers moving up the hill. She hurried back, but soon was stopped by other soldiers. The mountain seemed alive with them, and up at the top she heard the sound of guns. She turned this way and that to reach her home. The battle came nearer and nearer to her, and she was driven farther away with each shifting of the position of the soldiers. At length she lost her way and wandered afar, being guided back by the sound of the firing, which was resumed with greater fierceness later in the day. As she approached her home toward evening, her way was still blocked, but now by soldiers in blue instead of gray, and they were hurrying through the woods and down the ridges and defiles upon the eastern side of the mountain, in hot pursuit of the Confederates, who were retreating to London.

It was a small battle, as measured by comparison with those that followed, but there were thirty Confederate dead, and five that wore the blue, with wounded enough to keep the surgeons on both sides busy, and men were not as yet accustomed to the shedding of each other's blood. Besides, it is impossible during, and immediately after, a battle, to keep the reports of losses within bounds, and with what the soldiers saw of carnage, — which God knows was enough, — and what they believed of exaggerated reports, it seemed to them a great battle, — the first battle in Kentucky, and Zollicoffer was defeated !

A Tennessee company, moving through the woods early in the day in pursuit of a straggling band of Confederates who retreated before their greater numbers, came upon a burning cabin, which the rebels appeared to have fired before their withdrawal. They had not held it long, as was evident from the untrampled yard, and the little field still bearing its wealth of golden corn. Apparently a squad had fallen upon the cabin, perhaps had plundered it of its eatables, and, compelled to vacate almost immediately, had set it on fire. The Tennesseeans entered the clearing, and stopped to look at the blazing building and to take breath before pushing ahead. A little group gathered under a great pine with a mound below it.

"Somebody buried here, I reckon, Jack?"

"Yes. Somebody keered a heap for him, whoever he was. Look at them bright leaves, all tied in a wreath. Somebody's put them here, and hunted for all the bright an' purty ones."

"Some woman's done that. Reckon hit must a ben her man that's dead. 'Tain't ben long. The grave hain't ben thar many months. Say, Jack, what was that?"

"What was what?"

"Listen! Hit sounds lack a baby a-cryin'."

"It's in the house, as I'm a livin' man!" cried Jack.

A score of faces turned pale, that had looked that day on bloodshed without flinching. To see men killed was terrible, but this was unendurable. There was a child in the burning house, and there was not a moment to be lost.

"Who'll volunteer to go in an' get that baby?" cried Captain Cooper.

For a moment there was no response. Then Jack Casey cried, "I'll go!"

"Ef you go, I'll go with ye," answered Henry.

They moved around the house to find the best

way of approach. There were but two doors, and
the flames were bursting out of one. The door on
the other side was closed. The child's cry ceased
as they passed around, whether because they could
not hear him through the closed door, or because
the flames had caught him, they could not be sure.
Together the two men rushed forward, with half a
score hard behind them, and burst in the door.

"Git down, Hank, an' crawl. The smoke hain't
so bad."

But in the moment that the door was burst in,
the wind, rushing through, for an instant almost
cleared the room of smoke, but in another filled it
with flame. The one instant was enough. In it
they both saw dimly, in the corner nearest them,
the bed, on which the choking child had almost
ceased to cry. Jack seized the little one in his arms
and rushed out. Henry retreated to the door and
looked back to be sure whether the room had other
inmates, but was at once driven out by the flame.
The soldiers drew back to the edge of the clearing
and laid the little one on the grass. Then they
turned to Jack and Henry.

"Burn ye, Hank?"

"Nope."

"Git scorched, Jack?"

"Singed my har a little mite, but nary burn."

The child was also unhurt, though gasping for
breath. Asleep on the bed and covered with Mollie's saddle shawl, he had escaped the notice of the
rebels in their hasty visit, and had awakened barely
in time to be rescued.

What to do with the boy was the next question.

The Rescue of Cub.   Page 70.

He was a lusty young fellow of three or four years. His father, they judged from the grave near by, was dead. The mother — they had many and unfounded conjectures. Those were the days of wild tales of rebel atrocities ; and there were atrocities enough on both sides, in all conscience. But in the heat of that day when they first saw blood, in the anger and hatred of battle, the theory that commended itself to them was one that would have been instantly rejected after a few months of fighting, which was that the mother had been foully dealt with and grossly murdered, and the body left with the living child to perish in the fire which they had kindled to conceal their brutal deed.

They sent the boy to the hospital, Jack and Henry agreeing to see to him when the battle was over. "Jack an' Hank's Cub," the soldiers lovingly dubbed him, in affection for the child and the foster parents also ; for it was their fashion to dissemble their love behind rude sobriquets. Soon the name proved burdensome, and the whole company came to share, though in lesser degree, the paternal relation to the child, who thence became simply "The Cub."

It was four days before Jack and Henry saw their protégé. They were sent in pursuit of Zollicoffer to London, a dozen miles advance from the victory at Wild Cat. There they halted, and Zollicoffer's army turned aside to Mill Spring, yet held Cumberland Gap, though now somewhat insecurely.

The troops were in high spirits. They had fought a battle and won it. They had held their ground against two fierce attacks, and had driven the enemy from the field. They were advanced a good distance toward the Gap, and the way was clear to the Cumberland. Before them there was a fight, no doubt, at Cumberland Ford, and another at the Gap. But how could Zollicoffer now defend the Gap with his main force turned aside? Victory was already theirs. Cumberland Gap was theirs; and when its walls, like those of Jericho, should have fallen before them, there would be a clear entrance into the land of promise. They would drive out the rebels as Joshua did the Canaanites. Such literary and historical precedents as they possessed were from Scripture, and that was their stock illustration. They would capture the Gap like Jericho. Knoxville should be to them as Ai, and they would hang its military governor, Wood, of whom they had been hearing hard tales, as Joshua hanged the Canaanite king, and the righteous should dwell in the land; every man under his own vine, and every man under his own fig tree, all the days of Andrew Johnson and of Parson Brownlow.

At this time Andrew Johnson, on his way north to Congress, came to see the soldiers from his own State, and greatly encouraged them with the thought of an immediate deliverance for East Tennessee. General Thomas was becoming more and more anxious for such an advance. It would come as soon as transportation and reinforcements could be brought up. Meantime the soldiers possessed their souls in patience, and whetted their spirits for the victory that was in sight.

When the baggage wagons that had been at Livingstone and Wild Cat came to London, they brought little Cub. He was eagerly claimed by Jack and Henry, and the whole company, of which he was made an honorary member. He had cried at first, the teamster said, for " Mammy," but after the second night had ceased to mourn, and, from the first, had taken kindly to the soldiers. They set themselves to spoil him as rapidly as might be. They had a uniform made for him out of blue, and, short as were the troops of uniforms, it is to be feared that the commissary connived at the theft of a coat to be devoted to this use. They made him a wooden sword, and a military hat with a turkey feather, and taught him to shout " Forward, march!" and to exact obedience.

The whole company, from Captain Cooper to the big, black teamsters, loved the bright and happy little Cub. The whole regiment began to take an interest in him, and the other regiments to envy them. Rough, bearded men with children at home fondled him, and thought of their own little ones. Profane men, who began an oath, were suddenly stopped by some companion, and, looking about, saw Cub, and blushed. No one thought him a burden to the company. They would soon be at home, anyway.

Thus Cub had a merry time of it, and the soldiers were happy with him ; but, up on the slope of Wild Cat Mountain, a woman wandered, a raving maniac, sleeping at night on a lone grave beneath a tall pine tree, and asking men whom she met in her wanderings if they had seen anything of Joe, or of little Jim.

VI

The Fighting Parson

COLONEL WOOD, in command of the Confederate forces at Knoxville after the withdrawal of General Zollicoffer, paced up and down his room in indignation and perplexity. Before him lay several letters from his officers in East Tennessee, complaining of the bitterness of the Union spirit, and the difficulty which the troops were having because of it. Upon the table also were several recent issues of the Knoxville *Whig*, which he had been intently reading. A citizen entered the room.

"Good morning, Colonel Wood."

"Good morning, Mr. Sumner. I am glad to see you. Have a chair."

"I came over, Colonel, to have a little talk with you about Parson Brownlow. The grand jury, which is just beginning its session at Nashville, is likely to indict him for treason."

"He deserves it!" interrupted Colonel Wood.

"That may be, and yet I should be sorry to have it done. He is an extreme and abusive man, and rarely does justice to his opponents, but he is conscientious, and his intentions are good."

"Hell is paved with good intentions," replied the colonel.

"So I have heard. You used to be a minister, did you not, Colonel?"

"Yes; I am still a minister of the Methodist Church, and am preaching the Gospel of peace and of human rights in my present position."

"Well, you ministers might be a little more charitable toward each other than you and Brownlow seem to be. However, that is not what I came to say. I am sorry to have Brownlow arrested for treason. If he should be convicted and hanged, hundreds of Confederate sympathizers, like myself, who do not agree with him, and who have sometimes differed with him sharply, and who are most ready of all men to admit his infelicities of temper and of speech, but who respect his integrity and intentions, would be most sorry."

"I don't see how it is to be helped. He has brought it upon himself."

"That may be, but he has done it honestly and bravely."

"But, man, look at it from the military point of view. Here we are, in the midst of a hostile people. I need not hesitate to say to you that we have been greatly disappointed in the conduct of East Tennessee. We knew their sentiments before the war began. We knew that, separated as they are from the more wealthy portions of the South, their sympathies were more positively national and less sectional. We knew that, while few of them are rabid abolitionists, many of them are opposed to slavery, and few are bound to defend it by reason of property considerations, as is true in the remainder of the South. Still, we hoped that when the war had once begun, State pride would assert itself, and that the spirit of kinship with the rest of the South would animate them, and we should have thousands of them in the Confederate army."

"You did not know them, Colonel, that is evident."

"I know them now to my sorrow. They have resisted all our efforts to have them join the Southern army. A few have come, and most of these half-heartedly and over-persuaded."

"Over-persuaded is a good word, I think, Colonel."

"I admit that we have used harsh measures. But how could we help it? These villains have not a spark of honor. They take the oath in preference to going to prison, and then either evade it, or connive at measures which violate its spirit, and say that they have taken it 'from the teeth out.' They shoot our soldiers from ambush. We have lost scores of them, basely murdered in cold blood."

"The people have had strong provocation. Your soldiers have done no little looting, and have been guilty of intimidation and other crimes."

"Undoubtedly; it is impossible to hold in check so great a body of men in the midst of people who continually insult and harass them. But to return to Brownlow. In all these months of our occupancy his paper has been most bitter, and is increasingly so."

"Yes, it was more temperate when General Zollicoffer was here in person."

"General Zollicoffer's action I will not criticise, but I am disposed to think that his friendship for

Brownlow, his previous connection with the work of a newspaper in this city, and his own political sentiments made him err on the side of charity."

"I reckon he had more charity for printers, having been one."

"And for the old Whigs, having been one."

"More than you for preachers, having been one."

"The last few weeks his editorials have been past endurance. Have you read them?"

"Indeed I have, Colonel. Have you?"

"Read them? How could I help it? A score of copies are brought to me by indignant officers. Marked copies come to me by mail, one of them, I think, from the office of the *Whig* itself."

"What do you think of his call for Confederate troops?"

"It is insufferable. For three weeks he has been calling on the Confederate sympathizers to make good their boasts and join the Confederate army. Under guise of this call he has exposed the weakness of our hold upon the people of this region. He has referred again and again to the prospect of a draft. He has ironically urged the men of property and position to enter the army, and thus has bred discontent among the poorer people, from whom we had so hoped for a large number of soldiers. These now are saying, in echo of his editorial, that those wealthy Tennesseeans who shout most loudly for the Confederacy are most slow in offering themselves."

"There is rather too much truth in it to be comfortable," said Mr. Sumner, with a rather uncomfortable laugh. "I want the South to succeed, but I confess that I am a little slow about enlisting, with the Union forces moving, as they are said to be, toward Cumberland Gap, and with thousands of our own people, who have gone into Kentucky to enlist, eager to come back and visit upon the heads of all who have been concerned in the rebellion the evils which they have suffered. Besides all that, there is the danger of confiscation and financial ruin. You cannot wonder that men of means here in Knoxville are slow to offer themselves for military service."

"We will not discuss that, Mr. Sumner. Personally, I believe that men who believe in the justice of our cause should pledge as our fathers did for their independence, their lives, their fortunes, and their sacred honor. But to have this flung in our faces by Brownlow, and then flung up again by the men whom we have all but persuaded to enlist, is not pleasant."

"I can believe it. It is hardly less pleasant for us."

"That man deserves to be hung. He has kept ten thousand men out of the army. He has given aid and comfort to our enemies. He has scattered broadcast treasonable information. He has rejoiced over our misfortunes. He has stimulated the hostility of East Tennesseeans until we are on the crater of a volcano. If the Yankees should succeed in taking Cumberland Gap, I am not sure but they would rise and hang us all. And every week makes the situation worse."

"Colonel, do you think it possible that they can capture the Gap?"

"We could hold the Gap against any force if it were well provisioned and supported. But if General Zollicoffer should be defeated, what with the knowledge our soldiers have of the hostility in their rear, they would give up the Gap without a struggle."

"I am afraid you are right, Colonel; and if so, can you wonder that business men of Knoxville, whose sympathies are with the South, should hesitate to take a pronounced stand in favor of it?"

"I do not wonder, but I do not like it. However, there is one thing certain: Brownlow must be suppressed."

"That seems likely to be done. But can we do nothing to save him from arrest?"

"I am not anxious to save him. Yet, I would do so if I could honorably. He might take the oath, or a parole to be silent, and we could save the indictment."

"I am afraid it is no use to suggest that. But I intend to go to him. Will you come with me?"

"I have been on the point of calling on him, but I dread his abuse. I will go with you, if you wish. Perhaps he will be more courteous."

"Very well; let us go over."

The office of the Knoxville *Whig*, then one of the most famous of American journals, and the only Union paper published within the Confederacy, stood back from Gay Street, and was reached by a narrow alley. It was a plain, one-story building, with press room in the basement. The editorial and business office and the compositors were on the ground floor, and above the office was an attic in which the editor had a few books, among them

Helper's "Impending Crisis," for loaning which one of Brownlow's sons was arrested.

Down the alley that led past a business house built in front, Colonel Wood and Mr. Sumner picked their way to the sanctum of the *Whig*.

Parson Brownlow was reading the proof of an editorial when they entered his office. His dark face looked darker as they saw it in the shadow, and his heavy jaw had a determined look about its hard lines, which was not encouraging. He sat with his back to the window and looked squarely into their faces, and they looked toward him and the light as they talked.

"Mr. Brownlow," said Mr. Sumner, "Colonel Wood and I have called to consult you about your editorials in the *Whig*. Some of them seem to us a direct incitement to insurrection. You have even counselled the destruction of property and almost the destruction of life."

"I have said that the railroad that bears our loyal citizens south to die in rebel prisons ought to be eternally destroyed, and the men guilty of this outrage should pay the forfeit with their lives, and have offered to print in a roll of honor the names of men who would do it," said Brownlow.

"You will readily understand, Mr. Brownlow," continued Mr. Sumner, "that men having business interests in Knoxville and in sympathy with the South —"

"While careful to keep a whole skin themselves," interrupted Brownlow.

"Never mind that. You have had your say on that subject through the columns of the *Whig*. Now let me talk. We have labored long and hard to secure the building of railroads to Knoxville."

"And no man harder than I," said Brownlow.

"Gentlemen," interrupted Wood, "this is beside the mark. The question is not one of finance or of business interests. The matter of destruction of property is not now to be considered from its business, but from its military, point of view. Mr. Brownlow has incited his minions to rise and destroy the railroads. He has taunted us with our misfortunes, and has published them to our enemies. He has hindered enlistments, and has given aid to the miscreants who are waylaying and murdering our soldiers. Forbearance has ceased to be a virtue."

"Indeed it has," said Brownlow. "You hypocrite, parson at once and henchman of Jeff Davis! You have stolen the livery of heaven to serve the devil in! You preach on Sunday, and in the week encourage your drunken troops to enter my premises, brandish their weapons, throw filth at my house, insult my wife and children, and threaten my life!"

"I have done no such thing," said Wood. "I have tried to restrain my troops. You have goaded them to desperation. You have flaunted the Union rag in their face from the roof of the veranda of your house. You have abused them through the columns of your paper and in private and public speech."

"You are a lying hypocrite," said Brownlow; "a renegade minister of the Gospel. You have laid aside the robes of the sacred office you dishonored, to become a traitor against your God and your country!"

Colonel Wood rose from his seat.

"Mr. Brownlow, I will not bandy abusive epithets with you. I will at least be a gentleman. And I will not wait until my insulted manhood goads me to use my position to bring upon you the punishment in my power, and which you so richly deserve. It is an errand of kindness that has brought us here. Mr. Sumner is your friend. I, in spite of all your abuse, am a brother minister. We have come to say that this must stop. The grand jury is now in session, and, within a week, will have an indictment against you for treason. You know what will happen, if you are tried on that charge. Better men than you, and men who have been less flagrantly guilty, have been hanged. Now, sir, will you take the oath and escape this?"

Parson Brownlow rose to his feet and faced the colonel, his sallow face terrible to look upon in his wrath.

"Do you mean to insult me with your proposal to take the oath of allegiance to your hell-born and hell-bound government?" he demanded.

"Parson Brownlow, wait a minute," said Mr. Sumner; "I do not think you would be required to take the oath. We know your convictions, and no honorable man would ask you to falsify them. And I, and many of your neighbors who do not agree with you, would be perfectly willing to go your bond upon your simple promise not to utter or print treasonable words against the Confederacy."

"Such a promise, Mr. Sumner, I will never make. You may hang me, but you can never muzzle me. I have committed no offence. I have not shouldered arms against the Confederate government or the

State, or encouraged others to do so. I have discouraged rebellion, publicly and privately. I have protested against the outrages of this military despotism. I have refused to make war on the government of the United States. I have refused to publish to the world false and exaggerated accounts of the several engagements had between the contending armies. I have refused to write out and publish false versions of the origin of the war, and of the breaking up of the best government the world ever knew. All this I will continue to do, if it costs me my life. Nay, when I agree to do otherwise, may a righteous God palsy my right arm, and may the earth open and close in upon me forever!"

"Very well, sir," said the colonel, as he went out; "if you bring yourself to the gallows with your obdurate treason, your blood be upon your own head."

"Pray that it be not on yours," retorted Brownlow, "you have blood enough there already."

Mr. Sumner remained with Brownlow after the withdrawal of the officer.

"Mr. Brownlow, I am sorry that you insist upon a course which can but involve you in trouble."

"Why should it involve trouble? Does not this detestable government believe in the freedom of the press? Has not Jeff Davis himself said, and with reference to my paper, that he would not live in a government in which the press was not free? And now the whole Confederate government insists on breaking down the one newspaper in all these eleven States that dares to expose the evils of this cursed rebellion."

"I cannot talk of that with you, Mr. Brownlow; but, as a friend, I urge you to think of your own safety. I must say that I think it exceedingly unwise for you to continue the *Whig*."

"Then let me tell you, Mr. Sumner, that I have already determined to suspend the *Whig*. I know that my arrest is determined. I shall not wait to be arrested, knowing what trial would mean under the practices of this rebellion. I am now reading the proofs of what is to be for the present the last issue of the *Whig*. I am reprinting to begin with the articles which have been most criticised. I want them to stand as my unalterable declaration of principles. And here is my final editorial. I shall not leave until this last issue is printed and distributed. I may be arrested before I can get away. If I am cast into prison, I want this editorial to speak my final word to my constituency. I have said here what I think of the boasted freedom of the press in the Southern Confederacy. I have reviewed the course that brings me to prison. Here is a paragraph which you may care to read."

Mr. Sumner took the damp proof-sheet, and read:

"I shall in no degree feel humbled by being cast into prison, whenever it is the will and pleasure of this august government to put me there; but, on the contrary, I shall feel proud of my confinement. I shall go to jail, as John Rogers went to the stake, for my *principles*. I shall go because I have failed to recognize the hand of God in the breaking up of the American government, and the inauguration of the most wicked, cruel, unnatural, and uncalled-for war ever recorded in history. I go because I have refused to laud to the skies the acts of tyranny, usurpation, and oppression inflicted upon the people of East Tennessee for their devotion to the constitution and laws of the government handed down to them by their fathers, and the liberties secured to them by a war of seven long years of gloom, poverty, and trial. I repeat, I am proud of my position and my principles, and shall leave them to my children as a legacy far more valuable than a princely fortune, had I the latter to bestow.

" The people of this country have been unaccustomed to such wrongs. They are astounded for the time being with the quick succession of outrages that have come upon them, and they stand horror-stricken like men expecting ruin and annihilation. I may not live to see the day, but thousands of my readers will, when the people of this once prosperous country will look these wanton outrages upon life and liberty full in the face, and will ' stir the stones of Rome to rise and mutiny.' The people of this country, downtrodden and oppressed, still have the resolution of their illustrious forefathers, who asserted their rights at Lexington and Bunker Hill!

" Exchanging, with proud satisfaction, the endearments of home for a cell in the prison, or the lot of an exile,

" I have the honor to be, etc.,

" WILLIAM G. BROWNLOW,

" *Editor of the Knoxville Whig.*

"KNOXVILLE, October 24, 1861."

" How do you like it?" asked the parson, as Mr. Sumner handed him back the proof.

" It is characteristic," said Mr. Sumner.

" I shall go down with colors nailed to the mast," said the parson.

" I think, Mr. Brownlow, you had better leave the city as soon after publishing this as possible."

" I shall leave in a few days, if they do not arrest

me first. But I shall not go at once. I shall wait and see how it affects the rebels. I will not fire from ambush. They may arrest me, if they wish, after seeing my last utterance. But I shall not stay long."

Mr. Sumner took his departure, and called on Colonel Wood.

" Bear with the brave old man a little longer," he said, "and do not be in haste to arrest him, even if the indictment is found. The matter will adjust itself in a few days, and save you the criticism that would surely follow if he were to be arrested."

So Parson Brownlow published the last issue of the *Whig*, and waited about Knoxville for a week without molestation. Then he began preparations for an extended absence from home. He had had his say. He had waited after the firing of his last shot. He was ready now to go to prison or to exile.

Brownlow's enemies rejoiced, and his friends were relieved when he left Knoxville. He had been a thorn in the flesh of the Confederates for months, and that he was allowed to continue so long, spoke much for their forbearance. His unsparing invectives, his incisive taunts, his pious, but none the less vigorous, imprecations, were more than could be borne by a city filled with hostile soldiers, who suffered week by week under the lash of his tongue and pen. For a few days he rode about Blount and Sevier counties, collecting debts that were due him for advertising in his paper. He returned secretly to Knoxville and spent the first Sunday in November, and then withdrew again, and none too soon, for an event occurred which compelled him to flee for his life, and hide in the Great Smoky Mountains.

VII

Burning the Bridges

A GROUP of men were gathered on Friday, the 7th of November, in the woods near the East Tennessee railroad. The sun had gone down, and the short twilight was deepening into night.

"We're all here, boys, I reckon," said Jacob Hanson.

"Yes, all here," said Henry.

"I'm mighty glad you're with us, Hank," said his neighbor, Hensie.

"So am I. It ain't quite in line with my instructions, but it's helping the Union army."

"Yes, this railroad has been haulin' a stream of rebel fire right through East Tennessy the last year. What with the cotton States to the south, an' V'ginny to the east, we've had to take it from both sides along the line of this road."

"An' our friends sent south to rebel prisons, too."

"Yes; that was what made Parson Brownlow the maddest. He said to let the railroad that tuck our loyal men south to prison be etarnally destroyed."

"Well, that's about wut's goin' to be did. Have you got the fire?"

"Yep. You reckon we've got pine knots enough?"

"Plenty. We mustn't use more'n half on 'em at the first bridge. We'll need half for the other."

"What shall we use besides the pine knots?"

"Tear down the neardest rail fence and pile on top."

"Better let that liquor alone, boys," said Jacob Hanson, for some of the men were passing a bottle too frequently. "We'll need to be cool to-night."

"Who's at the head of this expedition?" asked Henry. "I didn't know about it till I got home to-night."

"Parson Carter, of Carter County. He's kin of your cun'l. He's planned the burning of six bridges to-night, taking in all the important ones for a hundred miles each side o' Knoxville."

"Parson Carter!" exclaimed Henry. "Why, it was to Rev. William B. Carter I brought my message from General Thomas."

"Sartin. Pap Thomas knows about it, an' so does Abe Lincoln, an' they want the bridges burned just as the Union army moves through the Gap."

"Put away that bottle, boys," again said Jacob. "Whiskey's all right in its place, but you've had enough fur to-night."

They made their way through the woods to where the railroad crosses a creek of considerable width. They looked up and down the track. No train was in sight. No soul was about.

"Henry, you fetch half the pine, an' the rest of you go for them fence rails," said Jacob; "and here, Sam, give me that fire."

Jacob Hanson moved to the middle of the wooden bridge, and blew and blew till the dull coal glowed, and, placing it upon a tie in the middle of the bridge, continued to blow, while he laid upon it slivers which Henry tore from the pine. In a moment a bright blaze appeared, and more pine was added. Jacob held the knots till they were well ablaze, and laid skilfully the dry sticks which Henry brought to him. It was some distance to a fence, and the fire was mounting high when the rails began to come. Eight sturdy fellows came carrying two long rails each, and one or two brought three. They went back and brought another load, and then a third, and Jacob and Henry laid them diagonally across the fire.

"Lay 'em criss-cross, Henry, not straight, like that. Lay 'em so's when they burn in two they won't drap inter the water. Thar. Leave open spaces for the fire to git through, thataway. Hit's as good as a grate an' a chimbly. Them iron tracks makes mighty good fire dogs, an' the fence rails is dry as punk. Ef hit don't all burn 'thout ketchin' the ties. No, they're gittin' lit. Now they're burnin'. All right, boys! Now fur the Holston!"

"You don't have no sorter doubt this is right, do you, Fry?" asked a man named Haun.

"Not a mite. Do you, Hensie?"

"Nary bit. Wen the Union army comes down, ef the railroad is here the rebs will jes' jump on the train an' git to kingdom come before the Union sojers kin ketch 'em. We mus' keep 'em here till the army comes. They've tuck away our guns so's we cyan't fight much, but we kin hold 'em wile the army licks 'em."

"I call this part o' the lickin'," said Henry.

"It's the railroad fetches 'em their provisions. Ef we fix 'em so's they'll go hungry a spell, they'll know how hit feels to some o' the people they've robbed."

It was late at night when they came to the bridge over the Holston. Near the little hamlet of Strawberry Plains the railroad spans the river. Here was a fine long bridge, built upon eleven piers. This was a more dangerous attempt. They paused near the bridge and laid their plans.

"Less git our rails an' have 'em near afore we set the fire," said Hensie. "They's a fence thisaway. Come, Fry an' Haun! Mr. Hanson, you bester git yer pine knots a-blazin' good afore we start, an' Hank, you git ye a big bundle of dry sticks."

Pursuant to this plan, the rails were piled out of sight at the end of the bridge, and all was in readiness for a start, when a shout was heard from the guard-house below the bridge.

"Hurry, boys!" cried Jacob. "Half o' you hold back the guard, an' the rest come with me!"

The sober members of the party for the most part stayed with Jacob, and the others engaged the guard. There was but one Confederate soldier guarding the bridge, but he was sober and brave. He faced his half dozen assailants without flinching, and wounded two of them before they got near him. In the darkness they became confused and got to fighting each other, and then alarmed the men upon the bridge with cries that a large body of soldiers was upon them. The fire was blazing high, and the whole party took to their heels, bearing away their wounded as they went. Then the brave

The Burning of the Bridges.   Page 90.

guard, whose single arm had driven away the burners, faint and wounded as he was, attacked the fire and saved the bridge.

The men were chagrined at their defeat, and the sober ones bitterly reproached the others. But it was no use crying over spilt milk, and besides they had succeeded with one bridge, and four others were burned by other parties.

"You don't reckon they's any doubt, do you, Hank," asked Hensie, "that the Union army is sure a-comin'?"

"Not a mite," said Henry. "That's what I come to tell Parson Carter. They was at London wen I lef', an' Cun'l Carter had some men on plumb to the Cumberland River at Barboursville. I shouldn't wonder ef they had took the Gap by this time."

"I hope so," said Haun. "I wouldn't mind so much, but I'd sorter hate to git hung. I got a wife an' a fambly o' little fellers, an' one's a baby. I'd sorter hate to git hung."

"They wouldn't none on us like hit right well," said Fry. "But the kingdom's a-comin'. They won't nobody git hung fur this. The rebs will be so skeered, wut with our burnin' the bridges an' the Yankees a-comin', they'll swim the streams to git over inter V'ginny an' to the cotton States."

"An' they'll come out lack Pharaoh's hostis," said Jacob.

"You're mighty right," said Hensie. "An' we'll sing to the Lord, for he hath triumphed gloriously. But I'd hate powerful to stretch hemp. Good night, boys!"

"Good night. We won't stretch no hemp. But you kin sorter be twistin' some for the rebs."

Thus the men went to their homes in mingled triumph and trepidation. The plan which they had just executed had been under consideration for months, ever since the suggestion of the destruction of the railroads in the *Whig*, and the event which had caused it to be decided upon was the news, brought by couriers, of whom Henry was one, detailed to bring the report of the victory at Wild Cat. Henry had found the plot in readiness for execution when he arrived at home, and, flushed with the joy of victory, he had joined his father in it.

Colonel Wood was finding his position in Knoxville anything but a bed of roses. He had tried to be at once a gentleman, a soldier, and a Christian minister. He preached at times in the Methodist Church, and endeavored to promote among his soldiers a spirit of reverence and fidelity. But his soldiers were not all as pious as might have been expected of the troops of such a commander, and the populace were in almost open rebellion. It was a relief when the *Whig* ceased its publication, and when in the first week of November it was reported that Brownlow had left, one thorn was withdrawn from the flesh of the commander. But there was other news that greatly distressed him. Following the defeat at Wild Cat, there was the most trying exhibition of effrontery on the part of the loyal citizens, and of fear and distress on the part of the Southern sympathizers.

Officers began to send in word that the people were getting out their hidden arms. One reported that the women were engaged in making flags, and that when discovered they did not even attempt to conceal their work. There was an outbreak of citizens against the soldiery in Knoxville. There were official reports of similar outbreaks elsewhere in East Tennessee.

In distress, Colonel Wood wrote to General Zollicoffer:

"KNOXVILLE, October 28, 1861.

"GENERAL: — The news of your falling back to Cumberland Ford has had the effect of developing a feeling that had only been kept under by the presence of troops. It was plainly visible that the Union men were so glad that they could hardly repress an open expression of their joy. This afternoon it assumed an open character, and some eight or ten of the bullies, or leaders, made an attack on some of my men, near the Lamar House, and seriously wounded several. Gentlemen who witnessed the whole affair say that my men gave no offence and were not at all to blame. The affair became general directly, and the couriers were sent to apprise me at my camp of its existence. I immediately marched Captain White's cavalry and one hundred of my men into the town to arrest the assailants, but they made their escape.

"The Southerners here are considerably alarmed, believing that there is a preconcerted plan for a united action among the Union men, if by any means the enemy shall get into Tennessee. Lieutenant Swan told me to-night that he heard one say this evening, as Captain White's cavalry rode through town, that 'they could do so now; but in less than ten days the Union forces would be here, and run them off.' I cannot well tell you the many evidences of disaffection which are manifested every day, and the increased boldness that it is assuming.

"Very respectfully,

"W. B. Wood, *Col. Com'g Post.*

"Brigadier General Zollicoffer."

There can be no doubt that this letter contains the exact truth. The relations of the citizens to the soldiers were strained to the breaking point. The case was parallel to that in Boston at the time of what is called the Boston Massacre. The only thing needed to goad the loyal men to action was the approach of the army of Thomas. This, and the suppression of the *Whig*, were the two events that brought matters to a crisis.

Colonel Wood began to be uncertain whether he had not erred on the side of mercy in letting Parson Brownlow escape. He knew every foot of East Tennessee. He was known to all the people. If he were to go out among them on the heels of this news, and speak at meetings and inflame the people, adding to all his other pleas that of his own persecution and exile, to what acts of mutiny might he not stir the people? Something dreadful was certain to happen, and it had been a mistaken kindness that had allowed him to leave the city.

These were the last thoughts of Colonel Wood as he lay down to sleep the Friday night after the departure of Brownlow. He awoke next morning with a start. There was pounding at his door. A messenger was there in haste.

"Colonel Wood! Colonel Wood! The bridges are burned!"

"The bridges?   What bridges?"

"Five railroad bridges, both sides of the city. That over the Holston was saved by the most desperate means!"

"This is the work of Brownlow!" cried Wood. "What a fool I was to let him go!"

He dressed and examined the reports. The bridges were widely separated, and must have been burned by different parties, acting in concert. The railroads on which Knoxville depended for its connection with the Confederacy, east and south, were, for the time being, useless. Knoxville was isolated, an island, in a sea of loyal and determined men. There was no telling how strong and far-reaching the movement was. The hand of Brownlow seemed apparent in it.

He telegraphed to Richmond, and received from Secretary Benjamin an order to hunt down the bridge-burners at all hazard, to try them before a drum head court martial, to hang them beside the bridges they had burned, and to leave their bodies hanging as a warning to others. It was a terrible order, but the Confederate authorities were at their wits' end how to suppress the constant mutiny among the East Tennesseeans, and had failed in every gentler method.

Colonel Wood set about executing this order, and said to his men, as they were drawn up on horseback before starting:

"Hunt down the cowardly bridge-burners; and if you find Brownlow, take no chances of his escape. If need be, shoot him without mercy."

Elizabeth Casey was wakened on Saturday night by a knock on the door. It is rare that any one knocks in East Tennessee. It is customary to sit on the horse outside the fence and shout. It is considered more polite. It is also at times more prudent.

"Who's thar?" she cried, starting, and getting out the gun.

"Hush up, Mis' Casey. Don't ye say a word. Jis' git yer dress on, an' don' stop for no extry fixin's, an' let me in. Hit's Steph Crowell."

"Wy, Steph!" she exclaimed, opening the door after a very brief delay; "wut's the matter? Wut on airth fetches ye hyur at sech a time o' night as this? Se' down thar. Wait. I'll blow up the fire, an' we'll hev a light."

"Don' make much light, Mis' Casey. I'll jes' light this leetle chunk o' pine. Thar. That's better. Mis' Casey, do ye know the way to Sevierville?"

"Yes, I know it as well as I know the way to the church house."

"Could ye find it in the night?"

"Wy, sartin, ef they was ary reason fur hit."

"Well, they's reason enough. I want ye to go an' save the life o' Parson Brownlow."

"I'd ride furder'n thet to save his life. Tell me, Steph, wut's it all about?"

"Do ye know 'bout the burnin' o' the bridges?"

"Yes, I heerd tell of it, an' was mighty nigh tickled to death. Them was brave men, Steph."

"Well, I hain't got nothin' to say about thet. You know I'm sorter on t'other side, Mis' Casey."

"You hain't nuther, Steph Crowell, an' you know it."

" Wall, I hain't a-goin' to dispute with ye, but hit's sorter important that ef I'm on the side o' the Union, I shouldn't be thataway too strong. I'm sorter lack the feller down to Tasewell that's got up in his store a pictur' of a nigger slingin' up his hat an' yellin' ' Dis Union furever ! ' Wen the rebs was thar he tole 'em them was his sentiments, an' they read hit ' Disunion furever.' Wen the Yanks comes, he's a-goin' to pint to hit jes' the same, an' let 'em read hit, ' This Union furever.' I'm sorter lack him, I reckon."

" That's a mighty bad way to be, 'cordin' to my way o' thinkin'."

" Wall, Mis' Casey, I hain't got so much time to argify with ye as I mought have under other sarcumstances, as the feller said when he run from the sheriff. Parson Brownlow's a-goin' to preach to-morrer in Sevierville, an' the cavalry's out a-scourin' the kentry fur him. I was in Knoxville las' night, an' the very ole devil's let loose thar. Wen the news come, 'peared lack the everlastin' bottom had fell plumb outen creation. The folks was mighty nigh skeered to death. Wood, he didn't know fur a spell wether he was foot or a-hossback ; but he knows now, an' he's a-goin' to hang Brownlow or shoot him, one, ef he kin git him in range."

" May the Lord cause him to fall into the pit he digs for the feet o' thet good man ! " ejaculated Mrs. Casey.

" That sounds a heap lack some o' Brownlow's sayin's. Ef hit warn't that he's a preacher, you wouldn't know sometimes wether he's a-prayin' or quotin' Scripter chapter an' varse, or jus' plain every-day sorter cussin'."

" It's my prayer," said Mrs. Casey.

" Wall, go ahead, then ; but ef you'll sorter leave me to do the prayin' now till mornin', I want you to do somethin' else."

" I'm afeard they wouldn't be much prayin' done ef it was left to you, Steph."

" I don' know. I think a heap more'n folks thinks I does sometimes, an', like as not, I'll be a preacher yit."

" You'll hatter break that fiddle, first."

" I reckon I hain't got no real loud call to preach yit, and the fiddle is sorter comp'ny ; but I want ye to git onter the horse I fetched ye, an' go to Sevier-ville. Hit'll be mornin' afore you git thar, an' the parson'll be a-preachin', like as not. You needn't be afeard o' breakin' the law agin disturbin' riligious meetin's, but tell him to git, mighty quick. He's as safe in Sevier County as anywere. Tell him to git inter the hills of the Big Smoky. I reckon some o' our fellers will hatter go thar, too, for the rebs is a-huntin' on 'em down."

" You think I had orter go, stidder you ? " asked Mrs. Casey.

" Laws, yes. Hit wouldn't do fur me ter go. I jes' come from Knoxville. I gotter git home, an' not a ben away from here. An' they cyan't nobody take no news along the straight roads from Knox-ville out, for they've proclaimed martial law, an' nobody can't git outen Knoxville without a pass. I stole a canoe to git out, myself, an' jes' let her drift. They won't nobody think hit quare me a-leavin' to come home, for they didn't see me, an' I won't be missed ; but ef I was to be found at Sevierville, I dunno but wut they'd hang me.   I'm goin' to the Hansons' now an' tell 'em the news.   They best be keerful, for I sorter reckon mebby they know more about them bridges than they'd wanter tell."

"I'll go, Steph.   Have ye got me ary nag ? "

"Yes, they's a fraish horse at the door."

"Putt my side saddle on him, wile I git my best clothes on.   It won't take more'n fi' minutes."

It took rather less than that, and Elizabeth Casey mounted, saying,

"Good-by, Steph.   I'll be back a-Monday.   I sorter wisht you'd be either hot or cold, but I dunno but you're a sorter lack Nicodemus, comin' to Jesus by night."

"Nary Nicodemus.   More lack the Ole Nick," said Steph, whose best wit was at his own expense. "Good night, Mis' Casey."

"Good night, Steph."

And with that Elizabeth was off.

VIII

Retreat from a Vanquished Foe

"HOWDY, Jack! Come hyur, Cub! Jack has you more'n's good fur him sence Hank went hum. Come over hyur an' I'll nuss ye. Git up on my shoulder, thataway! Now, up! Thar! See wut a big man! Cun'l Cyarter hain't nowar! He's a bigger man than ole Pap Thomas! Now, see him march!"

The strapping sergeant, Joe Hallet, caught Cub up on his shoulder and marched up and down before the tent with him.

"Now we'll march like a gin'r'l, stiff an' slow, thisaway! Now we'll march like we was goin' to fight ole Zolly, thisaway! Now we'll march like ole Zolly a-runnin' away from Wild Cat, thisaway!"

Joe put himself through all imaginable military paces with Cub upon his shoulder, Cub at times giving orders, which were promptly obeyed. A group of soldiers always gathered about the front of the tent when Cub was on parade. To hold him was a luxury. To "pack him" was an honor to be fought for. And many a soldier looked at him with a soul-hunger in his eyes. They were not all saints, those East Tennesseeans, and now and then they looted a store. When they did so, the first thing to be stolen, not even excepting the whiskey and tobacco, was the stock of baby shoes, which they tucked away in their knapsacks to take home to the little ones that rarely owned a shoe.

"Did ye hear the news from East Tennessy, Jack?"

"No; what news?"

"Wy, the Union men have heerd that we're comin', an' they've begun to organize an' git out the ole guns that they've hid, an' they've riz up agin the rebs. They licked 'em in Knoxville t'other day, an' mighty nigh druv 'em out. Ole Wood had to send to Zolly fur more troops. Zolly's gittin' mighty skeered about the Gap. He knows we're comin' up in front an' the home folks behind, an' he's sorter between the devil an' the deep sea."

"He's right about that."

"Yes, an' las' Friday night the Union men got together at Hiwassy an' at Lick Creek an' burned the bridges. They know we're comin' to smite 'em on the one cheek, an' they're gittin' good ready to have 'em turn the other, an' wen they do, they'll ketch it thar, sure's the gun's iron."

"Bully fur the bridge-burners! Haey!"

The Southerner cheers when he is mildly jubilant, but in his intensest moments he breaks forth into a yell that rends the air with indescribable effect. It was such a yell that now went up,—a yell of triumph over the patriotic uprising of their kindred at home and of hope soon to share with them a larger victory.

"Who's that yander?" suddenly asked one of them.

A horseman had passed the lines and was coming with news. His horse was wet and spattered and had been deep in the mud of the road.

"Hit's Lew Bailey," said Jack. Lew had been one of the several messengers sent into East Tennessee to report the Wild Cat victory and prepare the people for the incursion of the troops.

"Hi, Lew! Wut's the news?"

Lew drew rein for a moment and let his horse breathe.

"I got thar an' back all right," said Lew. "Had to come back by the Big Creek Gap an' through the edge of Whitley. But I'm here."

"Yes, you're all right. But how's the folks?"

"Tol'able. They're gittin' mighty anxious to see us. Heerd 'bout the bridge-burnin'?"

"Yes; we jis' heerd."

"Wall, they're arrestin' Union men right an' left fur that. Wood's proclaimed martial law in Knoxville. Brownlow's tuck to the woods. They'd hang him sure ef they got him. They've hung some a'ready an' goin' to hang more. Hank Hanson an' his dad was in hit. They hain't arrested them yit, but I reckon they will ef we don' git thar soon. The people cyan't stan' hit no longer. They want us to come right off. Ef we don' go mighty soon, they won't be none on 'em lef' wen we do get thar."

Lew rode on to headquarters to report, and the news quickly passed from mouth to mouth. The whole camp was aflame. Then word came that another courier had arrived from Crab Orchard with messages from General Thomas. There could be but one message now, they all thought, and began their preparations for breaking camp. In an hour the long roll beat, and the men fell in. Every heart beat high. Visions of victory and of home rose before the minds of two thousand homesick and loyal men. Colonel Carter took his position before the brigade.

"Attention!" The order rang clear and strong.

"You are commanded to prepare to break camp!"

A wild cheer broke forth from the ranks that swelled into a jubilant yell.

"Attention! Keep silent! By order of General Sherman, issued November 11th, General Thomas is to withdraw his command to the north side of the Kentucky River."

The men listened in mute astonishment.

Colonel Carter proceeded,

"As a Tennesseean I can understand your disappointment at this order, which is also a surprise and disappointment to me. General Sherman anticipates a movement of the joint forces of Zollicoffer and Johnston. He believes that they intend to join forces and penetrate between his two divisions, attacking Lexington and Frankfort. We are therefore commanded to fall back to Camp Nelson."

Colonel Carter gave the message with evident sorrow and chagrin. He did his best to explain the matter to the credit of his superior officers, but the explanation was lost upon his men.

Andrew Johnson was at the little tavern, and came out to inquire the cause of the assembling of the soldiers.

"Are you to advance?" he asked anxiously.

"I am sorry to tell you, Senator, that we are to fall back to Camp Nelson," said Colonel Carter.

"Fall back! In the name of Heaven, what does this mean?" cried Johnson.

"I am so ordered by General Thomas."

"And what is Thomas thinking of?"

"He has his orders from General Sherman."

"It is an outrage!" cried Johnson. "It is in-famous! It is an order that should be disobeyed!"

"Senator Johnson, I must not allow you to speak so in the presence of the soldiers. The order must be obeyed."

"Colonel Carter, do you know that your people and mine are suffering martyrdom in East Tennes-see? Do you know that all that is keeping them alive is the hope of the coming of this army? That they strain their eyes to see it coming, and pray God for it night and day? Do you know that the rebels are stricken with consternation at our approach and our victory at Wild Cat? Do you know that the Union men, rejoicing in our approach, and stimulated by our messages of encouragement, have risen against their oppressors, and have put their own necks in the halter for very joy of our coming, and the desire to do something to co-operate with us?"

"I know all that. I myself am an East Ten-nesseean."

"And do you mean to desert your own people in this extremity? Do you mean to turn your back on them in their distresses, and leave them to be imprisoned and hanged, when it is fully in our power to fly to their relief?"

"Senator Johnson, I have no choice. I am eager to press on. I believe that we could do it. But I cannot go against the positive command of my superior, and I must not allow you to speak so in the presence of the soldiers, who already have all that they can bear without mutiny."

"Bring me my horse!" cried Johnson, and he was soon riding post-haste to Crab Orchard.

"General Thomas, this is infamous!" he cried.

"I cannot help it, Senator. I have sent word to General Sherman that I am sure his fears are groundless, and that the messenger whom I sent would hasten back with other orders, if he should see fit to change them. He has not changed them, and I must obey orders, and so must my men."

"It is slavery," cried Johnson. "And our people are being ground down in tyranny, and we desert them in their extremity!"

"Senator Johnson," said Thomas, "the right of free speech which is yours in the Senate, must not here be exercised to the point of inciting the soldiers to disobedience. Senator as you are, if you say more, I will arrest you!"

And Andrew Johnson bit his lip, and in sorrow saw the order with equal sorrow obeyed.

General Sherman did his best in after years to explain that strange command, with what success must be judged by readers of his "Memoirs."[1] He was overwrought and nervous, and a score of newspapers declared that he was insane; and General Halleck relieved him from duty, saying, "I am satisfied that General Sherman's physical and men-

---

[1] A part of Sherman's prejudice against East Tennessee must be attributed to his just estimate of the difficulties of military operation there, but part also to his too low estimate of its military importance. As late as December 1, 1863, he wrote to General Grant: "Recollect that East Tennessee is my horror. That any man should send a force into East Tennessee puzzles me. Burnside is there and must be relieved, but when relieved, I want to get out, and he should come out, too."

tal system is so completely broken by labor and care as to render him, for the present, unfit for duty."

General Sherman to the end of his life resented the suggestion that his command had been an unnatural one, or that his mental condition was such as to prejudice sound military judgment. He contended that Johnston and Zollicoffer might have made the movement which he anticipated, and he never could understand why they did not. The reason probably was a very simple one, that they had far more reason to fear Sherman than he had to fear them, and the last place on earth where Johnston or Zollicoffer would willingly have gone, was between Sherman's two divisions.

For weeks the political leaders of East Tennessee had been in Sherman's camp urging him to come to the rescue of the loyal people of that region. He stoutly declared, and repeated the mistake in his book, that "the people of the whole South" were "in rebellion"; that before he could be secure in his present position, he must have sixty thousand troops from the North, and that for any offensive movement two hundred thousand would be needed. He did not overestimate the magnitude of the undertaking, but he reckoned without one important item — the loyalty of the mountaineers.

Why should not the Army of the Cumberland have marched into Knoxville before the close of 1861? Zollicoffer might have been driven from Kentucky within a month after the Wild Cat fight. He might have been driven from Knoxville before the winter set in. Knoxville cost us dear when months afterward it fell into our hands. Alas for the delay and loss of life that came from "assuming the people of the whole South to be in rebellion!" One hundred and fifty thousand loyal soldiers came from out the southern mountains to disprove that assumption.

Whatever the answers from a military point of view to the questions about that campaign, they did not suggest themselves to the East Tennesseans. Parson Brownlow wrote in 1862:

"It has been a matter of surprise that our army did not march upon East Tennessee long ago, capture Knoxville, and take possession of that great railroad. It was certainly owing to bad generalship in Kentucky."

Four days afterward General Sherman was relieved, and General Buell arrived to take his place, but the Tennessee troops were already back at Crab Orchard. The roads were bad. The winter was near, and General Buell, while discarding General Sherman's theory of danger from a Confederate advance, held that East Tennessee was not in itself worth taking; that to justify an advance into it there must be some ulterior point, which as yet he had not force enough to attempt. And so East Tennessee remained in the hands of the Confederates.

IX

A Loyal Deserter

IT is impossible to describe the effect upon the East Tennessee brigade of the order to retire from the movement against the Gap. The Confederates laughed long and loud over " the Wild Cat stampede "; but the men who had set their hearts upon fighting under the old flag for the redemption of their homes were filled with amazement and with shame. They pleaded, they protested, they cursed, they prayed, they even wept. They threw down their guns and declared that they would never move backward. But most of them finally fell in as good soldiers, though they knew, or thought they knew, " some one had blundered." But here and there a stubborn soul stood out.

" I enlisted to fight, an' not to run," cried Joe Hallet, " an' I hain't a-goin' to run, nuther."

" Ef I gotter run," said Lew Bailey, " I wanter run from some one that's a-lickin' me, not from some one I'm a-lickin'. I wanter fight an' let the rebs do the runnin'. I'll be durned ef I'll do both."

" Who's Sherman, anyhow?" demanded Sim Galloway.

" He's a fool, whoever he is!" said another. "Why don't they let Pap Thomas run this thing? He knows what's what."

Jack Casey sorrowfully prepared to march. His

cheeks were red with anger, and his head hung for shame. The tears dropped from his eyes as he thought of his mother and her defenceless position. Then there were Henry and his father, in prison, probably, by this time, and to be hanged, as likely as not. And the army that should be flying to their rescue was turning its back upon them there upon the gallows for their country's sake. He could not, he would not. It was not for this that he had enlisted. It was not for this that he would stay. He would go back to Tennessee and share the fate of his people. He would go back and defend his mother. He would go back and help to rescue Henry and his father. He would go back and die, if need be, but he would not run from the face of a beaten foe.

He packed his knapsack and filled his haversack with food. He gathered his simple belongings together and rolled up his blanket. Then he took Cub by the hand, and started toward the wagons that were loading for the march ; but he did not go to them. Starting off at an angle where the road forks beyond London, he turned into the forest toward the east. He set Cub on his knapsack with legs astride his neck, and walked as rapidly as he could away from the town and camp. An idea had come to him. He could not take Cub all the way back to Tennessee, as matters were at present, but he was within reach of Roundstone. He would make his way slowly there, and leave Cub with Henry's kinsfolks, and then go on unhindered, into Tennessee, and return sometime,—he no longer had the heart to think when it might be, when Tennessee was free again, — and take Cub home.   He can hardly be said to have felt guilty over his desertion. To him it seemed that the army had deserted, and that he was still in the fight.   He felt a mingled sense of shame and sorrow; but it was not because he felt condemned for his own conduct.

Jack made slow progress with Cub, who sometimes toddled along beside him and then had to be "packed."   They stopped two or three times at houses and got a cup of milk for Cub, but the people looked so curiously at Jack's uniform and at Cub, and asked so many questions, — kind ones, to be sure, for they were almost all loyal people, but questions that he did not like to meet, — that he began avoiding the houses and going through the woods to escape them.   For, proud as he was in having a greater loyalty than the army which had deserted him, he began to find that he could take little pleasure in having it known that he had run away from the army.   Such freaks does conscience play, justifying us to ourselves, and condemning us when we stand before others; and then, on the other hand, pleading our case when others accuse us, and unmercifully chastising us when it has us alone at its mercy!

It took him two long days to walk to Tigertail, which lies across the mountain from Roundstone. During those two days he struggled with his own conflicting feelings, yet ever justified himself to himself, but with a feeling of shame for the army which he had deserted.

Little Cub grew tired and often pleaded to be allowed to stop, but Jack pressed on.   Now and then he sat down and played with Cub and told him stories to rest him; and once a day, just after their noon meal, he spread out his blanket for a couch and let Cub take a nap. On the second night they slept on a thick bed of autumn leaves under the shadow of Torkletop Mountain, where the road winds through the Oxyoke Gap between Torkletop and Baldy, into the Roundstone valley. On the morning of the third day they emptied the haversack and climbed the winding road, and soon stood between the two great mountains that guard the approach to the valley, and looked down into the oval basin of the Roundstone.

Of all lovely valleys, Roundstone is the most charming. It is more than beautiful: it has an influence that is almost magic. The people of Roundstone would tell you so, and they are not given to sentiment. They would not know how to express it, but it is hardly too much to say that the whole community felt in a way that the creek was a sort of mirror of the life of the Holler. Not a few of its inhabitants have sat by one of the numerous springs which are its source, and wondered vaguely about the origin of life. They have followed its almost aimless wanderings through the valley, where it runs swift and shallow over the stones, and still and deep beneath the overarching beeches, and questioned whether the meaning of life is to be found in a mere search for the level which it finds in human relations. And they have stood by the Sinks, where the stream disappears, and wondered what follows when life seems to end, and what is the mystery of that unexplored cavern into which its waters are ceaselessly flowing, and where and what is the land where they emerge into sunshine again.

No one ever entered Roundstone through Oxyoke Gap without feeling something of the spell of the valley, which locally is known as The Holler. Jack Casey felt it as he entered the Gap that autumn morning in '61.

It was a clear November day. The air was keen and bracing and the sun was warm. It seemed like Indian summer in the valley and like the first pinch of winter on the hills. There was thin ice on the surface of Roundstone where it ran still, and the frost stayed all day on the north slope of the mountains. There had been no recent rain and no snow in the valley or on the lower hills, but Torkletop was white above the Gap, and Old Baldy stood up, magnificent in his antiquity, and lifted his hoary head with its crown of glory above the surrounding mountains, and extended his shadowy sceptre over the valley, of which he had been for unnumbered centuries the undisputed monarch.

Here and there Jack could see the smoke from a cabin, and almost directly across the Holler, a little to the south, stood one of the larger houses of the settlement. He moved down toward it, passing other houses, at which he inquired, and found that the house which he had seen from the Gap was that of Jacob Hanson's cousin, John Whitley. The sun was at its height as he crossed the foot-log over Roundstone and entered the yard.

A bright-haired, brown-eyed girl was spinning in the porch as he drew near. She started at sight of him dressed in blue and carrying a gun, but invited him to enter the porch and sit down.

There is many a skilful device of Cupid to set forth the charm of woman in the sight of man, but nothing which he has ever done can compare with that which he accomplished for the display of a woman's grace and beauty in the gentle art of spinning. The man who can see a pretty girl, devoid of self-consciousness, and with the freedom of a native grace, twirling the wheel and drawing out the thread, steady of hand and keen of eye, poising while it twists, advancing while it winds, and stepping backward while she draws another thread, — the man who can see all this, and watch the display of every curve and feature, the change of expression in face and eye, the poise of foot, the grace of ankle and the turn of hand, and not fall in love at first sight, is either hopelessly in love already or deserves never to be. And if Mr. Andrew Jackson Casey had not already been in love with her, he would have begun to love Jennie Whitley the moment he saw her in the porch that lovely November day.

And, if there be a thing which Cupid loves as a snare for the heart of a woman, it is a military uniform and the bearing of a soldier. Jennie Whitley, who already knew and respected Jackson Casey, did not regard him with diminished interest when she saw him before her dressed as a soldier.

"Howdy," she said. "I'm right glad to see you. Come into the porch an' se' down."

"Thank ye," said Jack. "I'm proud to see you."

"You're a sojer now, be you? So's my three brothers."

"Yes, I know.   I met 'em in Estill an' went to Camp Nelson with 'em."

"Is that so?   I'm right glad to hear it.   Seen 'em lately?"

"Not sence jes' atter the Wild Cat fight.   You heerd about that?"

"Yes.   Our boys was in it."

"Yes; they fit well."

"An' you holped whip Zollicoffer?"

"I reckon mebby I holped a little mite."

"What little boy's that you got there?"

"He's a little feller we found.   Hank an' I sorter took him.   Hank's gone back to Tennessy as a messenger."

"Is Hank a good sojer?"

"They hain't none better.   He's as good's they grow.   Where's your pa?"

"He went to the store for the news.   He goes every mail day now.   'Pears like he can't wait for news from the war."

"I reckon they's a heap more like him all over Kaintuck an' East Tennessy."

"You'll stop to dinner.   Pa'll be here right soon. Won't you take the little boy to the spring an' wash his face an' git him ready for dinner?   Or, hold on!—I'll git some water."

She brought him water and a clean towel, and Cub submitted, not without protest, to having his face and hands washed.   Then Jack washed his own, and combed his hair in the porch before a small glass which Jennie brought him.

"I hain't shaved sence I left camp," said he, viewing his face in the glass and suddenly conscious of a desire to look his best. "D'ye reckon I could have some hot water?"

She hastened to bring it, and he shaved himself in the porch while she went to the kitchen, where the dinner was already cooking.

Jack had completed his toilet, and looked and felt "better, two to one," as he expressed it, when John returned from the store. John was sorrowful and angry. He had heard of the retreat from London and the sorrow of the troops at the retrograde movement. It was not now at all certain that the whole mountain region would not be overrun. Roundstone, from its isolation, was relatively secure, but whatever the rebels wanted in the mountains was now at their disposal.

He quickened his steps when he saw a soldier in his porch. His first thought was that it might be one of his own sons returned from the army.

"Howdy, stranger, an' welcome! Sojer, I see."

"Yes. Is this Mr. Whitley?"

"That's my name. What's your'n?"

"Andrew Jackson Casey. I'm from East Tennessy. I've met your boys. I'm a neighbor of Jacob Hanson, an' a friend of his boy Henry. He's a sorter cousin o' yours, hain't he?"

"Yes; he's fust cousin. His mammy an' mine was sisters. I'm right glad to see a friend o' Jake's. Is Jake in the fight?"

"No; he couldn't git away right easy, but his boy Hank an' I slipped through the Gap an' 'listed together."

"I wisht you'd a-brought him with you. I hain't seed him sence he was a chap."

"He's back home now, detailed for messenger service."

"Be you on messenger service, too?"

"No, Mr. Whitley, I hain't. I wanter tell you all about it. I was in the Wild Cat fight. I was behind the fence with the other fellers when the rebs come up the hill, the front row with their hats on their bayonets till they got right clost, an' then they give a yell like all git out, an' come a-tearin' up the slope. We fired too high at first, them a-comin' up the hill an' we sorter excited like, but we didn't run an' they didn't stop. They kep' a-comin' an' a-comin', but we druv them back. Then 'long early in the evenin', 'bout two o'clock, they started fur us agin, an' agin we druv them back. We had kep' the top o' the mountin, an' we went over an' took the slope. They fit hard, but we met 'em face to face. Their guns was mighty pore an' so was our'n, — big, loud guns that take two thimbles full o' powder, an' a load big round as your thumb, — there's my gun! — an' three fingers deep in the bar'l, an' makes a noise when they go off loud enough to wake the dead, and kick like a steer, but they hain't much good, nohow. But we clubbed 'em back with the breech. We stobbed 'em with the bayonet. An' finally they jes' hadter run."

"I heerd about it," said John, excitedly. "I heerd how you alls licked 'em. But what's this about retreatin'?"

"I'm plumb shamefaced to tell about that. They's some mighty quare notions gits in the heads o' them officers. Thomas is all right, an' Garrard is all right, an' Carter is a hoss! But Anderson got sick an' had to git out o' the command at Louisville, an' Buell, they say, is goin' to take command; but he hain't come yit, an' while they're a-waitin', they give the command to Sherman. He come down to Camp Nelson while we was there an' made a long-winded speech to us. Thomas got mad an' left while he was a-talkin'. When he got done, the fellers begun a-yellin' fur Thomas to speak, but he swore he wouldn't do it."

"Thomas don't make no speeches, does he?"

"I reckon not, but he kin fight."

"How did the sojers like goin' back?"

"They hated it wus'n pizen. They swore they wouldn't do it, an' some on 'em didn't, but a heap on 'em did."

"Is that why you lef'?"

"Yes, I was jes' a-goin' to tell ye. I hate like sin to tell that I run away from the army, but it was thisaway. I lef' ma to home all alone. The rebs is rantankerous all around, an' I had to hide out for three weeks afore I left. I sorter had an *idy* that when we got into the army, we'd come marchin' back through the Gap, an' give the rebels Hail Columby. I hadn't no *idy* we'd enlisted to run. Well, just afore we got the order to go back, we'd got news from Tennessy about the Union men gittin' out their guns, an' the women a-makin' flags, an' all a-gittin' ready to welcome us an' help us drive out the rebs, an' how the Union men had burned the bridges, an' we's all fired up, an' ready to start, an' then come this news that Thomas had had a fool order to call us back. I thought o' mother, down thar alone. I thought o' Henry an' his pa, that had a sheer in the bridge-burnin', an' like as not in jail, an' goin' to be hanged, sure. I thought o' leavin' them all thar, an' runnin' like cowards when we'd jes' licked, an' I couldn't stan' it! I jes' packed up, an' says I, 'They kin go back ef they wanter, but I'm a-goin' back the other way. Ef I can't fight fur East Tennessy in the army, I'll go back an' fight thar outen it.'"

"I don' blame ye a mite! Nary mite!" cried John. "Did ye say Jake an' Henry is in jail?"

"Not as I knowed on. But the word was that they had a sheer in the burnin', an' the rebs was a-huntin' on 'em down."

"I'm afeard they'll git 'em. Looky here."

He took from his pocket the current issue of the Memphis *Appeal*, and pointed to an advertisement headed "BLOODHOUNDS WANTED," signed by two Confederate officers at Camp Crinforth. The advertisement stated that the hounds were wanted "to chase the infernal, cowardly Lincoln bushwhackers in East Tennessee and Kentucky."

"That makes my blood bile!" said Whitley. "Hain't it enough for them dirty slave-catchers to hunt niggers with hounds? Hev they come to that, that they must hunt white men, too? An' is the Gov'maint at Washington goin' to stand off an' see us et up by bloodhounds, an' call back their sojers when they're winnin' hand over fist? I don' blame ye a mite for desertin'! Go back an' fight fur your home! Go back an' die like a man, defendin' your old mother, ef ye hatter die, but don't leave

her thar alone at the mercy of the bloodhounds, an'
run away!"

"That's what I allow to do," said Jack. "An'
there's somethin' I'd like ter ast you about. Here's
this little feller, — Cub, we call him. He's a mighty
pert little feller. He's a orphan, and we got him
outen a burnin' cabin, whar the pappy was dead an'
the rebs had murdered his mammy an' sot the
house afire. I can't travel right easy an' pack him,
an' I hain't no sorter chance to keer for him jes'
now. I didn't wanter leave him with the army.
The fellers would a liked mighty well to have him,
I know, but he sorter belongs to me and Henry
together. I wonder ef you kin keep him here till
the war is over, an' I'll come an' git him, ef I live."

"We'll sorter hatter talk that over with Jennie.
She's boss inside the house. She's all I got now.
The three boys has all gone off, an' Jennie's the
only one that's lef'. Her ma died three year ago
come spring, an' she's ben my housekeeper ever
sence. She's a-callin' on us now to dinner. Less
go in. Yes, we're a-comin', Jen! Here, young
feller, come to yer granpap. Law, hit don' seem
but yistiddy I had shavers o' my own no bigger'n
him! An' now they're all growed up an' gone to
the war. They hain't nothin' grows so fast as chil-
dern. You'll be a sojer, too, one o' these days,
won't ye, young feller?"

"I's a sojer now!" cried Cub.

"Shore 'nuff! I reckon ye be. Wut be ye, a
cap'n or a cun'l?"

"He's a gin'ral, you'd think to hear him order
the fellers 'round. Here, Cub, set up on my

shoulder, like I was a hoss, an' show how you give orders!"

Cub mounted Jack's back and rode up and down the porch, giving orders and carrying off the honors with *éclat*, while John applauded and Jennie watched with interest, standing in the doorway.

"You best come in now," she said; "yer dinner'll be gittin' cold. Here, little man, you take this cheer beside yer pa, — beside Mr. Casey."

"Here, young feller," said Whitley, "you git up on this cheer! I'll turn hit 'round, so. Now you stan' up on the cheer, an' hole on with one hand to the back, an' retch with the t'other fur wut ye want. An' ef ye don' find wut ye want within retch, jes' ast granpap, an' you'll git it."

He paused a moment, hesitating whether to invite Jack to ask a blessing. His blue suit gave him a dignity that made it seem a proper thing; but he remembered his youth, and asked the blessing himself.

Cub got on finely at the table. His position was that which had been approved in the Holler for long generations. High chairs are unknown, and the rising generation stands on a chair at table and eats with one hand, while holding to the back of the chair with the other.

After dinner, Cub took his daily siesta, while Jennie washed the dishes, and he was still asleep when she joined her father and Jack in the porch.

"Leave off yer spinnin' fur a while, Jennie, an' fetch a cheer an' set with us. We're a-talkin' 'bout somethin' you'll want a finger in."

Jennie brought the chair, and walked with it past

Jack and her father, at no small inconvenience, and wholly without necessity, as it seemed to Jack, so as to sit beside her father. But that may not have indicated that she would not have been glad to sit beside Jack.

"Jennie, Mr. Casey's ben a-tellin' me about his plans an' what he intends to do. He's gotter go back inter Tennessy, an' hit tain't sartin how things is goin' to be down thar. This little feller is a orfling what he an' Henry picked up outen a burnin' cabin, an' they 'lowed atween 'em to keep him. But he cyan't tote him down to Tennessy, and he wants to know ef we'll sorter look atter him till the war is over. I told him that depends on you. I hatter do jes' what you say, ye know, an' sometimes hatter toe the crack mighty clost. But I 'lowed ef you didn't see no objection, we'd mebby try it. That's a right pert little chap."

"I don't see no reason why not," said Jennie. "He's a mighty fine little feller."

"Right smartly so. He's a major, sure's you're a foot high. Ye don't reckon you'd have no trouble takin' keer on him, do ye, Jen?"

"I don't guess it would be much trouble," said Jennie; "an' I git right lonesome sometimes when you're gone, now the boys is away."

"An' I git sorter lonesome myself thinkin' on 'em. 'Pears lack now they're gone, I think on 'em more as they was when they was little. I don't har'ly seem to real*ize* that they're men. I reckon this leetle feller'd be comp'ny fur us both. All right, Mr. Casey, we'll keep him!"

"Thank ye, Mr. Whitley. I 'lowed you'd do it.

Now I'll stay over night ef I kin an' hev a leetle more of a visit with Cub, an' then I'll sorter slip off 'fore sunup in the mornin', an' you kin say good-by to him fur me atter I gone, so's he won't take on, an' I'll git over inter Tennessy."

It seemed a short afternoon and a short night. Jack stole a little chance to talk with Jennie alone about Cub, enlarging on his precocity, which, if the regiment was at all to be believed, was phenomenal, and tenderly committing him to her care. With the sunrise he was off. John Whitley took him on his way as far as the salt works on Goose Creek, and bade him an affectionate farewell.

"Good-by," he said. "'Pears lack I'm sendin' off another boy. You favor my boys a heap. I'll look out for Cub, or Jen will. Do yer duty, an' God bless ye!"

Sunday at Sevierville

IT was a pleasant November Sunday when Parson Brownlow preached at Sevierville. The news of his appointment had spread far and wide, and would have drawn a large congregation at any time; but just now it was a matter of especial and widespread interest. The news of the bridge-burning, which had occurred on the Friday night before, was widely known, and added to the excitement. Whether Parson Brownlow had a share in it was not known; but many had read with a thrill an editorial in the *Whig*, remembered now with equal clearness by his friends and enemies, in which he had said,

"Let the railroads on which Union citizens of East Tennessee are conveyed to Montgomery in irons be eternally and hopelessly destroyed! Let the property of the men concerned be consumed, and let their lives pay the forfeit, and the names will be given!"

With Brownlow, was old Parson James Cummings, who first spoke. He was eighty-five years old and his white hair hung about his neck, but he was erect and had a martial bearing, and his spirit was strong and inflexible. He said:

"My brethren and sisters, my sands of life are nearly run. I am an old man, and my sun is near its setting. For forty years I have been a preacher of the Gospel, and I have borne among you an unblemished reputation for honesty and for sincerity. I fought in two campaigns under Andrew Jackson for this country, — for the *whole* country, not a part of it, — and I was a major in the War of 1812. I have defended this country against the British and against the savages. I have lived its entire history. I was born in the year that our country came to life. I want to live to see it reunited and happy. I am driven from my home for no crime, but because I am an outspoken friend of the Union. I do not falter. I do not fear. I am encouraged to firmness when I look back to him, against whom the mob cried, 'Crucify him!' but whose power was righteousness, and who came into the world to bear witness to the truth. O brethren, be strong in the Lord! Put on the whole armor of God. Take the sword of the Lord and of Gideon, and be ready when the hour shall strike to drive from your midst the invader and the spoiler! And pray for God's blessing on our hearts and our homes, on our glorious old rock-ribbed mountain loyalty, and on what is to be our fair and reunited country!"

There was perfect silence in the great congregation gathered from a radius of many miles, when Parson Brownlow rose to speak. He stood, tall and dark, smooth shaven, and with shaggy hair and brows, and began to speak in measured tones that soon rose in their key, and gathered power and volume till his tempestuous eloquence swayed the audience as a field of corn is swayed by the wind. Said he:

" My friends, I am glad to be here and speak to you to-day. I have left behind me my home and my business, and am a fugitive for the sake of my loyalty to our common country. I have not taken arms against the Southern Confederacy. I have committed no violence, but I have opposed with voice and pen the infamy of this treasonable attempt to break up this country, and for this I am driven from my home.

" My friends, I am glad to speak in Sevierville. It is a glorious name. It brings to our minds the days of the Revolution, when our fathers fought and won the battle of King's Mountain, glorious as that of Bunker Hill, the clans of these highlands gathering each under its own chieftain and winning a glorious victory. Among the leaders that day who were foremost in the fight, the one to whose genius more than to that of any other man the honor of the victory belongs, was John Sevier. This town may well be proud of its name.

" It was John Sevier who laid in these mountains the foundations of this glorious old commonwealth of East Tennessee. For we are a commonwealth by ourselves, my friends, in history, in politics, and all that distinguishes our public life. There is a line of separation that runs through Tennessee from north to south, and it follows the line of these mountains. It is in East Tennessee, where John Sevier established his commonwealth, which he named the State of Franklin in honor of the man who drafted the Declaration of Independence, that those principles are held dearest. That State has passed into oblivion; but the principles which it honored — the principles of the Declaration of Independence, the principles of the Revolution, the principles of Benjamin Franklin and of John Sevier — abide in our hearts to this day.

"My friends, we have fallen upon an evil time. East Tennessee has been voted out of the Union against her will and against her protest. Let me remind you of the way in which this glorious old commonwealth has been voted out of the Union through the fraud and villany of the Governor, Isham G. Harris."[1] Mr. Brownlow pronounced the name so as to bring a scornful emphasis upon the "sham," and went on at length concerning the elections of February and June.

"By such fraud and villany," he went on, "was this State carried over to the Confederacy, and East Tennessee with it, though even in that election, with thousands of illegal votes, with hundreds of timid men kept from the polls, East Tennessee protested against separation from the Union by a clear majority of 18,300! Glorious East Tennessee! She still stands unterrified and uncorrupted, five to one, for the Union and the flag!

"Now, my friends, what are we to do? We are taken out of the Union against our voice and vote.

---

[1] Governor, afterward Senator, Isham G. Harris, died in July, 1897, while this chapter was in the hands of the printer. Extreme as were the measures by which he carried Tennessee out of the Union, and severe as were Brownlow's strictures upon him, even Brownlow had later abundant proof of his honesty. When the Union forces occupied Nashville, Harris went south with the Confederate army, serving on the staff of General A. S. Johnston. He took with him the State school fund, amounting to half a million, and was himself counted a wealthy man. He returned at the close of the war, when Brownlow was Governor, and, though reduced to poverty by the war, had preserved the school fund intact, and turned it over to the Brownlow government.

We have had neither part nor lot in this infamy. We have seen our fields plundered, our neighbors conscripted, our brothers and sons driven to hiding in the woods, our polls corrupted, our leaders imprisoned. Wrongs less wanton and outrageous precipitated the French Revolution! Think of it! Citizens cast into dungeons without charges of crimes against them, and without the formality of trial by jury! Private property confiscated at the beck of those in power! The press humbled, muzzled, and suppressed, or prostituted to serve the ends of tyranny! The crimes of Louis XVI. fell short of all this, and yet he lost his head! The people of this country, down-trodden and oppressed, still cherish unshaken the spirit of their illustrious forefathers, — of Lee and Pickens and Sumter, of Jasper and Sevier!

"Friends, I may never speak to you again. With me, life has lost something of its energy. I have passed six annual posts on the western slope of half a century. Something of the fire of youth is exhausted. I have a bronchial trouble which may not long endure the exposure and the hardship to which I am now subjected. This may be the last time my voice reaches you before I die, — perhaps upon the scaffold, basely charged with treason. But if I were standing now upon the gallows, I would speak no other words than these, bearing my testimony against this monstrous rebellion, and calling upon you to be true to your record, to your ancestry, to your country and your God. If I am charged, as I have often been, with inciting you to insurrection, I reply that I am rather inspiring you to deeds of patriotism.   If I could, I would 'stir the stones of Rome to rise and mutiny.'   If I should hold my peace to-day, these rocks upon your loyal mountains would cry out their horror of the crimes to which we are submitted and their call to resistance.

"The Union army will soon be here.   Be ready to meet it.   Be ready with your weapons and your strong right arms.   Be ready with your flags and your loyal voices.   And when the boys in blue come marching through Cumberland Gap and through the mountain passes to your own fair land, from every hearthstone and fireside, from every schoolhouse and from every church, let this long shout go up to heaven, East Tennessee has been loyal to the Union, and will be, now and evermore!"

During the latter part of his address, Brownlow drew himself to the full height of his six feet.   His face that was dark and hard seemed almost trans-figured, and his voice that at first was slow and somewhat broken was like the sound of thunder. It was Sunday, and a religious service, but a long, loud shout arose and the mountains echoed it back again.

As Parson Brownlow ceased speaking, and before Parson W. I. Dowell, who was to have followed, began, there was a commotion in the back part of the congregation.   A woman, who had been riding hard, entered hastily, and called for Parson Brownlow.

"Parson," she said, "you must run for yer life. The cavalry are after you.   They're huntin' ye with orders to shoot ye without mercy.   They know you're here.   Hurry!"

Mrs. Casey's Warning to Parson Brownlow.   Page 128.

Having delivered her message, Elizabeth hurried away. She went to her horse, and was mounting, when the people came to her, and insisted that she should rest before returning. She went to a house, and received the generous hospitality of the people. At night she remounted and took her long way back to her home.

Before they left, both Brownlow and Cummings denied in the strongest language knowing anything about the conspiracy to burn the bridges. Brownlow declared that the false charges were knowingly made as a pretext for their murder.

"Let them kill me," he cried, "and this noble old man of God, who is also the victim of their malice! Let them shoot us down like dogs, or hang us on their accursed gallows! We can die, if need be! But our death will have a terrible retribution. The Union soldiers will avenge us sevenfold. The thousands of Union men in East Tennessee, devoted to principle and the rights of those who fall at the hands of these conspirators, will avenge their death! Let the fires be rekindled on the Union altars, and let the fire of the Lord consume these conspirators as it consumed Nadab and Abihu for presumption less sacrilegious! If we are incarcerated at Montgomery, or Tuscaloosa, or murdered for love of the Union, then let our friends and the friends of the Union take vengeance upon our murderers in the name of the God to whom vengeance belongeth! Let it be done, East Tennesseeans, though the gates of hell be forced, and the heavens be made to fall!"

Sevier County had voted on the question of separation from the Union in the preceding June, and against a scattering vote that aggregated 60 for dis-union, had polled 1528 for the Union. Brownlow knew full well that he was in the hands of his friends. He received the most abundant evidence of the support of the people to whom he spoke, and was hurried away with Cummings and Dowell to the remotest corner of the county, where he hid from the search that was diligently made for him.

Brownlow had other and later warnings. On Sunday night, William Rule,[1] a printer in the office of the *Whig*, left Knoxville by stealth, and rode, at the risk of his life, to warn Brownlow to escape. He found him on Monday, safe and undismayed, in Tuskaleechee Cove, in the Smoky Mountains.

Elizabeth Casey returned to her home on Sunday night, leaving the horse at Steph's as she went.

"Git home an' to bed to wunct," said Steph. "The rebs is all round. They've caught Haun. They got wind o' Hensie an' Fry. Jake an' Hank has run to-wards Sevier. They got acrost the river somehow," — Steph coughed a little, — "I dunno jes' how. But they're gone. Hit's lucky they didn't no man go your errand. An' you bes' be at home tendin' to yer own business right pert, if they call. I'm doin' more'n wut a rebel sym-pathizer ort to do, I'm afeared, but I got too tender a conscience. That's the cause o' the mos' o' my shortcomin's. Now, you git home."

---

[1] Later a captain in the Union army, and now editor of the Knoxville *Journal*, successor of the *Whig*.

XI

Exile and Prison

FAR back among the Great Smoky Mountains, close to the line that separates East Tennessee from North Carolina, is Tuskaleechee Cove. There, in a deep gorge which no wheeled vehicle had ever entered, a group of men gathered about a fire one day in November, in 1861.

Jacob Hanson raked the ashes from the top of some sweet potatoes, and tested them with a wooden fork. A dozen men watched the operation with interest.

" Done ? "

" Jes' right."

" How's the meat?" The question was addressed to a member of the legislature, who was broiling a piece of meat hard by.

" It'll do, I reckon."

" It's a mighty good thing we got that bear," said Judge Green. " They'd have had a hard time getting enough provisions from Wear's Cove for us, and the men below, too."

" He's tasted mighty good, I know that," replied Parson Cummings.

" Parson, ask a blessing."

Parson Brownlow raised his hands, and gave thanks for the bear meat and sweet potatoes which constituted their meal.

There were a dozen or more of them, all told, men of prominence, for the most part, and men exposed to special danger, either from outspoken patriotism, or from some overt act of resistance to the Confederate rule.

"This is getting mighty tedious," said one. "I don't like hiding out here like a pack o' groundhogs, with the men below a-guarding us like we was prisoners. I'd like to muster 'em all into a company, and go and meet the Union army."

"The Union army will be here soon," said Brownlow. "We shall see the end of the Confederacy in a few months. I expect to see it before I am a year older."

"A year! We can never stand another year of this!"

"Oh, *we* won't have to stand it a year! It may be a year before the rebellion is fully put down; but East Tennessee will be liberated in a few weeks."

"I hope so. This is the last of the bear, and we may not get another right off."

"Oh, well, we can get a coon now and then; and 'possums are mighty fat just now."

"We won't have many more sweet taters to eat with 'em."

"I'm 'fraid your right; and 'possums ain't much good without sweet taters. Is there ary sweet tater left in them ashes?"

"Just one more, Judge. You kin divide it with the parson there."

"Thank you, Judge. The law ought to divide with the Gospel."

"Who comes yander?"

"Somebody in blue. They've sent him up from below with news, I reckon. He ain't none of our men. The sojers mus' be comin'!"

"Hit's Jack Casey, as I'm a livin' man!" cried Henry. "Jack, hallo! Hello, Jack!"

"Hello, Hank!" called Jack, and quickened his ascent of the rugged and uncertain path that brought him to the fastness.

"Hand up yer gun. Give us yer hand an' I'll give ye a lift."

"Take the gun. I don't want no help. I kin git up," and Jack came clambering up the rocks.

"Ben eatin', hev ye? Got anything left?"

"Mighty little. Hungry?"

"Hungry! I could eat a horse with the saddle on!"

"We've got one tater, ef the parson and the jedge will give it up, an' thar's a little of the bar left that Hank killed t'other day. Thar, I reckon that'll keep you alive. Now tell us whar you come from, an' what's the news."

"Don't ast me no questions till I've et my dinner, an' then I'll tell ye."

"Wall, swaller yer victuals now an' chaw 'em atterwhile, ef you expect us to wait. Fur I reckon we're starvin' for news 'bout as much as you be for bar meat."

"Young man," said Parson Brownlow, "self-preservation is the first law of nature. We don't want you to starve to death, but we want you to tell us right off about the army. Where is it? Has it passed the Gap? Has it entered Knoxville?"

Jack stopped eating, and tried several times before he could swallow the bite in his mouth.

"The army has retreated," he said at length.

"Retreated!" every voice cried out in amazement.

"I hate to tell it. I'd ruther cut off my right hand. The army has fell back to Crab Orchard an' is goin' back to Camp Nelson."

"Did they get licked?"

"Licked? No! We licked 'em all out at Wild Cat."

"We know about Wild Cat," said Brownlow.

"Yes, don't tell 'em nothin' 'bout Wild Cat," said Henry. "I've told them all about that. Tell us what's happened sence."

"Gimme a drink o' water. I sorter choked on that bar meat," said Jack. "I hate like sin to hev to tell you. But we got to London, you know, an' had some men out as far as Barboursville, and found the way clear to the Cumberland River. We was all gittin' ready to foller, an' feelin' big as life, an' sartin sure we'd lick him, when all to once Cun'l Carter called us up an' said some one or other had told Sherman the fool yarn that Zollicoffer was a-goin' to nunite with Johnston over to Bowling Green, and push between Sherman an' Thomas, an' capture Lexington an' Frankfort, an' Sherman had ordered us back."

"Back where?"

"Back north of the Kaintuck River."

"An' Thomas done it?"

"He hated it like sin. He sent back to Sherman an' told him it was a lie, that the rebs wan't a-comin' in between 'em, but a-movin' away, an' he said he'd give the order, but he'd tuck pains to send the message by a officer that had got to come right back, so's to sorter give Sherman a hint to tell him to countermand the order. But Sherman didn't, an' the sojers was ordered back."

"Did they go?"

"Some on 'em did. They cussed an' cried and begged till Carter couldn't stand it, but it wan't no use. They just hadter go or desert. I deserted, an' I find a heap more did."

"You did wrong, my son," said Parson Brownlow. "The provocation was great, and you meant right, but you did wrong to desert the flag."

"It is a mysterious dispensation of Providence. I cannot understand it," said Parson Cummings.

"Providence — fiddlestick!" said the judge. "It's cowardice or treason!"

"Young man, proceed," said Brownlow.

"I run away. I hated to do it, an' warn't sure it was right, but I reckoned it was. I tuck Cub to Roundstone, Hank, an' found your kinfolks, the Whitleys. Ole man Whitley said they'd keep him, an' his daughter Jennie—"

"Omit that now," interrupted Brownlow, "and tell us what you learned as you came. How do the people talk? What have the rebels done? How is this to affect our future?"

"I got home, but didn't dast to stay. Ma was all right, but Hank and his pa had hadter hide here. Steph Crowell holped me right smart to git off unseen. Your folks told me to tell you howdy, Hank, an' your pa, too."

"What did you hear about the rebels?" asked the judge.

"They're gittin' mighty rantankerous sence they heerd the news. They're talkin' big about what they'll do ef they ketch Parson Brownlow an' the men that burned the bridges. They say the Yanks don't know when they do lick; an' when they do, they're so skeered, they run. They're huntin' for you alls. I heerd said they knowed you was in Tuskaleechee Cove, and a guard o' Union men in Wear's Cove, an' they're goin' to attack us to-morrow."

"To-morrow?"

"Yes; they're on the way now. I hurried to git word to ye."

There was an interval of silence. Parson Brownlow opened his Bible and read the account of the humiliation of Israel at Ai. His voice trembled; and when he came to the prayer of Joshua, the tears rolled down his swarthy cheeks and mingled with those of a dozen brave men.

And Joshua rent his clothes, and fell to the earth upon his face before the ark of the Lord until the eventide, he and the elders of Israel, and put dust upon their heads.

And Joshua said, Alas, O Lord God, wherefore hast thou at all brought this people over Jordan, to deliver us into the hand of the Amorites, to destroy us? would to God we had been content, and dwelt on the other side Jordan!

O Lord, what shall I say, when Israel turneth their backs before their enemies!

For the Canaanites and all the inhabitants of the land shall hear of it, and shall environ us round, and cut off our name from the earth: and what wilt thou do unto thy great name?

"Let us pray," said Brownlow.

They all fell upon their knees, and many wept, as the strong old patriot, with sobs and tears, poured out his soul before God.

"What shall we do?" they all asked, each of the rest, when the prayer was ended.

"Let us stay and fight them," said Henry.

"There couldn't be no better place," said Jack. "They can't git at us from but one way. They can't come up with horses. They can't fetch no cannon. They just gotter come up a few at a time. We kin keep 'em back."

"But we'll starve," said the judge.

"I don't see why. They's game enough, an' we kin go over to the other cove to-night an' gether some corn an' taters."

"There seems nothing else to do," said Mr. Cummings sadly. "I have long since beaten my swords into ploughshares, and have used the Sword of the Spirit, which is the word of God, to plough the soil of men's hearts for the sowing of the seed. It is hard for an old man who has preached the Gospel of peace for forty years to be driven to fight with carnal weapons, but I see no other way."

"We must prepare at once," said the judge.

"It won't do, friends," said Brownlow. "If the Federal troops were really coming, or even holding their own, we might do it. I shrink from bloodshed; and though I am called the Fighting Parson, you will bear me record that I am a man of peace.

Yet I would fight if there were any use. But we could not hold out long. If the rebels are not restrained by fear of the Union troops, they can bring against us force which we cannot hopefully resist. We must scatter, and at once. We must go forth two and two, or, at most, in groups of three, and hide where best we may, and wait for the coming of the Union army."

After much discussion, this plan was adopted. Jack set out with Henry and his father. Brownlow and Dowell set out at nightfall with faces toward Knoxville, and as day was breaking stopped at the house of a friend, six miles from home, and there learning that General Carroll, whom Brownlow knew, and whom he believed to be a Union man at heart, was about to succeed Wood in command at Knoxville, he sent to him a letter, conveyed by his friend, Colonel John Williams, asking to be allowed to return to his home, and to be assured protection.

General Carroll answered this letter six days afterward, and the letter reached Brownlow three days later, promising him protection to the extent of securing for him a fair trial. Brownlow felt the importance of proving in advance, if possible, that he had not been concerned in the bridge-burning, and sent his affidavit, with those of Cummings and Dowell, that none of them had known in advance of the plan to burn the bridges. The letter was not delivered, as the messenger who conveyed it received other word on his arrival at Knoxville. Confederate friends of Brownlow, Mr. Sumner and others, had sought from Hon. J. P. Benjamin,

Confederate secretary of war, a safe conduct for Brownlow out of the Confederacy. Secretary Benjamin wrote to General Crittenden, who had recently assumed command, saying that he was unable to give a formal passport, but would be glad to know that Brownlow was out of the Confederacy, rather than a disturbing element within it. On receipt of this, General Crittenden wrote to Brownlow, that by calling at headquarters within twenty-four hours, he would receive a passport into Kentucky, and would be accompanied thither by a military escort. Brownlow eagerly obeyed, and reported at headquarters in Knoxville, where arrangements were made for his removal two days later. But on the intervening day, he was arrested for treason, and imprisoned.

There is no evidence that General Crittenden or Secretary Benjamin dealt with Brownlow in bad faith, though at the time it was impossible not to believe that this had been the case. Both Benjamin and Crittenden appear to have been surprised and grieved at the act, which originated with the Confederate district attorney. But, fair or foul, he was arrested, bail was refused, and the man who had returned with assurance of protection and safe removal was cast into prison.

The jail in Knoxville was crowded full on the sixth day of December, 1861. One hundred and fifty Union men were there confined, too thickly crowded to allow all to sleep at once. The jail contained no article of furniture, table, or bed, or bench. A single water bucket and a tin cup did service all around, and was refilled at intervals from a dirty hogshead near at hand. The food was scanty and of poor quality, the jailer being, as is often the case in the South, the proprietor of a hotel, and feeding the prisoners largely on the remains from the dinners at his hostelry. It was hard lines in the jail when Boniface had an unusual run of custom at his other boarding house.

The guards were insolent, profane, and obscene. Occasionally, a negro was placed upon guard ; and his delight in the magnifying of his office was almost intolerable, partly because he could be more over-bearing than any white man, and also because the prisoners, while few of them owned slaves, agreed with Parson Brownlow in " not regarding the chief end of man as nigger."

Most of the prisoners were in the single open room ; but back from the door was an iron cage, in which were confined men charged with capital offences. Of these there were four, all accused of bridge-burning ; and the negro guard stood at the outside of the cage, and threw bits of lead and pebbles through the bars at them, and called them vile names.

The short December day was drawing toward a close. The prisoners were glad to see it go, yet looked with more of sorrow to the night, in which the floor must be spaced out to one set of sleepers, who were to be wakened when the night was half gone, that the rest might lie down. There was a prospect, so they heard, that a large number were to be taken south in a few days to be imprisoned for the war. They all dreaded that fate, as they did the hangman, yet longed for any relief from the ills which they were suffering.

The door swung open and another prisoner entered. He was tall and dark, and stood erect, reaching almost to the low ceiling. Most of them recognized him at once, and the men in the cage gave a sudden cry,

"Parson Brownlow!"

The parson walked to the cage, straining his eyes to look into the shadow within.

"What, Hanson, Jacob Hanson! And your son, too! And Jack Casey! Ah, friends, I'm sorry to see you here! And who is this? Haun? Why, yes, I remember you. C. A. Haun? Certainly, I know you. And you, too, are charged with bridge-burning! And here are more of my friends, all about me here."

"We're all your friends, Parson," said an old man at his elbow.

"What, Tate, you old Calvinist! You here! Ah, yes, I know! You cheered the flag when it passed your door! Give me your hand, you noble old Baptist! You are wrong about the doctrine of the perseverance of the saints, but you have the virtue. And here's another old father in Israel, Parson Post. You prayed for Lincoln instead of Jeff Davis, didn't you? I heard about it. I'm glad to be with you."

"We're having a dreadful time, Parson," said one of the old men. "We ain't got no place to set down, nor nothin' to set down on. We can't eat what they send us to eat. The air is fit to smother us. When it's cold we almost freeze, and when it's hot we nearly die. When some of their brutal soldiers get drunk, they put them in here to sober off, and they curse and abuse us day and night."

Brownlow heard these and many like complaints. He heard sad tales of friends at home, of unjust charges, of false accusations, and of harsh treatment. At length he quieted them all, and said:

"Gentlemen, these things are hard to bear, but let us bear the yoke patiently. Don't take your confinement so much to heart. Rather glory in it, as patriots, devoted to your country and your principles. What are you here for? Not for stealing; not for counterfeiting; not for murder; but for your devotion to the Stars and Stripes, — the glorious old banner under which Washington conquered, lived, and died! You will yet enjoy your liberties, and be permitted to die beneath the folds of the star-spangled banner, the sacred emblem of a common nationality!

"Be of good cheer. The Federal Government will soon crush out this wicked rebellion and liberate us, if we are not brutally murdered; and if we are, we die in a good cause. I am here with you to share your sorrows and sufferings, and here I intend to stay until the rebels release me, or execute me: or until the Federal Government comes to my rescue. Do not be cast down. Above all, don't count this a disgrace. I regard this as the proudest day of my life."

It would be cruel to dwell upon those days. It would be unjust not to remember that some of the officers sought to relieve the sufferings of the prisoners, above all that the Confederate surgeon, Dr. Gray, who was unfailing in his attentions to the prisoners, secured them a few rude comforts, benches, a table, some pallets for the sick, and exercised a humanity which the prisoners long remembered. There were incidents of kindness such as his, which seemed forever like the spirit of the Good Samaritan. There were also instances of abuses too sad to recall; too brutal to be named.

Southern prisons are dreadful places, even to this day; and that at Knoxville, in a time when to ordinary motives for ill treatment there was added that of political hatred, was the scene of some gross indignities inflicted upon men whose only crime was their loyalty. May God forgive the brutalities that were inflicted by both armies in their military prisons! There is nothing that evokes more of the fiend in a brutal man than to place him, armed and in power, over men against whom he conceives himself to have the right of belligerent hatred.

One of the things for which the prisoners watched with most of eagerness, and one that brought them most of sadness, was the news that came to them by other prisoners who were constantly arriving. A new group from Jefferson County came one day and brought news of the capture and execution of Hensie and Fry. The hearts of those charged with bridge-burning fell, and they sorrowfully asked for particulars.

"Hit war Cun'l Leadbetter hunted on 'em down," said the new arrival.

"Who's he?" asked Henry. "I never heerd tell o' him."

"I know him," said Brownlow. "He's a Maine man. No Southern man can be as brutal as a renegade Northerner. He adds to the passion he has learned in the South a deliberation and calculating cruelty which a Southern man cannot equal."

"He tied the knot with his own hands," said the new prisoner. "He had 'em hung so near the track that men could hit the bodies with canes from the keer winders. An' he ordered the bodies to hang four days."

"The bloody scoundrel!" cried Brownlow. "When the Federal army comes into East Tennessee, that infernal murderer shall hang from the same limb!"

"Hit was specially hard for Fry," continued the prisoner. "His wife come an' begged to see him afore he was hung, but —"

"His wife?" asked Haun. "Dave Fry hain't got no wife."

"Hit warn't Dave Fry," was the reply.

"What Fry was hit, then?"

"His cousin Bill."

"Lookyhere!" cried Jacob Hanson. "You mean to say hit warn't Dave Fry was hung?"

"I tole you hit war his cousin," replied the prisoner.

Jacob started to speak, but Henry checked him.

"Look out what you say, pa. Ye cyan't do Bill no good now, and hit tain't no use to git Dave inter trouble."

"Be careful, too, for your own sake," said Brownlow. "These walls have ears. Don't confess that you know too much about it."

There was an awful silence throughout the jail for a full minute. The men in the cage looked at each other until they all grew pale, and in the dim light of the jail their faces were terrible to see. The prisoners gathered about the cage and waited breathlessly.

"If you can say anything without danger to yourself or others," said Parson Post, "we're very anxious to hear. Be careful, though. Speak low."

Jacob started to speak several times before he succeeded. Then he said, in a low voice:

"I hain't a-goin' to say who was thar, or who warn't. I hain't a-goin' to confess that I know nothin' about hit. But men,"—his voice sank to a whisper,—"I'll say this much. As true as God's in heaven, they've hung the wrong man!"

Then there was a long and terrible silence, and the men in the jail dared hardly to speak, or even to think. As they thought of it afterward, there was no hour of their sad prison life that seemed to them so unutterably dark as that period of silence and horror that followed Jacob Hanson's declaration.

The next day forty prisoners were marched out and taken to the prison at Tuscaloosa, Alabama, for the war. It was a sad scene when they departed to that almost hopeless incarceration, but it left more room. Before night, however, thirty-one other prisoners were brought in, and a dozen drunken soldiers were sent in for the night. The latter made the jail a howling pandemonium. Indeed, there seemed to be a general spree among the Confederate soldiers, and drunken men were placed on guard without. Three times during the night a drunken soldier thrust his gun through the window of the jail and discharged it, by accident, he said.

A few days afterward, Haun was taken from the jail and hanged. He was a young man of twenty-seven, and left a young wife and a family of little ones. Still a few days later, they took Jacob and Henry Hanson, and hanged them on the same gallows.

The details of the hanging, the prisoners might never have known, had it not been that the guards about the jail brought back reports of the execution, and told them, with every evidence of delight, to the prisoners, whom they constantly threatened with like fate. From these it appeared that the father was compelled to witness the execution of his son, before he was hanged himself. Both died unmoved, declaring their loyalty to the Union and the principles for which they had suffered.

There was more hesitation about Jack Casey. He was known to have been associated with the Hansons, whose guilt was clearly proved. The evidence against him was circumstantial, but strong. Against it, he could only declare that at the time of the burning he had been in the Union army. But this, if it proved anything, proved him to have been a deserter; and the word of a deserter was trusted little, when there was so strong a motive for his lying. Besides, when captured, he was fleeing from the officers, in company with the Hansons, who were his almost certain partners in the crime. There were other lines of evidence; and one man, whose evidence was procured through Lieutenant Sam Marshall, broke the force of his alibi by swearing that he had seen Casey near the scene of the bridge-burning, the night before it had happened. The military court felt the necessity of taking strong measures. It was almost impossible to convict these men, who were so strongly bound together. It was worse than folly to turn them over for trial to their own courts. The military tribunals had been far more liberal in these doubtful cases than their instructions would have warranted. They sentenced Casey to be hanged.

It was a sad mother who came to the jail to see her son Jack for the last time. She had ridden all night, on horseback, and arrived early in the morning. She cast herself upon her son's neck and wept as if her heart would break. She could give up her son to die upon the field of battle, but to see him die upon the scaffold, and for an offence of which he was innocent, she could not bear.

"My God, what a sight!" cried Brownlow. "May these eyes of mine, that have seen many sad sights, never look upon one like this again!"

He tried to think of some way to prevent this terrible murder of an innocent man. Could nothing be done?

He tore from his note-book a leaf, and wrote upon it a despatch to Jefferson Davis. Soon the time allowed the poor woman to take a last farewell of her son expired, and they led her from the cage, weeping bitterly.

"Here, madam," said Brownlow; "your son must not die. He is innocent. Bad as this rebellion is, Jefferson Davis does not wish to hang innocent men. It is too late to establish his innocence, but we may appeal to the pity of the President at Richmond. The telegraph office is near. Hasten there and send this message:

> "'KNOXVILLE, Dec. 27, 1861.
> "'HON. JEFFERSON DAVIS:— My only son, Andrew Jackson Casey, is sentenced to hang at four o'clock this evening, on a charge of bridge-burning. As he remains my earthly all, and all my hopes of happiness centre in him, I implore you to pardon him.
> "'ELIZABETH CASEY.'"

Jefferson Davis had a tender heart. Like the great-hearted Lincoln, he more than once took counsel of his sympathies, rather than his judgment, preferring to err on the side of mercy. He saw in imagination the mother and the doomed son. He pictured to himself the grief of the aged woman at the execution of her only boy. His eyes filled with tears.

"I cannot decide as to the justice of the sentence," said he; "but I will save his life."

Two hours before the execution should have taken place, the jailer entered the prison with Elizabeth Casey. In her hand was a slip of yellow paper.

"I am to release you from the cage," said the jailer, "and give you the freedom of the prison until you are taken south. Your sentence is commuted to imprisonment during the war."

The mother rushed forward to meet her boy, and with a cry of joy fell fainting in his arms, her hand still clutching the yellow paper which bore the news from Jefferson Davis that her son was not to die.

XII

Jack's First Journey by Rail

THE month of December was almost gone, and with it the year 1861. The hours dragged heavily in the Knoxville jail. The days since Christmas had been dreary enough. The soldiers were unusually bibulous, and the jail was never free from the presence of some who were sobering off. The guards were just drunk enough to be ugly, and their ill-treatment became so unendurable that one of them was disarmed and soundly thrashed by a prisoner named Turner. The officers were probably glad of the event as an aid to discipline. At any rate, Turner received no punishment, and for a day or two the prisoners were treated with a little less of inhumanity. Parson Brownlow watched the fight with the keenest interest, and applauded its issue; and even Jack Casey, who was then in the cage under sentence of death next day, could not repress his joy.

The day after Jack's reprieve, occurred one of the periodical deportations which always caused a flutter of excitement. No one knew who were to be sent south until the names were called. The officer who on this day had charge of the shipping of prisoners was himself a trifle the worse for his Christmas drinking, and in no very amiable mood. He had forgotten his list of prisoners,

too, and there was a vexatious delay while he sent
for it.

"Come, now.   More lively when your names
are called!   We've no time to lose!   Sick?" he
demanded of one old man.   "Git up here, you old
liar!   You'll be sicker afore you're done with this!"

Twenty-two prisoners were called off, Jack among
the rest.   They were marched through the streets
under a heavy guard, and locked into a box car, to
be sent to Tuscaloosa.   The train was a slow one
and the stops were frequent, and the short day was
at its close when it entered Chattanooga.

Here there was a delay; and at length the prisoners were ordered out, under guard, and were transferred to a car on another train.   They eagerly
looked about them, as they passed from one train
to the other, for some opportunity to escape, but
found none.

Jack's eye took in as much as time and the darkness would permit while the prisoners were being
loaded into the car.   There were several cars ahead,
— freight cars, and one or two flat cars, — and then
came the freight car which contained the prisoners.
Back of this was the caboose, in which the eight
guards and the trainmen stayed.   Two guards were
stationed upon the top of the prisoners' car, and
were relieved at intervals of two or three hours.
But the prisoners had judged from the sound of
their walking upon the roof that the guards on top
did not regard their post as hazardous, and made
occasional excursions to the caboose to warm themselves within and without, leaving only one man on
the roof; and they thought there had been one or

two brief intervals during the day in which all the guards had been in the caboose. This had given them little comfort, however; for these times, if they occurred, were of brief duration and when the train was in motion, and they were securely locked in.

The car was locked. The last breath of outside air had been breathed. The last chance of escape seemed gone. In darkness and silence the prisoners huddled inside the car. An hour passed, and the train was slowly creeping south. It would take them all night to ride the two hundred miles to Tuscaloosa, and the end would come all too soon. Another hour passed. Two men who were sick, one with rheumatism and the other with dysentery, lay in the corner moaning, one with pain and the other with cold. The others began to rise and move about the car, kicking their feet against the sides to warm them.

As Jack passed about the car, his foot struck a loose board in the end next the caboose. The guards had not noticed it in the dusk. It was as if, in the previous loading of a beam of timber, or other long and heavy article, the end of the car had received a blow that started the nails in three of the narrow matched boards, directly under the small end door and over the bumpers.

Jack dropped on his knees and examined the place. The nails had been pushed out nearly an inch, and might easily be knocked out entirely. Could an opening there be of service to them? They could not hope to escape by that way, and at first it seemed he had made a useless discovery. He called a council, and together the prisoners evolved a plan which had in it some promise of success.

The night was raw, and the guards on top grew cold. About the middle of the second watch, the prisoners were rejoiced to hear them both, as they thought, clamber down the ladder at the end of the car and enter the caboose.

"Now's the time, boys!" said Jack, and gave the loose boards a vigorous kick, and then another, and another.

At the third kick, the middle board gave way. Jack reached out for the coupling-pin. They were ascending a short grade, and he could not draw it. Oh, if they would only go down hill for a moment! The ascent seemed miles in length. The guards would surely return. The cars began bumping together. They were descending a slope. Now for it!

"Pull the furthest pin, Jack, so's we kin hev two!" said a prisoner at his ear. Jack reached, and withdrew the farther pin, and brought it inside; then pulled back the boards that still hung by the nails at the top, and waited.

They began to go up hill again. Jack peered out. They were leaving the caboose behind. It had stopped. It was far back. They rounded a curve and left it out of sight.

"Glory!" shouted Jack.

"Whoop-ee!" cried the prisoners.

The sick men moaned, and one of them pleaded pitifully.

"Oh, boys, don't leave us!"

"Pull in the other pin and the link," said Jack's monitor.

Jack drew the other pin, and reached out to take the link. As he was drawing it inside, a pair of legs came down the end of the car, and a foot swung uncertainly, feeling for a hold. They were mistaken in thinking that both guards were in the caboose. Only one had gone within. The other, seeing that an accident had occurred, and ignorant of the cause, had laid his gun upon the roof of the car, and was descending to investigate. It was no time to falter. The soldier was standing insecurely on the bumper, and holding with one hand to the brake-rod, while with the other he felt for a hold on the small end door. Jack stepped back, and gave a short run and a mighty kick. The boards burst off, and they and his foot struck the knee of the unstable guard. He lost his footing on the bumper and his hold upon the door. A moment he held with one hand to the brake; but swung round, and fell heavily upon the track.

The other prisoners had taken the two heavy coupling-pins and the link. The man with the link was busy at the door in the other end, and two with the pins were at one of the side doors. The latter first effected an egress, and a half dozen of the most reckless jumped out in the dark, with the train in motion. In time, the end door gave way, and Jack crawled through and drew the pin. The car slacked up, and soon stopped on a short bridge. The caboose was two miles behind, and the train was speeding on in the darkness. One of the prisoners climbed to the top, and secured the gun of the soldier. Others armed themselves with the coupling-pins, and all, save the two that were sick, scattered into the woods,—some to be recaptured, some to perish in the wilderness, and some, after untold trials, to escape.

When Jack crawled out of the window to uncouple the car, he did what was for him an unprecedented thing. He had never ridden before on the cars; and to climb between them in the night seemed, as indeed it was, a perilous venture. He felt for something to hold to, found the brake-rod of the car ahead, and clung to it with one hand, and stood with a foot on each bumper, while he leaned down to draw the pin.

The sweat was starting from him. His hand stuck to the frosty iron. He got his balance. He found the pin. He waited till the tension lessened, and drew the pin and handed it through the window. Just then the car gave a jerk as the train began an ascent, and he saved himself from falling by holding fast to the brake with both hands. When he regained his hold, the cars had separated, and he was speeding on with the train.

Jack was appalled when he realized his situation. The cutting-off of the cars would soon be discovered, and he would be found alone of all the prisoners. He crouched down upon the bumper and thought fast how he could make the best of his deplorable condition. He could not get into the car. The end door was locked. He might have climbed to the top, but was not sure but he was safer where he was. If he could be sure of finding an open door, and could enter it without too great danger, he would prefer to climb to the top and explore from car to car. But if he did not succeed, his danger would be increased. He decided to stay where he was, and, if discovered, to jump off.

He was fortunately saved from any rash step, and relieved from his dilemma, by the slacking of the train as it approached a station. Here, as it later appeared, they were to meet a train from the south, and here, he knew, they must discover the loss of their cars. The train ran upon a siding and slowed up. As the rear car passed the switch, a lantern flashed full in Jack's face; but the switchman had turned to close the switch, and did not see him. Jack let go his hold and quickly ran on the other side, along in the shadow of the train, until he came to some piles of railroad ties, and hid behind them.

He watched the switchman's light as he followed the train to where it had stopped. The light stopped at the end car and then went hurrying down the track to the engine. Then other lights came back. There were excited shouts and curses. The train from the south came in, but was stopped and held.

Soon the engine of the south-bound train cut off and ran back after the lost cars, the tender carrying two men from the north-bound train and two more hastily picked up at the little station.

Jack crept under his own train to the side of the other. He had ample time, and felt from car to car for an open door. He found none. It was a through-freight train, loaded for the most part with cotton, bound for Virginia. He stumbled over a pinch-bar lying beside the track. It was a heavy, clumsy tool for any other than its proper use, but it was a godsend to Jack. Slipping between two cars, he felt for the hasp and padlock that secured the end door of one of them, and, using his bar with vigor, pried off the staple and opened the door.

The inside was filled with cotton bales. There was a very narrow space above them in the car. He crawled in with difficulty, and with greater difficulty turned back and slid the door shut. He crawled half the length of the car, and found in the middle a narrow space that had not been filled, between the layers of bales in the two ends. Here he could stand erect, and find elbow-room and a fighting chance.

He began to take courage. His situation was not hopeless. If he could remain here without detection, he might hope to get far enough from the scene of escape to avoid suspicion when he should again appear among men. He could hardly wait for the train to move. The trainmen were quite as impatient as he. His heart stood still as he heard them pass his car cursing. But it was the delay that vexed their righteous souls. They cared little about the prisoners, but only wished they had been in Washington — or some worse place — before they had caused them this trouble. For the men of the other train and the drunken, faithless guards they had anything but gentle words.

It was a full hour, and must have been past midnight, when the noise of the other engine was heard. Without waiting to make inquiries, the north-bound train took on its two employés, and, amid a volley of curses, started on its way.

They made few stops before reaching Chattanooga. Jack lay down on the best bed he had enjoyed for weeks, and slept soundly until awakened by the stopping of the train.   There was a long wait and a deal of switching then; but at last, soon after sunrise, they crossed the Tennessee River and were on their way again.

Jack determined to stay where he was as long as possible.   His chances were improving with every mile.   He must get through the Confederate lines somehow, but he could not be in any worse place than he had been.

They passed through Knoxville early in the afternoon.   Jack feared that they might stop and leave him there, but they only stopped to change engines, and moved on.   Their progress was slower now, and it was night when they stopped at a small station near the Virginia line.

The prisoners had had two days' scanty rations served on leaving Knoxville.   Jack had had something to eat and had slept a part of the day. Nightfall found him somewhat rested and ready for adventure.   He waited an hour after the cars had been run on to the siding, and, satisfied that they were at their journey's end, crawled back along the cotton bales, slid open the end door, slipped out between the cars, and, shouldering his bar, escaped to the woods and turned his face toward the north star.

XIII

Jack's Return to his Regiment

THERE was never such a boy as Cub. Everybody admitted that. And it was the more remarkable, considering how many other boys he resembled. There was not a soldier in Carter's brigade who was not reminded of some " young un " whom Cub " favored." There was not a fond old grandmother in Roundstone Holler who was not given to tracing resemblances, and who did not give especial attention to Cub. Take him for all in all, if the concurrent testimony of those who knew him in childhood is to be believed, we shall not look upon his like again. This is true also of a large number of other small boys, according to the testimony — and who would dare dispute it? — of parents and admiring friends. Considering how many interesting babies there are in the world, the presence in life of so many commonplace grown people must forever remain an inscrutable mystery. But Cub belonged quite out of the ordinary category, and even mothers with boys of their own sometimes found it safe to exclaim, with what mental reservations it is not our purpose to inquire, —

" Sech another boy ! "

Cub's first Christmas in Roundstone was a great event. He woke betimes and climbed out of bed, and ran to the chimney-corner, where he found the most wonderful boy doll, dressed all in blue and with a soldier cap. His eyes and nose were cunningly painted on his white cloth face. His shoes were of the same material as his clothes. No purchased toy could have given half the pleasure that was afforded by that remarkable specimen of the skill of Jennie. It was his only present, and it was enough. Children on Roundstone never think of receiving more than one present, and that is why they so enjoy Christmas. It has been demonstrated that the joy which Christmas brings is in inverse ratio with the number of presents which a child is accustomed to receive.

Cub marched up and down the porch all Christmas day, shouting orders to his soldier doll, and calling "Christmas gift!" — which is the Holler's equivalent of "Merry Christmas!" — to all passers, and now and then shouting for the Union and the flag, and hanging Jeff Davis to a sour-apple tree.

No one has quite the same appreciation of the Civil War as one who lived through its scenes as a boy, and whose earliest and most indelible impressions are associated with its most stirring events. Cub drew in the military spirit with the air he breathed, and when he was told that if he cried at having his face washed — as, being a boy, he did — he would never be a soldier, he made his best attempt at heroic and stoical silence, though convinced that no soldier could have so severe a test of courage.

The days of "Christmas week" sped rapidly.

They were short, dark days, and nature was preparing for the dismal and incessant rain which fell in January. But no day went by that did not bring some neighbor with news, that was often old before it reached Roundstone. There was likely to be trouble over near Somerset, and there was hope that Zollicoffer would be driven back by a different route from the Gap. Thomas was massing his forces, and had ordered the scattered detachments of Carter's brigade to be ready to march to Somerset.

On New Year's Eve, a drizzling rain was falling, and the air had that creeping chill which penetrates all garments and coils itself next the skin, like a cold and slimy serpent. Cub and Jennie were in the chimney-corner, and she was knitting and teaching him his letters out of Webster's " Old Blue-Back " speller, and telling him the wonderful stories in the back part, which in Roundstone Holler is known as " the grammar " of the book, — about the ox that was gored, and the dairymaid who tripped in the midst of her day-dream, and the rude boys at whom the farmer threw first grass and then stones. John was popping corn in a long-handled skillet, his face getting red as the coals over which he held it as he bent over his work. The corn was popping with a merry rattle against the tin cover, when there came a faint hallo at the fence, and the dogs began to bark. John was too intent upon finishing the popping of his corn to stop, and Jennie went to the door.

" Come back, Tiger ! Here, Watch ! " she said, and the dogs came to her. " Hallo ! " she called.

" Howdy ! " The voice was faint, and she heard

the wooden latch of the gate click. There was something in the voice that sent the blood to her cheeks. Without waiting to ask who was there, she called, "Come up to the house!"

He came, reeling up from the fence, and caught at the porch to steady himself. He stood erect with an effort, and addressed a "good evening" to Jennie, and, as she stood aside, entered the house. A moment he stood, holding to the door for support, and then, on first feeling of the warmth of the room, dropped fainting upon the floor.

"Pa!" cried Jennie, as John was lifting the cover from the skillet. "Quick! It's Mr. Casey!"

John sprang to his feet, and was quickly at Jack's side. He was drenched to the skin, and cold.

"Git the whiskey bottle, Jennie!"

Jack was soon sitting with his head on John's knee, sipping the whiskey and hot water which Jennie held for him.

"I'm all right now," he said. "I was tard, an' a leetle mite faint. I hain't had nothin' to eat all day."

"Don't talk now. Jen, you run an' git Jack some hot milk with jes' a thimbleful o' corn juice in it, an' give me a dry shirt fur him, an' some hot water in a bucket fur his feet, an' a blanket to wrop him in, an' a dry towel."

Jennie obeyed these commands almost simultaneously, and started for the hot milk, while John was stripping off the wet clothes. Cub had stood in wonder for the few moments that had been consumed, but now he rushed to Jack, saying,

"Christmas gift, Jack! Don't you know me?"

"Cub!   Bless yer ole heart!   I seed you every minute in my mind while I've ben a-tryin' to git hyur.   You look jes' the same, but it seems so long sence I've ben hyur, an' they's so many things happened, an' I feel so much older myself, I sorter had an *idy* I'd find you a head taller."

John rubbed Jack dry with the towel, and brought a glow to his back and limbs; and placing him in a chair before the fire, wrapped in a blanket, with his feet in the bucket of hot water, gave him the milk which Jennie brought.

"Now, ye kin hev that an' thet's all ye *kin* hev fur now, only a handful of this popcorn ye kin hev to chaw wile you're drinkin' yer milk.   In the mornin' ye kin hev more.   Or ef ye wake up in the night, ye kin mebby hev a leetle more. But you're mighty nigh starved an' sick, an' victuals is too scase now to kill a man with 'em."

"Pa, don't!" said Jennie.   "We've got victuals enough!"

"Oh, yes, we've got enough, thank the Lord! But we hain't got none to waste in killin' good men."

"I reckon he's right," said Jack; "but some more would taste mighty good!"

"Well, ye kin hev 'bout half a glass o' milk an' another handful o' popcorn.   No, take hit out o' the other side o' the pan.   That got burned a leetle mite.   I want ye to eat the best, what ye do eat."

"He kin have all he wants, cyan't he, Jennie?" asked Cub.   "Nice old Jack!   *My* Jack!" and he fondled Jack as if he were a big dog.

"Wall, Jack, hit's time to put ye to bed. I'm goin' to put ye right here in my bed clost to the fire. I'll take the bed in the other corner."

"I'm goin' to sleep with Jack," said Cub.

"Ye goin' to jilt Jennie?" asked John. "Thar, Jen, yer nose is broke now. Cub's gin ye the mitten, shore."

"I'd sorter like to have him," said Jack. "I hain't had nobody nor nothin' that was my own for seems lack a hundred years."

Jack got into bed with a hot brick at his feet, and Cub soon came down with Jennie, dressed in his union night-suit, which Jennie had made for him, and looking like a little polar bear as he scampered about the room. He crept in beside Jack, and Jack drew him close to himself, and said, —

"God bless ye, Cub! Good night, Miss Jennie. Good night, Mr. Whitley. This hain't much like prison!"

Jack woke in the night and drank the glass of milk that had been left for him, and ate another saucerful of the popcorn, which latter, however, he found himself constrained to share with Cub, who also wakened; and in the morning he was almost himself.

"No, ye hain't nuther," said Mr. Whitley. "I reckon I'm the boss o' my own house. Ye hain't nuther a-goin' to git up an' go on. Ye gotter lay in bed to-day, an' rest an' git sorter fatted up, an' in 'bout a week, wen the rain holds up, ye kin go back to the army. I reckon you're right 'bout hit bein' a mistake to leave, but I sorter gloried in yer spunk!"

"Happy New Year!" cried Cub, waking and rubbing his eyes.

"Ah, thar, ye young rascal! Got ahead o' yer ole granpap! You'll ketch a good lickin' fur thet! Now see ef ye don't!"

Cub laughed at the prospect of a whipping from "granpap," and Mr. Whitley took him by the feet, held him head down, Cub screaming with delight, and carried him to his own bed, where he tumbled him over and over, catching him by the heels and turning him in repeated somersets on the bed, and demanding each time he turned him over whether he now intended to be a good boy, and Cub calling each time,

"No! No! I won't be dood! Do it aden!"

Jack rose on his elbow and watched the sport with eager eyes. Then he sank back in the bed, finding himself weaker than he had thought, and closed his eyes with a sense of restful gratitude.

Breakfast came soon, and none too soon for Jack, but he was restricted in the amount of his food by John Whitley, who insisted that times were too hard to kill good men by overfeeding them. But at dinner he took a little more, and at night ate as much as he wished of popcorn and milk. And that was the way that Jack celebrated the New Year of 1862.

Next day he was up and about, but was glad at times to lie down again. John hailed Dr. Culvert as he passed, and had him look at Jack. But he only said that Jack was doing well, though he had "grazed a spell o' fever mighty clost."

"I'd give him a dose o' quinine," he said, "jes' fur good luck, ef 'twarn't that quinine's gittin' so scase an' high. Hit's about impossible to git, and they's a heap a-needin' on it. I look at a feller's tongue an' feel his pulse twict afore puttin' my knife blade inter my quinine bottle, these days."

He forbade Jack's rejoining the army for a week at least, and that was a comfort to Jack, who proceeded to settle down for a week's visit with a clear conscience. He felt comparatively secure about his mother, from whom he had learned, when he saw her last in jail, that while the Union men about his home were suffering quite as much as ever, the withdrawal of troops into Kentucky had reduced somewhat the plundering of homes and the danger to the women so remote from the towns as his mother.

That week was an oasis in the memory of both Jack and Jennie. They already counted themselves old friends, and were strongly drawn together by their mutual interest in Cub. No words of love passed between them, but their friendship ripened into warm affection.

It rained all that week, and was still raining when the week expired. John insisted that he should not start in the rain, but Jack declared that he would not wait a day beyond the doctor's orders. So John called in the doctor again, who said that Jack was well, but that it was resky to start in sech a rain, and that he had best stop over Sunday and see ef it didn't hold up. Sunday was three days distant, and Jack stopped with mingled satisfaction and impatience, but declared that he would start Monday at sunup, if it rained pitchforks and red-hot cannon balls.

"Ye shan't start off alone," said John. "I'll take ye a step on yer way."

So Monday morning they mounted their horses, and started through swollen branches and over roads that were badly washed out for Somerset and the Union camp. They rode hard that day, and stopped over night at Barboursville. The next night they were across the Cumberland from Williamsburg. The river was past fording, and they had some difficulty in finding a ferry. But at length a man was found with a crazy old skiff who set Jack over for a half dollar in paper money, which sum, together with another dollar for emergencies, John Whitley provided.

Jack pressed his hand as they stood on the bank together, and John started back to where he was acquainted and could get a lodging a mile back.

"Thank you, Mr. Whitley," said he. "You've been like a father to me."

"Sorter gittin' ready to be," said John, dryly.

That was the sort of remark that passed, and still passes, for a joke on Roundstone, and had the added value of conveying parental permission, which was always deemed desirable, but to be sought by indirect approaches, and granted without definitely saying so. To mention the matter of Jack's interest in Jennie in so many words would have been presumptuous in Jack and quite indelicate in John. When this explanation is made, it will be seen that John's dry joke combined a good many admirable features. He chuckled over his skill in saying it, for indeed it was necessary that something should be said, and it was his last chance. He repeated to himself the remark, and that of Jack, to which it was a reply, half the long way home. He found an opportunity to repeat it to Jennie soon after he had put out the horses.   He told it to her as he was pulling on his dry woollen stockings in the chimney-corner and while she was getting him something warm to eat.   He told it with a grave face ; but when he saw that Jennie blushed, he laughed.   When Cub asked him what he was laughing at, he laughed louder, and said, as he drew up to the table, stroking Cub's hair,

"You'll know sometime, Cub," and then he laughed again.   For that also was a joke.

Jack found a detachment of soldiers at Williamsburg and spent the night with them.   He had been sick, he said, and had been away from his regiment. They took him into their barracks, and he spent a comfortable night.   The next day a guard was to leave for Somerset with a wagon train, and he accompanied it.   It had begun to rain again, and the mud was fathomless.   They were three long days on the way, and every night they were wet to the skin.   It was late Friday night when they arrived, and on Saturday Jack reported to his regiment.   It was hard lines, but the things which cheered him most were the thought that he was going back to fight for the Union, and the memory of John Whitley's joke.

Jack had once or twice had misgivings about his welcome, but he was not prepared for the reception which awaited him.   Among the officers of his regiment (and the officer of the day, as it happened, that day) was a pompous, rather corpulent, West Point graduate, who had recently been sent to them, and whose soul was vexed, as indeed it had reason to be, with the lack of discipline among the East Tennessee soldiers and their readiness to drop out of service when, in their judgment, the army had ceased to serve its proper ends. It was unusual to capture a deserter among them, and when one was found, he argued, an example should be made of him. He insisted that Jack should be court-martialled.

Then it was that Jack stood up in his boots and delivered himself of an oration.

"I hain't a-sayin' that it hain't law," he said, "but I say afore God and men that it hain't right. I fit like a sojer when they was fightin' to do, an' I only run away when the army quit fightin' an' went to runnin'. I've ben in prison an' under the gallows fur the sake o' the Union. I've ben shot at an' sick an' starved fur the ole flag. I've ben sent south to die in a rebel prison pen. I've gone through fire an' water to git back. An' I hain't a-goin' to be shot now by the side I come to fight fur. I'm willin' to die fur the Union ef I must, but it hain't no Yankee bullet that's goin' to kill me. I'll appeal to Abe Lincoln. He's a mountain boy, an' has got wild-hog sense, ef he is Pres'daint. I'll appeal to Cun'l Carter. I'm willin' to admit that I'm a returnin' prodigal, an' I hain't astin' to hev no fatted calf killed. But I'll be hanged ef it's Scripter to kill the prodigal to feed the fatted calf."

Jack had no idea of being personal in his last allusion. He could not see what the officers laughed at, nor why the officer of the day colored. Just what would have happened is not certain, had not General Carter, who by this time was a brigadier, entered headquarters.

"General," said one of the officers to whom Carter turned with a look that was a question as to the cause of the immoderate laughter, "this man appeals to you."

"He is a deserter," said the officer of the day, — "a deserter, who has just been recaptured, and should be court-martialled. He is an insolent fellow, beside."

General Carter took a seat and turned to Jack.

"Well, sir, what have you to say for yourself?"

"Cun'l Carter, excuse me, Gin'ral," said Jack, " I don't know what these officers is a-laughin' at. But I jes' wanter tell you how it is. I know you, Gin'ral Carter, but I don't guess you remember me. I fit under you at Wild Cat. I never runned away from the enemy, an' I didn't run away from the army till the army turned back at London. Then I was plumb catawampus. I was plumb ashamed to run. I had lef' my ole mother all alone in Tennessy, a-watchin' fur us to come through the Gap, an' drive off the rebs. An' when we was ordered back, jes' 'peared lack I couldn't stan' it. I jes' got up an' skedaddled. I got home, but I couldn't stay there, an' I went to hidin' out along o' Parson Brownlow an' some o' the men that burned the bridges, an' the rebs broke up our camp, an' captured a heap o' the men, me an' two of my friends amongst the rest.

"They tuck us to Knoxville, an' treated us lack beastis, an' they tuck my friends out an' hung 'em. They sentenced me ter hang, too, but Jeff Davis tuck pity on my mother an' let me off, an' they sont me ter go ter Tuscaloosa. I got away, and started back to the army. I got wet an' mighty nigh starved, an' was tuck sick an' had to stop on the way. The day the doctor said I mought come back, I kim. I 'lowed I'd mebby be called up to tell why I didn't stick by the army, but I hadn't no *idy* they'd talk about cote-marshallin' me. An' when I got back, atter all I done went through, an' the officer o' the day said I'd gotter be cote-marshalled, I jes' tole him I'd went through fire an' water to git back, an' I'd ben shot at an' sick and starved an' mighty nigh hung fur the Union, an' I wasn't a-goin' to be shot by my friends ef I cud help it. That's all. I warn't sassy to him. But Cun'l, I mean Gin'ral, I've told you God's truth. They didn't capture me, no sech thing. The officer he was mistakened. I swear on a stack o' Bibles a mile high, I *kim* back, all the way from a hundred mile south o' Chattanoogy, whar I escaped from the rebs. I *kim* back, an' no man never captured me an' fetched me back. An' I tole him 'twarn't Scripter fur me ter be hung."

"He said, General," said one of the officers, "that it was not according to Scripture to kill the returning prodigal to feed the fatted calf. The officer of the day felt that there was something personal in the allusion."

The laughter broke out again, and Jack stood unconscious and embarrassed.

"You may return to your company," said General Carter. "The army has better uses for such men than shooting them. The officer of the day is right about punishing deserters. We have been greatly troubled, and have felt that severe measures must be taken. But I do not think, and I do not believe that he thinks, now that he has heard your story, that this is the case to begin with. You are a brave man, and I am sure will not desert again. Go to your company and do your duty."

General Carter rose and offered his hand to Jack. It did not occur to Jack that this was an unusual thing, or one that should have embarrassed him. Rather his embarrassment began to leave him, and he grasped the general's hand with a strong, true grip, and gave it the mountain pump-handle shake, saying :

"Thank ye, Cun'l. I'm mighty proud to see you a gin'ral. Ef you want anything hard done, jes' send fur me, an' I'm there. I'm mightily obleeged to ye. I knowed you'd understand, fur you're from East Tennessy yerself."

"That's a noble fellow," said General Carter, as Jack went out. "He has in him the making of a soldier."

XIV

The Battle of Mill Spring [1]

IT was a dreary Sunday morning in January.
The mud was deep in the roads from Logan's
Cross Roads to Somerset, and had been stirred
to the consistency of glue by the tramping of
the troops, the passage of cavalry, and the deep cutting of the artillery, making deeper the ruts that in
places were declared to have no bottom. A mule
team, the soldiers affirmed, dropped into one and
disappeared, all save the ears of the mules. It had
rained almost incessantly since the new year, and
this was the nineteenth day of the month. The
battle which yesterday had seemed imminent, now
seemed unlikely to occur for several days ; for the
Cumberland separated the armies, and Fishing Creek
was swollen full to the tops of the banks.

Carter had left his position at London, to which
he had been returned, and where he kept an eye
like that of a mountain wild cat on the Gap, ready
to pounce on the rebels whenever they should come
out of their holes, and had come without direct orders
from Buell, who was now in command, to the help
of the army before Mill Spring. For Buell had
informed Thomas that his own larger plans must
not suffer by sending reinforcements to the minor
campaign in the mountains of Kentucky.

<hr>

[1] Called also the Battle of Fishing Creek and of Logan's Cross Roads.

The Tennesseeans were creeping out of their damp blankets under the dripping tents and getting into their muddy clothes. There was no little grumbling, for their wagons had been kept back by the rain, and rations were short; but there was little time to cook breakfast.

Just at daylight, the half-dressed men were surprised by the sound of a vigorous attack upon the Kentucky troops near by. The Confederates had made their way down the road to the right, and had fallen first on Wolford's Kentucky horsemen with such suddenness as almost to capture their horses. Behind the cavalry, and next to receive the attack, was Col. Speed S. Fry with his Kentucky infantry. To protect the exposed wing came Colonel Manson with his 10th Indiana, and Van Cleve with the 2d Minnesota. Both these men fought with our friends in later battles as generals.

Carter's Tennesseeans, two thousand strong, were hurried through the woods to the left, where they took position in the edge of the timber, facing a corn field through which the Confederates were stubbornly fighting their way. In spite of their surprise, and with no superiority in numbers, the Union forces were quickly and effectively placed, commanding three sides of this field. While the Confederates fought with might and main, they were met in front with equal courage, and from either side there poured in upon them a heavy cross-fire.

The Tennesseeans had just a moment for breath, after taking position, before the battle waxed hot upon the left. The West Point officer, who had wanted to hang Jack, improved that moment by

showing the men how to transform a rail fence into a
series of rude forts with sally ports between. Taking
the inner ends of the rails, they moved them inward,
pair by pair, beginning with the top, making of the
fence a row of triangular pens, breast-high in front,
in which the two regiments were distributed.

"Boys, that West Point officer is good for somethin', hain't he?" asked Jack.

"I'll never say agin that he hain't," said Sergeant
Hallet. "This is as good a fort as I want."

It was a simple device, and one often followed
later by both armies, and no stone wall served better
in giving confidence to raw men when fortifications
must be constructed instantly and under fire.

"Here they come! Ready, boys!"

Up through the stumps of the cornstalks the
Confederates came. They had marched nine miles
through the mud and rain. Their powder was wet
in many cases, and often guns refused to fire, the
soldiers pulling the trigger over and over, and unable to tell in the noise of battle that the wet load
was still in their guns, sometimes ramming down
load after load upon the wet powder and impacted
ball. Yet there was firing enough, and the woods
were soon full of smoke and fog, and the rain kept
up its dreary dripping.

Out of the smoke and fog, a regiment came up
against the rail pens, and fought like fiends for possession of them. It was a Tennessee regiment, commanded by another Colonel Carter, and Greek met
Greek.

Twice they came up and fell back. Once they
drove the men from the pens, but with a savage

Jack Meets an Old Acquaintance.   Page 175.

yell the mountaineers charged and drove them back. Jack, with five companions, regained the pen from which they had been driven, and fired their guns across the rails point-blank into the faces of the enemy. The Confederates wavered and their colonel fell, but that instant a young lieutenant rushed ahead and rallied them, leading them to the very line of the fence. There was not a loaded gun in the pen where Jack stood, but Jack seized his gun by the muzzle and with its clubbed breech struck at the officer's head. The lieutenant sprang aside and threw up his sword to ward off the blow. The sword arm received its full force, and the sword fell from his hand. He fell to the ground and was up again in a minute, his right arm hanging painful and useless. He took the sword in his left hand, and attempted to lead on the charge, but the fire from front and flank was more than flesh could bear. He reeled as he turned, and two men supported him as he was borne to the rear. Yet in that single instant, while Jack's gun was falling upon the upraised arm, he and Sam Marshall recognized each other.

The nominal leader of the Confederates in this battle was General Crittenden, but the man whom the soldiers trusted was Zollicoffer. Crittenden was declared to have left Mill Springs drunk, and the men under him protested against his commanding. But they were willing to fight under their old leader, who was second in command, for Zollicoffer was a good, true man, and they trusted him. The one thing needed then to make complete their discomfiture occurred in the death of Zollicoffer.

The soldiers affirmed that Colonel Fry shot him, and sang a doggerel song which said,—

"Up jumped Colonel Fry,
And shot him in the eye,
And sent him to the happy land of Canaan."

But the tale told on the ground for many years was that old Jack Christian had started out that morning with his squirrel rifle on his shoulder to go to the house of a neighbor, and found himself unexpectedly between the armies. Making the best of his way out, he was near to escaping at the Union left, when a horseman bore down upon him through the fog. Confused and alarmed, he drew his gun to his shoulder and fired, and Fry, charging with his men a moment later, found dead in the dripping woods the real commander of the Confederates. Whether this was true or not, Jack Christian believed it true, and later became insane, brooding over his killing of so good a general.

It was useless fighting after the Confederates knew that Zollicoffer was killed. Fatigued and hungry, depleted and discouraged, they broke and retreated, but halted at a ravine a short distance back, and made one more stand. It was a forlorn hope. The artillery, which up to this time had taken little part in the fight, opened fire, and the Union infantry bore down upon them, with Wolford's daring cavalry. They broke again, and this time hopelessly. They ran through the mud and rain, demoralized and breathless. They threw away their guns, and then their haversacks. They abandoned their cannon, and left their way strewn with dead and wounded, and every kind of baggage. They ran to Mill Spring, nine miles, through mud of fathomless depth, and rain that never ceased falling. The camp was soon alive with shells, which Thomas sent flying after them. They left the camp. They left their cannon mounted. They left their provisions and camp utensils. Wet and weary, without food or shelter, and already dropping with fatigue, they started through the wilderness into Tennessee, some to perish by the way, and others to arrive at Knoxville, the shattered remnant of what had once been a splendid army. General Sherman proved to have been right in his estimate that two hundred thousand men would be needed for offensive warfare in the army of the Cumberland: the mistake was in assuming that these must all come from the North because of the solid disloyalty of the South. Zollicoffer, after the most desperate exertions, had enlisted few Kentuckians. But of the seven infantry regiments that drove back his army, three only were from the North. The other four, besides Wolford's dashing and fearless horsemen, were from the loyal South, — the 1st and 2d Tennessee, and the 4th and 10th Kentucky.

Throughout the country there rang a shout of joy. It was the first decisive engagement of the West. It proved that the smaller victory at the Wild Cat Mountain had been no accident. The soldiers sang with savage triumph,—

> "Zollicoffer's dead,
> And the last words he said
> Were, 'Here's another Wild Cat a-coming!'"

N

The people of the North who had been wearied and discouraged by delays about Washington, took heart again at this small, but decisive and important, victory.   Had it been promptly followed up, the results might have been even more important than they were.

General Thomas was himself surprised by the magnitude of his victory.   He had been quite content with the thought of driving back the rebels.   When Colonel Fry asked him afterward, why he had not followed his advantage with a demand for the surrender of the entire army, he thought awhile, and answered,—

"Hang it, Fry, I never once thought of it!"

It was the more of a pity that omniscience should not have been joined to the omnipotence which the soldiers attributed to General Thomas.   They had great faith in his ability to give orders and secure obedience, and they long repeated how the turning-point of the battle had been his rising in his stirrups and shouting,

"Attention, Creation! By kingdoms, right wheel!"

But if Thomas, who was slow as well as sure, underestimated the importance of an immediate forward movement, still more did Buell,[1] who in plan-

---

[1]   "EXECUTIVE MANSION, WASHINGTON, January 6, 1862.

"MY DEAR SIR : — Your despatch of yesterday has been received, and it disappoints and distresses me. . . . .   My distress is that our friends in East Tennessee are being hanged and driven to despair, and even now I fear are thinking of taking rebel arms for the sake of personal protection.   In this we lose the most valuable stake we have in the South.   My despatch to which yours is an answer was sent with the knowledge of Senator Johnson and Representative Maynard, of East Tennessee, and they will be upon me to know the answer, which I cannot safely show them. They would despair ; possibly resign to go and save their families somehow or die with them.

"I do not intend this to be an order in any sense, but merely, as intimated before, to show you the grounds of my anxiety.

"Yours, very truly,   A. LINCOLN.

"Brigadier-General BUELL."

ning the larger operations toward the Mississippi, had little strength to spare for what he counted a wholly minor effort on behalf of East Tennessee. The roads were almost impassable, the Confederates had fled, and there was no immediate call for advance, which was, indeed, extremely difficult, on account of the constant rain and the condition of the roads and streams.

Late on Monday, Jack's company was pushed across the Cumberland to Mill Spring. The Confederate camp was already in possession of the Union soldiers. Jack was detailed to assist in the burial of the dead, and he looked among them for men he knew, and was glad not to find Sam Marshall there. He went to the hospitals, and did not find him. But a young woman who lived on Mill Spring Hill, and whose home had been used for Zollicoffer's headquarters, gave him some information about the man whom he had struck. When the surgeons first arrived at the camp, and began their work among the wounded, she was required, in the absence of other help, to assist them. The surgeons from the two armies met in friendship, and attended to men as they came to them, without distinction of rank or side. It was a Union surgeon whom she was assisting, and he came to a young Confederate officer suffering from a fracture of the right arm, which had been greatly aggravated by his nine miles' retreat. He was eager to be attended to, and in need of immediate assistance. Yet he scornfully refused the Union surgeon's aid, and waited for a Confederate. A few bitter-spirited men on both sides, she said, had done the same. The surgeon with a curse had left him, and it was long before a Confederate surgeon came to his help. By that time the work of the surgeon she had been helping was over. It was well toward morning, she said, and she was coming with water, when the physician, seeing her pass, stopped her for a moment, and asked her to hold the ends of the splints while he put on the bandages. The wounded man was suffering greatly, and spoke most bitterly of his wound, and of the man who had struck him, whom he said he recognized, and he would have his life to pay for it. She remembered him well, — a tall, handsome fellow, with flashing black eyes and courage like a lion, but with a spirit so bitter that she shrank from him, even while gladly helping him. The officer was a prisoner, but was so badly wounded that he was not guarded. When he got away she did not know, but in the morning he was gone. Having told Jack this story, the young woman appealed to him for help.

"We are loyal," she said. "My father is in Thomas' army, and now will surely come to us. We have suffered from the rebels, but have been protected by them. We have looked forward to this day with hope and prayer. Now the Union soldiers that have come to our house scorn our professions of loyalty. They treat us worse than the rebels did. We are almost starved for want of food. They have eaten all we have. You are a Southern man, and know that there are loyal people in the South. Secure us protection till my father comes."

There was many a woman in the South who made the same appeal during the four long years of the war. Some spoke untruly and were believed, and abused their trust. But some, alas! spoke truly and were not believed. And there is no sadder tale that is told to-day by those who lived in the South during the four years of horror, than that of loyal people suffering at the hands of those who should have been their protectors.

"I'm done with my work," said Jack, "an' I've got nothin' to do till my reg'maint comes up. I'll stand on guard afore this door, miss, an' ef ary man tries to cross the threshold without right or leave, I'll put a bullet through his skin, whether it's covered with blue or with but'nut."

"Thank you," said the young woman's mother, as she came to the door, and Jack explained his mission, and the daughter enlarged upon his kind offer. "Thank you; I am glad that some men in the Union army know that there are loyal people in the South."

A few hours later, Jack's regiment came up, and with it came also the owner of the house. With a cry of joy, the women embraced him after months of separation and danger, and when they told him of Jack's kindness, and the father turned to thank him, Jack had gone.

NOTE. — I am constrained to add to this chapter a quotation from Parson Brownlow concerning General Zollicoffer :

"He was a man who never wronged an individual out of a cent in his life; never told a lie in his life; as brave a man personally as Andrew Jackson ever was; and the only mean thing I ever knew him to do was to join the Southern Confederacy."

XV

A Duel in the Dark

ALL this while Knoxville was quivering with excitement. The officers who had fought at Mill Spring — Crittenden, Zollicoffer, Carroll, and Wood — had all been in authority in Knoxville, and were well known in the city. Most of the troops had passed through Knoxville on their way to the field. When the broken fragments of the army came back, dripping, starving, and terrified, with the news of Zollicoffer's death and the disaster that had hopelessly befallen the army, the city went wild. The Confederates expected an instant advance that would compel the surrender of the city; and the loyal people, who were becoming depleted, rejoiced greatly. But General Buell, tried by the lack of discipline and constant annoyance of his raw troops, feared to undertake such an expedition under the conditions which then existed. So Thomas was ordered to join Buell's main army; and Carter, the watch-dog of the Gap, returned to his old station at London.

There Carter went into winter quarters. The soldiers were quartered all about in the mountains, guarding the different roads, making occasional raids upon the Confederate outposts, and subsisting as best they were able on the barren country. It was hard for the soldiers, and not less so for the people. The roads were so bad as almost to cut them off from their base of supplies. From Crab Orchard the streams were past fording much of the time, and in the brief intervals of their subsidence, the roads were so gullied out by the rains, and so steep and rocky beside, as to be well-nigh impassable. Desperate were the efforts to relieve them. It was said that one might have walked on dead mules from London to Crab Orchard, and still the troops nearly starved. Scurvy broke out among them. The 10th Indiana, out of its nine hundred men, had but two hundred fit for duty by spring.

The soldiers broke over all attempts at discipline, and foraged and stole without mercy. The poor Union people of the region, who had suffered from small crops because their sons and husbands were in the army, and had been once pillaged by the rebels, had now to suffer even worse plundering, because of direr need, at the hands of their own friends.

Jack escaped all this. Soon after their return to London, he found himself one morning unable to rise. The camp surgeon, who came to see him, said :

" You're in for a run of fever, and the hospital is full. You couldn't get home, could you ? "

" Not home," said Jack ; " but ef I had a horse and some one to go with me, I reckon I might get to some sorter kinfolks o' mine at Roundstone."

" I'll get you a furlough," said the surgeon, " and see about a horse."

It was a hard day's ride, but the weather was clear and cool, and Jack was nerved to the fatigue by the prospect of a home and a bed. He had often to rest by the way, but just in the dusk of evening Jack and his companion, Sam Loomis, passed through the Oxyoke Gap and drew rein before the house of John Whitley.

"Hello, thar! Who's thar? 'Light an' come in!" called John.

Jack and Sam made their way to the door, and Jack sank wearily into a chair before the fire, his face flushed with fever, and his hands shaking with fatigue.

"Hit's a bad penny come back," said he, with a faint attempt at a joke.

"I see, I see!" replied John, heartily, "an' come back wus'n wut it was wen it went away. Git off yer duds now, an' git inter thet bed, an' I'll see wut I kin do fur ye. Se' down thar, young man, tell I git this feller inter bed, an' I'll go with ye an' putt out the beastis."

As they were going out soon after to attend to the horses, John hailed a passing neighbor, and asked him to send word to Dr. Culvert that he was needed. Then they put the horses in the barn, and gave them some "roughness," as John called the bundles of blade fodder, and produced from a place of concealment ten short ears of corn, which he divided between them.

"Hit tain't 'nough," said he; "but a company of sojers passed through here a spell ago, an' didn't leave us much for ourselves, let alone the hosses."

"Which army?"

"The Lincoln army. That was the wust on it. They was hungry, I reckon, an' so was their hosses, an' they needed wut they could git, but they mought a ben a leetle mite more human about it. Hit's sorter hard to take sass from yer friends, an' be called an ole reb wen yer mighty nigh starvin' fur the Union, an' got three sons bein' shot at in the Union army."

It was late in the night when Dr. Culvert arrived. Low as was his store of quinine, he administered it to Jack.

" He'll pull through all right," he said, " an' he wouldn't a ben sick at all ef he'd a stayed here, an' not went back to the army fur a few weeks. But he hain't a-goin' to be much sick, though he won't do no more fightin' till spring."

From time to time he called, and found Jack " runnin' along " with the fever which, after three weeks, broke and left him weak and convalescent. During this time Jennie was the most faithful of nurses, and Cub was constantly trotting in and out, devoted to his guardian, and asking daily, —

" Ain't you well yet? Well, when *is* you goin' to get well ? "

At the close of a fortnight, Ephraim Whitley came home from his regiment on a furlough. There was little to do, he reported, and provisions were short, and they were glad enough to have some of the men at home. He and Jack, already firm friends, rejoiced to meet in Ephraim's home, and together they passed more cheerfully the weary days of Jack's convalescence.

One night in March, when Jack was getting to feel almost himself again, and Ephraim was preparing to return, a stranger called and asked for a night's entertainment for himself and horse, which was readily granted. John went out with him to put his horse into the barn, and the stranger asked permission to bring into the house a heavy sack which he had been carrying behind his saddle.

"Hit'll be all right here," said John, "but fetch it inter the house ef yer wanter. Wut yer got in it?"

"Salt," said the stranger. "I've ben to the salt works at Manchester, an' I'm a-takin' two bushel o' salt to my folks down in Tennessy."

There was nothing unusual in this; but precious as salt was, the place that was safe enough for the horses, which in all pioneer countries are the most valued of chattels, was safe enough for the salt.

"Fetch hit in, ef you'll feel any easier about it," said John. "Hello, Eph! Come out an' give this man a lift with his bag o' salt."

"You needn't mind. I kin pack hit," said the stranger.

He carried the salt into the living-room, though John rather plainly hinted that it would be less in the way in the kitchen, and set it down in the corner farthest from the door, and threw his overcoat upon it. Then he turned to greet Eph, who was sitting by the fire, and Jack, who was lying in his clothes upon the bed. He started visibly at their uniforms, and said:

"Ah, sojers, I see! I didn't know as they was ary sojer round this holler?"

"They hain't many," said John; "but a heap has gone from here to the war. These is my boys, one on 'em my own boy an' t'other sorter kinfolks. I got two more boys in the army."

The stranger, not without some appearance of
constraint, began a profuse and unstinted com-
mendation of John for sending his sons to the
field, and a profession of loyalty to the government. It was so earnest that it quite compelled
their admiration, and drew out John's heartiest hospitality. Eph, too, found himself warming to the
stranger, but Jack lay with closed eyes, listening and
saying nothing.

John took the stranger into the kitchen for supper, and Eph would have gone with him, but Jack
motioned him back.

"Eph," said he, "they's somethin' wrong with
that feller. You watch him mighty close. You
see that he sleeps in the loft to-night, an' we'll
see wut's in that sack."

"Why, wut do ye think?"

"I don' know. But I'm dead sure he's a spy
or a smuggler, one. He's got somethin' inside
that bag besides salt."

Supper being ended, the stranger sat in the chimney-corner, and entertained them long with his stories. He was genial, and had a hearty laugh, which
to Jack seemed a trifle strained. At length he said
he was tired, and if they didn't mind he believed
he'd lie down.

"I'll show ye to the loft," said Eph, and took
a candle.

"Ef ye don' mind, I'd a leetle mite druther sleep
by the far. I got a tech o' rheumatiz, an' I'd jes' a
leetle mite druther sleep down stairs, that is, ef hit's
jes' as convenient."

John started to say that it would be just as convenient, but stopped when he saw that Eph knew what he was doing.

"Well, I'm sorry, but hit tain't right convenient fur ye to sleep down here. You see my friend here hain't got well yit, an' I sleep with him to look atter him, an' pa's gittin' sorter old, an' we don' like to send him up stairs."

This was dangerously near a lie, for John would have resented being considered an old man, and he often slept in the loft.

"That needn't make no difference. Jes' let me sleep with him," said the stranger. "I'm used to double-teamin'."

"No, they hain't no use o' that," said Eph. "You kin jes' as well hev a bed to yerself," and he led the way to the loft.

John Whitley began to see that all was not right. While Eph was up stairs with the stranger, he sought an explanation from Jack, who told him of his suspicions.

"Shore enough," said John. "They hain't no manner o' doubt of it. We'll see wut's in thet sack."

They partially undressed and lay upon the beds. The fire had been covered, and the room was dark. At a signal from Jack, Eph rose and blew the coals enough to light the wick of a candle, which he handed to Jack, and then took down two guns from the forks above the fire, and gave one to his father, taking the other himself. Carefully walking in their stockings over the creaking floor, they gathered about the sack. Eph set down his gun and drew the ram-rod, and then untied the sack. Jack held the light in one hand and the mouth of the sack in the other, while Eph with his left hand held the opposite side of the bag, and with his right thrust the rod deep into the salt.

" I've hit suthin'," he said, and baring his arm, followed the ramrod down into the bag, and brought up a package wrapped in paper.

" They's more," said he, " but less see what's in this."

They stood about it while Eph untied the string, and was about to unwrap it, when suddenly there came a pistol shot from the head of the ladder, and John Whitley fell, mortally wounded, on the floor of his own house.

With a cry of surprise and anger, Eph and Jack turned toward the assassin, and as they did so, a bullet passed over them and lodged in the log wall of the house. The murderer was making for the door with all speed. Eph seized him midway, and Jack dropped the candle to take up a gun, and the light went out.

Eph seized the stranger's hand, as it was levelled to shoot again, and threw it up, with the pistol in it. Then they struggled in the dark for possession of the weapon, and each for the other's life. It took less than a minute, but it seemed a night. Jack turned to the fireplace, and tried to light the candle, but could not blow the coals into flame. Just then the kitchen door flew open, and Jennie stood in the door with a light and Cub holding to her wrapper, and at that instant the pistol, held by the two struggling men, went off while pointed upward, and the murderer fell, shot under the chin.

Jennie cast herself upon her father's body, weeping and lamenting. Jack gently led her away, and he and Eph got him on the bed. He was not bleeding greatly externally, but had been shot in the side at a downward angle through both lungs, which were rapidly filling with blood from internal hemorrhage. Eph went for Dr. Culvert, and he soon came, but nothing could be done. The murderer had died instantly, and John Whitley had passed away before the doctor came. They laid out the two bodies in the same room, the father on the bed, the murderer on the floor where he had fallen, and they covered the one with a sheet, and the other with the coat which he had thrown over the bag, and sadly, tearfully, and with a sickening sense of horror, waited for the day.

"Less see what he was a-smugglin'," said the doctor, and completed the undoing of the package.

"Quinine!" he said, as he laid six one-ounce bottles on the table.

There were ten of those packages, sixty ounces in all, in the bag, and the stranger was smuggling them south to the fever-stricken soldiers of the Confederacy. There was nothing for which men ran greater risks. Many a man lost his life in an effort to convey to the south the fever-soothing drug. Dr. Culvert kept one package for himself, and Eph and Jack took the other fifty-four ounces to the Union camp. It was welcome in both places, but it had cost the lives of two men, and one of them was as true a patriot as ever gave his life for his country.

Besides the great loss of life in the two armies,

East Tennessee lost an estimated aggregate of twenty-five hundred Union men during the war. Some of them were put to death by military tribunals. Some died in Southern prisons for conscience' sake. Some were shot in guerilla warfare, outlaws but patriots, some were assassinated, and some fell defending their homes and their loved ones against assault. All the border States suffered in like manner. Some of the men who fell deserved their fate, being desperadoes and using the war as the occasion for plunder. But among the rest were not a few who died as bravely and as worthily as John Whitley.

XVI

If Thine Enemy Hunger

THE winter of 1861–2 departed from the Cumberland Mountains, "unwept, unhonored, and unsung." There was cheering news from Forts Henry and Donelson, and Andrew Johnson was at Nashville as military governor. That was something to be thankful for. But it was, after all, discouraging to see how little good it did to the people in the eastern part of the State. It left them one less thing to hope for. There was good news from the Mississippi and the Big Sandy, but these were somewhat vague and remote regions; and so far as the mountain people had heard of outside military movements, they were those of McClellan, whom they had come to hold in the highest esteem. Almost entirely overlooking intervening operations, they watched eagerly for news from " Little Mac," and not even their own sorrows depressed them more than his inaction and reverses. It is a thing almost to be wondered at, but it is declared on the best of evidence, that the failure of McClellan's peninsular campaign was the most discouraging news that, in all the history of the war, saddened the hearts of the mountaineers.

Elizabeth Casey lived a quiet, and for the most part an uneventful, life. Having few home duties, she was in demand as a nurse for the sick, and found abundant occupation that winter. She watched eagerly for the news, and gave herself to the careful study of the routes by which the army was moving, or might move, for the sake of following the wanderings of her soldier boy, and for the pleasure of the occupation and the participation which it seemed to afford in actual military life. She studied such maps as could be found at the court-house of the topography of the region around Cumberland Gap, at first to assist her imaginings of the routes by which the soldiers would come into Tennessee, and later, as she found herself attaining a degree of knowledge of the subject, with the hope that it might some time be of service. Conversation — and there was ample time for it, and the old people who had travelled most about the mountains had most desire to talk and hope and conjecture — enlarged her knowledge.

She had a mind that was active, and a will that was strong, and at times she imagined herself riding over the mountains to her boy, if he should be wounded, or to save him from threatened danger.

One morning toward the end of January she heard a faint voice outside her door, and hastily opening it, found on the rude stone step that led up to the porch a Confederate soldier. For a moment she shrank back, and then drew near, for she saw that the man was not drunken, as at first she had thought, but wounded and had fainted.

She drew him into the house, and dashed water in his face, and as he began to show signs of returning life, she gave him stimulants, and got him upon

o

the bed.   All the time it seemed to her that she knew him, but who he was she could not remember.

"Give me something to eat," he pleaded.   "I'm 'most starved."

She made him some gruel, and he took it and fell asleep.   That day and the next she kept him, allowing him to talk little, caring for his shattered arm, and nursing him back to strength.

"I don' har'ly know as I ought to do it," she said ; "but pore boy, ef he is a rebel, he's got a ma."

On the morning of the third day, he raised himself in bed, and said :

"I'm goin' to dress me, an' go home.   You've saved my life, an' I'm mighty thankful."

"Don' go till yer able," she said.   "Besides, I want you to tell me now about the war.   You come from Kaintuck ?   Has they ben a fight ? "

"Yes, they has," said he.   "They was a big fight at Mill Spring."

"Tell me about it," said she.

"We got licked," said he.   "Thomas licked us awful.   We had to leave our dead an' wounded, an' run.   Zollicoffer's dead.   Our boys are scattered all the way from here to the Kentucky line.   The most have gone to Knoxville, but Knoxville has got to go now.   They warn't no use o' me a-goin' there, so I started thisaway towards home.   I live about six mile across the Holston from here.   I ought to know you, but I ain't been in this cove often, though I know a right smart o' people over thisaway."

"I thank God ye got licked," said she.   "I'm heart an' soul agin this wicked rebellion.   I hope this is the end o' hit."

"You're Union?" he asked. "You're kind, though. I've passed some houses where they set the dogs on me because I was a reb. They'd have taken me prisoner, ef they dared, and give me up to the Union army."

"You needn't have no fear o' me," she said. "They hain't no Union army here to give ye up to. I won't do ye no harm. I'm bein' good to ye for my boy's sake that's in the Union army. Mebby some rebel woman that's got a boy in the war mought be good to him some time for her boy's sake. Now you mustn't talk no more. Jes' lay down an' rest to-day an' to-night."

"I'll rest a spell this mornin'," he said. "I ain't har'ly able to get on. But before night I can get over to some friends o' mine that live less'n two mile from here, an' stay there to-night, an' by mornin' I can git home."

He rested that day, and toward evening rose and found himself able to stand and walk a little.

"I'll be a-goin' now," he said. "I'll take it easy, and git acrost to my friends by dark. God bless ye for what you've done for me. You've saved my life. We must be friends now, ef we are on different sides. I'll have to be 'round home a spell now. Some day I'll ride over when I get strong. Seems like I ought to know you, anyhow."

"'Pears like I ought to know you, too," said she, "but I can't somehow place ye. I'm right sure I've seed you afore ye had a beard, an' when you wasn't so pale. That makes a right smart o' difference."

"My name's Marshall," said he, "Dr. Sam Marshall."

"Sam Marshall!" she cried. "Be you the man that got some one to swear away the life o' my boy? Be you the man that sent my boy south to die?"

"Good Lord, woman, who are you?" he cried, a suspicion of the truth crossing his mind.

"I'm Elizabeth Casey, Jack Casey's mother. An' you're the man that got old Pete Stevens to swear that my boy helped burn the bridges. You villain! You perjurer! You lyin' scamp! I wisht I'd a lef' ye to die on my door-step afore I saved the life o' the man that tried to murder my boy!"

Sam steadied himself by the post of the porch, and began speaking thickly, —

"I'll tell you two things, Mis' Casey. One is, I didn't git no one to swear false against your boy. Leastwise, not as I know of. I hunted up what ev'dence I could find, and when Pete Stevens said he seen a man near there that favored the man I described as Jack, I had him taken to Knoxville, an' he identified Jack as the man. I hain't a-sayin' he was right or wrong. I hain't a-sayin' I wasn't glad to find him an' get his ev'dence. But I swear on the Holy Bible I never bribed no man to swear a lie. That's one thing I got to tell you. There's another thing. Yer boy ain't south in jail. He's got out. I don' know how, and I don' know when. But I seen him plain as I see you in the battle o' Mill Spring. He's the man that broke my arm, an' I've swore to have his life for it.

"I'll tell you another thing. Ef I'd a knowed you lived here, I'd a died afore I'd a tuck a crust from you, or crossed the threshold o' his door. I was so weak an' faint night afore las', I hardly knowed where I was at, an' I ain't right well acquainted over here anyhow. I knowed I mus' be nigh the Hansons, an' I didn't dast to go there. I tried to git two miles furder to where I know some folks that would have taken care o' me. I knowed they'd see me five miles furder an' at home as soon as I could go. But I give out, an' had to stop. I'd a died afore I' a taken a pinch o' yer salt. But that can't be helped now. As to yer boy, I've swore to God I'll kill him when I see him, an' I never broke no promise I ever made, an' I hain't a-goin' to break one I swear to."

Weak as he was his cheek flushed. He gathered strength and started toward the road. Elizabeth ran back into the house and pulled up a loose board in the floor. From a hiding-place below she drew out Jack's long gun that had been his father's. Sam was out of the yard, and starting weakly down the road when she got to the fence, and levelled the gun across it.

"Stop!" she cried.

He stopped and turned back.

"Sam Marshall," she cried, "ef I'd a knowed you was the man ye be, I don' know whether I'd a let ye die on my step or not. But one thing I know. No man is a-goin' out o' this yard alive a-swearin' to kill my boy. I've give my only son to this war. I've put him where he has to stand an' be shot at by men sech as you. I've seed him right under the shadder of the gallows for the love he has for the flag, and the love his mother has that let him fight for it. An' now, Sam Marshall, as God's in heaven above us, ef you don't take back

that wicked oath, an' promise that if ever ye see
my boy in trouble you'll do for him what I've done
for you, then I'll put a bullet through yer heart,
and God judge between you an' the mother that
kills ye to keep ye from murderin' her boy!"

Sam Marshall was no coward, but there are few
men who face certain death in passion without wavering.   A moment he hesitated.

"Speak quick!" she cried, and she raised the hammer of the gun.

"Let me think," he asked.   "It's a mighty hard
thing to decide."

"Say quick what yer goin' to do!" she cried, and
he heard the click as she set the double trigger.

"I'll promise," said he, "I'll never do yer boy
no harm ef I can help it, doin' my duty."

"You'll be a friend to him?" she demanded.

"Yes, I will, God help me!"

"Then go," she said; "an' ef you ever break
this promise that ye make to-day, a mother's curse
and the blood of a murdered son rest on your soul
forever."

She lowered the hammer of the rifle and returned
to the house, and Sam Marshall walked feebly down
the road and was lost to sight.

XVII

Parson Brownlow's Release

"WHAT are you doing there, you villain ?" demanded Parson Brownlow through the bars.

"Washin' my face. Didn't ye think hit would look purtier ef hit was washed ?"

"It was black enough, but your soul is blacker. Don't you know that we have to drink the water from that hogshead ?"

"Well, sir, I'll have you to know that the water where a Jeff Davis soldier washes his face is plenty good enough for any Lincoln screamer or bridge-burner to drink!" replied the soldier.

"The time will come," retorted Brownlow, "when you will lift up your eyes in hell, being tormented in the flame, and will plead for a drop of water on the tip of your tongue!"

There was no way to remedy the abuse but by protest. Parson Brownlow was capable of so vigorous a use of the English tongue as to be a terror to evil-doers, even when in full power. He had, moreover, the ability when he was righteously indignant, to use Scripture in a way that added to its sanctity all the effectiveness of ordinary profanity. Thus he kept up the spirits of the prisoners, and soon proved a white elephant on the hands of the prison authorities.

Moreover, he got access to the papers, and published far and wide the fact that he had returned to Knoxville under the written promise of General Crittenden, by authority of Secretary Benjamin, that he should have a pass out of the Confederacy. He did not choose with any misguided notion of respect for those in authority, the words in which he charged the Confederate government with breach of faith in the matter. General Crittenden felt the force of these charges against his honor, and so did the Confederate secretary of war. Moreover, Brownlow dipped his pen in the gall of his most biting sarcasm, and published articles which represented him as rather enjoying an experiment which his imprisonment permitted him to make. He was anxious to know, he said, which was the higher authority in the Confederacy, the secretary of war and a major general on the one hand, or a dirty little drunken attorney, such as the man who had caused his imprisonment. He wrote as much to Secretary Benjamin at Richmond, and added, —

"Just give me my passports, and I will do for your Confederacy more than the devil has ever done, — I will quit the country!"

At times Brownlow, whose health suffered in jail, believed that he would die in prison, and at other times he believed that he would certainly be hanged. He composed a speech to be delivered under the gallows, and afterward published it as a statement of his principles.

Secretary Benjamin was a good deal disturbed by these matters. He wrote to Knoxville that he felt that his official promise, while not intended to be a protection against legal action, had so compromitted the honor of the Confederate government that if Brownlow should be convicted, he must himself request President Davis for a pardon. It was useless to prosecute Brownlow after that, and he was released, but on the same day of the entering of the *nolle prosequi* in the civil court, he was arrested by the military authorities, and placed under double guard in his own house, where for a long time he was sick, and under the authority of the same Colonel Leadbetter who had hanged Hensie and Fry, and whom he denounced as the prince of villains, murderers, and tyrants. In the middle of February, Leadbetter was superseded by Colonel Vance, a gentleman of high character, who relieved him from most of the annoyances of his imprisonment. It was well for Brownlow that this change of jurisdiction came. With the reverses of the year, the Confederate soldiers grew almost desperate. It seemed to Brownlow that "the rebels had suddenly been filled with the malice of hell." The guard about him was now increased to ten men, no longer to confine, but to protect him.

It had seemed to the local authorities that the imprisonment of Brownlow was a necessity, in spite of the promise of the Confederate government. The Knoxville *Register*, when there had been a prospect of his release, protested against the action of the War Department at Richmond as being " worse than a crime, — a blunder." It said :

" Brownlow has preached at every church and school-house, made stump speeches at every cross road, and knows every man, woman, and child, and their fathers and grandfathers before them, in East Tennessee. As a Methodist circuit rider, a political stump speaker, a temperance orator, and the editor of a newspaper, he has been equally successful in our division of the State.

" Let him but once reach the confines of Kentucky with his knowledge of the geography and population of East Tennessee, and our section will soon feel the effect of his hard blows. From among his old partisan and religious sectarian parasites he will find men who will obey him with the fanatical alacrity of those who followed Peter the Hermit in the First Crusade. We repeat again, let us not underrate Brownlow."

Thus the local authorities held Brownlow against the will of the Confederate government, not because they wanted him, but because they knew the loyalty of East Tennessee, and feared to allow him to depart. Like the man who caught the bear on the opposite side of the tree, they wanted some one to help them to let go.

After a double defeat of the Confederates at Mill Spring and Fort Donelson, when the town was filled with flying soldiers, and many of the pronounced Confederate sympathizers of the town were hastily moving south, no thought of prudence restricted Brownlow's joy. He reminded the rebels, some of whom he had known, that they had boasted of their intention to " die in the last ditch," and he complimented them upon the eagerness of their search for the ditch, and the prospect of their finding it. He expressed his estimate of the courage of the new troops, who from time to time were passing through

Knoxville north, and waking the town with their hilarious and often drunken boasting, that, —

"A company of them can demolish any unarmed woman in the country!"

On Friday, February 28, appointed by Jefferson Davis as a day of fasting, humiliation, and prayer, Brownlow applauded the appointment, affirming that, —

"If ever a set of men needed to humble themselves before God and confess their sins, it is the men associated with Jeff Davis in this infernal rebellion."

This became intolerable. On Sunday, March 2, Secretary Benjamin ordered Major Monserrat, who had succeeded Colonel Vance, to remove Brownlow to Kentucky, and that officer was only too glad to obey. The very next morning he started, under a guard of ten men, who were ordered to protect him at all hazards, and to treat him courteously and kindly.

Brownlow had no little difficulty still in getting through the lines. Both Generals A. S. Johnston and Hardee at first refused to honor his passes. The truth was that the Confederates were then in such terror that they dreaded to have Brownlow's knowledge of their weakness and confusion taken to the Union army. But the two weeks that he was detained at Shelbyville were to him a sort of ovation. The Union people thronged him, the women sent him flowers, and the rebels chafed under his bitter words.

It was hard for them to kick against the pricks. They dreaded to let Brownlow go. They dared not wholly disregard the authority of Richmond and send him back, and they could not forever keep him where he was. Jonah was not a more uncomfortable guest; and they proceeded to throw him overboard. On March 15, they sent him under escort and a flag of truce, and soon he entered Nashville, where Andrew Johnson was establishing the military government, and Buell was resting after his victories and planning for other ones. Brownlow was at once in demand, and received a welcome that a king might have counted an honor. He was eagerly questioned by Buell for military information, and greeted by the officers and men of the Union army with every token of affectionate regard. He was called from his room in the St. Cloud Hotel to address the crowd that thronged the space below. That his right hand had not forgotten its cunning, and that his tongue was as vigorous as ever, is evidenced by his own report of his speech delivered on that occasion, in which he proposed the sentiment, " Grape for the rebel masses, and hemp for their leaders ! "

XVIII

How a Woman Saved an Army

WITH the coming of the spring of 1862, operations began against Cumberland Gap. General Carter had held on all winter in the face of great discouragements. General George W. Morgan was ordered to join him with three additional brigades, and advance upon the almost impregnable fastness, then often spoken of as the American Gibraltar, — the key to East Tennessee. There had been a time, just after the battle of Mill Spring, when it might have been had for the asking, if any strong force had been sent against it. But the delays had been such that it remained now the one Confederate foothold in Kentucky. Garfield had driven Humphrey Marshall from the Big Sandy; Forts Henry and Donelson had fallen, and with them Nashville had surrendered; Island Number 10 had been given up, and the Mississippi was open to Vicksburg; the battle of Mill Spring had cleared central Kentucky; and the only point in the middle West, where the Confederate line bent to the north, was where Union sentiment was strongest, and where men who had refused all possible encouragement to join the Confederacy were enduring great hardship for the hope of fighting for the flag. It seemed a wrong and anomalous thing that such should be the case. The plan which

Nelson had originated, and McClellan had approved, and Thomas had been eager to adopt, and Lincoln had unceasingly advocated, the plan which Carter had waited all winter to start in motion, seemed about to materialize in the capture of the Gap and the relief of East Tennessee.

General Carter wanted a man for extra-hazardous service. He sent for the colonels of his two East Tennessee regiments, and made diligent inquiry after a young mountaineer whom he remembered as having deserted after the battle of Wild Cat, and who had rejoined the army before the battle of Mill Spring. It was found after some inquiry that the man he sought was Jackson Casey, then absent on sick leave, but reported as convalescent, and likely soon to return.

"Where is this man Casey?" he asked.

"At Roundstone, a day's ride away," was the reply.

"Is he well enough to travel?"

"Captain Cooper has word that he is ready to return when needed."

"Good! Let a trusty officer be detailed to convey a message to him. It will be better for him not to return to camp."

Late that night an officer rode up to the Whitley home, and obtained shelter for the night. Supper over, he drew Jack aside and communicated his instructions. He was to secure a horse and ride at once into Tennessee, near his old home, and direct a body of men who were preparing to leave the State to unite with the Union army. In February, Governor Harris had called out the entire militia force of the State, commanding every able-bodied man between eighteen and forty-five to join the Confederate army. Large numbers of Union men, who had been held at home up to this time, finding that they must fight for the Confederacy if they remained, were planning how they might escape to Kentucky. A band of several hundred was forming in Knox and Blount counties, as General Carter had been informed, and the route by which they were planning to come, following up the valleys, was, because of prospective Confederate movements, a dangerous one. The entire party was liable to be captured en route.

General Carter, himself an East Tennesseean, counted on the help of such bodies as this in his operations against Cumberland Gap, and wished to afford them all possible assistance in joining the Union army; but he felt that to come to London at that juncture would be extremely dangerous, and advised, instead, that they effect a union with the troops stationed at Boston, near the state line, in Whitley County.

Jack proceeded on his mission, not without some uncertainty, for he was putting his head within the halter again. But he rejoiced in the trust confided to him. In citizen's clothes, and armed only with a revolver and bowie knife, he rode out of Round-stone, and turned through Crank's Gap into Virginia, and thence into Tennessee.

Before Jack left Roundstone, Joe Whitley came home for a few days, and there was a conference among Eph and Joe and Jack — for he was now taken into the family — as to the best way to provide for Jennie. With the news of Jack's mission,

a way seemed to open.   Jack would go into Tennessee, and returning, as he must another way and on
foot, would leave his horse with his mother, and start
her toward Roundstone to stay with Jennie for the
remainder of the war.   This provided satisfactorily
for both, and Jack was glad to remove his mother
from the scenes in which she was living.

Jack passed safely and without undue fatigue
through Crank's Gap and over into the corner of
Virginia.   He was about crossing into Tennessee,
when, looking down the narrow road before him,
he saw a horseman who had dismounted, and was
examining the hoof of his horse.   Jack hesitated
about going on, but it was not easy to go around,
so he spurred on, and soon overtook the man.
Though he was in citizen's clothes like himself,
Jack easily placed the man as a soldier, and readily
supposed him to be a Confederate.   The same idea
was in the mind of each, and neither stopped to
think that the other might belong to the Union
army, as they were then well within the Confederate
lines.

Jack saw that the man was troubled.

"Howdy, stranger," he said.   "In a hurry?"

"Not much," said Jack; "but I ain't used to
wastin' much time when I want to git somewhere."

"That's the way with me; but I'm sorter in
trouble."

"What's the matter?" asked Jack.

"My horse lost a shoe 'bout six mile back, an'
I couldn't find no place to git him shod.   I've jes'
had to ride on an' now he's lame.   Look at that
hoof crack."

"Mighty bad, ain't it?   I hope you warn't in no hurry?"

"Wall, I warn't in no tearin' hurry, as the feller says, but I was sorter anxious to git on.   Stranger, how'd you swap horses?"

"Same's ef you didn't have none."

"Wall, this hain't much of a horse jes' now, that's a fact.   But he's a mighty good one when he's shod.   I'll give ye two hundred to boot.   An' they hain't a prettier ridin' nag in Kaintuck than this one."

"Looky here," demanded Jack, "I wanter know what you're in sech a hurry to git on fur?   It looks to me sorter suspicious.   I've got an *idy* you're a Union spy, tryin' to git information for the Yanks."

"Wall, stranger, you're shootin' inter the wrong side o' the tree, that's all.   Seein' you're on the same side, an' I'm in a fix, I'll tell ye what.   I hain't no spy, but I'm a messenger, an' I've got despatches fur Kirby Smith.   Now ef you got the heart of a Southern gentleman, I know you'll let me have yer horse."

"Not by a jugful," said Jack.   "I've got some despatches myself."

"Wall, le' me take your horse, an' I'll deliver your despatches."

"Not much," said Jack, "but I'll deliver your'n."

"No, I couldn't give 'em up.   But I'll tell you what, I mought tell you what I know, an' ef you git through afore I do, you kin give the word. You know Morgan's movin' to attack Cumberland Gap, an' he's sent Spears with one of his four bri-

gades to clar out Big Creek Gap. Kirby's got
men a-watchin' on him, an' has been a-gittin' word
every day how the work was gittin' on, an' how
fur that brigade is a-gittin' from the main body at
Cumberland Ford. The word I've got is that they
hain't right sure whether Morgan means to clar that
out jes' for a bluff, or whether he raley intends to
leave Cumberland Gap one side an' come through
Big Creek Gap. Anyhow, they allow that the work
is mighty nigh done. He's got the obstructions
mighty nigh clared out, an' is as fur from Morgan's
main army as he's a-goin' to git. Either he'll go
back right soon now to the Ford with the rest, or
the rest will come up to whar he is. An' the word
I've got is, that now's the time for Smith to slip
through Woodson's Gap, and cut off Spears' brigade as he goes back through Big Creek Gap, an'
he kin bag the hull brigade without encounterin'
Morgan's main army at all. That's the word."

"I'll hurry on an' take it," said Jack. "Don'
you reckon you best le' me take the papers? Kirby
may want them."

"Wall, I donno but I best. Wait till I pull off
my boot. No, I don' guess I best give up the
papers. But that's the hull o' the message, I know.
I wisht you'd le' me take your horse."

"Cain't do that," said Jack; "but you needn't
a'hurry with your lame horse. I'll take the word all
right."

Then Jack turned toward home, and hastened
with all his might. That evening he pulled up at
the house of Steph Crowell.

"Steph, Steph! Hello, Steph!"

Steph came to the door.

"Howdy, Jack, howdy!" Then correcting himself he said, "No, hit tain't Jack. I was mistakened. I don' wanter testify that I've seed Jack Casey round here in citizen's clothes. You resemblify Jack Casey powerful, as the feller said, but I see ye hain't. How ye ben?"

"Right pert. But, Steph, I want to swap horses."

"I'm allers willin' fur a good trade. Wut'll ye give to boot?"

"Whatever you say, Steph, an' I'll see that you git the money, but I ain't got it with me. But I mus' have a fraish horse right off."

"I reckon that would be a right good beast you're ridin' ef he warn't so used up."

"He's a fine animal. I never straddled a better one. But I've rode hard. Fetch out your'n, an' fetch him over to the house while I ride over an' see ma a minute."

"Meanin' over to Mis' Casey's? I'll come over in ten or fifteen minutes. I reckon though, ef the hoss is a-goin' to travel to-night, I best feed him fust. I'll come over half a hour atter you git thar."

Jack hastened home and found his mother. Glad enough was she to see him, but she repressed her eagerness to question her son about himself when she saw that he had a message for her.

"Quick, ma! Git yerself somethin' to eat, an' git ready to ride. I want ye to go through the mountains to-night and take a message to Cumberland Ford."

She lost no time in discussion, but hastily prepared the last meal they were to eat together, while

he told her his message. The word about the army
was told in detail and repeated carefully, that there
could be no mistake. He also told her minutely
about the way that she must go, the mountain paths,
the passes through the ridges, the best places to ford
streams, and much more, but this she knew almost
as well as he. The matter of her home at Roundstone was told in less detail, but she accepted it, not
without a heart-throb at leaving the home that had
been hers, but without protest.

She gathered into a reticule some things which
she wished to take with her, having respect to the
necessity for light travel and haste, and Jack agreed
to see that the rest of the family belongings of value
were stored in the cave.

By this time Steph was at the door, and Jack and
his mother went out together.

"If you don' mind, Steph, I'll ride as far as your
house with mother, and leave this horse at your door.
Thank you, old friend."

"Good-by, stranger, I hope ye won't regret yer
swap. You do favor Jack Casey more'n ever I
seed two men favor each other. Good-by, Mis'
Casey. I hope ye'll have a good ride, wherever
you're goin'."

"Good-by, Steph. And God bless ye."

At Steph's gate Jack kissed his mother and tied
his horse, and then went to the house to rest that
night and be off with the dawn, hindered hardly
an hour by the task of secreting the property.

Thus Elizabeth Casey started on her perilous ride
in the night to save the Union army from the raid
of General Kirby Smith. It was a long, dark ride.

The woods were full of dangers, seen and unseen. The roads were wretched, and in places she had to ride where there were no roads. She was turning her back upon her life-long home, and parting again with her son, perhaps forever, but her heart was brave and her purpose true.

Who shall record the heroic deeds of women in the Civil War? Poets sing the fame of the general who rides from afar to save the day, but how few know the tale of the noble woman of East Tennessee, who, mounted on the horse that her son had brought, rode through the darkness and the wilderness, through swollen streams and hostile camps, where no man could have ridden unhalted, and brought the warning that saved from capture a whole brigade! The government was appealed to later, to make some fitting testimonial in honor of the brave deed, but nothing came of it. Yet General Morgan gratefully records that what saved the command of General Spears, as he was clearing the way for the approach to Cumberland Gap, was the heroic ride of that brave woman, who had already given her son, and now risked her life besides.

They tell wonderful tales of that ride, all through the Cumberland Mountains: how she galloped down a road that was held by the rebels, and when the sentinel called his "Halt! Who goes there?" answered, "A woman, and I won't halt," and dashed by him, knowing that he would not fire upon a woman; how she urged her horse up a rocky slope where never horse had carried a human soul, and where, as they verily believe, only special

Providential intervention saved her from certain death; how she forded streams that were swimming deep, and came through dry, as the Israelites passed through the sea; how once her horse fell beneath her on the edge of an abyss, but she rose unharmed and mounted and rode on again, the horse seeming to gather strength and courage from her own indomitable will, — these and a score of other incidents they relate of that ride of a heroine to save an army.

The day was breaking as she stopped on the top of the mountain that separates Kentucky from Tennessee, and sat for a moment to rest her panting horse after the climb, silhouetted against the sky that was lighting with the dawn. Just as the sun was rising she stopped for a half hour to feed her horse and remove her saddle, and then was riding on again. The sun rose to the meridian and began to decline, but her hand still held the rein, and the faithful horse moved on.

That afternoon there came riding around the clean-cut end of Pine Mountain where the Cumberland has sawn it through, a mud-bespattered horse, and a tired but triumphant woman, bearing word to General Morgan of the danger awaiting Spears' brigade.

Messengers were sent out. The brigade was recalled. And when, next day, Kirby Smith passed through Woodson's Gap, and with a swoop like that of an eagle descended upon the valley where Spears' brigade had been, the prey had taken its flight, and the Confederate army returned from a bootless journey.

XIX

The Plucky Women of Scott County

FOR several days in April a number of men were at work steadily and stealthily in the woods on the bank of the Clinch River about twenty miles north of Knoxville, building a boat which might ferry seventy-five men across the river at once. Having completed their task, they hid the craft in the woods, to prevent, if possible, the rebel pickets from finding it until it should have served its end.

On the night of the anniversary of the ride of Paul Revere, Jack Casey made his way to this boat and waited for company. A group of seventy-five men, largely from the vicinity of Knoxville, who had rendezvoused at Bull Run Creek, first appeared, and rejoiced to find the boat in possession of its friends. They were gotten on board at about two o'clock in the morning, and set ashore on the opposite side. The boat returned for another company that had appeared, and the first, who had already marched twenty miles in the rain, unslung their haversacks, and sat down to rest. Before the boat returned they were alarmed by the cry that the rebel cavalry were after them, and hastily formed in line, placing in front the men, less than one-third of their number, who had been able to secure any kind of weapon. It proved a false alarm. The two horsemen who approached were friends, coming to guide them until daylight. Three hundred thus crossed that night, and seventy-five, comprising another company, were captured in their attempt to reach the rendezvous. These, with four hundred others, captured the preceding day, were taken south, and then given their choice of imprisonment or of enlistment in the Confederate army.

At almost every house, as they marched by, a man would come out and silently join the column. The men as they passed saw many a sorrowful silhouette in the doorways, many a fond farewell, as fathers and husbands and sons stood for a moment on the threshold with arms about their loved ones, and then hurried out in silence to join the company, which now about held its own in numbers; for while many joined its ranks, some who could not keep up, and were already wearied with the march and chilled with the rain, gave out, and dropped into some hospitable cabin by the way.

When daybreak came, they could go no farther. They found a secluded place in the hills, and, first eating a meal from their haversacks, threw themselves, wet as they were, and without shelter from the rain, upon the sodden earth. A few acted as sentinels, and these, in two hours, woke the entire company, bringing in a man whom they had captured, who professed to be a rebel, but who talked so confusedly that they could make little of what he said. They took him for a spy, and hastened on, commanding him to stay with them on pain of being shot. It appeared in time that their prisoner was really a Union man, who, having been captured

by the Confederates and escaped, had come among
them by accident after a night of wandering, and
fearing them to be enemies, and being greatly per-
turbed, made the confused answers which had so
frightened them. But they did not learn this for
some hours, which was well for them. The cavalry
were in hot pursuit, and arrived at their brief resting-
place an hour only after they had left. But for
their false alarm and utmost haste, they would all
have been captured.

The men had no commander, but trusted to their
guides. Jack had brought general information concerning the route that must be chosen, but at different points they followed the lead of individual
members of the party, who knew in detail some
portions of the way, and at times they found ready
guides in loyal men through whose neighborhood
they passed. · They saw few houses, however, and
marched all day without another halt for rest.

When it had grown dark, and they had now been
tramping for twenty-four hours with only two hours'
rest, Jack called a halt, and there was no one to
question his authority, nor did any wish so to
do. They were miles from any human habitation.
The deep ravine in which they huddled together
seemed in the darkness and rain a haunted place.
They ate a supper from their long-soaked haversacks, and lay down on the wet ground, in a pouring
rain, to spend a night in what they ever afterward
called "Camp Misery."

Still the enemy followed them, being baffled only
by their choosing a way so rough as to be impracticable for cavalry, and night by night they stopped

to rest a few miles nearer the land that was sheltered by the Union flag. After five days of marching, they passed through Scott County, which adjoins the Kentucky line, and were stopped for a time early in the morning by the swelling of New River, but found after an hour of search one small canoe. It would not ferry over the men, but it would take in a few trips their precious firearms. A single cabin was in sight on the other side, but not a soul could be seen. The men loaded their guns into the canoe, and themselves plunged into the water. On the other side they reclaimed their arms, and, in doing so, accidentally discharged a gun. Then suddenly life appeared in the cabin. A man ran to the barn, mounted a horse, and rode off at all speed, to warn the neighbors that the rebels were coming.

They ascended the river bank to the cabin, and found, as they had suspected, that the warning conveyed by the horseman had been of the supposed approach of the rebels, and that the "jay-hawking" might now be looked for at every foot of the way. This information was given with evident satisfaction by a resolute and toothless old woman, with a snuff-stick between her gums.

"But we hain't rebs. We're fur the Union," said the men.

"Be ye Union, shore enough?" asked the woman, removing her snuff-stick.

"Yes, we're Union, every man of us, an' we're goin' over into Whitley to fight for Lincoln."

"Laws a massy! An' them men'll be a-shootin' on ye every mile o' the way from here to Kaintuck! Here, Marthy! Marthy! You run up the branch an' holler to Sue and Peggy! Tell 'em to come right off!"

A tall, long-limbed girl of sixteen answered the behest, and in ten minutes there were four women at the house: the old woman, the young girl, and two neighbors.

Meantime the old woman went into the house and got a red shawl. With a needle she quickly basted some stripes of white cotton on one side, and mounted it to a sapling which one of the soldiers cut at her command. It was ready by the time the women were on hand.

"Gals," she said, "these men is Union, an' our men thinks they're rebs. They don't know one man from another, the men don't, an' they'll shoot 'em, sure's yer borned. But they won't shoot women. We gotter go ahead an' keep the men from shootin', till they find out who they be."

The Tennesseeans recognized the propriety of accepting some such offer. They were dealing with men who were not accustomed to be trifled with, and who would stop to ask no questions before shooting. That they were coming from the south, without warning, was *prima facie* evidence that they were rebels, and they would meet a warm reception from the men of Scott County. They were an odd lot, old men and boys for the most part, too old or too young to be drafted, and with certain rough and ready ideas about the value of human life, and the best way of settling difficulties. They lived in that border county, and built their stills on the state line, and settled questions of jurisdiction at long range. They were steady of nerve, and not over tender of conscience, and they could see from behind a rock a man whom they believed a rebel, and could watch his approach, as he appeared above the sights on the two ends of the four feet barrel of their mountain guns, and then, when the blade on the muzzle just filled to a hair the slot in the hindsight, they could press the hair trigger with the steadiest nerve, — those Scott County bushwhackers! But they were loyal, every man of them, and the strong men having gone to war and left the old men and boys to defend the women and the homes, that was the way they did it. And they were a terror to evil-doers all the way from Pine Knot to Brimstone Creek.

Never did an army have a better advance guard, or one that promised more for its safety than that which the old woman organized on the north shore of New River on that April day. The sun was beginning to shine, and the dingy green of approaching spring was on the hilltops. The season seemed to have changed in a day from the dearth and cold of winter to the almost realized promise of spring. And this was gladdening the hearts of the men, whose every mile hitherto, and every night of rest until the last, had been passed in a constant rain. And best of all was this reception by a people who were near enough the protection of the Union arms to come out openly and be their friends.

"Toe the mark, here!" called the old woman to her three companions. The four women marched abreast, waving the flag, and talking or singing as they walked. The men followed a short distance behind them, and stepped with new alacrity, and filled the road from side to side, for a long distance.

The Plucky Women of Scott County.   Page 221.

At each house they passed, the women stopped and called out other women, until there were a dozen of them, and as they approached places which they knew were favorable to ambush, they called laughingly, —

"Shoot, ef ye wanter!   We're a-comin'!   Don't we look lack rebs?"

Soon men, who were hiding beside the road, stood up and let down the hammers of their guns, and joined the procession.   When some of the women had to drop out and return, their places had been taken in advance by others, and at no time during the day, after the number reached its full, were there less than a dozen in the lead.   The warning had gone a matter of six miles, as one neighbor had sent the news ahead to another.   But for the whole fifteen miles from New River to the state line, the loyal women of Scott County led the way with cheering and with song.   Behind them came the men of Scott, and behind these came the heroes of the parade, the men from Knox and Blount, who were going to fight for the flag.

When any of the women turned back to go to their homes, as they did from time to time in groups of two and three, the men cheered them, all down the line, and waved their hats and kissed their hands.   Just as the sun was setting, they passed over the state line and entered the camp at Boston.   The soldiers saw them coming, and received them with open ranks, cheering the hardy men of Tennessee and the plucky women of the good old county of Scott.

XX

The Capture of Cumberland Gap

CUMBERLAND GAP, an almost impregnable natural fortress, had been greatly strengthened by the Confederates during their occupancy. Morgan found that he could approach the Gap, but that his force was insufficient to capture it by assault, especially with the sudden activity of Kirby Smith on his flank. Smith was drawn off toward Chattanooga by a diversion of Buell at Morgan's request, but Buell sent word to Morgan, on the 10th of June, that he must depend upon his own resources, and look for no further aid from the main army; moreover that Buell contemplated larger operations, which might be seriously injured by any failure of Morgan, who therefore had better attempt no offensive measures.

But the hard-worked soldiers, who had spent weeks of labor in cutting roads, in hauling cannon by hand over the Pine and Cumberland mountains, who had lived for months on the hope of an attack upon the Gap, would hear to no word of remaining longer upon the defensive. At one o'clock on the morning of June 18 the command started forward, in two parallel columns of two brigades each, over roads that they had cut either out of the virgin forest, or through the obstructions which the Confederates had thrown across them. It was a high day with them all. They were advancing almost against orders, and their right to the attempt was to be demonstrated at the point of the bayonet. They had waited too long for this day not to greet it with enthusiasm.

They made a brief halt for breakfast as they entered the valley of Yellow Creek. Their hearts beat high, and they were confident and eager. In the midst of the meal, a Union man rode among them with the news that the rebels were retreating before them. They had looked for a desperate battle. To win the Gap without a fight was news too good to be true, and almost too good to be desired. The advance was sounded. The meal was left half eaten. The army was in motion again, up the valley of Yellow Creek. Along the way they found evidence that they had been told the truth. They came to the outposts and found them deserted. Up the slope they came to a masked battery, and found its guns spiked. They rushed up the road, where the rocks slope like the roof of a house. They pushed past each other in their eagerness. They left the road and went scrambling up the side of the mountain. No orders could restrain them. No discipline could hold them back. They were thirsty, and passed a spring, many of them without stopping to drink. They had no breath to cheer, but they climbed with grip and nail.

The advance reached the great saddle, and met the advance from the two brigades approaching from the other road. They joined in a cheer which was caught up below and echoed hoarsely from thou-

sands of parched throats. Up the steep they
crowded, companies all broken, lines all disregarded,
the flags ahead, and the strongest of limb and purpose hard after them. They paused for breath in
the Gap, and for a swallow of water at the spring,[1]
from which no thirsty soul could drink without gratitude to the good God who made it there, and most
were content to stop.   But after an interval of rest
a group of the bravest started up the slope on the
steeper side, above the Gap.   A color-sergeant belonging to De Courcey's brigade, which had entered
the Gap from the other side, saw the movement, but
was too exhausted to go farther.

"Give me your flag!" cried Jack.

"Place it on the very top!" cried the color-
bearer.

Up, up the steep path they went, already tired,
but all eager to be first upon the summit, a hundred, perhaps, of the foremost, who were sighing for
more worlds to conquer.   Their companions still
arriving in the Gap, and the officers who were standing a little apart with their field-glasses, watched
with interest from below. Jack looked down and
saw the cloud of witnesses, and it put fresh enthusiasm into him. He pressed on, passing one and
another, until there were hardly more than a dozen
ahead, and they were almost at the top. At that
moment a brawny fellow, who was in the lead,
glanced over his shoulder and saw Jack struggling
up.   He stopped and wheeled about, and halted
those who followed him with a wave of his hand.
He caught his breath enough to speak by the time

---

[1] This fine spring has been ruined by the blasting of the tunnel beneath the Gap.

Jack came panting to the place where he and his comrade stood.

"Stop!" said the strapping fellow to those ahead of Jack. "Stop, and let the flag go first!"

Jack passed on, the others following hard after, and behind these, four or five score hardy fellows panting up the slope between them and the notch. Jack scrambled over the low embankment and ran to the great gun, Long Tom, which stood in position on the very crest. He climbed upon its carriage, the big fellow giving him a lift, and stood upon the breech of the great cannon, waving the flag where all below could see. A cheer came up from the Gap, a cheer that had been pent up for months, a cheer that had in it the ardor that had come from hard struggle and great privation for the sake of the Union. And the great mountain range that opened its arms to take the Union army to its very heart echoed back from its two great peaks the loyal shout, and from the highest pinnacle of the Cumberlands there floated that day the flag with the stripes and the stars.

This was glory enough for the most of Morgan's command, but not for Carter's brigade. Carter asked permission to pursue the enemy through the defiles of Tennessee, which he knew so well. He was allowed to go forward as far as Tazewell, and to send detachments short distances from there. He returned, reporting that the Confederates had fled beyond Tazewell and to the Clinch Mountains, or even farther. As a military movement his march into Tennessee was hardly more than a reconnoitre. But to his men and to the people it was a triumphal entry. Many of the soldiers passed their own homes. From time to time, along the way, a man in the ranks would quicken his steps as he recognized familiar landmarks, and would note with eagerness the succession of well-known objects that marked the approach of his own house. And there at the fence they would be waiting, — the wife with the baby in her arms, the children standing along the rail fence, — and the man would drop out of the ranks to embrace his wife and kiss the children, and hold for a moment the baby to his heart, while his companions sent up a hearty and a homesick cheer. There were old men that came tottering to the door, and stood leaning on their staves, thanking God, like Simeon in the temple, that they had lived to see that day. There were women at every house, cheering and waving and saluting the flag. There were lusty children that shouted their joy at the top of their boyish lungs, or prattled it in broken baby accents. And there were those who could not cheer nor wave nor speak, but who stood weeping tears of joy when they saw the Union flag that had returned to East Tennessee.

XXI

A Great and Forgotten Battle

CUB was playing one day in August, down by the creek, and Jennie was spinning in the porch, while Elizabeth hatchelled the little crop of flax which they had pulled by hand, and were preparing for the loom.

"Hetchellin's mighty hard work," remarked Jennie. "You let me do thet a spell, while you spin."

"No, I'm mighty glad of a chance to do it," said Mrs. Casey. "It's lucky we're so fur to one side the armies don' hardly ever come through the Holler. All the flax I had last year in Tennessy the sojers tromped down."

"I reckon this war hain't a-goin' to las' much longer, don' you?"

"I don' see how it kin, with our side holdin' the Gap. Hit seems mighty quare they hain't gone on to Knoxville. They mought jes' as well."

"But, as long as the Union side holds the Gap, the rebs won't come inter Kaintucky, will they?"

"No, I don't reckon they kin. They's other gaps, but none like that. They mought get over into the west part o' the State, but now that Fort Henry and Fort Donelson has fell, they hain't no show for that."

"Why don't the Union sojers go on, do you reckon?"

"I don' know.   'Pears like they git all hesitated up, an' don' know what to do.   Ef I was in command at the Gap, do you s'pose I'd leave that railroad for the rebels to send cotton an' corn an' fodder from Georgy, an' rebel sojers from V'ginny, an' let 'em travel back 'n' forth an' send Union men south to prison, when it'd all be ours for the astin'?   I reckon not.   I've a plumb notion to git on a horse some day an' ride to Gin'r'l Morgan to the Gap, an' say, 'Ef it hadn't a ben for me ye wouldn't a got here.   Now you're here, ye got to go furder, or ye needn't a come.'   But still it's something, that while he's thar the rebels can't come in here.   But it's mighty hard on the folks in East Tennessy.   Here comes Cub.   What's the matter, Cub?"

"Sojers is tomin'!" cried Cub.

"Sojers?   I reckon not.   Run down to the fence, Jennie, an' see."

Jennie ran to the fence and back in haste.

"They be a-comin', shore enough," she said, "an' I'm afeard they're the rebs."

"The rebs?   That's impossible!" cried Mrs. Casey.

But it was true.   While General George Morgan was holding the Gap with his small force, Kirby Smith had left General Patterson before the Gap to prevent trouble from Morgan, and had passed from Chattanooga, through East Tennessee, and into the mountains of Kentucky, and was now hastening toward the blue grass.

"Git some water, Jennie," said Mrs. Casey. "Hit's a hot day, an' they'll be thirsty.   Reb or

Union, I won't refuse no thirsty man a drink, but they gotter keep outer this house."

She examined the rifle above the fireplace, and hid it in one of the beds, while Jennie ran to the spring, and brought a bucket of water, which she refilled again and again. Elizabeth went to the fence in front with a gourd, and met the first men to pass.

"Here's water," she said, "an' you're welcome to it. But we're two women, livin' all alone with a little boy, an' we hain't got no more to eat than we need ourselves. We hain't got no contraband goods here, an' we hain't a-goin' to have none o' you men a-comin' in an' pesterin' us. Jest take yer drink o' water an' go on."

The men were in haste, and thankfully received the water, which, though the force was a small one, disappeared far more rapidly than Jennie could bring it, and no one attempted to molest the women.

"Do you reckon you could give us a snack to eat?" asked one man, toward the rear. "We're gittin' our forage as we go, an' the fellers in the van sorter gits ahead of us."

"You kin have what little we got cooked up," said Elizabeth; "but you mus'n't take wut little we got to live on for the winter."

Jennie brought out of the house a few corn pones, and a high pie, the latter made of several layers of biscuit dough alternating with apple sauce.

"Tell me who ye be," asked Elizabeth, "an' where yer goin'?"

"We're Kirby Smith's men," said the soldier. "The main army's goin' over the big road through

London, but we're scatterin' out so's to git enough ter eat. We're goin' to the Big Hill now, an' I reckon we'll see the Ohio River afore we stop."

"I reckon you'll see some other things afore ye see that," said Elizabeth.

"Sich as which?" asked the soldier.

"Sich as bayonets, an' sich like."

"Well, we hain't seed much to skeer us this fur," laughed the men.

"You better go back," said she, "while ye kin get back with hull skins."

"They hain't nothin' a-gwine ter hurt us," said one of the men. "We hain't killable. Ef Yankee bullets would kill us, we'd a ben dead a right smart spell ago. We got so much lead in us now we don' dast ter go in swimmin'."

"That's a pity," said she. "Mos' on yer need a swim right bad."

"Wall, good-by, marm. Good-by, miss. We'll come back atter while."

"You'll come back a heap faster'n ye went. That is, ef you're so's to be able to walk."

Thus the good-natured banter passed between the women and the soldiers. But the women saw them out of sight with great anxiety.

Toward night the last company came down the road, and camped beside the creek. One of the officers came to the gate to make inquiries concerning the roads to Manchester. Elizabeth was preparing supper, and Jennie met him.

"Miss Whitley!" he exclaimed. "I had no *idy* of meeting you here, but I'm mighty glad to meet you again. You remember Dr. Sam Marshall?"

"I remember you," said Jennie, flushing slightly.

"I've wanted to say," he hurriedly went on, "I know that I didn't appear well when we met afore. Like as not it was my fault. If you thought ill of me then I'm mighty sorry; for there's no one in the world I'd like so much to have think well of me as you. Miss Whitley, don't try to stop me. Don't run away from me. I ain't goin' to say anything more, only that the first time I seen you I loved you. I haven't any *idy* you feel so towards me, but I can't help thinkin' that if you knew me better — if I could explain — if you'd just count me a friend till I had a chance to show you what sort of feller I really am —"

He was going on almost breathlessly, but Jennie stopped him.

"It's no use, Dr. Marshall," she said. "I don' think ill o' ye, p'tic'lar, but I couldn't love a man that's a rebel."

"Is that the only reason?" he asked. "This war'll be over after a while. Then we can talk about that. I don't want you to say you love me — not now. Leastwise I don't expect it. But is that the only reason why you couldn't?"

Jennie bit her lip and hesitated. "No," she said at length, "it ain't the only reason."

"You love Jack Casey!" he exclaimed. "Tell me. Is that the reason?"

"Dr. Marshall, if I do, I hain't never told him so yet, and I ain't a-goin' to tell no one else. Good night."

She turned and went into the house, and Sam Marshall wandered down to the Sinks, and listened

to the swirl of the water as it disappeared, and
thought his own life-current had suddenly sunk into
a like abyss.

When Jennie arose next morning the soldiers
had moved on, and she and Elizabeth waited, as
did thousands of Kentucky women, for the dread
tidings that were soon to come.

It was on the 23d of August, 1862, that Kirby
Smith met a small Union force, mostly of Kentuckians, on the wooded slopes of the Big Hill,
which lies between Rockcastle and "the free State
of Jackson," as they used to call the mountain
county named for Old Hickory. The hill is fourteen miles across, and it was hard climbing, to say
nothing of fighting, on that hot day. There were
a few experienced troops that had come from Cumberland Gap, and the rest were home guards. The
soldiers who had been under fire circulated among
the new recruits and encouraged them. The Whitley brothers were there, and to their company were
added some new recruits from the neighboring
county of Estill.

"Howdy, Mr. Murray, I didn't know you was in
the war."

"Yes, I 'listed two months ago. I hoped that
you young fellers cud put down the rebellion without me, but hyur I be. Where's your friends from
Tennessy ?"

"Cousin Henry got killed in the war." Eph
shrank from telling that he had been hanged.
"Jack Casey is with his reg'maint at the Gap."

"'Pears like them men at the Gap mought a
saved us this trouble."

"So it does. But it don't seem like nobody realizes the importance of pushing on into East Tennessy. I've heerd tell that Abe Lincoln has insisted on it from the start, and Thomas and Nelson has always believed in it. But they always put some one in command that don't. An' so the rebels has that railroad, and they can bring their forces from V'ginny or the cotton States just as they please, an' dump 'em down thar right at our door. Ef we'd go on while we're at it, an' git that railroad an' hold onto it like grim death, they wouldn't be no more raids like this."

"Nelson's in command now. He believes in invadin' East Tennessy."

"Yes, but he's got all he kin do now to keep back the rebs that's here. He can't do no invadin' now his self."

Here the long roll beat, and the men fell in at their posts. There was a scattering fire in the distance, and soon the woods were alive with men in gray. To the new men it was uncanny to see the Confederates pushing their way up the hill, with flushed faces and with unslackened speed. They fired, as it seemed, into their faces, but really above them, as do all raw troops, especially when shooting down hill; and it became a thing of terror to see the enemy come on, scrambling over rocks, pulling themselves up by branches of trees, and hardly minding the leaden hail that was poured down the hill. Up and up and up, panting and yelling, and seeming to blow the smoke of battle from their nostrils, and now the enemy was at the crest, and fighting hand to hand for possession of the ridge. The crooked Union line wavered and broke.   A few men fled, and then the road was full of them.   Then the Confederate advance drove itself like a wedge into the gap they had made, and the terrified home guards turned and ran, pell-mell, toward the blue grass.

On the western slope of Big Hill there is a clear and beautiful spring, whose waters ripple in a cool rill all the way down the mountain side.   When the retreating soldiers came to this, they halted for water, and here a handful of the old troops made a stand, supported by the braver ones that were new.   Here again the enemy came upon them, but, met in the narrow mountain pass by a determined body, they were repulsed, and their superior numbers driven back, and under cover of this advantage, the Union soldiers retreated to the foot of the hill.

A week later occurred the forgotten battle of Richmond.   The terrible struggles about the Confederate capital later in the war drowned out all memory of another Richmond.   But here, in the edge of the blue grass, a few miles from the Big Hill fight, occurred what was up to that time the greatest battle in Kentucky, and one whose results struck terror to the heart of the entire North.

General Nelson was not dismayed by the defeat of his troops at Big Hill.   He left General Manson [1] in charge of the army, with instructions to oppose the Confederate advance, and fall slowly back to the Kentucky River, while he prepared to make

---

[1] "I immediately sent couriers with orders not to fight the enemy. . . .   What the motive of General Manson was in bringing on an action under the circumstances, and marching five miles to do so I will leave him to explain to you.

"W. NELSON, *Major General.*"

a stand at his own well-chosen position. He was
driving about in a buggy, selecting points to be occupied by his troops, when he heard the sound of
the cannonade. Lashing his horse into a run, he
hastened to Lancaster, ten miles on the way, where
he secured a fresh horse and pushed on. Over six
feet high, and bearing his three hundred pounds
lightly, he was one of the most commanding figures
of the war, and those who saw him that day lashing his horse furiously along the Richmond pike fell
back before him.

As Nelson approached Richmond, the firing,
instead of receding, came nearer, and he knew that
it boded ill for his army. The Union forces, under
General Manson, had gone out to meet the Confederates, and taken position beyond Richmond, a
few miles toward the Big Hill. Behind their slender
defences of fence rails stood the new men, and against
them, hardened to service and flushed with victory,
came the hosts of Kirby Smith. To have won their
way inch by inch up the steep side of the Big Hill
had been to them a thing of little difficulty; and
now to meet their foe upon the level and face to
face, they counted hardly worth the name of fighting. With a yell and a volley, they came to the
attack, while the Union soldiers with set teeth
awaited the onset.

There was a short struggle and a sharp one, and
the dead and wounded were on every side. The
Confederate artillery came up, and belched out its
fire and sent its round shot bowling over the rolling
fields and tearing through the ranks. The raw recruits fought bravely against great odds until the

fight became a hand-to-hand contest, and then the Union soldiers broke and retreated toward the town.

As Nelson came into Richmond, he was met by the retreating soldiers. He was in a frenzy. The defeat of his army meant the surrender of Lexington and Frankfort, perhaps also of Louisville and Cincinnati. He drew his sword and ordered the fugitives to halt. He cursed the women who ran to him for protection, and threatened the life of every man who did not turn back. The soldiers feared him more than the enemy, and gathered to his support. Only one man withstood his authority. A soldier from Indiana, making toward the rear, stopped when ordered by Nelson to return, and held up a wounded arm.

" But, General, I'm wounded," he said.

The infuriated Nelson struck him over the head with his sword and pushed on. The poor fellow fell against a fence, and holding himself up, leaned his wounded head upon the fence, which showed his blood stains for many a year. When, a few months later, Nelson was shot dead by an Indiana officer, the people of Richmond looked at the stains upon the fence, and thought his death a retribution for his striking a wounded Indiana soldier.

Furious as Nelson was, he was yet able to display great military genius. He selected a new position, and gathered the fugitives to maintain it. Just outside the little city, in the cemetery, he rallied his men. Hiding behind tombstones, and protecting themselves behind the fence, they made a desperate stand. But again the rebels pressed upon them in front and flank, while their cavalry threatened the rear. Their guns seemed never empty. Their yell was terrible to hear. The gaps in their ranks seemed to heal as fast as made. Nelson's utmost efforts were unavailing. His men broke and ran, leaving on the field five hundred dead and twelve hundred wounded. That in its day was an awful roll of dead and wounded, and showed how hot had been the struggle ere the new troops gave way. Nelson left no stone unturned to redeem the fortunes of the day. When his soldiers had been driven from the cemetery and through the town, and he himself was wounded, he rallied them for a last desperate stand upon the Lancaster pike; but all in vain. His men were hopelessly routed. They fled beyond Camp Nelson to Lexington and then on north, hardly stopping till they reached the Ohio River; and Kirby Smith pushed on into the rich blue-grass region, where he captured hundreds of fine horses and gathered stores of provisions, and his men lived on the fat of the land.

There was consternation in Ohio, for on the flank of Kirby Smith was John Morgan's band of cavalry, which a year later made such a disastrous raid, and even now was learning how to do it. And Smith's whole army moved northward at its leisure, Bragg also moving into Kentucky by a parallel route, occupying towns which the Union troops had held, and practically taking possession of the entire State. Lexington and Frankfort were evacuated. Cincinnati and Louisville were in terror. The officers of Ohio became anxious for the safety of the State archives, and General Buell marched with all haste from Nashville to protect the cities of the North.

General George W. Morgan and his forces at Cumberland Gap, cut off from their base of supplies and surrounded by forces greater than their own, were in imminent peril of capture or starvation, and in all Kentucky there was no adequate force to oppose the advance of Smith and Bragg. General George Morgan at length determined to retreat, and did so, taking his command with him across the mountains to the Ohio River, and leaving Cumberland Gap to the Confederates. Thus did a successful movement end in dismal failure, and the mountains were left again in undisputed possession of the Confederates.

A few miles south of Richmond, on the pike toward Berea, stands a little red brick church, whose walls show to this day the marks of cannon balls. Inside, on the narrow benches, thick as they could lie, were the wounded men. In a corner near the pulpit, side by side, lay Mr. Murray, and Bill and Joe Whitley.

"I shall soon be well," said Mr. Murray to Becky, who came with her mother the day after the battle. "And Joe'll recover, too, but Bill won't live many days. He's a brave man, and wants to see his sister. Can you ride and fetch her to him?"

Becky consented, and her father told her how the boys had received their wounds. They were the last men to fall back. Joe stood with the flag where the fire was hottest till the army fled, and was shot just as the retreat began. Bill looked back and saw him fall, and, turning, caught him and the flag together in his arms, and with Eph's help bore them from the field. It was that return to save Joe and the flag that cost Bill his life; for just as they crossed the fence a ball struck him, inflicting a fatal wound.

"Shall I go for your sister?" asked Becky of Bill.

"I sorter wisht ye would," he said; "an' ef I don't live till ye git back, tell her all sech things as a feller ort to say to his sister. An' God bless ye an' Joe. I don't blame him fur likin' ye. I — I — I could a sorter keered fur ye myself ef it hadn't a been I knowed you an' Joe liked each other."

Becky rode alone to Roundstone, and returned with Jennie and Mrs. Casey. They left Cub with a neighbor. The two girls rode one horse, and brought a large bundle of bedding for the wounded men. And a prettier picture could hardly have been than these two girls on horseback together, with their fair faces and white sunbonnets. Bill was dead before they returned, and with sad hearts they turned to the nursing of the living.

There was much for women to do in those days, and not all could remain away from home. Nor, as the men were prisoners of war, were all allowed to do so. In a few days Mrs. Casey went home, as Mrs. Murray had already done, and the two girls were left together at the hospital, caring for their friends, who were to be sent south as soon as they were able. The days were all too few. Almost reluctantly they saw the daily improvement of Joe and Mr. Murray. The latter was first able to be moved, and together they bade him a sad farewell, as with a score of others from the hospital, he departed to Andersonville. But Joe recovered more slowly, and with one or two discouraging relapses, and was still too feeble to be removed in October, when the battle of Perryville drove the Confederates from the State, and Joe was left in Kentucky with his friends.

He was still too weak to make the long, rough journey to Roundstone, but they obtained a carriage in Richmond and took him to the home of the Murrays, where Jennie left him.

But who shall tell of the mingled feelings in the hearts of those young women, who were but two of thousands of loyal and true Southern women of their time, each with her love and pride, her sorrow and fear? They were happy in the recovery and escape of Joe, and both mourned the brave and kind Mr. Murray in his living death in a distant prison. And Jennie's heart, which was still sore for the tragic death of her father, was broken anew by the loss of her brother Bill and anxiety for Jack, from whom she had not heard since the evacuation of the Gap. The narrowness of their vision, their ignorance of the great movements of the war, increased their uncertainty and anxiety; and the only things that remained unshaken and immovable were their love for their friends, their trust in God, and their devotion to the cause of the Union.

Mrs. Casey, from her visit to the hospital, returned by another way; the Confederate occupation of the Big Hill making it difficult to get back to Roundstone by that route. So she went to Berea, where there had been a school, that was now broken up, and through Boone's Gap to Livingstone, and so across Wild Cat Mountain.   Here she spent the night with a family of Tennessee refugees who had occupied a cabin which they had found vacant after the battle a year before.   Finding further progress northward difficult, and having undisputed possession, they had remained.

"Did you ever hear," she asked, as she was leaving, "'bout a house the rebels burned at the time o' the battle?"

"They burned more'n one house," said the man. "What fur house was you thinkin' 'bout?"

"I wasn't thinkin' 'bout no house in p'tic'lar, only I heerd that they burned up a house with a woman in it."

"Lack as not they did, the dirty devils!" said the man.   "They done a trick as bad, I've heerd. They burned up a house with a baby in hit, an' hits ma went crazy."

A sudden idea came to Elizabeth.

"Where was it at?" she asked.

"'Bout a mile from here, down that holler, an' up yan spur o' the hill.   See that lone pine, thar in the edge of a leetle deadenin'?   That's hit."

Elizabeth asked no more questions, but turned her horse's head that way.   She found the pine tree in the edge of the clearing, and the chimney and doorstone where the burned house had stood. The place answered to a description she had heard from Jack, and her heart sank within her.   She made her way to the pine, and there were two graves instead of one.

R

She turned and rode sadly away, and reined in her horse at the next cabin and asked for a drink.

"Am I on the big road to London?" she asked the tall, lank woman who came to the fence with a gourd, a baby at her breast, and a two year old clinging to her skirt.

"Yes, this here's the road," said the mother, hushing the ravenous young babe, and bribing him to silence by allowing him to proceed with his dinner while she talked. "This is the road. How d'ye come?"

"I come down the road from the top o' Wild Cat, but I sorter got out of the way, I reckon. I come by a place where they's ben a house burnt, up here about three-quarters."

"Oh, yes. That's Joe Cameron's house, I reckon. Him an' Mollie lived thar. Did ye hear about it?"

"No, I didn't. How was it?"

"Wall, hit was thisaway. Joe an' Moll they got married an' lived up thar, an' Moll was allers sorter quare. She was sorter cold lack, but she could love an' hate lack death, only she didn't show hit lack other folks. An' wen Joe died, two year ago las' winter, she acted so you couldn't har'ly tell wether she keered or not. But we knowed she did, a heap."

"Them's the kind that keers the most, a heap o' times," said Elizabeth.

"Yes, an' she did. She wouldn't live nowhurs but jes' thar, an' she lived thar an' sometimes uster go out an' sleep on Joe's grave. Did yer see Joe's grave under the pine?"

"I seed some graves there," said Elizabeth.

"Yas, thar's two thar now. Time o' the battle, a year ago, Moll come down here with three peck o' beans she wanted my ole man to pack for her to the store when he was a-goin' light, an' wen she got back the battle was on, an' she couldn't git home till night, an' when she *did* fin'ly git thar, the rebs had burned her house an' the baby in it."

"What did she do?"

"Do? Good laws a massy, you'd better ast what she didn't do! She warn't jes' rightly at herself afore, an' wen that happened, she jes' went stark crazy, an' she wandered all over the mounting, astin' folks ef they'd seed Joe or the baby. The neighbors uster pack her up somethin' to eat, an' the teamsters sorter got to know her, an' lef' her a snack now an' then. But wen winter come we was all mighty nigh starved out, with what the armies had et up, an' we tried to look atter her, but some days we didn't see her. An' we made her a sorter shelter by the grave, but a heap o' times she wouldn't sleep in hit, an' one mornin' atter a storm that froze everythin' hard, an' the ice so slick you couldn't har'ly stan', let alone climb the mounting, my ole man started up with somethin' fur her to eat, an' he found her dead, froze stiff on Joe's grave. He come back, an' he says, says he, 'Pore Moll, I reckon she's found Joe an' the baby.'"

Elizabeth rode on in silence.

"I won't tell Jack an' Jennie," she said to herself; "it wouldn't do no good, an' it would make 'em feel bad."

XXII

The Secret of the Sinks

IT is not always the largest event which fills the largest angle in memory. The little village of Manchester forgot a hundred thrilling and important events of the war even before its close, they trod so on each other's heels. There was always something happening about the salt works, three miles away, where the water from saline springs, piped through wooden spouts, is boiled down by a process painfully slow, and whatever affected the salt works affected Manchester; for he who enters the Goose Creek Valley has the option of going up the creek or down the creek, with the further provision of frequent fording of the creek, whichever way he goes. But some minor events were never forgotten. For instance, it is remembered by many, and mentioned always with sadness and something akin to horror, that when George W. Morgan was retreating with his Union army from Cumberland Gap, and John H. Morgan with his dauntless riders was hanging on his flanks, just as the Union troops were preparing to move out of Manchester, where they had halted for a day, there was a pause caused by the execution of a Union soldier who had murdered a comrade. The very minute that the fatal shots were fired by ten soldiers, five of whose guns were loaded and the rest blank, as if in echo of their shots, there came the sound of the firing of the Confederate cavalry, attacking one of the Union wagon trains.

Many men in and about Manchester lost their lives during those terrible four years; and they were buried and forgotten. But so long as the world stands, the village will not forget the incident of the retreating army shooting one of its own soldiers, and the two antiphonal volleys that seemed more awful than the roar of a battle.

It was on the night before that very morning in September, 1862, that an incident occurred which has always been remembered as in some measure distinct from the other events of the war as they affected the life of Roundstone Holler. To Roundstone it was the climax of the war, and it gave to the Sinks a new and unuttered, but awful interest. Besides the men whom the Holler had sent into the Union army, there were some in irregular organizations with occasional military experience. Some were old men and boys, organized for home defence under " Captain" Ben Bailey, whose two sons, Lew and Rastus, were in the army. But there were two marauding bands: one of which rendezvoused at Gooserock, across Oxyoke from the Holler, and called itself a band of " Southern Regulators," commanded by Tom Jackson; and the other, which had its headquarters at Drip Rock Cave, and was under a desperado named Palestine Seagrave, professed Union sympathies. There was little difference between the last two bands. Both were lawless, and both fought for plunder. Their choice of sides was relative, and not absolute, excepting as the mutual hatred engendered made adherence to one set of principles compulsory. Both bodies hated Old Ben and his band, which had dealt out summary justice to one or two members of each. But each had enough to occupy the attention of the dozen or twenty desperadoes who composed it, without courting direct conflict with him and his larger company, which numbered near fourscore loyal boys and old men from Roundstone Holler and five miles round about. Up on the top of Scalp Dance Hill he lived, in a secluded and naturally fortified place selected by his grandfather, who had been Roundstone's first white settler. Just at the end of the path which is practically the only way to gain access to his house, are the Sinks, Roundstone's everlasting mystery, where the creek disappears under the Jellico Mountain. Back of the house, in the edge of the timber, stood Captain Ben's still. This has been destroyed thrice in recent years by revenue officers, in league, as the family believe, with the devil and the makers of the infamous red whiskey from Cincinnati. It was a poor return on the part of the government, all the Baileys believe, for their services in the time of the war; and they have given several revenue officers what they count their just deserts. At the time when Captain Ben was in his prime, revenue officers were unknown in the Holler. There were no worse things then than rattlesnakes, panthers, and bushwhackers. From his house Ben could view the whole surrounding region, and from here the blast of his horn would be heard two miles on a clear day, and further yet at night; and the word was passed on by the women, while the men hastened with incredible speed to their trysting place at the Sinks, where the roads meet that come down the valley on both sides of the creek.

The two bands of Jackson and Seagrave continued their depredations until the autumn of '62, ranging further and further from home under the growing and wholesome fear of Captain Ben, and always with mutual hatred and some fighting of each other. When Kirby Smith invaded Kentucky, however, the band that called itself Union thought it time to consider the soundness of its politics, and when Cumberland Gap was evacuated and the Union troops were fleeing northward with the Confederate cavalry dogging their flanks, the error of their previous affiliation seemed manifest. So there was a determination on the part of the men to fall in with the Confederate rear and plunder the Union baggage trains.

Against this proposed course, so the story goes, for it is derived from somewhat meagre data, and for obvious reasons when the sequel is known, the captain, Pal Seagrave, protested. Whether from a lingering spark of conscience, or from a conviction that the interests of the plunderers would best be served by remaining as they were, he sat on his horse, and swore to shoot any man who went to the rebels, and ordered them into their saddles for a long ride. They were hardly mounted when they came face to face with Tom Jackson's command, en route for Manchester, where they hoped to find opportunity to plunder the Union rear as it moved on. Both sides drew their weapons, and a battle seemed imminent, when Pal called a truce.

"Looky here, Tom Jackson," he said, "these here men o' mine is bound ter go with the South. I swore I wouldn't go, an' I could er held 'em ef hit hadn't a ben for meetin' you. They'll go now, sure. Fur I know mighty well ef the shootin' begins here right now, some o' these hell hounds o' my own'll shoot me so's to go to the devil along o' you. Now, they hain't no use o' these men killin' each other. They mought's well go together. But they cyan't have but one captain, an' considerin' the past, this earth hain't big enough to hold both you an' me. Draw yer pistol, or you're a dead man!"

At the word both men drew, and Jackson fell at the first fire.

Still holding his smoking pistol, Seagrave said:

"Men, I'm yer captain now. I jes' want ye to bury the hatchet, an' let bygones be bygones, an' I'll lead ye to Manchester agin the Yanks. But ef they's ary man that objects to me fur captain, let him say so right here."

He cocked his pistol and waited for a reply. There were some dark looks from the newer contingent whose recent commander he had just shot, but no man questioned his right to command. He proceeded:

"The Yanks is a tryin' to drive a lot o' beef cattle afoot through the mountings to the Ohio River. Ye didn't know that, did ye? Wall, I knowed hit. An' I know whar they'll stop tonight, too. An' I allow ter be thar about sunup or a hour afore, an' see ef we cyan't scatter them cattle in the woods, an' pick 'em up later on."

This announcement evoked interest from even the new members of his command, and a yell of approval from the old ones.

"Now, you men, I don't want ye to go ter openin' no old sores. I want each detachment to elect a leftenant ter command that part o' the company, an' I'll command the hull. An' when ye git that done an' a grave dug, I wanter tell ye somethin' else that'll interest ye all, an' be a sorter frolic fur early in the evenin'."

They rode aside into the woods, and scooped out a shallow grave, where they buried Captain Tom, as brave and wicked a man as ever escaped the hangman, and soon were deep in the more congenial work of electing officers. Pal sat on his horse between the two bands, as they separated to decide, each for itself, who should be its second officer. When they had made their choices, they came together, and he announced the decisions for the ratification of the united company, called the men elected to his side, and laid out his plan for the campaign. After a brief conference with his officers, he addressed the company:

"Men, we've got something ter submit fur yer approval. Yer don't none on ye bar no love p'tic'-lar to Ben Bailey. Now afore we leave these parts ter be gone a spell, an' while the Union folks is all mixed up, let's visit him to-night afore we start, an' git a drink an' settle his hash. Then ef we want, we kin fetch our cattle back here with some sorter safety, an' pasture them in the coves about Goose-rock, but hit won't be no use as long as he lives."

There could have been no better way of cementing the sympathies of his lately united band than by such a proposition. It was received with the greatest enthusiasm, and the rest of the day was spent in perfecting the organization and equipment of the company, preparatory to this and a more extended expedition.

The mountain soldier had the limitations of his virtues, among which was his tendency to drop out of the ranks for a day or two, whenever his regiment passed near his home. Usually, knowing well the mountain roads and passes, they had no difficulty in overtaking their regiments, a few days' march further on. Jack Casey and Lew and Rastus Bailey came through Oxyoke Gap that day, and intended to stop for a night and part of a day, having learned that the Union van would halt for a short rest at Manchester while the wagon trains came up. There was mingled joy and sadness at the Whitley cabin over the return of Jack and the doleful retreat. To give up the Gap, seemed like the carrying away of the gates of Gaza, and they knew well to dread the flying foxes with firebrands at their tails. But they had learned to take disappointments as a matter of course, and they made the most of their meeting. It was near night when Jack came, and the supper was soon past, and he and his mother and Jennie and Cub sat together about the fire, for the night was cool, and fuel, thank God, was plenty, spite of the war !

Up on the hill above the Sinks, Ben Bailey talked with his sons, as they sat in the firelight, but with the doors barred as ever. The old man was bitter in his comments on the evacuation.

" Nothin' ter eat but mules ? " he cried ; "wall, let 'em eat mules, then ! Marion and his men — yer gran pap was one on 'em — would have ben glad o' mules ! But talk o' bein' starved out, an' yit a-drivin' off hull droves o' cattle ! By mighty, hit's a shame ! "

The young men attempted some mild defence of the retreat, when the old man's ear caught a sound. Without a word, and with a gesture for silence and obedience, he rose, took down his rifle and revolvers, and slipped out through the shed room at the back of the house. The sons took their guns and followed. A minute later the house was surrounded by armed men, who first made sure that every way of escape was cut off, and then began demanding admittance. Quickly and noiselessly the three men slipped to the edge of the clearing, where they had a view of the door, and then looked back, just as the door was opened from within and a gleam of light shot out.

" Hit tain't the sojers, boys," said the old man ; "hit's Pal Seagrave's gang. We'll move over the rocks an' down the path to the Sinks, an' knock them galley west ! Don't fire now ! "

There was a howl of rage when the guerillas gained the interior of the house and found that Ben was not there. They threatened and abused his wife and daughters, demanding to know where he was hidden, but could learn nothing. At that moment, the sound of a horn broke the silence of the night, so full and clear that it must have been heard for miles. The band knew the sound and feared it.

"Less go," they said.

"Stop!" said Seagrave.   "Before we go, there's one thing I kin do, anyhow.   I'll burn out this vile nest!   You women, git out o' here!"

Driving them out, he took the tongs and lifted the forelog into the furthest corner of the room, where it soon began to blaze, then rolled out the backlog into the middle of the floor, and scattered the brands in every direction.   The bandits waited to be sure that the fire had made such headway as to prevent the women's returning to put it out. Afterward they hastily visited the still, and filled their stomachs and canteens, and then rode down the mountain.   It was steep and rugged, and the way was narrow and rocky.   It was the only way in which an equestrian could get to or from the house, and a very difficult one at that.   Ben had counted on this fact when he decided to slip down the hill and give battle at the Sinks.   From homes near and far men started at the sound of his horn. They knew where to assemble, but had they been in doubt, the light from the burning house soon formed a second signal.   No watch-fire ever kindled on Scalp Dance Hill — and many had been lighted there in the early days — shone out more widely or brought more eager response than that flame.

"Go up the road to the left, Lew," said Ben, "and you, Rastus, go to the right.   Stop the men that come, an' have them range to cover the Sinks on both sides.   Don't let a man git by!   Don't fire till ye hear my gun from the mushroom rock above the Sinks.   Then pick yer men, an' fire fast an' sure!"

Jack Casey sat by the fire with his mother and Jennie. Cub had just gone to bed. Suddenly they heard a sound, and Jack started.

"What's that?" he asked.

"That's Captain Ben's horn," said the women.

Jack took his gun from the antlers, and started without another word.

"Jack," said his mother. He half turned at the door with a look of inquiry.

"Yes, go," she said.

Fast as Jack went, there were others there before him, and Lew Bailey was there, just as the flames began to break out of the house, assigning the men their stations according to his father's orders. Others came, some on foot and some on horseback, till there were a dozen on that side, and no less a company out of sight on the other side. The flames were now leaping high, and the light shone down the mountain, lighting the road above the Sinks as if it had been noon. In his haste and passion, Pal Seagrave had lighted his own funeral pyre. The bandits felt their hearts quail as they emerged from the darkness of the long defile down the mountain side into the glare of light that was like the eye of God. Yet they were not without hope that their work had been too quickly performed for the gathering of any large body of Ben's men. But Pal Seagrave thought of the man whom he had shot that day, and felt in his heart that he was riding to his doom.

A hundred yards up the hill above the Sinks, behind a rock that shaded and hid him, but with the whole scene in view, Ben Bailey crouched with

his rifle and two revolvers.   He watched the cavalcade as it wound its way down, the horses stumbling
over rocks in the haste of their riders; and picking
out the hindmost he levelled his gun at him.   Then
suddenly changing his mind, he turned it upon the
man at the head of the company, just as he was
turning from the hill road into the glare of the main
road above the Sinks.   He drew a careful bead.
The knife-blade sight on the muzzle just showed in
the notch of the hindsight, and he pulled the trigger.
Pal Seagrave threw up his hands with a cry, and
reeled in his saddle, and fell.   The men in the rear
halted an instant in indecision, and the last one
dropped, struck by Ben's first pistol shot.   At the
same instant, from both sides of the road, there was
a volley of bullets, sent with unerring aim, out of
the darkness that was like pitch, into the fatal glare
of light that had come to seem unearthly.   Those
that survived the first fire made a wild rush, some
on one side the Sinks, and some on the other, hoping to escape while the men reloaded; but these
were picked off by a scattering fire, and in the rear
was Ben with his two six shooters, and an aim that
never missed.   It was short and bloody work.
Then Ben blew his horn, and, leaping to the top of
the rock, gave his orders for the securing the frightened horses.   These were soon tethered to swinging limbs, excepting those that had escaped back
up the hill, which were safe enough, and could be
found in the morning.

Then Ben came down to the Sinks, and his men
gathered about him, amid the dead and wounded, —
if there were any wounded.

"Men," said Ben, "we've done a clean job, an' the world is a heap better off. An' hit won't do nary grain o' good ter have nothin' said about hit, considerin' how the war seems to be goin'. Stand out here in the light, every man o' you, an' take off yer hats with yer left hand, an' raise yer right hand ter heaven, an' swear ter God that ye won't tell livin' man what we've done, nor what we've got ter do yit, an' we'll finish this job while we're at it."

"Pa," interposed Lew.

"Shet up!" said Ben. "I don't take my orders from men that's ben trained under officers that gives up the Gap! You an' Lew go up ter the house an' keep the women thar a spell, an' see ter gittin' 'em a place ter sleep."

"I'll go too," said Jack. "They can stay at our house to-night."

"Yes, you go too. We've got our own ways o' fightin', an' know how ter do it."

The young men ascended the hill, securing two horses as they went.

"What d'ye reckon he 'lows to do?" asked Jack, with a feeling of horror.

"The Sinks," said Lew, grimly.

"Wounded an' all?" asked Jack.

"I don't reckon we'd best ter ast wether they *be* any wounded," said Rastus.

At the top of the hill they found Mrs. Bailey and her three daughters, and conducted them by a narrow and perilous foot-path along the ridge and down to the Whitley home. There they spent the night, but no one slept save Cub. The women asked a few questions, and took the enigmatical answers as did the women in twenty other homes. The fire burned down after a while, and no one came up from the Sinks.   Late arrivals in answer to Ben's horn were met by sentinels, saying that the fire was over, and they were to go quietly back to their homes.   The sun had risen before there was any return of the men who had been left at work, but there was evident activity about the Sinks all night, as shown by the light of the torches. Then the whole company rode up to the Whitley gate, and partook of the corn pones which Elizabeth had baked for them, anticipating their need of a warm bite as they went home.   They came to the fence and stopped for a moment.   Every man was mounted, and those who had ridden the night before, now each led a horse.   There was not a 'word about the fight.

"We had a right bad fire, didn't we?" asked Job Crosby.

"Yes," said young Moses Davis, with a faint facetiousness.   "Wha' d'ye reckon sot it?   Lightnin'?"

"No, ye fool," said Captain Ben, "they warn't no lightnin' las' night.   The forelog rolled out onter the floor, an' the house ketched from that."

That remained the authentic explanation, and the fire on Scalp Dance Hill entered into the history of the Holler without specific mention of attendant circumstances.   There was a raising a few days after, and Captain Ben furnished his new home, quite as well as his old abode, with the proceeds of two horses which he sold, — the one in London, and the other at Barboursville, — and the still was again in

The Secret of the Sinks.   Page 257.

successful operation, as the good feeling at the raising attested.

The two bands of Seagrave and Jackson were missed at once from the neighborhood, and the story that they had fallen in with the rear of the Confederate army accounted for their absence to complete satisfaction. But this information was conveyed with a quiet suggestion that their return need not be expected. The Holler breathed more freely after that, and one horror of the war was removed. As to what finally became of them, there are two theories extant — one that they joined "John Morgan's Horse-thieves" in a body, and were killed or captured in one of his raids; and the other that perhaps old Ben knew something about it.

Jack and the Bailey boys went on that day and rejoined their regiment near Manchester. They noticed as they passed the Sinks that there was fresh earth here and there that might have covered blood stains, and that certain rocks were wet from recent washing; but there were no other signs of the conflict, and the Sinks seemed to moan more sadly than was their wont, but told no tales.

XXIII

In Secret Service

THE winter of 1862 found Jack and his Kentucky friends with their regiments in Nashville. General George W. Morgan had fallen under criticism for his desertion of Cumberland Gap, and had been relieved from his command. General Buell had been censured for not following up his victory at Perryville, and for allowing Bragg and Smith to leave Kentucky with rich stores of provisions and hundreds of fine horses, and had been succeeded by Rosecrans. Andrew Johnson was opposed to Carter, and had asked to have him removed to make room for General Spears ; and Carter was placed in command of a hastily organized brigade of cavalry, with which he made a brilliant raid into East Tennessee, and returned with his small command to Kentucky. Meantime his old brigade was taken to the front, and for a time hung in mid-air with little to do or hope for.

A feeling of discouragement had settled on the army and the country. Men were deserting by thousands. Soldiers surrendered without provocation for the sake of being paroled, and thus released from further military duty. The army had lost confidence in its leaders and in its own *esprit de corps*. The idea of a ninety days' picnic was effectually gone, and in its place as yet had come no spirit, such as afterward manifested itself, of intense and dogged patriotism, capable of enduring a series of reverses.

" Looky yan, Jack !" cried Joe Hallet one day. " See them fellers in nightcaps !"

A dozen men in uniform, with white cotton nightcaps on their heads, were marching down the streets of Nashville and among the camps, preceded by a fife and drum playing " Dixie," and followed by a band of hooting little darkies.

" Who d'ye reckon them fellers be ? " asked Eph Whitley.

" Some fellers in disgrace, I reckon," answered Jack.

Inquiry developed the fact that these were men who had surrendered for the sake of being paroled, and on their return to camp they had been sentenced to bear this punishment by order of General Rosecrans.   The incident had its result in a very general discouragement of needless paroles.

" We hain't the only fellers that surrenders to keep from fightin'," said Lew Bailey.

" We hain't the fellers that does it a tall," said Jack.

" I know we hain't; but I meant the rebs does hit as well as the Yanks."

" That's so.   They git mighty tard o' the war ; 'specially them that's ben forced inter the army."

" Warn't hit you, Jack, that marched them seven fellers inter camp at the Gap ? "

" Yes, but it warn't but mighty little credit to me," said Jack.

"I never heerd jes' huccum ye to git 'em. How was it?"

"I've tole it a heap o' times," said Jack; "I reckoned all the fellers had heerd it. I'm shame-faced to tell it agin."

Most of his companions in the barracks had heard it; but a good story was much prized in those days of camp tedium, and Jack told his adventure.

"Wall, it was when we was holdin' the Gap, an' meant to keep a-holdin' it. One day, long in the last o' August, I got outside the lines down by Powell's River, an' I got sorter tard walkin' an' was powerful hot, an' I come to a place whar the water run deep, an' looked cool an' nice, an' thinks I, I'll jes' have a swim. So I tuk off my cloes, an' went in. I didn't 'low they was a reb in ten mile o' where I was, an' I splashed, an' dove, an' had a mighty good time. I hadn't had a swim all summer, an' it felt mighty good. Wall, I was in there, an' a-gittin' 'bout ready to come out, an' I looks up ter the bank, an' I sees some fellers in but'nut come down to the bank where my cloes was. They pinted thar guns at me, an' yelled, —

"'Hey, thar, you infernal Yank! Come in outen the wet!'

"Wall, thinks I, they hain't no use a-talkin', I cyan't fight a hull reg'maint, naked as I was. So I says, 'I s'render. Lemme come ashore an' git on my cloes,' says I. So I went ashore, an' they stud around me while I dressed, sorter pokin' fun at me fur gettin' ketched thataway, an' I was a-feelin' mighty peaked myself. When I got my cloes on, one on 'em says,

"'You're mighty shore you've s'rendered, be ye?'

"'I hain't no manner o' doubt of it,' says I. 'I wisht I had.'

"'Wall,' says he, an' he an' t'other fellers was sorter a-laughin' all the while. 'So do we,' says he. 'Thishyer war's played out,' says he. 'We've had ter fight so fur,' says he, 'or go south ter prison; but it's gittin' mighty tarsome,' says he. 'Now,' says he, 'we're your prisoners, an' you jes' surround us, an' take us inter camp.' So I tuck 'em ter camp. They warn't but seven on 'em when I come to count 'em; but when I was in the water, an' they had their guns pinted at me, 'peared lack they was a reg'maint."

"What did they do with 'em in camp?" asked a soldier.

"I d'livered 'em up to Cun'l Byrd; an' he says, 'It's a plumb shame to send them fellers north to prison,' says he. 'I'll parole 'em an' send 'em home,' says he. But they dassent *go* home, that was the trouble. So he ast Gin'ral Carter 'bout it; an' Carter he sends fur me, an' he says to the men, 'Whar ye from?' says he. 'From Morgan County, East Tennessy,' says they. 'I know Morgan County,' says he. 'They hain't no rebels there,' says he. 'We was rebels 'cause we hadter be,' says they. 'We're in favor o' the Union,' says they; 'but last Apr*ile* we was a-tryin' to git inter Kaintuck to enlist, an' we was captured, an' gin our choice to go south to prison, or to enlist; an' we enlisted fer the rebels.' 'Wall,' says Carter, 'I'd parole ye ef I could send ye home. But that hain't no use: they'd pester ye to death.' Says he, 'Would ye enlist in the Union army ef ye had a chance?' They all said they'd be glad to do it, an' he tuck 'em in.

"An' I bet a pone he hadn't no better men than them was, too."

"While you was foolin' 'round the Gap," said Eph, "we fellers was ketchin' it at Richmond and Perryville."

"I reckon Perryville was right smart of a scrimmage," said Jack.

"Ef any man's ben in a fight like that," said Eph, "an' says he wants another, he's a blame liar."

"You must a got badly skeered there," said Jack.

"I was skeered to death fus' gun went off. Afore night I didn't mind it no more'n the blowin' o' the wind. But I warn't any less skeered. A feller gits so skeered atter while hit skeers all the skeer outen him."

"You warn't skeered, war you, Lew?" asked Jack. "I've heerd you stood up behind the wall when every feller that showed an inch o' hat was shot through the head, an' you yelled to the fellers not to run."

"So skeered I didn't know whether I was foot or hossback."

"It takes a brave man," said Jack, "to own that he is skeered."

"I dunno wy a feller should be skeered," said Zeke Holcomb, who was a notorious coward in time of danger, but a man of prodigious courage afterward. "I fit at Perryville, an' I warn't skeered."

"Ye hadn't no call ter be," said Sim Galloway, who was lately returned from his wound.

"Where was you, at Perryville, Sim?" asked Jack.

"I was part way in a holler log, bigges' part the time," said Sim. They looked at his pale face and laughed, for they knew how he had received his nearly fatal wound.

"Why didn't ye git *clar* in, Sim?" asked Eph.

"I got in as fur's I could," said Sim, quietly. "Zeke Hocum was in ahead o' me."

Sim seldom indulged in a joke; but this one made his reputation as a humorist, and Roundstone quotes it to this day concerning Zeke Holcomb and his descendants.

"You fellers that fit at Perryville didn't waste no love on Gin'ral Buell, did ye?" asked Jack, as the laugh ceased.

"Ye could put it all in yer eye," said Eph. "Ever see him?"

"I seed him wunct," said Lew. "While we was a-movin' to-wards Perryville a new reg'maint — the 75th Eelinois — stopped at a well ter fill their canteens. We was right behind, and they was delayin' the hull column. Buell he rode up an' ordered 'em ter move on. But they was plumb crazy fur water. Buell he tries ter ride up to the well ter cut off the bucket, an' he couldn't force his hoss through. I seed them fellers look at him, tryin' ter ride over 'em, an' heerd some on 'em swar ter kill him the fus' battle. That same reg'maint was put in the front at Perryville, — raw men, jes' out from home — an' they fit well. They lost three hundred men that day."

"I seed Buell fust day o' the Perryville fight,"

said Eph. "We'd had a scrimmage to get to a puddle in the dry bed o' Doctor's Creek. We'd druv off the rebs, an' got a drink, an' filled our canteens. Wen we got inter camp I says to myself, ' I'd as lives have half that water outside o' me as inside,' an' I poured out half a canteen full inter a tin, an' got off my shirt for a bath. Jes' then some one stopped afore the tent an' yelled, ' Pour back that water!' I looked out, an' thar sot Gin'ral Buell. Says he, ' When men are fightin' an' dyin' for a drink, water's too sacred to use fur a bath.' I poured hit back inter my canteen, an' next mornin' I needed it for wounded men."

"He had mighty little patience with new men," said Jack; "but he was a brave man an' a good gin'ral. You lost your flag at Perryville, didn't you, Eph?"

"Lost hit by gittin' it shot to pieces. That was the flag the Gov'maint furnished. We still got the one the women made."

"You best keep that, or you'll ketch Jesse from Joe and Becky."

An orderly came up to the door of the barracks, and asked for Jackson Casey.

"That's me," said Jack.

"You are commanded to report for immediate duty at the office of Colonel Truesdail," said the messenger.

"Who's he?" asked Jack.

"Don't you know who Colonel Truesdail is? He is the chief of the army police," said the orderly.

"All right, I'll go. Good-by, boys. I'll meet ye in Chattanoogy an' keep Christmas week."

" Good-by, Jack, ef ye don' come back. Hanged ef I don' wish he'd send fur me. I'm tard a-doin' nothin'."

Jack promptly reported, and was made acquainted with his business. The chief of the secret service watched him narrowly as he talked.

" Did General Carter send you on special service into the enemy's country last spring ? "

" Yessir."

" You are a Tennesseean ? "

" Yessir. *East* Tennessy."

" I want you to go with another man, whom I have sent for, and who will be here soon, and find what you can of the movements of the rebel forces about Murfreesboro. Find whether they are going into winter quarters, or are likely to attack us. Find the condition of their horses, the feeling of their troops, and the sentiment of the people between here and there. Keep to the east of Murfreesboro. Don't try to enter the rebel lines. I have other men who are to do that. I have yet others who are to observe their movements to the west. Go as far as Smithville, and if you are able, get on to McMinnville, and be back in a week. The man with whom I send you is a man I know, a Kentuckian named Abe Ryan. He ought to be here now. Here he comes. No, I am mistaken. Stay here till I return."

The colonel rose and greeted the man who entered. " Good morning, Captain Garnett," he said, and the two retired together to an inner room, where they were closeted for some time. Jack marked this man Garnett well. He was tall, dark, and reserved, but had an eye that took in every detail of his surroundings, and Jack took him at once to be a spy of importance.

While they were thus engaged, an orderly showed another man into the room where Jack was sitting. Jack conjectured that the newcomer was his companion, Abe Ryan, and this conjecture proved correct.

Soon Colonel Truesdail came to the door, and parted from his guest on the threshold.

" From now until Christmas," said he, " give us every possible detail. But do not needlessly risk yourself. Remember, you play against heavy odds."

The dark man said little, but went out, and the two men in waiting were invited in.

Colonel Truesdail explained their duties more at length. They were to proceed in citizen's clothing around the Confederate army, taking note of the outposts and sources of supply, observing the country, and learning what they could from the people. They were to keep together, if possible, and if they separated from force of circumstances, they should make their way back as best they could, with all the information they could gather. Their ostensible errand south was to look after property in Chattanooga, concerning which the colonel had information in captured papers. They were to impersonate the two sons of a man who had recently died there, coming from Kentucky to attend to their father's estate. The clippings from some Chattanooga papers, with certain captured letters which he gave to them, were to be their vouchers if they needed to account for themselves.

Studying these, they were able to make a very fair story of their errand, and donning the clothes provided for them, dark gray suits of Kentucky jeans, they set forth.

They spent their first night with a man named Hooper, suspected of being a rebel sympathizer, who lived on the bank of Sam's Creek, some twenty miles from Nashville. They found these suspicions unjust. Hooper was a true Union man, and poor almost to the point of starvation, and accepted gladly the money they paid him for their lodging, yet with regret that his poverty made necessary any limit to his hospitality. From him they learned of the frequent escape of Confederate prisoners confined in the penitentiary at Nashville, and of the way in which they were set across the river by a neighbor named Rook.

Still further south they found what had been a good farming country well stripped of provisions by the Confederates, who seemed to be massing at Murfreesboro. The third night they stayed together in a little tavern in Smithville. They had proceeded without molestation, and were gaining information every hour. Another day's advance, they thought, would be enough, and would enable them to return by another route, and they hoped with equal security.

They went to the dingy little room that was assigned them, and found no lock on the door.

"Never mind," said Ryan, "I've got a little trick here that's good for that."

He shut the door, and drew from his pocket a gimlet, which he screwed into the crack between the door and the casing, turning the handle so as to leave a bar across the edge of the door.

They removed their outer clothing and lay down; but they were hardly asleep before there was a pounding at the door.

"Hey, thar, you blamed Yankee spies!" cried a voice without. "Open this door, or we'll knock it in!"

They rose in haste and silence, drawing on their boots and coats.

"The winder!" whispered Jack.

"Yes!" said Ryan.

The pounding at the door was increasing, and there were calls for an axe to break it in, when they raised the sash, and slipped through, dropping upon the low roof of the kitchen, which was directly under. Here they crawled to the eaves, and dropped to the ground on the back side of the hotel, but saw, as they slid down the shingles, that the front of the hotel was guarded by a squad of cavalry with pine torches. The night was dark, and it was difficult to keep together. The torches of the soldiers served the spies well, for they marked the position of their pursuers. The two sides of the hotel that were on streets were guarded, but there were no torches in sight to the rear. The prospect of escape seemed good, but the barking of a dog in the stable yard brought a torch around the house, just as the crash of the door showed to the soldiers inside the vacant room, and thus marked at once their escape and the way by which they had gone.

Across fences and fields they made their way, making pursuit difficult, but losing all sense of direction, and eventually finding themselves pursued as they emerged into the road, taking opposite directions, and losing each other in the dark. Ryan found his way towards Hartsville, and after six days of wandering returned to Nashville. Jack wandered all night, and when the morning broke, and he was able to take his bearings, he judged that he was proceeding toward Murfreesboro, a conjecture which he verified at a cabin where he inquired of two elderly people. There he obtained some food, but not without being asked questions, which showed that his hosts were on the side of the south and suspected him. He paid for his meal, and bought two pones that were in sight on the table, and stuffed them in his pockets. The old couple warmed a little at sight of his money, but apparently were the more suspicious of him for having it.

Jack hastened away, certain that any inquiries made about him there would be rewarded with exact information concerning him. He had told his Chattanooga story, and started south toward where the road would lead into a pike. But coming to the pike, he paused to consider his situation. He had nothing now to gain by going south, so he turned his face northward and followed the pike.

He soon became convinced that he was pursued. Bands of horsemen were riding along the pike inquiring at houses as they went, and keeping a sharp lookout at the sides of the road. At the top of every hill he came to the pike, and took a look about and then left the pike for the field or wood.

Late in the afternoon, as he emerged from a field that had grown up to scrub oak and sassafras, he came back to the pike at the top of a knoll, to find horses tethered to the fence upon the opposite side. He drew back into the bushes and looked again. On the opposite side of the road was a small cemetery, and a score or more of people were gathered about an open grave. There were three carriages and a dozen horses. Jack thought quickly. He would get down to the road, where the pike cut through the hill, and mount one of the saddle-horses and ride away. He slipped down into the low cut. He was so near that he could hear the weeping of the friends about the grave, and the tones of the burial service which the minister was repeating.

Jack hesitated as he stood with his hand on a bridle. To steal a horse was, of course, to be pursued at once, and while he could make a few miles better progress, it was only to have his way ahead made more difficult. He looked about again, and now saw that one of the carriages was of a pattern new to him. Such a thing as a hearse was unknown in his part of Tennessee, and at another place he might not have been able to imagine its use; but its shape and the nature of the occasion told him at a glance. It was long and low, with a narrow pane of glass on either side, but there was ample opportunity for a man to hide within. He quickly undid the door and crawled inside, fastening the door behind him, and was hardly within before the people began descending from the cemetery, and the driver of the hearse untied his horses and mounted the box.

"Hello, there!" Jack heard the voice with the clatter of hoofs beside the hearse. The driver reined in. They had gone not twenty rods from the cemetery.

"Have you seen a man go along the pike afoot?"

"Nary un. Who d'ye want?"

"I'm hunting a Yankee spy, and he's come this way."

"I hain't seed him," said the driver, and started on. Jack gripped the hilt of his pistol and waited the issue, but there was no further inquiry. They passed a sentinel. They were within the Confederate lines. They entered a town. The short day drew to a close, and night had fallen when the driver unhitched his horses, and backed the hearse into a shed, growling that it seemed unusually heavy.

XXIV

Out of the Frying Pan

JACK crawled out of the hearse, cramped and cold, and cautiously crept into the village. No great time was required to convince him that he was in Murfreesboro, the headquarters of General Bragg. His sensations were most unpleasant. He crept along the shadow of the houses, uncomfortable and perplexed. Soon, however, his blood began to move, and with it his courage rose. The streets were full of life. Soldiers, citizens, and women of the town mingled and moved to and fro, with happy conversation and unrestrained laughter. The people whom he first met regarded him with no suspicion, and Jack at length ceased to avoid them. It was ten days before Christmas, and Murfreesboro was in her best clothes and happiest spirits. Jefferson Davis had just been upon a visit there, and people were coming and going from every part of the South. The town had never been so festive. The sight of so much good cheer could but infect Jack with something of its own contagion.

Moreover, he said to himself, while it might have been hard enough for him to have gotten inside the Confederate lines in any ordinary way, and quite as hard to get out, being in, he was probably in as safe a place as he could find south of

Nashville. Emboldened by the thought, he walked openly upon the street, meeting people as he had occasion, and attracting no attention. So he re-called to himself his ostensible errand, and prepared to give such account of himself as might be neces-sary. He went to the City Hotel, a brick struct-ure on the public square. It was full, but they directed him to another and less pretentious tavern.

"Yes, I reckon we can take care of you," said the genial proprietor; "but we're mighty full. Got two in mighty nigh every room. We can eat you all right, but I ain't right sure if we can sleep you. D'ye mind goin' in with another good man? Mr. Coburn, can you take in a bed-feller? Here's a gentleman from Kentucky, just got in from Chat-tanoogy, — missed the stage an' got in late. He looks sorter peaceable. I reckon I'll put him in with you, if nary one of you mind. Mr. Coburn, make you 'quainted with Mr. Saunders. If you two men have any trouble together, jest call on me. I'll settle matters."

Jack turned to meet his new room-mate, a pleas-ant, well-dressed young fellow who wore his hat on the side of his head, and removing it to shake hands with Jack revealed his hair well oiled and brushed low upon his forehead. He was a bit of a dandy, and looked for a moment askance at Jack's clothes, but was reassured by his face and manner.

"Glad to meet you, Mr. Saunders," he said to Jack. "I reckon we can get on together."

"I reckon so," said Jack. "I can stand it ef you can."

They went to their room, and Jack made his

T

toilet.　He told his story, how he had been to Chattanooga to settle his father's estate and was trying to get back to Kentucky, but had no passes further, and must wait for them to come.

"No trouble to get passes here," said Coburn. "I can get you all you want in a week or two.　But the trouble is to get through the Union lines."

"I can get through them," said Jack, "if I can get out of here."

"How?" asked Coburn.

"I ain't right sure how," said Jack, remembering that he would better not be too confident.　"I'll wait a day or two and see what comes to me."

Coburn told his story with equal readiness.　He had been in Murfreesboro several weeks on business connected with an army contract.　He had come to know the guests of the tavern, a number of army officers, and a good many people of the village. He seemed to have money, and, while not over-burdened with wit, was withal a pleasant companion. Jack saw that he looked again at his clothes.

"I must get some new clothes," he said.　"I had a sorter hard time gettin' here, and got these tore and soiled."

"I'll go with you to-night, if you say so," said Coburn, "and help you pick out some.　I know the best place in town."

Jack gladly accepted the offer.　He was well supplied with money, and the suit which he purchased was within his means; but all clothing cost money in the South just then, and Coburn's taste was less modest than his own.

It thus came to pass that Jack's first appearance

in Murfreesboro by daylight was in good attire, and he could not help noticing as he was shaving before the glass that he was not an ill-looking fellow. Coburn noticed it, too, and with satisfaction. He began at once to assume the air of proprietorship over Jack, and show him about and introduce him to his own acquaintances as " Mr. Saunders, my friend from Kentucky." However pleasant or valuable such a friendship might have been at another time, Jack was not minded to reject it now, and it proved for him the Open Sesame to a somewhat wide acquaintance. After breakfast he cautiously referred again to the subject of a pass.

" No trouble about that," again said Coburn, " but we must wait a spell till things settle down, and we know for sure that Rosecrans is goin' into winter quarters at Nashville. Then it'll be easy enough. You got to wait anyhow, and things will be all right here by the time you get word from Kentucky."

"I was hopin' to get home for Christmas," said Jack.

" It'll be too late for that," said Coburn; " but you'll have a right merry one here."

Jack was not altogether happy about it. He knew that Rosecrans had no thought of going into winter quarters. Still his situation was so much better than he had any right to hope, that he possessed his soul in patience, and went for a walk about town.

Walking in front of a fashionable house on Main Street, he saw the door open, and a man come out whom he had seen before. Behind him in the door stood the hostess and several friends, some of them Confederate officers.

"Good-by," said the hostess, in a tone of good-natured raillery. "I just believe you're going off so's to get shut of giving me a Christmas gift."

"No, indeed," said the departing guest; "I'm coming back before Christmas, and I'll bring you something."

"Don't believe him," laughed one of the officers. "He looks solemn, but he's a gay deceiver."

"I know," said the lady; "out of sight, out of mind."

"I'll be in sight again soon. A bad penny, you know. Good-by."

"Good-by." And the door closed behind him.

Jack's heart beat fast. He slackened his pace till he saw that the man was coming his way, then moved ahead out of sight of the house, and allowed himself to be overtaken.

"Captain Garnett," said Jack, in a low tone. The stranger's dark face colored a trifle and he seemed to start. Then, with composure, he said,

"You are mistaken, sir."

"Wait," said Jack, as the spy was passing ahead; "I know you, Captain. I have seen you in Colonel Truesdail's office. I'm in the secret service, too."

"What are you doing here?" demanded the captain.

Jack quickly told his story, and the captain listened with interest.

"Can you help me through the lines?" asked Jack, anxiously.

"I could," said the captain, "but I want you

here. Stay at the tavern where you are. Be at ease, enjoy life, make friends. Do you need more money? I will leave you some. Keep your eyes open and your mouth shut. I shall be here again in four days. Tell me then all you can learn, — not from officers, I meet them, — but from the people and from your own observation. I want everything that can be learned, — movements of troops, planting of batteries, location of outposts, gossip of the people concerning the armies, — everything. I come and go, and stay but a few hours. You stay and be eyes for me; but no tongue, you understand. We must not be seen together. Here is money. Meet me here in four days. I will report you to Colonel Truesdail. Good-by."

Jack returned to the tavern, disappointed but content. As soon as he felt sure of his duty, his occupation began to develop cheerful features. Coburn was waiting for him, and had secured for him an invitation to a party which he was to attend that night. And that was where Jack met Bessie Granger. Brisk of movement, ready of speech, a soldier's daughter, and in politics a veritable little spitfire, but the merriest girl, with a quick temper and a warm heart, she was a revelation to Jack, who had never seen a woman like her. Her mother was dead, her father was fighting in Virginia, and she lived with her married sister. It was evident that she had from the first at least a friendly interest in Jack. A vigorous little rebel, she showered good-natured abuse upon all her men friends who were not in the Confederate army, and, with a not un-natural inconsistency, passed by a half dozen uniformed admirers to bestow her favors upon Mr. Jefferson Saunders, better known to the reader as Jackson Casey.

Fortune, given to carrying coals to Newcastle, rarely gives to a man so many simultaneous favors, added to the pleasant consciousness of doing his duty. Jack had no trouble in picking up information. The tavern was a centre for its dissemination. Coburn was a mine of it. The gatherings which Jack attended almost nightly, composed of young people of the town and younger officers and soldiers, fairly buzzed with gossip and news. It was a merry group, and Jack proved popular among the young men, and distanced all competition in his almost involuntary strife for the favor of Bessie Granger. People who noticed how well Jack was prospering there ceased to ask what was keeping him in Murfreesboro. Jack saw this, and it added a reason for his "shining up to her"; for that was the way he described to himself his attentions. Coburn, who had introduced him, and who was attentive to Bessie's best friend, urged Jack on. In all this Jack did not plunge recklessly into flirtation. It was a new world to him, and for a time he followed the lines of least resistance. Indeed, when it was seen that Bessie was disposed to be kind to him, it was counted matter of course that Jack would gladly follow his advantage. That Bessie admired him was not so strange, after all. If his speech was uncouth, it was less so to Southern than to Northern ears. But as an offset to this there were his native grace, his handsome face, his liberal supply of money, his generosity, his ready wit and warm heart. Bessie felt that she had discovered a rough diamond, and no man could wish for a more pleasant discoverer.

The days passed quickly. Captain Garnett came and went, and came again, and again was gone. He told Jack little, but from his questions Jack saw that his information was of importance, and that a crisis was approaching. Three times, just before the battle of Stone River, Captain Garnett made his way back and forth between the armies. Christmas came and went. Murfreesboro made merry on the edge of the volcano of approaching battle. In some of the most aristocratic houses the American flag was nailed to the floor, and the party danced upon it. General John Morgan was married to a Murfreesboro lady just before Christmas, and his wedding was one of the great events of the season. Jack had no share in these functions; but his own group of friends did not lack for Christmas festivity, and he danced the Virginia reel with Bessie Granger.

So pleasant and so natural was all this that now and then Jack had to pull his real self together, and remind himself that the man underneath the new store clothes of Mr. Jefferson Saunders was the plain mountain soldier, Jack Casey. It came to take an effort to recall himself to himself. Doubtless he played his part the better for thus losing himself in it; and so far forth he was glad, for he had lost all fear of betraying himself. But just when he was playing his rôle the best, and rejoicing in it, there would come a twinge of conscience. Jefferson Saunders was fast falling in love with

Bessie Granger. But Jackson Casey was be-
trothed, not in word, to be sure, — but that was
little comfort, — to Jennie Whitley. Bessie was a
bird of bright plumage, — "pretty as a red bird,"
was the quotation which he borrowed to describe
her, — but Jennie was the wood dove with the
true heart. So Jack Casey vowed that he would
not so far forget himself as to be untrue to Jennie
Whitley. But Jefferson Saunders remained, and
could hardly do else than remain, on good terms
with Bessie Granger.

The Sunday after Christmas Jack saw Captain
Garnett again.

"You need not stay much longer," he said to
Jack. "There will be a battle before the year
ends."

"May I leave before the battle?" asked Jack.

"Yes; I shall return once more, but not within
the town. Meet me Tuesday night in the edge of
the woods to the left of the Manson pike, this side the
river. Have all the information you can get and
go with me."

"You go to Nashville, now?" asked Jack.

A moment the dark features of the spy relaxed
into a smile of triumph. "I dined to-day with
General Bragg. I am to dine with General Rosecrans to-morrow," he said.

XXV

On This Side of the River and on That

IT was a merry Christmas in camp, in and about Nashville. Eph Whitley and his companions among the Kentucky troops spent a happy holiday. To be sure there were sad memories and homesick longings. But provisions had become plenty since the completion of the railroad, and there was shelter and good cheer. But the thing that most of all made the men happy was the prospect of a move. The army had been reorganized, and their division was commanded by the white-haired General Van Cleve, who as a colonel had fought at Mill Spring. They were ordered to be in readiness to start at a moment's notice, and throughout the day they inspected their arms, and made ready to break camp.

The month had been a hard one. There had been frequent minor engagements at the outposts with varying results. On the 11th of December Franklin had been captured in a Union raid, and some loss inflicted on the enemy. But the battle of Huntsville had resulted disastrously, and the troops had behaved so badly as to afford no little ground for censure. The whole army felt the stigma of the implied charge of cowardice, and was ready to prove its mettle. But Christmas day passed, and the order to march did not come. On Friday morn-

ing, the 26th, there was a general movement. The
8th Kentucky was well to the front, but the 1st
Tennessee remained in Nashville, much to its
own disgust. Unlike the preceding, this day was
most disagreeable. A soldier soon assumes the
privilege of grumbling, even at what pleases him,
and there was no lack of it this day, though the
men were glad enough to march, even through the wet.

"Eph," asked Jim Galloway, "why d'ye reckon
they didn't start us out yistiddy, lack they said they
would?"

"I reckon they was a-waitin' fur fallin' weather,"
said Eph with grim humor.

The army marched that day and the next, engag-
ing the enemy's pickets and skirmishers at times,
but continuing their way toward Murfreesboro. On
Saturday night they camped on the north bank of
Stewart's Creek, and the Confederate pickets were
just on the other side. The Union forces became
convinced that they were fronting no large body of
troops, but only skirmishers sent to dispute their
passage.

The army made no advance that day, but all the
morning and early afternoon the 8th Kentucky
watched the men across the creek, and fired whenever they saw a head appear behind a tree, though
with little if any effect; and the rebel sharpshoot-
ing was also ineffectual.

Early in the afternoon Eph saw a Confederate and
called to him,

"Hello thar, Johnny!"

"Hello, Yank. Gwineter shoot?"

"No. Not now. Let's quit this fur a spell."

"All right. *You* mought as well. You hain't a-doin' us no more harm than a tom-tit peckin' at a spruce log."

"Wall, you hain't a-doin' us no harm. You tell your fellers to quit their shootin', an' we will."

"All right. Hit's a go."

"Boys," said Eph, "this hain't no way to spend the Sabbath. I reckon we're stopped to-day because ole Rosecrans don't like to march on Sunday. Less quit this firin' an' have a truce."

The word quickly passed along the line on both sides of the creek, and the men began to come out of the bushes and gather on the banks of the stream.

"Hello, Yanks!" said a rebel. "Who proposed this here truce?"

"We did," said Eph.

"Hit's honest Injun, is it?"

"You're right, it is."

"All right. Hit's a go, then, till sundown."

"Whar be you Johnnies from?"

"From Alabam. Whar be you from?"

"Kaintuck."

"Got any whiskey?"

"That's what we live on."

"How'll ye swap some for coffee?"

"We never drink it while the worm goes."

"What be you fellers a-comin' down here for, anyhow?"

"You'll find out when we meet you at Murfreesboro. Be you goin' to stand thar, or run?"

"That's tellin' tales outer school. But from here to Murfreesboro you'll travel the bloodiest ten mile ever you walked."

"I reckon so.   But hit won't all be our blood."

The conversation was getting rather too political, and both sides felt that it was a pity to waste the little time they had together in any unkind words.

Just then a Confederate officer rode down to the stream.

"What's this?" he asked.

"We've agreed to a truce till sundown," said his men.

"All right, boys," said he. "Keep it faithfully."

Then turning toward the stream, he rode in a few paces, and let his horse drink.

"Hello, boys," he said to the Union men.

They saluted him as they would their own officer.

"I'm Captain Miller, of Stewart's Cavalry, and these are my men. Don't fire on them, and they will keep their truce with you. Have you any papers to swap?"

They inquired among themselves, but found no newspaper.

"We lef' Nashville in the rain," Eph said, "an' what papers we had got wet. I'm sorry."

"Never mind," said he. "Here's a Chattanooga paper. I'll give you mine, anyway," and riding a few steps further into the stream, he threw it over, and rode back.

"Thank ye, Captain," said Eph. "Ef we meet you or your men in battle, we'll spare ye."

"Thank you, boys. This is a better way to spend Sunday than in useless waste of powder."

"Yes. A heap better than shootin' bullets inter the timber. This is most as good as goin' to meetin'."

"Boys, have you a chaplain with you?"

"Not with this comp'ny. They's one with the reg'maintal headquarters but we hain't seed him to-day."

"We have no chaplain," said the captain. "Our chaplain took small-pox in the hospital and died."

"I reckon we could find a preacher," said Eph.

"Thar's a Illinois reg'maint up on the hill that's got a chaplain. He's a right good feller, too. A reg'lar shoutin' Methodist. He'd come, I know. Sim, you go 'n' ast him."

"I will ride back in half an hour," said Captain Miller, and so rode away.

Many an Illinois regiment knew Chaplain Barnes, and many a soldier loved him. He was short in stature, and rather stout but not corpulent, and was lithe in his movements. He was an able preacher, a forceful stump speaker in temperance and anti-slavery campaigns, and carried the interests of the soldiers upon his heart. The soldiers loved him, and called him, somewhat roughly, but with a robust appreciation of his whole-hearted, enthusiastic preaching, the "Bully for Christ" chaplain. A story, which the good chaplain declared to be more or less apocryphal, was often told as indicating the origin of the name. The regiment had received official mention for good conduct at Perryville, where it was put into the front, though only a week from home, and the men were enthusiastically cheering the officers who had received particular honor.

"Bully for Colonel Gooding!" they cried, and then, "Bully for General McCook!"

"Bully for Abe Lincoln" was the next cheer,

and then, noticing the chaplain vociferously joining in it, they shouted,

"Bully for Parson Barnes!"

"Boys," said he, "I thank you for cheering for me, and I say with you, Bully for all the good men you've been cheering. But I want you to say, and say it with all your hearts, Bully for Christ."

The chaplain always declared that that was not just what he said, but that was what the soldiers told.

In a very little time the chaplain appeared. Men were not always ready to listen to sermons, and he was glad of an opportunity to preach. The day was mild and clear, and the Sabbath hush was on all the earth. The little minister came walking with a quick step down among the men at the bank of the creek, and greeted both sides with cordial words.

"Boys, can you sing?" he asked.

Eph Whitley's father had led the singing at Roundstone ever since any one could remember; and all Roundstone knew Eph as the best singer among the young people of the Holler. He started a weird, camp-meeting melody which both sides knew, and sang together,

> "I am bound for the promised land,
> I am bound for the promised land,
> Oh, who will come and go with me,
> I am bound for the promised land."

To this refrain were sung successively the stanzas of "Am I a soldier of the cross."

Chaplain Barnes mounted a low rock on the shore of the stream and opened his Bible. Captain Miller returned and sat on his horse, a little back among the trees, on the other side. Clear and strong the chaplain said :

"My friends and brothers on both sides of the stream. We have been singing together, and singing truly, that we are bound for the promised land. In spite of all the wickedness and cruelty of this wicked and cruel war, I am glad to believe that that is true of many of us on both sides.

"My text is in the twenty-second chapter of the Book of Revelation, and the second, third, and fourth verses.

"'On either side of the river was there the tree of life, which bare twelve manner of fruits, and yielded her fruit every month : and the leaves of the tree were for the healing of the nations. And there shall be no more curse : but the throne of God and of the Lamb shall be in it : and his servants shall serve him. And they shall see his face.'

"My brothers, I do not know the full meaning of this text, but I feel that I know a little more of it for our meeting here, and I am sure that the tree of life does grow on both sides of this river.

"We stand separated from each other and from our own future by just such narrow streams. How narrow a river separates us from to-morrow, and yet with the rising of the sun we shall be taking each other's lives ! How narrow a stream separates us from each other in all our convictions, and how much of prejudice and misunderstanding has existed on both sides to bring about this awful war, and caused us to forget that the tree of life can bear more than one manner of fruit !

"How narrow a stream separates us from the new

year! This is the last Sunday in the old year and almost the last day. The old year with all its accomplishments and all its mistakes is before God, and we must give an account for it, and begin the new one. How narrow a stream separates us from the other world. We may not even live to see the end of this year and the beginning of the next. Oh, my brothers, if the tree of life is to bloom for you on the other side of the river of death, it must be planted here! We sing that,

> " 'On the other side of Jordan,
> In the sweet fields of Eden,
> Where the tree of life is blooming,
> There is rest for you.'

"But I read that on this side of the river, as well as on that, is there the tree of life. My friends, the leaves of that tree must heal this nation. And while we do our awful duty now, and strike our hardest blows, let us remember that we strike our brothers, and pray God for the healing of this nation with the leaves of the tree which grows in the garden of God.

"God bless you all, my brothers. The same kind of heart beats under gray that beats under blue, and we are one in spirit to-day. Together we join in this worship. Together we join in song. Together we join in thoughts of home and love and duty, and the same kind of love and hope is growing to-day in hearts on both sides of this little creek. So may the same graces abound in our lives on this side of the river of death that we hope to have in the heavenly paradise."

On This Side of the River and on That.   Page 289.

Then the little parson lifted up his voice in prayer, and the whole company knelt with him upon the banks of the stream, and there were tears dropping from many eyes.

"Let us sing in closing," said he,

> "'On Jordan's stormy banks I stand,
>   And cast a wistful eye,
>   To Canaan's fair and happy land,
>   Where my possessions lie.'"

Eph led the singing to one of the minor airs which both sides, being Southerners, knew so well. The song was hearty, but the chaplain did not know the tune.

"Boys," said he, "I don't quite know those tunes. And I want to sing with you. Let's sing one more hymn. Let us sing, 'There is a land of pure delight,' to the tune of 'Varina.' I guess everybody knows that."

They all knew it, and sang with him,

> "Sweet fields beyond the swelling flood,
>   Stand dressed in living green :
>   So to the Jews old Canaan stood,
>   While Jordan rolled between.
>   Could we but climb where Moses stood
>   And view the landscape o'er,
>   Not Jordan's stream, nor death's cold flood,
>   Should fright us from the shore.''

Then he pronounced the benediction, and went away. Captain Miller also rode back to his tent. And the men, as the dusk came on, built their fires down by the stream, and made their coffee, and drank each other's health. On the coals they broiled the rabbits which both sides had found in considerable numbers, and whose chase had served as diversion all the morning. There was swapping of broiled rabbit for hard tack, and it may even have been that in the excess of good fellowship some flasks from the Kentuckians went across the stream in exchange for canteens of hot coffee. The men visited until dark, and then with good words on either side went to their tents. The night fell without the firing of a gun along Stewart's Creek, and the peace of God's Sabbath reigned on this side of the river and on that.

The next day the Union army took up its march again toward Murfreesboro. There was skirmishing, but at long range, and the men of Eph's regiment looked to see whether they were firing at men on foot or horseback, and if the men were mounted, it is to be feared that their aim was not very true.

"Hello, Kentuck," said an Illinoisan to Eph. "Stole our parson and had meetin' yesterday, did you?"

"Yes; an' he's a main good one, ain't he?"

"You're mighty right. He's the man that invented the word 'skedaddle'; but he's the bravest man in the army."

"Did you have preachin' yistiddy?"

"No; we had a funeral."

"That's nothin' outer common. Was it an officer?"

"No; General Palmer had commanded us not to commit depredations. We obeyed the order over the left. Some of the fellers in our company found a sheep, and were skinning him when Palmer rode along.   They just whipped a blanket over him and got out a deck of cards and were playing seven up by the time he got there.   He looked at the blanket and didn't say anything, but rode on.   The fellers in our mess had caught a hog.   We had lots of time yesterday, and we were skinning him, and he caught us in the act.

"'Ah,' said he, 'a body!   A corpse!   Some poor fellow gone to his long home!   He must be buried with military honors.   Call the officer of the guard.   Officer,' says he, 'these men have lost a comrade.   A dear friend has passed away.   Provide them with spades, and see that they dig a grave, wide and deep.   Be sure they dig it deep.   And let them bury their friend with military honors.'

"He sat there on his horse, sober as a judge.   But there was a twinkle in his eye.

"Well, we had to dig the grave, and we wrapped the hog in an old overcoat and buried him under guard.   And General Palmer said, 'Peace to his ashes!' and rode off.   But when we got him buried and the guard returned, we thought of the resurrection, and it wasn't long till Gabriel's trumpet blew."

"You dug him up, did ye?"

"Well, I ain't saying what we did.   But we didn't eat salt horse for supper, I can tell you that.   And we had all the better appetite for pork chops and tenderloin for our exercise digging the grave."

XXVI

The Battle of Stone River

THERE is always a reaction from unrestrained mirth. After Christmas Murfreesboro grew thoughtful. Two days before the end of the year a shudder of apprehension seized the town. The Yankees were coming. They had left Nashville two days ago. They would be here in two days more, and then there would be a bloody battle. All hopes of going into winter quarters were at an end. Discipline in the army became rigid. People began seeking permission to leave town, and for the most part readily obtained it. Coburn was among the first to leave. Jack could easily have gone now, but his orders held him for another day and night. He was eager to be gone, to be in his own place in the ranks, away from this false position, away from the hollow part which he was playing, and away from Bessie Granger, before he should be tempted to say what he must not say. Bessie asked him about the approaching battle and its probable effect upon his plans. He could not give her such answers as she desired, nor could he well reply when she asked, what more than once she had asked before, why so brave a man as he was not a soldier. Jack determined to be kind to her, and no more; to explain to her his situation at the earliest moment when his duty would allow him to speak; and to avoid, if possible, all future relations with the secret service.

On Tuesday night he made his way to the appointed place, in hope of meeting Captain Garnett. But the hope all but forsook him when he came to the place. The pike was full of soldiers crossing the river to take position beyond. All day in the rain he had seen the troops moving to the left. He now divined the meaning of it. He had news now, and of importance. He must if possible see Captain Garnett. But the movement which made his news of importance prevented the captain's coming. The hours went by till the sky grew gray, and all night long he watched in vain. After hours of ineffectual striving to make his way through the lines, Captain Garnett had given up the attempt, confident, however, that his information was correct. It was correct, and on it had been formed the plan of Rosecrans to move out from the left and throw Van Cleve's division across the river upon the Confederate right, which was believed to be the most favorable point of attack. It was all the more so now that the Confederate left was so extended, but the news which Jack obtained, which would have been worth ten thousand men to Rosecrans, was that Bragg had formed precisely the same plan, and had thrown his left across the river, three miles further down, to strike the Union right, and that everything depended upon being able to strike first.

When Jack returned to the tavern in the dawn of the last day of 1862, the battle had already begun, and from the firing he knew that Bragg had struck first. He changed his dripping clothes, put dry cartridges in his revolver, swallowed a hasty breakfast and waited.

It had rained all night, and Eph Whitley and his 8th Kentucky comrades had lain without fire in the dripping woods between the pike and the river. With the first light of day they were astir, and after a cold bite of hard tack moved toward the left to the ford. The water was icy cold, but they plunged into it, and came up on the other side ready for another march and an attack on the forces a half mile beyond. They were hardly across the river when the sound was heard of a heavy battle on the right, and the order came to recall the division and support the exposed wing. Two brigades were left in charge of Colonel Price, and Eph's regiment was with them. The rest of the division rushed through the woods, their garments dripping from the second fording, and met the whole right in retreat, with the rebels in full pursuit. Bragg's movement had been magnificently planned and brilliantly executed. With a shorter distance to move, the Confederates had the advantage of the first attack, and they carried everything before them like a storm.

In every battle there is a sorry picture at the rear. Cowards and stragglers are in every fight, and men who prove brave enough afterward sometimes run like sheep at the first fire. But the Army of the Cumberland never before or afterward saw what it saw that day, whole regiments in swift retreat, and the overborne troops pushing their way by thousands through the fog to the rear. Up and down rode Van Cleve, the blood dropping from a wound in his foot, and his white hair streaming in the wind. A new plan was arranged. A new line of battle was formed — a line which receded, but was not again broken. Rosecrans now became anxious for his left wing, and rode back to the ford whence he had called Van Cleve.

"Who commands this brigade?" he demanded.

"I do," said Colonel Price.

"Can you hold this ford?"

"I'll try, sir," said Price, looking about at his depleted body of men, and up to where Breckinridge held his four brigades of splendidly drilled Confederates.

"Can you hold this ford?" again demanded Rosecrans.

"I'll die right here, sir," said Price.

"Can you hold this ford?" thundered Rosecrans.

"Yes, sir, and I will!" replied Price.

Eph looked to the right and the left into the faces of his companions, and read in every one of them the answer of their commander. "Yes," said he, "we will!"

Twice that day Bragg ordered Breckinridge to move over and attack the centre. That he did not crush the Union army into fragments that day was due to the failure of Breckinridge to obey. For Colonel Price kept his word and his position at the ford.

Early in the afternoon the Union troops took their final position, and from the ground then occupied they never receded. They formed in a semicircle bending outward, with the ends resting on Stone River. Against this new line the Confederates hurled themselves four times. The cannon roar was deafening. The roll of the musketry was incessant. Men fought like demons, no longer firing as earlier they had sometimes done into their own ranks, but volley upon volley straight into the faces of their enemies. Each army had lost immensely; but each was stronger in morale and in possibilities of victory than when the fight began. To kill men or to be killed ceased to be a thing considered. On the one side there was determination to break the line, on the other to hold it, and neither side thought of life or death or anything save that. The fighting ceased as the day died, and the night fell bitter cold, and the Union line stood firm.

New Year's day broke clear, but cold. There were dead by thousands, and wounded more than could be cared for. Bragg telegraphed to Jefferson Davis that God had given a happy new year to the Confederate cause, but neither he nor Rosecrans cared to begin the battle that day.

On Friday Rosecrans pushed his left further across the river, and that day the battle was fought at the other end of the line. It was Bragg's desperate attempt to force the issue. He had expected the Union army to retreat the night before. Breckinridge, against his earnest protest, was thrown with all the impetuous force of his four fine brigades against the Union left. The charge of Breckinridge at first was irresistible. The Union troops fell back. It was the most magnificent movement of the battle, but for the Confederates the most disastrous. On the hill above the ford the Union General Mendenhall massed fifty-eight cannon, and rained down upon the advancing Confederates, the flower of the South, a hundred shots a minute. Since the world began, flesh and blood had never stood under such a storm of iron hail that smote whole ranks to the earth. The Confederates stopped as they pressed through the cotton field, and from the bolls at their feet took cotton and stuffed their ears against the awful thunder of the artillery, and pressed on. The Union infantry now rallied, and poured in their murderous fire of Minié balls. Southern dash and ardor at its best met equally at its best Northern endurance and determination. The Confederates advanced and were repulsed, advanced again, and again were driven back. A third time the wave of battle advanced and receded, breaking on the adamantine rock of the Union front, and leaving two thousand Confederates dead and dying men upon the field. Night fell, and was welcome, for both sides were weary of slaughter.

Saturday brought a storm and little fighting. The Union army was gladdened that day by the coming of a wagon train of supplies, guarded by a hastily picked up brigade under General Spears. Among his men were the 1st and 2d Tennessee, which regiments were sent to reinforce Van Cleve's command. The arrival of these fresh troops, and the great loss sustained by Breckinridge, greatly disheartened Bragg, and on Saturday night, under cover of a heavy fire, his army began its retreat.

In the town, the excitement seemed to subside when the battle really began. There was anxiety still, but of the calmer sort. The roar of the battle seemed somehow to steady nerves that had been unstrung by the uncertainty of the past days. Soon the wounded began coming in. The churches were filled with them. All the public buildings became hospitals. The Union University and the Soule Female College were filled with bleeding, suffering men. There were more than the surgeons could attend. The townspeople began offering their services. Jack hastened to the university, and was soon at work, caring for the more slightly wounded, whom the surgeons could not attend. He rejoiced that this much, at least, his duty as a soldier did not prevent. The need for nurses grew. The surgeons were far too few in number. More women came to help, and here and there a man was sent from the ranks, who was known to have knowledge of surgery or skill in nursing. Jack was busy, when a voice at his elbow asked,

"Let me help you, won't you, please?" and looking up he saw Bessie.

She had never looked so pretty to Jack in her party dress as she did now, with pale face, but set teeth and pleading eyes.

"Yes, help me here," said Jack. "I thought at first you was an angel."

She held the bandage on a wounded leg while Jack wrapped it round and round, and then together they went from man to man, attending to minor wounds, bringing water to quench the terrible gun-shot thirst, and assisting the surgeons in the more difficult cases. The work continued all day, and grew harder and more abundant as the day wore on, till the plucky little Bessie was wearied to the point of exhaustion. Jack almost forced her to go home for refreshment, and took himself to the tavern, whence, after an hour of rest, he went again with Bessie to the university, and they worked together far into the night.

There is something about work in such relations that creates a new world for those who engage together in it. A day of it, and it seems to have been forever. The past recedes and all but vanishes, and the awful and absorbing present fills all that ever has been and all that is to be. When, long after midnight, Jack parted with Bessie at her door, it seemed an age since morning when they had begun their work together. If one such day seems an age, four of them become an eternity.

With the first reliable news from the battle, Murfreesboro thanked God and took courage. The Confederates were winning. The Union army had been driven back. But the first night and the next day met them with adverse news, for the Union forces were not dislodged. On Thursday night there was another outbreak of joy over the false report that the Nashville pike was crowded with the wagon trains of the retreating Yankees. Bragg believed it, and so did the army and the town. But Friday brought the awful carnage and defeat of Breckinridge, and the dead had to be hurried from the overcrowded hospitals almost before their last breath was drawn, to make room for the thousands of wounded. Then the people's heart sank like lead. Jack could hardly resist sharing with the people about him, and especially with Bessie, the varying emotions which the alternating tidings brought.   The only thing which made it possible for them to work together without his betraying himself was that they were too busy to talk much.   All day and almost all night they labored.   They lost count of the days.   The time seemed unrelated to other time.   The years of the past were like a dream. One night, — it must have been Friday night, — Jack took Bessie home as the day was breaking, and himself sought his bed in the tavern.

"You're the pluckiest little girl ever I seen," said he, as they approached her home.

"I'm afraid I shouldn't have been so brave," she replied, "if — "

"If what?"

"I don't know."

"What did you start to say?"

"I started to say that I thought it was largely the help of your presence and courage that made me brave.   I thought I had better not say it, but you have made me do it."

She spoke half reproachfully.   They were at the steps of the house.   Jack looked down into the tired face and it lighted up.

"A man couldn't help being brave with you," said he.   He could hardly resist the impulse to take her in his arms.   "You're plumb tired out," he added.   "You must sleep now till noon.   Then I'll come for you."

The day dawned, and darkened again with a storm. Jack ate his breakfast and lay down, but was too tired to sleep.   The effort which it had come to require to recall himself to himself was little short of violent.   He must define to himself his own position. Did he love this pretty, plucky little Southern girl, or was he still in love with Jennie? His heart turned to Jennie when he had time to think of her, but she and all associated with her seemed very remote just now. Yet duty was near. Whatever else he remembered or forgot, he must remember what brought him here, and what was his duty as a soldier.

He went out into the storm and walked toward the river. Here the Confederates held both sides, but far down the stream was Van Cleve's division, strongly reinforced and holding the ford, and above it on the hill frowned Mendenhall's murderous fifty-eight cannon that had wrought such havoc yesterday. To get through the lines by land was clearly impossible, and to cross the river here was of no avail. If only he had a boat, and it were night, he might hope to escape. He walked up the bank of the river. Boats were few, but he found a round-bottomed log canoe below the brick house, near the railroad bridge. It was locked, and the paddles were gone, but Jack marked its position, and the location of the troops above. It was two miles, at least, to the ford, and the night would be dark.

He turned back to the town. The rain was falling, and it was not yet noon. He stepped into the Methodist church on his way back, to see how the wounded fared there, and met face to face in the door, Sam Marshall. Marshall laid his hand on his sword, and Jack drew his revolver.

"Hold on!" said Jack, in a low voice. "Let's settle this outside."

They passed to the rear of the church, which was crowded inside with wounded.

"What are you doin' here?" demanded Marshall.

"I'm carin' for wounded soldiers," said Jack. "What are you doin' here? Why ain't you at the front fightin'?"

"I was there till they called me here," said Sam. "But what I want to know is, what are you doin' inside these lines?"

"Sam Marshall, if you insist on astin' that question, you an' me might just as well fight it out an' be done with it. You know what I'm here for, an' I hain't a-goin' to be betrayed an' hung, nuther. If you an' me can come to terms, all right. If not, then they won't but just one of us leave the hind side o' this church house alive."

"By heaven, I'd like it so! I've swore to kill you! But I've promised your mother I wouldn't. But if you're here as a spy, no promise holds. I won't kill you, but I'll see you hung."

"No you won't. They hain't nary one of us goin' ter stir from this spot till we come to terms, or one of us gits killed."

"I wish I'd a died before I ever touched your mother's food! I swore to her I'd never harm ye. But I can't let you go with information to the enemy. I'd ruther break a hundred promises, and die, too!"

"Sam Marshall, let me tell you this. I reckon I've done all the harm I can this trip. I hain't got no information now that's good for anybody. I couldn't get through the lines, as I know on, if I had. Mind you, I'd git information if I could,

an' I'd git out with it if I could. But all I'm a-doin'
here now is to put in my time lookin' atter these
wounded Johnnies. If you think it's your duty,
we'll fight, and there'll be one less rebel nuss or
surgeon, one, afore we git through."

Marshall hesitated. "If you'll promise —"

"I won't promise nothin'. I've told you the
truth. I'm goin' back to the university, where
I've been workin' night an' day for four days,
savin' the lives of rebels. If I git a good chance,
I'm goin' back to the army."

"The sooner the better, then. And we'd best
keep out of each other's way. I won't betray you
without fair warnin'. That's all I can say."

"I'm agreed. Only, you understand, I ain't
astin' no favors. If you think you ort to fight,
don't let your promise hold you back. Do yer
duty, an' I'll do mine. But I reckon we might
as well wait till the battle's over, an' the hull question may settle itself."

"Casey, you ain't a coward, I'll say that for you.
I don't know as I'm doin' right, but I'm tryin' to.
Whatever I do, I'll do without any grudge on old
scores. They might as well go by the board. If
you can get out inside twenty-four hours, I wish
you would, for I ain't right sure what I ought to
do. But I'll stay here, and you stay at the other
hospital, where you are at, and I reckon we'll both
have enough to think about for this day without
killin' each other."

Jack went now for Bessie; and as he went, his
determination grew to leave the town that night.
There was skirmishing, and now and then a

wounded man was brought in fresh from the field; but more were brought who had not been picked up the day before. The storm was heavy, and Jack thanked God for the pitiless rain that made the yet more pitiless fighting impracticable for that day.

They stood a moment in the house before they started into the storm.

"Bessie," he asked, "do you know the people that live in that brick house on the river above the pike?"

"Yes," said Bessie, "I know them well."

"I want to borry their canoe to-night," said Jack. "Do you reckon I could get it?"

"What do you want of it?" she asked, suddenly turning.

"Nothin'. That is, I've important business on hand to-night."

"I reckon I could borrow the boat," said Bessie; "but they'll wonder what I want it for at such a time, that's all."

"You needn't mind," said Jack. "I'll tell ye if I need your help. Mebby I won't git to go."

As he thought about it he reflected that it was not best to ask Bessie's help in the matter. It would necessitate too many explanations. He would break the lock, and make some shift for a paddle. But if possible he would go. They worked together in the hospital that afternoon, but Bessie saw that he was preoccupied. They were both weary, and there was somewhat less to do than on former days. They left early in the evening, and Jack parted with Bessie at the door. He lingered a moment, for he did not intend to return.

"Good night," he said, "and get all the rest you can."

"Stay a moment," she said. "You are not in earnest about leaving town to-night?"

"I ain't right sure," said he.

"But if you go, when will you return?"

"I can't quite say about that," he answered. "As soon as the battle is over, I reckon. I can explain matters then. I can't now. I may not go. If not, I'll see you to-morrow. Good night."

It was an unsatisfactory parting to them both. Jack turned toward the tavern, seeking something of which to make an oar. After some searching he discovered a clapboard, which he shaped into a clumsy paddle. Then he went to his room and reloaded his revolver, and borrowed a hammer to break the padlock of the boat. As he went out into the street he found a new reason for his going. The cannon had begun firing in the distance, but under cover of this feint, Bragg was withdrawing his forces from the town. This was news to be taken at once to the Federal camp. He made his way around to avoid the troops who now filled the muddy streets from side to side, and in half an hour approached the river. Under the rocky bank, he found a low, round-bottomed, dug-out craft half full of water. He bailed it out with his hat, and stepped ashore to break the lock, and there stood Bessie.

"Here is the key," she said simply, "and here are the paddles."

"Bessie!" he exclaimed.

"If you must go," said she, "I must go with you and bring back the boat."

x

"But I can't let you," said he. "You'll risk your life. I can't come back with you, and I won't send you back alone in the dark. I won't go — but I must go. No, no. Bessie, my brave girl, let me take you home, and I'll go alone."

"If you must go," said Bessie, "I go too." And stepping lightly into the boat she sat in the stern. Jack said no more, but unlocking the boat, pushed off.

"I trusted you," said she, "and knew that if you must come, I ought to help you."

"They may fire on us," said Jack. "When we touch shore and the sentinel challenges us, I'll jump out and push you as far as I can. Bend low in the boat, and pull into the current, fast."

There was need of caution. Two hours Jack paddled to gain as many miles. "You're not going too far, are you?" she asked.

"No," said Jack, and gladly noticed that she did not know that the Union troops were across the stream, and thus had no suspicion of his real errand. He would not undeceive her to-night, but land on the same side from which they started. The waters ran swift and shallow at the ford. Above them was the hill with its fifty-eight black-throated cannon. Jack turned the boat about, and cautiously approached the shore, stern on.

"Halt! who comes there?" rang the challenge of a sentinel. Jack knew the voice. It was Eph Whitley.

"A friend!" said Jack, and then in a lower tone, "Keep still a minute. I'm coming ashore."

While still several yards from the bank, he

A Night Ride on Stone River.   Page 307.

pressed Bessie's hand warmly, whispered a good night, and stepped out into the water knee-deep. He gave the boat a push with all his might, and Bessie bent to the paddle. In a moment he was on shore, and the boat and Bessie were out of sight.

Eph called the officer of the guard, and Jack told him that Bragg's army was in full retreat. The news spread from lip to lip, and brought comfort to thousands of soldiers camping that night in the rain.

"You must a had a hard time rowin' here in the dark," said Eph. "You come right by your own reg'maint, too. They've just got here under General Spears, and are camped on the other side between us and the bridge." This was good news to Jack, and he soon found his own company. But for the sake of one day more of good standing in the sight of Bessie Granger, he was glad to have rowed one unnecessary mile, and to have landed on the other side.

The 1st Tennessee spent Sunday in repairing the railroad bridge. Few troops entered Murfreesboro that day. All day long in the rain the people of the town were moving out. Vehicles of every sort were pressed into service. The only carriage the town possessed when Rosecrans entered was th hearse in which Jack made his entry. It was a sad day to the town, and a sad one for Bessie Granger. The hospitals were left. Bragg had no time to take his wounded, and left his surgeons and nurses with them. Bessie went to the university and worked a while, but soon returned home to escape from questions concerning Jack, whom many wounded men missed. No arm had been more strong, no hand more tender than his, and no one in the hospital had seen Bessie without him. She went to her home and watched the endless procession pass; but Jack did not come. She half repented her expedition the night before, yet rejoiced in the share she had borne in it. She could not fathom the mystery of his departure, but she trusted him. She could not understand why his evident admiration of her stopped short of an avowal of affection, but thought him possibly deterred by her superior culture. She gave up trying to unravel the tangle and simply looked for Jack.

Monday morning, bright and early, Jack dressed himself in his army blue, but threw over it his store overcoat. He had obtained permission to precede the army and settle his bill at the tavern, agreeing to join his regiment as it passed through the town. He made a brief stay at the tavern, and quickly sought Bessie. Sad and dispirited she was watching for him, and flung the door wide as he entered.

"I knew you would come!" she cried. "I trusted you!"

Jack's heart gave a great leap when he saw her, and it filled his throat. There was but one thing that he could have said easily in that moment, and that was to tell her that he loved her.

A moment he stood and held her hand, and then without a word flung off his overcoat, and stood before her in his regimentals. She recoiled from him as if he had struck her. Then she sank into a chair and covered her face to hide him from her sight, and wept as if her heart would break.

"Leave me, leave me!" she cried.

"I must leave you, Bessie," he said. "But I wanted to tell you first."

"You have betrayed me!" she cried. "You have deceived me! You are a traitor to the South and to me!"

"Listen to me, Bessie," he said. "I'm no traitor to any one. I've been in the Union army from the start. I've done my duty there. I can't now make you understand it all, but you can understand now some things I couldn't explain at the time."

"I only understand that you have been false to me, and to my country!" she cried. "I am a fool to cry for you. Leave me! I hate you!"

The sound of a fife and drum was heard approaching.

"Bessie," he said, "that's my reg'maint. I've got to join it in just a minute. If I had time to explain, some things wouldn't seem so bad to you as they do. If I'd been quite so bad as you say, I wouldn't a come back to you this morning. I reckon I've done wrong, but I don't quite see how I could help it. I don't blame you for hatin' me; but, Bessie, I don't feel thataway to-wards you. I'd like a chance to explain, sometime, but I can't do it now. Good-by, Bessie."

The regiment was coming up the street, and the tune was "Dixie." Jack turned on the threshold.

"Good-by," he said again.

"Oh, come back!" she cried. "I don't know what to say. I don't know what to do! No, go!"

Jack turned back and stood a moment beside her as she sat weeping. He stooped and took her hand. She did not resist, and as he dropped it, he thought

her fingers clasped his own a little. "Good-by,"
he said; "I'll come again, sometime, if you'll let
me."   And then he ran to join his regiment.

Spears' brigade was sent through Murfreesboro
in pursuit of the Confederates. No strong attack
was made upon them, but an effectual skirmish was
kept up throughout the day, and the rebels were
followed several miles, with frequent minor fights
and some loss. General Spears, in his report of the
battle, especially commends the conduct of "the gallant Tennesseeans" who took part in that fight.
Certainly among them all there was none who fought
with better zest that day than Jack. He rejoiced
in the opportunity of fighting. He rejoiced in the
attempt to restore himself in some measure in his
own esteem. He could not feel that he had been
wholly to blame, yet he had somehow to reinstate
himself in his own good graces. He was glad that
Bessie had not wholly refused him permission to
see her again, but he did not regret that his duties
prevented his doing so at once. For a few days he
was kept beyond the town with his regiment, and
then he was ordered to Nashville to report the results of his work in the secret service. When the
mail went north, he rode on the box of the hearse
with the driver, with a guard before and behind.
When he arrived in Nashville, Colonel Truesdail
commended him for his service, and asked him if he
would not like to engage in that kind of work for
the rest of the war. But Jack thanked him and
declined. He was glad if he had done well, he
said, but it wasn't the sort of work he liked. It
sorter left a bad taste in his mouth.

XXVII

Fort Sanders and Lookout Mountain

FOR six months after the battle of Stone River, the Army of the Cumberland was comparatively inactive. There were several minor engagements, mostly about points where there had already been fighting, as at Fort Donelson and Franklin, but there was little progress. The Tullahoma campaign, which was an aggressive movement on the part of Rosecrans, and which ended in driving Bragg, more by manœuvring than by fighting, out of Tennessee, occupied less than two weeks in the summer, from June 23d to July 4th. Then Rosecrans advanced to Chattanooga, and the world knows the rest.

Jack was not with the Army of the Cumberland on this campaign. In the early spring the 1st Tennessee was at its old stamping-ground at Camp Nelson, and the Second Regiment was at Somerset. There they were provided with horses, and were known from this time on as "Tennessee Mounted Infantry."

"Wall, Jack, how d'ye like ridin'?" asked Sam Loomis.

"I can stand it ef the critter can," said Jack; "but a heap o' the time it's about all I can do to git enough fur myself to eat, let alone the horse."

"Who d'ye reckon'll be our gin'ral now?"

" I heerd we're likely to have Carter agin."

" I hope so.   Spears warn't no fool ; but Cyarter's the bully."

" How'd he come to leave us ? "

" Hit was Andy Johnson done it.   He wanted to git Spears in."

" Wall, he mought a worked for a wuss man, but I hope we'll have Carter agin."

A few weeks later both regiments were encamped near Somerset, under command of General Carter, who had a brigade of eight thousand troops, mostly raw, and six thousand of them Tennesseeans.   One night Jack and his regiment camped at Logan's cross roads, close to the site of their camp two years before at the battle of Mill Spring.

" War's funny business, hain't it, Jack ? " asked Joe Hallet.

" It looks thataway a heap o' times.   What you thinkin' bout now ? "

" Oh, here we be, two year atter fightin' here, right back agin, same's before, we on this side the river, and the rebs at Mill Spring on t'other.   We don't make much progress, do we ? "

" They have made progress.   But it's mighty discouragin'.   'Pears lack the gen'rals don't know as much as they'd orter.   They hain't no manner of excuse for doin' any fightin' here a tall.   Ef we'd a ben up to snuff a tall, we'd a druv the rebs so fur south while we was a-drivin' on 'em they wouldn't a come back till the day o' jedgmaint, an' late in the evenin' at that ! "

" What d'ye reckon's the matter ? "

" The tap root of the trouble is that the rebs has

been allowed to stay in East Tennessy.   We've let
'em stay there, first because our gen'rals didn't know
that the folks there was loyal.   Then we've let 'em
stay there because we thought we couldn't live on the
country, and couldn't take wagon trains for supplies, an' they never seem to think that we ort to
be able to live where the rebs can.   An' that where
the rebs git out so easy we could as easy git in.
An' then they let 'em stay there because they think
they'll do as little harm there as anywhere.   But all
the raids inter Kaintuck comes from there."

" I begin to believe the gen'rals is as big fools as
other folks."

" Wall, they be an' they hain't.   Now there was
Sherman.   He made a powerful big blunder two
year ago when he was in command here.   But they
do say he's done some o' the tallest kind o' fightin'
sence."

" That's what I heerd tell.   But gen'rals don't
know everything, by a long shot."

" No, they don't.   Now there's the battle o'
Perryville.   They wouldn't nary one of the two
gen'rals a fit there, ef they hadn't both a blundered
an' hadter."

" I've heerd that's so.   Both thought they was
fightin' part o' the other's army stidder the hull on
it, but they mighty soon found they was wrong."

" Then, there was the battle o' Stone River.
Both gen'rals had sense enough to make a mighty
good plan, but nary one on 'em had sense enough
to know that the other had sense enough to make
the same plan."

" Not knowin' makes a heap o' trouble."

" Yes, an' they's another thing that makes a heap o' trouble, one gen'ral thinks the other side has got the biggest force. He allers thinks thataway. It's sorter lack a fish when you got him on yer hook, he's allers so much bigger'n he is when ye git him landed. Wall now, a heap o' the time both gen'rals is skeered of each other. One is afraid, an' t'other dassent. An' they never stop to think that the other fellers is jes' as much afeard as they be."

" I reckon that's about hit."

" Sartin, that's it. An' then they's another trouble. When we've licked, we don't hardly ever foller up the thing, an' hit 'em again, or ef we do, we go slow as the seven-year itch."

" Yes, Buell had orter licked Bragg wuss atter Perryville."

" In course he'd ort. What business had we to let Bragg take all them wagon trains outen the State, an' all the best horses in Kaintuck ? "

" But then, Rosecrans done the same at Stone River."

" Yes, they all do the same. They spend month atter month a-gittin' ready to do somethin', and then hit 'em a little, an' say, ' Now you hurry an' git outen here right quick, or you'll git hurt,' an' then the rebs moves on 'bout twenty mile, an' sends out their cavalry to raid our wagon trains, and we git good ready atter while to move on agin."

" Hit's sorter lack see-saw. Hit's sorter lack a game o' checkers. Here we ben fightin' fur two year an' better, an' now we're both on us back in our own king row, an' both sides movin' back'ards an' for'ards in their double corners."

"But a heap o' good men gits moved off'n the board."

"Yes, an' some on 'em kings."

Narrow as was this view of the progress of the war, there was much to confirm it as witnessed on their horizon. The fall of Vicksburg, which came that summer, and the repulse of Lee at Gettysburg, were great events, but in a way remote from them, though they broke the back of the Rebellion. But their great event in the summer was a raid into East Tennessee, under the gallant General Sanders, himself a Southern man, and a relative of Jefferson Davis. On this raid, in which Jack bore his part with honor, they captured a few hundred prisoners, destroyed some Confederate property, and burned the railroad bridge at Strawberry Plains. It was counted a successful raid, as it accomplished its end, and with trifling loss to the men involved. But it seemed a deplorable thing that the Union army could find no better and greater thing to do than that for which the ignorant mountaineers, in their misguided attempt to do something to help put down the Rebellion, had done two years before and paid for with their lives.

On this raid Jack paid a hurried visit to his old home, close to which they passed. He called at the home of the Hansons, and there fed his horse and ate a meal. He found them well, but greatly saddened by the death of their father and brother. Martha Hanson inquired with especial interest concerning Eph Whitley, and Jack was glad to tell her of the goodness and courage of her lover. Jack remembered that he had promised Henry Hanson

to look after his sisters, and he opined that so far
as Martha was concerned, his task would not weigh
upon him if Ephraim Whitley should survive the war.

"Hooray, boys!   Have ye heerd the news?"
Sergeant Jack Casey came running into camp
near Somerset, one hot day in midsummer.   The
soldiers who were lying in the shade where they
could find shade, in undress uniform of all sorts,
roused to hear it.   News had come to have a lan-
guid interest, but was always acceptable.
"What's the news?" asked Dan Schofield, an
iron-gray old trooper, removing his cob pipe, and
deliberately blowing the smoke at a horse-fly that
was buzzing about his nose.
"We're goin' to march."
"Mighty hot weather fur that," replied Dan.
"Whar be we goin'?" asked Sam Loomis.
"Inter East Tennessy."
"Git out!" said Dan.   "Ye cyan't fool me!"
"It's a fact, shore's the gun's iron," said Jack.
"Hit's ben a fact ever sence the war begun, but
hit don't never happen."
"Wall, it's a-goin' to happen now.   Gen'ral Burn-
side has come, and he's goin' to make it his chief
business to capture East Tennessy.   Rosecrans is
a-goin' to hold Bragg at Chattanoogy an' lick him
thar, an' we're a-goin' to strike straight fur Knoxville."
"How d'ye hear?"
"Cun'l Byrd tole me.   They hain't no secret.
We're all goin' to know it come mornin'."
"I hain't a-goin' to tell ye ye lie, but I've heerd
so often that we're goin' inter East Tennessy that

I've sorter made up my mind to die on the other side er Jurdin, as the preacher says."

"They hain't no lyin' about this," said Jack. "The news comes straight. An' Burnside's headquarters is a-goin' with our brigade."

"By jolly! We'll hatter patch up our cloes, and keep our horses curried, won't we?"

"You kin expect orders to march to-morrow, I'll tell you that now."

The camp was soon astir with the bustle of preparation for the breaking of camp.

"Fellers," said old Dan, as they lay before the tents in the moonlight that evening, "fellers, you young chaps don't know what it is to want ter git home. I lef' a wife dyin' with the consumption, an' nine young uns to home. I hated to leave 'em like pullin' teeth, but I wanted to fight fur my principles. I ain't one o' the tender-hearted sort, but when hit comes to talkin' about goin' back to East Tennessy, hit breaks me all up."

"I reckon we know somethin' about it," said Jack. "Some on us has got wives, and more on us hopes to have; an' we've got mothers and sisters, too, a heap on us."

"I know. But this is different. Wall, I wish the Lord we *would* go, and mebby we *be* a-goin'; but I've ben disappinted so often las' two year, I'm hanged ef I'm a-goin' to believe it till I enter the valley o' the Sequatchie."

The grizzled old veteran coughed a little, and drawing from his pocket a twist of tobacco, he cut it into his cob pipe with a wicked-looking bowie knife, and asked his next neighbor for a light.

"Dan," asked Sam Loomis, "how fast does a baby grow?"

"What d'ye mean, how fast?" asked the older man.

"I mean how long does it take a baby to git too big fur a par o' shoes like them?"

He fished in his knapsack and brought out a pair of baby shoes, carefully wrapped in a red handkerchief.

"'Bout six months, mebby," said the authority on family matters.

"I've ben packin' on 'em nigh onter two year," said the younger soldier, sorrowfully. "Hit's our first young un, an' was borned 'bout a month atter I lef'. I 'lowed when I got these I'd git home by the time he could toddle around the floor."

"You'll hatter loot another store an git some bigger ones. I'm afeard he'd outgrow another par afore we raley git back."

The young fellow's voice was husky.

"Blast yer smoke!" he said. "That's mighty rank tobaccer yer usin'. Lemme have a pipeful on it."

"Here, fellers," said Jack, "this won't never do. We're gittin' sorter lack a funeral. This hain't no way to be a-gittin' ready to go home. Less sing somethin'."

They tried one or two hymns, which did not quite seem appropriate. "I am bound for the promised land" came the nearest to it, but did not quite fill the requirements. Sergeant Joe Hallet started and sang with a little help from the few who thought they knew it, and a number of well-meant but discordant attempts at assistance from those who knew that they did not, a song beginning,

> "Hey, Betty Martin, tip-toe, tip-toe!
> Hey, Betty Martin, tip-toe fine!"

Then, to the surprise of all, old Dan sang his first and last song in camp. It was a wonderful thing, not to be judged at all as a musical performance, yet it was voted a hearty success. It had an intricate refrain, whose burden was pretty Jennie Jenkins. No one ever could learn it, and Dan next day was impolite to a man who asked to be taught that chorus; so all he could remember, and he was not certain that was right, was the closing or the refrain,

> "To my double, fiddle, treble,
> To my purty Jinnie Jinkins, oh!"

Joe Hallet was getting hilarious, and he started "Skip t'-m'-loo." The men who had handkerchiefs tied them around their left arms, and thus were labelled as girls. There was a shortage of girls, to be sure, but that was in keeping with the actual situation; and the men's thoughts were somewhere else as they seized their partners, and sang their praises,

> "Pretty as a red-bird, skip t'-m'-loo!
> Skip t'-m'-loo, my darling!"

And then some one started, "When Johnny comes marching home." It was a good while since they had sung it. The idea of going home was not as constantly in mind as it once had been, but they made out well. Again they recalled their former dreams : how the girls would sing, the boys would shout, the ladies — they pronounced it la-dyes in singing — they would all turn out, and they'd all feel gay when Johnny came marching home.

The next day verified the news. They were to start without delay, and start they did over ground long since familiar, by Mt. Vernon, London, Williamsburg, and Boston, by Marsh Creek and Chitwood, through Scott County and into Morgan. General Burnside accompanied this brigade, and sent his main army by other routes. Carter's brigade was proud to escort the general of the army, and did some brilliant fighting on the way. They marched like the hosts of Joshua, advancing to redeem the land promised to their fathers from the Canaanite. They fought with a fierceness born of their plucky Scotch-Irish blood. They rammed down their bullets with a prayer or a curse, according to the religious experience of the individual; but it all meant the same, and drew a fine bead, and when they pulled the trigger, said Amen. Nothing was able to stand before them. They swarmed through Big Creek Gap. They descended on Knoxville, like the wolf on the fold. They beset Cumberland Gap behind and before, and captured it and all its host. They flowed along the valley of the Holston, like the waters in the freshets of spring, and bore all opposition down before them like a flood. They began their irresistible march on the 20th of August, and rested not until near the middle of September; and then Knoxville, and the river, and the railroad, and the Gap were all shadowed by the Union flag.

There was rejoicing in Knoxville. The loyal citizens of the town welcomed the Union army with heartiest words of good-will. General Carter was appointed provost marshal-general of East Tennessee, with headquarters at Knoxville. Burnside's host began to pass down the valley and across the hills toward Chattanooga, where he hoped to effect a junction with Rosecrans, and join him in another conquest of the still unconquered Bragg. On the 11th of September, Colonel Byrd occupied Athens, and on the 29th, after a skirmish, he entered Sweetwater, which villages lie well on the way to Chattanooga. But before Chattanooga was reached, the Confederate General Williams appeared to the east of Knoxville, marching down the railroad to attack the city. He was repelled; but soon the outposts toward the south were also attacked, and in October Byrd's advance was recalled to the defence of Knoxville, which was endangered by the coming of General Longstreet.

Since the Federal occupation of Knoxville, some slight defensive works had been thrown up about it; but it now became a matter of the greatest necessity that these should be strengthened to oppose the superior numbers of Longstreet and the impetuous dash of his men, before which, thus far, nothing had been able to stand. To give time for this work, the cavalry were disposed to protect the city from approach; and a temporary organization of the mounted men, left without a commander by the promotion of General Carter, was effected, with General Sanders at the head. The men knew Sanders and admired him. He had led some of them in their raid upon the Holston bridge the year before, and they understood his coolness, courage, and determination.   Under his command they fought with enthusiasm.

Longstreet crossed the Holston River below the city, and approached it from the west.   The key to the possession of the city in this direction was an earthwork, which later was named for General Sanders.   This was incomplete when the enemy approached, and time was of the utmost importance to complete it.   A mile west of this work, between the river and the railroad, and covering the road that leads from London, Sanders took his stand on the night of November 16th.

The next morning the Confederate forces moved against this screen of cavalry that thinly shut them out from the city.

" Boys, d'ye reckon we're here to fight, or jes' to sorter skirmish with 'em for an hour or two ? " asked Sam Loomis.

" We're here to fight," said Jack.

" We can't never hold our ground against Longstreet's whole army."

" We're to hold it till they send word that the fort's finished," said Jack.

" I hope they'll work mighty fast then, for this here ain't no army to send out agin Longstreet."

" They hain't no better army to send agin him," replied Jack.

" Man for man, that's so.   But Sanders hain't got but a handful o' cavalry."

" Quit yer jabberin' thar," said old Dan.   " You ast a heap o' fool questions.   Ef Sanders says to hold this hill till the fort is finished, we'll stand here ef hit takes till the pit freezes over."

All that day they held the line. At first the rebels advanced against it with easy and confident expectation of pushing back the cavalry and doing their real fighting at the fort; but as they met with strong resistance, they added to their strength, and renewed the attack again and again. All that day the infantry surged against the line of horsemen, and all day long they were held at bay. Night put an end to the attack, and the weary men rested on their arms.

Late that night Burnside sent for Sanders and for his chief engineer.

"Colonel Poe," he asked the latter, "how long will it take to make those works defensible?"

"I think I can have them done by noon to-morrow," was the reply.

"General Sanders, can your men hold their ground till then?"

"I think so, sir. They can hardly press us harder than they have done to-day."

"Your men are heroes, every one. You shall have every horse and sabre that we have; but we can spare no infantry, for the city must be defended on every side. Hold the line till noon, and we will drive them back."

Poe and Sanders went out together.

"Come with me to my quarters, Sanders," said Poe, "and rest a few hours."

"I will," said Sanders, "for I am weary."

"Poe," said Sanders, "I'm afraid it will take longer than noon to finish that fort."

"I am afraid so, too, Sanders, but I think by that time it will be defensible. But every spadeful of earth that we can add after that hour will make the city that much more secure."

"Of course."

"Sanders, if we are hindered in our work by the artillery firing, do you suppose that you can hold that line past noon?"

"It is murder to hold it for a minute longer than is necessary; but if the safety of the city depends on it, I will hold it until we are forced back, even if it is after noon."

They lay down on the same blanket, and dropped asleep, but soon Sanders was recalled to his command. When the day broke, the attack was renewed, and with evident determination to break the line without more ado. The Union soldiers had made for themselves frail defences of fence rails, and stood behind them, dishevelled and powder blackened, fighting fiercely. Once the rebels pressing down the road with a wild yell broke through the line, and drove the Tennesseeans from their rail pens. Sanders saw the movement, and walked calmly to the place, standing in one of the vacant cribs with half his height exposed to the rebel fire. It was only a moment that he stood alone. Fifty men were at his side in an instant. Jack fired his carbine into the struggling mass of Confederates, and, fixing his sabre bayonet, rushed into the mêlée. The rebels were surging against the rails. Jack drove his bayonet through the shoulder of one of them who was climbing over. Old Dan met in single fight a swarthy Texan who was raising his sabre to strike at Sanders, and when the blow fell, it was on the head of grizzled old Dan, and his sabre was in the Texan's breast.

Hour after hour the men in the fort watched with admiration the unequal contest, and bent their energies anew to the work of completing the fort. Noon came, and still the cavalry, dismounted and fighting hand to hand, held the enemy at bay. Sanders looked at his watch, then turned and scanned the earthwork, and turned to the fight again.

One o'clock, and again he turned and looked.

"They're doing well, boys," he said. "Hold on a little longer."

Two o'clock, and still the fight went on.

"Hold it an hour, boys," he cried, "just another hour, and we will fall back!"

The fight grew more furious. The rebels realized that if they were to reach the fort that day they must speedily break the line. Rallying again they came on with an ear-piercing yell, and broke full on the middle of the line. It wavered. Sanders saw it weakening, and hurled himself into the place that was beginning to break. There was a cheer, and the men rallied to his support. There was a moment of murderous fighting, and then again the rebels fell back; but the gallant Sanders fell at the front, mortally wounded.

It was useless to hold the line longer. The curtain of cavalry that for two days had shut in the city from Longstreet's approach withdrew like the gathering of a scroll, taking their wounded and the body of their leader. "They buried him darkly, at dead of night," that the officers scattered along the line might attend his funeral; and the whole army mourned the death of a hero.

As Jack was turning to leave, he heard a voice faintly calling him from the rail pen next to his.

"Why, Sam," said he, "you're wounded, ain't you? I'm mighty sorry. Come, I'll help you to the town."

"I'm afeard I'm done for, Jack. Look how this arm is splintered. An' see how it bleeds."

Jack twisted his handkerchief around the shattered arm, and helped his friend to the rear.

"Cheer up, ole feller," he said "you ain't a-goin' to die."

"I reckon I hain't good fur much more fightin'."

"I'm afeard not, Sam. I reckon you'll hatter go home an' git sorter 'quainted with that baby that was born atter you enlisted."

It was hard getting him to the rear, but Jack succeeded, and saw him safely in the hospital. That night they told Jack that Sam would recover, but must lose his arm, and Jack went next day to assist the amputation. Something dropped from its quivering fingers when the knife severed it, and Jack picked up, and reverently tucked under the pillow, the pair of little outgrown baby shoes.

The next day Longstreet's hardy soldiers bore down upon the new fort, which by order of General Burnside was named Fort Sanders. Never was there a more determined dash; never was there braver defence. But the lives of the brave men who fell with Sanders had purchased their value in the strength of the place, and Longstreet's hardy men fell back without advantage.

Then ensued a siege, with wet and foggy weather, and no fighting of importance. The other works were strengthened ; but it was confidently expected that the main attack would be made on Fort Sanders. A lot of rusty telegraph wire was procured, and stretched from stump to stump over the ground across which the attack must proceed. Provisions grew scarce in Knoxville, and the garrison must have starved, had not the loyal people above the city, at great risk, floated down provisions to them in the night, which served to provide half rations. Longstreet began to expect that he would capture Knoxville without more fighting, such as had cost him so dear.

But word came to him from Chattanooga, which caused him to hasten his plans. Bragg was not succeeding as well as he had hoped. Rosecrans had been relieved from his command, and Grant had come. Rosecrans had been full of plans for the saving of the Union army, and freely gave them to General Grant, who naïvely remarks in his account of the campaign, " My only wonder was that he had not carried them out." Grant was now carrying them out, and Bragg was by no means happy.

This made it important that Longstreet should have done with Knoxville, and hasten to help Bragg. So on Sunday, November 29, 1863, he began action by pouring upon Fort Sanders his heaviest artillery fire. For twenty minutes the rain of metal continued, and then stopped : and out of the woods there swept the lines of Longstreet's splendid army. The night had been cold ; the morning was dull and foggy. The men got entangled in the meshes of the wire. The guns tore great gaps in their ranks. The musketry poured in its shot upon them. They broke all lines. They ignored all organization. There was never a more splendid exhibition of individual courage than when, disentangling themselves from the wire, those men rose up and pressed on, singly and in squads, toward the fresh clay of Fort Sanders. Water had been poured on the fresh earth. It had frozen thinly. Sometimes the men slipped upon it, and again they broke through. They floundered in the mud of the ditch, but they ploughed their way through. They sank deep in the fresh earth of the parapet, but they slowly made their way up the slope. They fell by scores as they slowly climbed the redoubt, but they came on. They planted their battle flags on the crest. They met the garrison with empty guns and fixed bayonets. They climbed over the dead bodies of their comrades and strove with the gunners for possession of the cannon. But no human flesh could stand before such fire as they received. Musketry belched in their faces. Cannon hurled grape among them at point-blank range. Shells rolled by hand over the parapet exploded among them as they struggled in the ditch. And behind the new wall of earth stood men with fixed bayonets, and courage grim and desperate as their own. Broken and shattered, the splendid fragments of Longstreet's fine brigades fell back, hopelessly repulsed.

A week longer Longstreet sullenly besieged the city. There was no further attack — that would have been murder. But by Tuesday large wagon trains belonging to his army could be seen moving eastward. On the following day troops were seen taking their departure. There was no further move apparent on Thursday, but there was a general indication of discouragement. On Friday night Longstreet withdrew his army from about the city, and the siege was raised.

With great joy the soldiers and citizens hailed their deliverance, and at once communications were opened with Chattanooga. Then they learned for the first time, how a few days previous to their own fierce fight at Fort Sanders, the Union forces had scaled the palisades of Lookout Mountain, and had swept over the slopes of Missionary Ridge, driving Bragg's men before them, capturing their guns, and turning them on the retreating foe. Thus by a double victory East Tennessee was freed from the power of the Confederate government.

A few days later the news of these victories reached Roundstone and Estill, bringing joy and hope. Joe Whitley had taken long to recover from the wound which he received at the battle of Richmond. He was able in time to be about, and to ride back and forth from Estill to Roundstone; but he gained slowly, and after a year of waiting he had reported at Camp Nelson and was honorably discharged from the service. He would be well in time, the surgeons said, but probably never very rugged. So the war was over for Joe, and he moved back and forth between his two homes, the old home on Roundstone, and the home that was to be his in Estill.

"Joe," asked Jennie, "why don't you jes' marry

Becky an’ be done with it ?   You cain’t go to the war agin.”

“We’re waitin’ for Mr. Murray to git home from Andersonville,” said Joe.

But the months passed by, and Mr. Murray did not return, and at length it seemed to all a wise thing for the young couple to be married.

“Becky,” he asked, “what preacher would ye like to have marry us ? ”

“I’d like to have Mr. Fee,” said Becky.

“You mean the abolitionist ? ”

“Yes ; the man at Berea.   He used to come out here an’ preach, an’ stopped here over night once or twice, and pa always liked him.”

“I’d like myself to have him.   But the blue grass folks druv him out, didn’t they ? ”

“He is back,” said Mrs. Murray.   “I heerd last week about him bein’ back, an’ preachin’ over on Horse Lick.   He’s moved back with his wife, an’ they’re at Berea now.   They hain’t started the school agin, but he’s preachin’ thar.”

“Less go over thar an’ git married, Becky.”

“I’m willin’,” said she.

A few days afterward Joe and Becky rode up Berea ridge, inquiring for Mr. Fee.   He was at his home, and had gathered there the children of the neighborhood, and in lieu of any other school, was, with the aid of his wife, instructing them.   He was a small man, but Joe marked him as one who, if a soldier, would go without flinching to the cannon’s mouth.   He had in him that dogged, stubborn courage that makes sometimes the fanatic, and again the hero.   He had shared the early efforts of

Cassius M. Clay, and was still at his work in spite of war and mob. Mrs. Fee came with him to the door. She was a cheery, cordial little woman, with a womanly insight into things, and knew at a glance what had brought the young people.

"You must get down and stay to dinner," said she. "Let's have the horses put out, and we will get acquainted." Mr. Fee greeted them no less heartily, but soon withdrew to his study to finish a tract against the evils of caste distinction; for, slavery having been abolished, he was seeking more worlds to conquer.

The announcement of dinner brought him from his study, and during the meal he talked pleasantly and without bitterness of his experiences, his wife occasionally adding a bright touch to the narrative.

The meal finished, Mr. Fee took his Bible and read the chapter concerning Isaac and Rebecca, and Mrs. Fee interrupted the reading to remark that Rebecca was the name of this bride, whom she believed to be worthy of her name.

It was a simple but impressive marriage service. There was no ring, there was no elaborate ritual. The pledges which they made were few, and the fee was a pittance. But two young hearts went out into life together with a benediction resting on them, and an ideal before them, which they never forgot.

There was something sacred about that ride homeward. The world seemed other than it had been, and in after days they tried to make the rocks and trees appear just as they did that day, but with only partial success. Life was transfigured for them, and the inspiration of that day never wholly forsook

them.   Among the truly happy homes in Estill
County to this day, after years of life, bringing joy
and pain, there is none that is brighter than that of
Joseph and Rebecca Whitley.

"Joe, who is that sittin' on the porch?" asked
Becky, as they came in sight of the house.

Joe looked, and could hardly speak.

"It looks like —" he said.

But Becky with a glad little cry urged her horse
ahead, and had dismounted in a trice, and when
Joe came up she was clasped in the arms of her
father.

Mrs. Murray had prepared her best supper, and
they were sitting happily at the table when there
was a shout at the gate, and they rushed out to
welcome Eph Whitley.

"Home on a thirty days' furlough!" he explained.
"Captain Wilson's home, too, and five of his men.
Gin'ral Thomas gin orders that we was to have a
month off for bein' the fust men on the top o'
Lookout Mountain."[1]

"Did ye take the flag?" eagerly asked Joe.

"The flag! I reckon we did. Hit was the fust
flag on the summit, an' when we waved it from the
big rock on top, hit was cheered by a hundred
thousand men!"

Joe's eyes flashed with excitement, and then grew
dim.   "I wisht Bill could a ben thar," he said.

---

[1] "The following named officers are granted leave of absence for the period of
time set opposite their respective names: Capt. John Wilson, Co. C, 8th Kentucky Vols., 30 days, for gallant and heroic conduct on the morning of the 25th
day of November, 1863, at the battle of Chattanooga, in advancing with five
enlisted men and placing the Colors of the 8th Kentucky Vols. Inft. on the peak of
Lookout Mountain, in the face of the enemy. . . .
"By Command of Major General Thomas."

There are huge tablets in bronze on Lookout Point, telling the valor of regiments able to pay for perpetuating the glory of their deeds on that spot. But the bravest of all those deeds is not thus recorded. One must go to the records of the War Department, or into the mountains of Kentucky, to learn how the flag that first looked down from Lookout Point upon its image in the Tennessee, was that made by the loyal women of Estill County, and borne aloft by Captain John Wilson and his brawny men of the 8th Kentucky. It came home at length with honor, and still is venerated by the women who made it, and the men who bravely carried it, in the battle above the clouds.

XXVIII

Mary Gossett's Baby

ONE day in the autumn of 1863, a woman, passing along Roundstone Creek, stopped at the Whitley gate and asked Cub for a drink. Cub was afraid of her, and ran to the house to call Jennie. Jennie came to the gate with Cub clinging to her skirts.

"Come in," she said, "an' rest a spell."

"I don't guess I'll stop," said the woman. "I'm in a hurry, sorter."

"Come in while I git ye a drink, anyhow."

"I'll put myself level on a cheer a minit on the porch. I'm sorter tard."

"I should think ye would be. Hit's plumb hard walkin'. Did ye come fur?"

"A right smart piece," said the visitor, in a tone that forbade further inquiry.

Jennie brought the water and gave it to the woman, who was evidently greatly fatigued.

"You best stop a spell," said Jennie. "You're plumb used up. We'll have some dinner right soon now."

"Be they ary sojer about?" asked the woman, cautiously.

"Nary one. I don't reckon they'd hurt ye, nohow."

"I dunno. I dunno. But ef they hain't none

here, they won't hurt me. I reckon I'll stop, fur I'm mighty nigh tuckered."

"Take off yer sunbonnet an' make yerself to home," said Jennie. "I'll hurry up the dinner."

"I'll keep my sunbonnet on, right whar hit is," said the stranger, a little resentfully, "an' I don' keer fur no dinner. I jes' wanter rest."

Elizabeth returned soon afterward from the woods, bringing with her the first ripe papaws, which were to serve as a relish for the frugal dinner. Jennie was working in the kitchen, preparing a hoe cake.

"Ma, they's a sorter quare woman settin' in the porch. I just wist you'd go an' see her."

"How d'ye mean quare?" asked Elizabeth.

"I reckon she's all right. She don't act like no fool nor nothin', but she don't seem to be rightly at herself."

"I'll go see," said Elizabeth, and went to greet the stranger. In a moment there were such cries from the porch as brought Jennie in all haste from the kitchen.

"Wy, 'Liz'beth Casey! For the land o' goodness!"

"Well, I never! Mary Gossett! How under the canopy o' heaven did you come here?"

"I—I don' har'ly know how come I here," stammered Mary. "Hit's a sorter long story."

"Don't tell us nothin' till atter dinner," said Jennie. "You'll feel better then."

"I didn't 'low to eat," protested Mary.

"Matter o' cose you'll eat," said Jennie. "I got the hoe cake mighty nigh ready."

"Wall, ef hit don' make no trouble, mebby I will. I *do* feel a sort of gallness in my stummick."

She washed her face without taking off her sunbonnet, and kept it on at the table, though Elizabeth gently suggested its removal.

After dinner, which she ate with evident relish, she offered to help about the work, but Elizabeth and Jennie both objected.

"You hain't a-goin' to do nothin' o' the kind," said Elizabeth. "I'll tell you what you're a-goin' to do. You're a-goin' right into the room an' lay down on the bed an' take a nap o' sleep, while Jennie an' me does the dishes. Then when you git rested, we'll se' down an' have a good visit."

Mary was too weak to protest, and allowed herself to be led to the bed, where she lay down, still wearing her sunbonnet, and soon was fast asleep.

Late in the afternoon Jennie tip-toed through the room on some errand, and the sunbonnet had fallen back, exposing a head that had been totally bald, and was just beginning to show the promise of a growth of hair.

"Ma," said Jennie, "I don't reckon we best to say anything more about her a-takin' off her sunbonnet. She hain't got no hair."

"She useter have," said Elizabeth, "as purty a head o' hair as ever I seen. Don't ye recollec' seein' of her the night o' the Hansons' frolic?"

"I remember now, but I wouldn't a knowed her. Mebby she's had some fever or somethin'."

"I reckon so. An' she's sorter sensitive, anyhow. But she ain't crazy."

Mary slept the better part of the afternoon, and

in the evening, when the dishes had been washed, they
all sat about the fire and waited for her to tell her story.

"You don' think I'm crazy, do you, 'Liz'beth?"

"Not a mite, Mary.   I know you're all right.
But you've been sick, hain't you?"

"Yes.   I've had measles, 'n' had 'em bad."

"That's a pity.   I never did hear o' growed
people a-havin' measles till this war come on.   Then
'pears lack they hain't nothin' too bad to have."

"That's huccum I to hev 'em," said Mary.   "I
got 'em in the army."

"Tell us all about it," said Jennie.

"Hit all begun when Bill jined the army," said
Mary.

"The Union army?" asked Elizabeth.

"No.   The rebel army."

"You don't mean it!   Bill hain't no reb?"

"Yes, he is.   He hadter be."

"Pore feller!   I know he's fur the Union."

"So he was.   But hit was thisaway.   Less see.
When did you leave East Tennessy?"

"Hit was last April* was a year ago —   Spring
o' eighteen an' sixty-two."

"Wall, hit was jes' atter that.   You know Bill
had been a-hidin' out, sorter not wantin' to leave
me — cause I was sorter lookin' to be sick, an' not
well nohow."

"I knowed about that," said Elizabeth, "an' I
'lowed to be thar an' help you through, ef I hadn't
a come off suddent."

"I know," said Mary.   "Wall, the baby come in
July, an' I didn't har'ly reckon I'd ever git up agin.
But afore that, they lef' word for Bill that ef he'd

z

jine the rebs he wouldn't be sent off south, but jes'
enlisted an' sorter kep' about nigh home, to gyard
Knoxville ; but ef he didn't, they layed out to hunt
him down an' send him to Andersonville or Tusca-
loosy, one."

" That was mighty hard," said Elizabeth.

" Wall, Bill had kep a-sayin' ever sence he'd
knowed how I was, says he, ' I'll see ye through,
Polly,' says he — he allers calls me Polly — ' an'
then by that time I reckon the Union sojers'll be
here, and mebby I won't hatter fight, but ef I do,'
says he, ' thar's whar I'll fight,' says he."

" Wall ? "

" Wall, he had a mighty hard time on it, specially
atter the Gov'nor gin out that proclamation orderin'
all able-bodied men inter the rebel army. Bill he
wanted to go north then, but 'peared lack I
couldn't let him. I was a-feelin' mighty bad every
day, an' I sorter had a presentmaint that I wasn't
a-goin' to live through it, an' I baiged him notter
go — "

" I don't wonder," said Jennie.

" Wall, you wouldn't wonder ef you'd a felt as I
felt. Wall, when they sent that word to Bill — "

" Who sent it ? "

" The rebel captain at Rutledge. He was a-tryin'
powerful to git enlistmaints. He lef' word at the
house fur me ter tell Bill he'd hunt him down an'
sen' him south ef he didn't enlist, but ef he did he
wouldn't likely hatter go off at all.

" Wall, Bill come in next even' 'bout an hour
b' sun, an' I tole him, an' Bill he warn't a-goin' ter
do it.

"'I'll go north,' says he, 'an jine the Yanks.'

"But I jes' held to him. 'Oh, Bill,' says I, 'don' leave me now. Go in an' list. What odds is it, anyhow? The Yanks don' know nothin' about us, or ef they do, they don' keer. Jine the rebs, Bill, an' stay till I die!'

"'Ye hain't a-goin' ter die, Polly,' says he sorter tender, an' sorter skeered, too. 'I'm afeard I be,' says I, 'an' who's a-goin' ter keer fur the baby, the baby that's a-comin'?' Bill he sot a-thinkin', an' I was a-cryin'. Says I, 'Oh, Bill, do this, an' I won't never ast you for nothin' agin!'

"Bill he sorter hesitated, an' jes' then they come a noise o' horses a-gallopin' down the road, an' the nex' thing they was three rebel cavalrymen at the fence. Bill he started to run out the back door, an' then he looked back at me an' turned on his heel right in the middle o' the floor, an' come over an' kissed me an' says, says he, 'Don't cry, Polly, I'll do it!' An' he went out o' the front door an' met the sojers at the fence, an' when I come out they was a spreckle-faced feller settin' on one horse, an' he had a sergeant's braid on his coat sleeve, an' he was a-holdin' up his hand fur to show Bill how, an' Bill was a-holdin' up his hand an' a-swearin' to be a rebel. That night was the fust he'd slep in the house sence Aprile; an' the next day Bill went to Rutledge an' enlisted."

"I cyan't har'ly blame ye, Mary," said Elizabeth.

"Wall, Bill was about home mighty nigh half the time then till the Yanks advanced on Cumberland Gap. But then they gethered all the men in and tole 'em to be ready to move. An' then you know the Yanks tuck the Gap — I mean the fust time, was a year ago — an' Bill an' his company was jes' acrost the river from the house, an' expectin' fur to hatter go furder south when the Yanks moved on Knoxville.

"Bill was with me when the baby was borned. You'd orter see him, 'Liz'beth. He's the cutest little feller! Bill named him Jefferson Abraham Gossett. He said the Abraham was fur him an' the Jefferson fur me; fur he uster sorter devil me about me makin' a rebel outen him. But then, as I was a-sayin', when they moved jes' acrost the river I agreed with Bill to signal over ef the Yanks come. An' shore enough, one day down come a rig'maint full hickory, an' stopped an' ast me fur the ford. I tole 'em the way to the upper ford."

"The lower one's a mile nearer," said Elizabeth.

"I know it. An' then I run out an' hung up a red rag, an' then I heerd two guns go off on the other side, an' I know'd that Bill had seed the rag. That's how the Yank's didn't git Bill an' his company. They was gone back into the hills afore the Yanks got thar.

"But the Yanks come back next day, right mad, an' arrested me fur signallin' to the enemy. They made me leave my baby — "

Here Mary began sobbing, and Elizabeth and Jennie cried with her.

"The Yanks hain't much better'n the rebs!" cried Jennie.

"No, Jennie, the *men* hain't, but the *cause* is," said Elizabeth. "What else, Mary?"

"They tuck me to the Gap, an' I baiged 'em to

let me go back; but they said it was me that kep'
'em from baggin' a hull company, an' it was a crime.
They 'peared lack they didn't wanter try me thar,
so they kep' along from day ter day, an' when they
come ter thinkin' o' leavin' the Gap in the fall, then
they sent me ter Camp Nelson on the Kaintuck."

"We know whar it is," said Jennie.

"Wall, thar they was sorter good ter me, an' I
'lowed I'd git to go back, but they said I'd hatter
wait fur orders from Washington, an' I waited month
atter month, an' while I was waitin' I tuck sick with
the measles. I wasn't real strong, nohow, an' I had
'em hard. My hair all —"

She stopped and pulled her sunbonnet tighter and
began again.

"I got most well an' then had a relapse, and was
wuss'n ever. Wall, when I got well the las' time
they didn't gyard me nor nothin' but jes' lef' me
runnin' aroun' the hospital, an' I kep' a-thinkin'
about my baby. He's more'n a year old now ef
he's a-livin'. I reckon they'd all sorter forgot
huccum I thar. They warn't never nothin' said
about it, but they didn't no word come to let me
go, an' I jes' couldn't stan' hit no longer. So two
weeks ago I run away."

They understood it all then, and gave Mary all
assurance of affectionate sympathy. They looked
at Cub, sleeping now, and pitied this poor mother.
They kept her with them two days — she would stay
no longer — and then Elizabeth took her behind her
on a horse — she was so light and frail as hardly to
add to the load — and set off with her through the
woods to the East Tennessee line. It was a two

days' ride to where she left her, and the waters were flowing to the south, indicating that they had passed the watershed which is the boundary between the States. Then Elizabeth took leave of her, and Mary resumed her lonely journey.

"Keep right acrost the headwaters o' the Clinch," said Elizabeth, "an' when ye strike the headwaters o' the Holston, foller down. I don't reckon ye'll find any sojers of ary kind. Ef ye do they won't pester ye. An' God bless ye an' the baby."

XXIX

The Heart of Bessie Granger

SEVERAL months had now passed since Jack had seen Bessie Granger. He thought of her often, and with a mixed feeling of admiration and of wounded self-esteem. But more and more it came to be apparent that their attraction toward each other had been the result of the somewhat unreal conditions in which they had met, and not because of common interests that would have been likely to last.

"I wonder why she wanted to fall in love with such an ignorant fool as me, anyhow?" he often said to himself. But as Jack was young and handsome, and had good sense and some rude graces, and especially as thousands of women as wise as Bessie Granger are constantly falling in love with men less worthy, that question need not have given him great concern.

He wished he was well out of it. He had not said when last he saw her what he had meant to say. The approach of his regiment, the outburst of her passion, and his admiration for her had caused him to be less frank than he had meant to be. He was not sure, when her passion had spent itself, whether her regard for him would reassert itself. She had cast him off, yet had somewhat relented. He had shown her that he was a Union soldier, but had told her nothing of Jennie. He was not sure how far he had seemed to commit himself to Bessie, nor whether he had at all honorably released himself. He did not know whether he was bound to her or not. He wished for nothing so much as permission to march through Murfreesboro, that he might meet her in his own character, with opportunity to be openly honest and have the matter settled.

For as Jack returned to his real self he found, and the months had proved it, that the image of Bessie began to fade out of his heart, and there appeared more plainly another which hers had never wholly obliterated, but like the dissolving view of a stereopticon had all the while been dimly on the screen and now grew in brightness.

Whatever his thoughts in waking hours, it was Jennie that he saw in his dreams. Sometimes he saw her face as he had seen it in freshness and beauty at the Hansons' party, when a look of sincere admiration for him had transfigured it. Then he saw her as he had seen her at the spinning-wheel. Then he saw her as he had never seen her in life, with a look of sad reproach because of Bessie Granger. Then her face appeared as he had seen it in the candle-light when she stood in the door with Cub, on the night of her father's murder. And Cub! Ah, Cub! Dear little fellow, how he loved him, and how Jennie loved him! If anything had been lacking to anchor his affection to Jennie Whitley, and make it certain that he must give up all thought of Bessie Granger, it would have been found in the mutual interest which he and Jennie had in Cub. But he could not in honor offer himself to Jennie till he should again see Bessie. But what if she still loved him? He felt like a thief as he thought of it, and remembered her unquestioning trust and courage on the night of their ride in the canoe, when she had risked her life for him.

Meantime, fortunately, he had duties enough to occupy his thought a good share of the time; and no man could say, whatever Jack Casey's deflection from duty on the one occasion of his meeting with the fascinating Bessie, that as a soldier he was ever otherwise than reliable, constant, and brave.

After the siege of Knoxville, the cavalry and mounted infantry were scattered in detachments through the mountains to protect Knoxville against further assault, and the people against marauding bands of guerillas. Unfortunately, Burnside did not follow Longstreet, or wholly drive him from the State, and bodies of Confederates remained in the eastern counties, greatly to the distress of the people.

Hundreds of Tennesseeans now came in from their places of hiding to enlist in the Union army; and these were organized, as well as possible, into companies and regiments. In one of the companies thus formed, when the list of officers was read, there appeared a name which had received a commission "for gallant conduct on the field of battle," Lieutenant Andrew Jackson Casey.

Jack's office was no sinecure. His men were ignorant and undisciplined. They were well mounted, and most of them lived less than two days' ride away, and began at once to exercise their accustomed freedom in going and coming at will.

"That's what we jined the army for," said one delinquent. "Good heavens an' arth, leftenant, we hain't had our freedom with the rebs hyur. I reckon we kin have it now."

Then not a few of the later enlistments were of men who had been doing more or less fighting on their own account, and had come to enjoy the methods of guerilla warfare. General Carter had not a little trouble because of the depredations of his own troops.

"What have you got in your blanket, there?" asked Jack one day of a raw recruit whom he met coming into camp with his blanket bulging suspiciously above his knapsack.

The soldier sheepishly attempted to evade the question, but when pressed, unrolled the blanket and displayed a beheaded goose.

"Didn't you know they was orders agin committin' depredations?" Jack demanded.

"I hain't committed no depredations," said the man.

"What do you mean? You've ben stealin' poultry."

"No, officer, I hain't. I done hit in self-defence."

"In self-defence?"

"Yessir. I was comin' to-wards camp, along whar the road runs beside the creek, an' I seen this goose an' two others a-comin' down to the warter. I stopped an' looked, an' my mouth sorter wartered for 'em, but thinks I, ' No, sir,' thinks I, ' I'll obey orders.' Wall, I went ter pass, an' blamed ef the hull three on 'em didn't stretch out thar necks an' hiss at me, thisaway, ' Sh-sh-sh-sh ! ' ' By golly,' says I, 'I might stand that ef I was a private citizen, but bein' a sojer of this great an' glorious nation, hit tain't right. Hit's an *insult* ter the Gov'maint.   As long's I wears the blue,' says I, 'no goose shall assault me.'   I jes' hauled out my sabre an' made a clean sweep at him an' cut off his head, an' the rest o' the inemy retreated, an' I fetched this one a prisoner inter camp.   I'll send ye over a slice on her to-night, leftenant."

There was one comfort in it all.   Whenever there was any real fighting to be done, the men could be counted on, and Jack heartily hoped for some. But the winter passed, and the summer dragged itself along, and there was only fighting with straggling bushwhackers.

One day there was brought into camp a man charged with being a rebel spy, and the men, who had a zeal not always according to knowledge, were for hanging him at once.

"Let him have a fair trial," said Jack.   "I'll hang nobody.   I'll send him to Gen'ral Carter."

The man was brought to him, and said,

"Hit's a lie, officer, I ain't no rebel spy."

"No, I reckon not," said Jack, extending his hand.   "How d'you come on, Steph Crowell? They won't hang you this time, I reckon.   I'll pay you now the boot on that horse."

"Ef hit tain't Jack Casey, Solomon was a sutler! Wall, I reckon I never needed a friend much wuss. But by gum, Jack, I wouldn't a knowed you in them shoulder straps.   Yer face looks sorter peculiar, as the ole woman says, but I couldn't somehow reconstruct yer name."

"I'm glad to see you, Steph. You ain't a-goin' to git hurt by *my* men, now I can tell ye."

"Daggoned ef I wouldn't like to be one o' yer men myself, ef hit warn't fur the company I'd hatter keep. I never seed sech a tribe in my life."

"They're all right, Steph, only they don't know right how to do things. Why don't you enlist?"

"Wall, I've had a heap o' reasons, so fur. At fust I didn't know which way the cat would jump. Then I sorter got to helpin' a leetle sendin' information to the Union army, an' I sorter thought I was a-doin' about as much good an' boardin' to hum. I don't like the beds yer give fellers to sleep in, in the army. They hain't no place to throw yer boots under 'em."

This was Steph's method of stating his objection to sleeping on the ground.

"Do as you like. They shan't hurt you."

"Wall, I've found that hit's mighty uncomfortable haltin' between two opinions, as the preacher says, an' the next ossifer in these parts may not happen to owe me any boot on a hoss trade. I reckon I'll enlist."

One day, late in the summer, a paroled Confederate soldier was brought in by Jack's men, who had refused to honor his pass till it had been approved by Jack.

"Sam Marshall!" cried Jack, "you here, and paroled? I didn't reckon you'd ever give a parole."

"Howdy, Jack," said Sam. "I'm mighty sorry to trouble you, but mebby the account stands a little bit to my credit now on that Murfreesboro deal. I wouldn't a ben paroled, but I had to be or go north to prison, one, an' I don't hanker after Camp Morton much more than you do after Andersonville. You know after the battle o' Stone River they took me from the field for hospital service, an' left me behind with the wounded till the Union surgeons could care for 'em, an' sent us back later under a flag o' truce. At Chattanoogy they done the same, only the Union men wouldn't send me back. They noticed my shoulder straps, an' when they found I'd done the same thing before, an' had ben a-fightin' sence, they said I wouldn't hardly rank as a non-combatant. So they was goin' to send me to prison ; but as I had stayed in good faith, they sorter compromised an' said ef I'd go home an' not bear arms agin till the close o' the war, they'd let me go. I reckoned the war was about over, anyhow, when Bragg was defeated there, an' it warn't much to promise. So I promised, an' got my passes, an' went to Murfreesboro an' visited a girl I knowed there an' had promised to marry, an' I got married an' stayed there a little spell, an' then come north with my wife, thinkin' I'd git back home an' go to practisin' medicine agin. It's ben mighty slow travellin', but I got this far, an' I don't reckon you'll stop me now."

"No, your pass is all right. And, Sam, ef you don't mind, I don't see no use now of you an' me not bein' friends. I'm mighty thankful to you fur what you done fur me in Murfreesboro. I don't reckon no harm come of it."

"I'm willin' to be friends. I'd like to have you meet my wife."

" I'd like to meet her.   Where is she ? "

" Back where the pickets stopped me."

" I'll send for her."

In a few moments she arrived, a pretty figure, her face covered with a sunbonnet after the manner of the land.

" My wife, Lieutenant Casey.   Bessie, this officer's an old friend o' mine."

Jack raised his cap and she looked down at him under her sunbonnet.

" I think we've met before," she said.

" Sam," said Jack, " I wish you much joy.   Miss Bessie, you've got as brave a man as they is in Tennessy.   Sam, I reckon I knowed your wife afore you did, an' ef any man has a right to give his blessin' an' to wish you well, it's me, I reckon, an' I do it with all my heart."

The story was told in a word.   Sam had remained some weeks in the hospital at Murfreesboro, and Bessie had resumed the work at which she had proved so efficient, and in which she tried to forget some unhappy memories.   And thus two aching hearts were caught on the rebound.

Among Jack's recruits were several escaped Confederate conscripts who gladly sought enlistment in the Union army.   Some of them were soldiers of fortune, who fought none the less merrily when, as now, they did it with necks in a halter.   Others were heartily for the Union, but had joined the Confederates under extreme pressure.   Of these was his old neighbor, Bill Gossett.   No man of Jack's command was more faithful or courageous.

On this day he was on sentry duty, and noticed

as he met the sentinel whose beat was next to his, on the other side of the road, that his comrade was tipsy and ugly. Several times he tried to pick a quarrel with Bill, but Bill turned each time at the end of his beat without harsh words. At the other end of his walk, as he turned back, he saw the drunken soldier trying to stop a woman who was endeavoring to make her way through the line.

"Halt!" he yelled, "ye cyan't git through without a pass!"

"I don't need no pass," said she. "I'm jes' a-goin' to my baby."

The soldier raised his gun.

"Halt, or I'll shoot!" he cried.

The woman made a rush and went by.

"Halt!" he cried again. "I won't tell ye no more! Halt, or I'll kill ye!"

"Don't shoot!" cried Bill. "Hold on thar!"

He ran toward his companion to stop him, but seeing that he was bent on shooting, and would fire before he could reach him, stopped and levelled his own gun.

"Drop yer gun, you fool," he cried, "or yer a dead man!"

The sentinel looked toward him and then at the fleeing woman, and pulled the trigger.

There were two reports so near together that they sounded like one. The drunken sentinel fell, shot through the heart, and the woman staggered a few steps and fell in the road.

With a cry that was terrible to hear Bill rushed to her side. He pushed back the sunbonnet and kissed the face beneath.

"Polly! Oh, God, my wife!"

"Help!" cried Bill. "Get a doctor! quick! My wife is shot!" But there was no camp surgeon attached to Jack's command. A half dozen men came out at the noise of the firing, and looked for a moment helplessly at each other. Then one started on a run to Jack's headquarters.

Lieutenant Casey was standing before his tent still conversing with Dr. and Mrs. Marshall, when a soldier ran up breathless.

"Leftenant," he called, "they's a woman shot down here!" There was a man shot, also, but no one thought of that as important then.

Jack turned to Sam Marshall.

"I reckon I'll hatter conscript you for a spell," he said.

"Glad to help," said Sam, taking his pill-bags from his saddle.

"Let me go, too," said Bessie. "You both know I can help at such times."

The three hastened to the line together, and Jack gently drew Bill away while the doctor and his wife bent over the wounded woman.

"Badly wounded," said he, "but she may recover."

"She's *gotter* recover!" cried Bill. "Ef they's a God in heaven that's kind and just, my wife hain't a-goin' to die."

"Don't say that, Bill," said Jack.

The doctor and his wife were busy a long time dressing the wound.

"She mustn't be moved for a few days," said he. "Can you set up a tent just inside the lines an' keep her there?"

A tent was quickly brought and set up, and they moved Mary thither.   Bill sat by the cot.   At last she opened her eyes.

"Polly," said he, gently, "d'ye know me?"

"Oh, Bill!" she cried faintly; "is this heaven? Did he kill me?   Whar's the baby?"

"The baby's all right, Polly.   Yer sister Marthy's got him.   An' you hain't killed, an' this hain't heaven; but hit'll be mighty like it when you git well!"

Then the doctor came in and said that Bill must come away and let his wife rest.

"Let me stay, Doc," said Bill.   "I won't say nary word."

"Come away for an hour.   You can go back later.   My wife will look out for her for a spell."

So Bill came away with great reluctance.

"Doc," said he, "hit's a God's blessin' you was here."

"I hope she'll get well, Bill."

"They hain't no hope about it.   She has *obleeged* to git well.   I'm bound to hev her git well."

"Well, Bill, I hope so, but she's a mighty sick woman.   I'm glad you've got confidence.   I'll leave her with you an' Providence."

"Leave her!   Lookye here, Sam Marshall, you ain't a-goin' ter leave her.   No livin' man don't know what I've suffered the las' year.   An' now I swar on a stack o' Bibles a mile high I hain't a-goin' ter take no chances on Polly's life.   God hain't brung her back ter cheat me outen her now.   I'll take my place by the roadside where she fell, an' I swar I won't see ye pass that spot alive till my wife's outer danger."

"Stay, Sam," said Jack. "I'll furnish you a tent an' put up yer beastis, an' send word on home that you're all right. Stay an' doctor Bill's wife an' some sick fellers that I've got here in camp, an' I'll send you on with a escort when you're done."

"I'm anxious to get through the lines," said Sam.

"I'll put you through," said Jack. "I'll send you on when you're ready, an' while you stay you shan't be under no restraint."

"Doc," said Bill, "yer jes' gotter stay."

"I'll talk with my wife," said Sam. "I reckon I can stay till you can get a surgeon from Knoxville."

"I can't get none, I reckon," said Jack.

When Bessie came out of the tent, Jack said, "Mis' Bessie, I'm a-goin' to conscript you an' your man for a spell till that woman's better or wuss."

"I reckon," she replied, "if Sam stays here caring for *your* wounded as long as you stayed in Murfreesboro caring for ours, it would be about an even trade, wouldn't it?"

"I reckon so," said Jack, "an' he shall have as good company as I had there."

So the Marshalls stayed for a week in camp with Jack, and by that time Mary was out of danger. They rode on then to their home, and Bill was given leave of absence and an ambulance to convey Mary back to the little cabin that had been their home, and was to be again. There her sister came and brought the baby, and there daily rode Dr. and Mrs. Marshall, and Mary grew stronger from visit to visit.

One day Jack rode out to see them and his old

friends about home. Bill was holding the baby on his knee, and sitting beside the bed. Mary lay there, pale but happy, the sunbonnet replaced by a little cap that Bessie had made, beneath which was beginning to appear a flaxen tress that reminded Bill of the beautiful hair his wife had worn.

"Howdy, Bill! Howdy, Polly! You're doin' finely. At this rate I'll soon call Bill back to service. That's a fine boy you got there, Bill. Hello, young feller! What's your name?"

"His name useter be Jefferson Abraham," said Bill, "part for my politics an' part for my wife's. We wasn't sure then how the cat would jump, an' we was sorter like the feller that prayed, good Lord, good devil. But we've changed now. So his name is Abraham Lincoln Jackson Marshall Gossett."

"Look out or the name will kill him," said Jack. "Who's the Jackson for? Me, or old Hickory?"

"Both, sorter," said Bill.

"He's storyin'," said Mary. "Jackson's for you."

"And the Marshall's for me," said Sam, just then entering with Bessie.

"Or your wife, one," said Jack.

"Well, it ain't much odds. And seeing it takes the place o' Jeff Davis, it's a good thing to let the name have just enough rebel to save it."

"Stop your nonsense," said Bessie, leaning over and kissing the boy. "The rebel part is the only really good part of the name. That is — Abraham Lincoln is all right, and there are worse Yankees than Lieutenant Jackson Casey. But Marshall is the best name of all for this baby. In fact, it's the only one I should want for myself."

XXX

The Thaw in Nashville

NO campaign of the Civil War was so picturesque, and none has been so widely sung, as Sherman's march to the sea. In its picturesqueness lay a large portion of its military value. When Sherman turned his back on Hood's army, and went south through unprotected territory, carrying out very literally his theory that "War is hell," some one else had to fight Hood.[1] Thomas was at Nashville, and his army, comprised of the ragged ends of three corps, was scattered from the Ohio River to Alabama, and from Virginia to Missouri. To gather these together, and make of them a fighting body, was no small task. Especially was this true of the cavalry, which was given into the charge of General Wilson. By the most strenuous exertion the men were gathered together at Nashville, and an effort was made to provide them with horses, for many of them had been dismounted in their scattered posts, and others had come by rail, leaving their horses behind them.

One day in November, 1864, Lieutenant Jack Casey arrived with his band of tatterdemalions from

---

[1] "Thomas advised [Sherman] against his plan. . . . Grant suggested to him to resume that of following Hood. . . . Lincoln, as he himself said a little later, 'was anxious, if not fearful,' but did not interfere."

— Cox, "March to the Sea," p. 5.

the mountains. To make the command effective, the regiment, which was not full, was doubled by the addition of raw men; and Jack was given command of a company, with orders to impress horses as best he could, and mount and drill his men.

Perhaps there was no part of the war which the cavalry enjoyed more thoroughly than that opportunity of impressing horses. No beast with four legs was safe about Nashville. Farmers reluctantly parted with the animals with which they had hoped to plough their fields the coming season, and men of wealth saw the dust gather on their empty carriages. Governor Andrew Johnson's carriage horses were taken, and the street railroads were left without means of operating their cars.

By rare good fortune, Jack and his crowd struck a town near Nashville, where a circus was in progress. There were a few broken heads among the canvasmen and drivers, but no blood was shed, and in the end Jack's company was all mounted. A long-haired, cadaverous mountaineer secured the trick mule, and rejoiced in the sport which his manifold misfortunes afforded to his companions. Steph Crowell was at his best, on a wonderfully spotted animal, but mourned after the first rain to find that many of the spots were painted, yet found satisfaction in the fact that the horse was intelligent and strong, and still was as spotted as Joseph's coat. Jack secured a remount in a thoroughbred that could leap hurdles. One or two of the venturesome fellows discussed the question of mounting the elephant and camel, and all made the most of their free admission to the show.

Wilson succeeded in mounting a considerable cavalry force, and determined to use that arm of the service, as it had not been used in any previous battle of importance, in the main attack, and not simply in skirmishing and flank movements intended to cover the operations of infantry.

On the 30th of November Hood advanced to Franklin, which two years before had been captured by Rosecrans from Bragg, and there met the Union advance. It was a discouraging thought that so long after what had been thought a decisive victory, the same ground should have to be fought over again. As yet, Thomas had not all his force in hand, and had no intention of fighting, but hoped to withdraw his army to Nashville. Hood, also, intended to defer battle till next day, but his officers were smarting under his rebuke for allowing a Union brigade to escape the night before, and were eager to prove their courage. They proved it, poor fellows, for few battles proved so fatal to officers as Franklin. Twelve Confederate generals and many colonels were killed or wounded there.

At four o'clock, most unexpectedly, the battle began. The line of battle was short, and the heavy fighting was confined within a small area, in the centre of which was a house occupied by a family named Carter. The family consisted of an aged man and his daughters, with a son who was a paroled Confederate soldier. There was another son, a Confederate officer somewhere in the army,—they knew not where. They were assured that there would be no battle that day, when suddenly the firing began, and they were imprisoned in the house in the very focus of the fight. After an hour of fighting the cloud of sulphurous smoke obscured the light so as to seem like an eclipse. For some time still the firing continued, and then, as at a signal, both sides ceased. The silence that ensued was uncanny and fear-oppressing. In that silence, because of the unnatural dark, the cries of the wounded that lay between the armies were terrible to hear.

The battle was soon renewed. The first advantage had been on the side of the Confederates, and in the uncertain light they supposed it greater than it really was. They rushed forward again and again. They continued the fight long after dark. On both sides men fired at the flash of each other's guns, yet sometimes lay down and were safe within reach of each other's bayonets. Two Confederate soldiers made a safe and cosy nest for themselves in the asparagus bed beside the Carter smoke house where they could have shaken hands with the Union soldiers in the trench at the end of it. When morning came, after a night of dread and constant danger, the Carter girls found their brother, the young officer, in the trench behind the house, mortally wounded. There he had lain helpless through the night, almost at the door of the home where he was born.

The Union army fell back under cover of the night, and went into its intrenchments at Nashville, and Hood moved north and beset the city, making his siegeworks strong. Thomas continued strengthening his position; but as Thomas already had intrenchments, it seemed that all the advantage of delay was on the side of Hood. General Grant began telegraphing Thomas to move out and fight Hood, but Thomas waited to increase his force of mounted men. After a week's delay, the weather suddenly turned cold ; rain fell, freezing as it struck the earth, and the ground was a sheet of ice. Thomas was still more reluctant to move ; and to Grant's repeated orders he replied that he would move when conditions permitted.

After nearly two weeks of delay, General Thomas called a meeting of his generals, and asked their advice about attacking the Confederates. He laid before them the urgent despatches of the Secretary of War and telegrams received daily, and sometimes twice a day, from General Grant, at first advising, and later commanding, him to move, and finally threatening him with removal from his position if he did not start at once.

"What is your opinion, gentlemen?" asked General Thomas.

In such councils the lowest officer usually speaks first. But General Schofield, who stood next to Thomas, and would naturally have succeeded him in case of Thomas' removal, first spoke his own conviction, that General Thomas was right. This chivalrous act of Schofield impressed the whole council.

"What do you think, General Wilson? Can your cavalry stand on this ice?"

"General Thomas," said Wilson, "I would not start till there is a thaw, no matter who commands it. If I had my men dismounted behind Hood's present intrenchments, and had to repel an advance over this ice, I would guarantee to do it if my men were armed with nothing more than a basket of bricks."

"Judging from the way they got their horses, I think that your men might be trusted to provide themselves with bricks," said Thomas.

"Or make them, with or without straw," said General McArthur.

"Gentlemen," said Thomas, "I am willing to move when we can move and win. I am willing to resign my command, if that is desired. But so long as I am in command, I cannot sacrifice brave lives without prospect of success. I am weary waiting for a thaw, but it cannot long delay in this climate. As soon as that comes, we will move with vigor, and when we move, we will win." So Thomas waited for five days more. As at Chickamauga he telegraphed " I will stay till I starve," and won the title "The Rock of Chickamauga," so now under circumstances not less trying he proved immovable.

General Grant meant what he said, and followed his last telegram with orders to General Logan to hasten to Nashville and succeed Thomas. Then, becoming still more nervous, he started to command the troops at Nashville in person. Logan had got as far as Louisville, and Grant as far as Washington, when there came a thaw.

In a dense fog, early in the morning of the 15th of December, the cavalry under General Wilson moved through Nashville, and around to the right, to fall upon the Confederate left, while the infantry advanced in a smaller and parallel arc. When the fog lifted at nine o'clock, it was an inspiring sight that the watchers saw from Nashville. The cavalry had made their wide detour, and were tethering their horses to charge on foot ; and the rush was majestic

and irresistible. The rebels had been saying that
the Yankees had brought their weather with them.
This day burst forth from the fog into sudden sunshine, and there was fighting hot enough for the
warmest-blooded Southerner.

By noon the infantry had driven the Confederate
right from its position, and the cavalry had over-
lapped it, using their horses for advances and fighting on foot.

At one time when the cavalry were fighting at a
distance from their horses, a sudden dash of the
Confederates upon their exposed front drove them
back in some confusion. It was only for a few
minutes, but it nearly resulted in the capture of
Captain Casey. Jack had gotten deeply into mud,
and in the retreat was almost overtaken by the
enemy as he was in the act of climbing a stone wall.
At that moment Bill Gossett looking back saw him,
and with Steph Crowell rushed to his relief. In a
deadly fire they ran, pulled him over the wall, and
helping him by both arms, ran with him back to
their companions and horses. Then they mounted
and charged again. While the cavalry moved, the
infantry supported every advance, and the Confederates were mown back as by the swing of a mighty
scythe.

Nothing could have been finer than the deliberate
but resistless dash of the cavalry, unless it was the
splendid charge of Post's brigade up the slope of
Montgomery Hill, with its colonel at its head.
Montgomery Hill was to Nashville what Round Top
was to Gettysburg, and the capture of that eminence
completed the movement on the right.

Then came the dash for the centre, which was undertaken by General Wood, who protested that it was suicide, but who went in as though success were certain, as indeed it proved. Perhaps in no great battle of the war, except Missionary Ridge, was the whole panorama of the fight in so full view; and Thomas watched from the city the progress of every movement. The fight was stubborn everywhere; but the result was the same on all sides. The example of the cavalry in the early morning on the right became the inspiration of each succeeding movement, and when night set in the Confederates had been driven two miles. But they threw up intrenchments during the night, and found the position into which they had been driven, though much less favorable for offensive action, even more advantageous for defence than that which they had abandoned. So both sides bivouacked on the field.

The morning of the second day saw little fighting, as both sides were moving for positions and erecting temporary fortifications. The rebels had made good use of the night in rearing or occupying stone walls, with head-logs above, and the hills which they had taken were steep and easily defensible. The gallant Colonel Post opened the battle with another splendid charge, on Overton's Hill, such as the day before had resulted in the capture of Montgomery Hill, the cavalry still swinging outward from the right. He led his three regiments, one of which was a new regiment of brave colored men, to the very breastworks, and the men fought with great courage; but at the critical moment Post fell, the colored regiment broke under the terrible fire, and the movement failed with a loss of five hundred men.

The thaw had come, indeed, and now it was difficult to move across the ploughed fields that were sticky with mud. But the cavalry wheeled still further, and secured in succession all save one of the pikes by which Hood had approached the city, and by which he must retreat. Then, leaving their horses, with incredible toil they dragged two captured guns through the mud and up a hill to the rear of the Confederate position. Just as this was accomplished in the rear, General McArthur in the front sent word that, unless forbidden, he proposed to order a charge up Overton's Hill, now the key to the Confederate position. It seemed a great risk, but consent was not withheld. McArthur selected McMillen's brigade, which had seen service in many campaigns, and knew its leaders and its duty. With fixed bayonets, and without shot or cheer, they emerged from their intrenchments and went up the slope. Unlike new men, they scattered as they ascended, and their loss, though heavy, was greatly lessened, and no loss dismayed them. Jack's company was just panting up the hill behind, and the guns were slowly coming up through the mud, when he discovered McMillen's infantry silently but resistlessly ascending Overton's Hill.

"Hurry up them guns!" he shouted. Another pull at the ropes by panting men and the guns were brought to the summit, their wheels solid with mud. A moment, and they began to belch their fire and pour their shot into the midst of the Confederates. The rebels looked from the charge in front, to find themselves assailed in the rear. With despairing energy they turned their faces again to the slope, up which with majestic sweep the Union troops were moving, and hopelessly emptied their guns among them. It was useless. The wavy, scattered line seemed proof against their balls. There was a struggle at the breastwork, a hand-to-hand grapple, and then the Confederate flag came down, the Stars and Stripes went up, a mighty cheer arose, and the Confederates broke and fled.

General Wilson gathered his cavalry again and sent them in pursuit. Long after night had fallen they followed the enemy down the pike, until it grew too dark to discern friend from foe, and the pursuers mingled with the pursued.

Riding through the woods, Jack got separated from his men, and in the darkness rode suddenly against another mounted man. Their horses stopped, and the men's knees touched. Each raised his sabre ready for a blow.

"Hold on!" cried Jack. "Let's not strike till we both know who we be. Be you Yank or reb?"

"Reb," said the other. "Who be you?"

"Yank," said Jack.

They paused, and each one's pause might have been fatal; but for some reason, neither could tell why, they did not strike.

"Look here, Yank," said the rebel, "I reckon ef we should fight here in the dark the chances would be about even, don't you?"

"I reckon they would," said Jack.

"Like's not we'd both git killed," he continued.

"I shouldn't wonder."

"Yank, I'll resk my sheer ef you say so, but this sorter killin' don't seem ter me jes' like fightin' in the field. I got a wife an' three babies to hum, an' I don't see no need o' goin' to kingdom come an' leavin' them to some other man to support, an' I'm afeard you wouldn't do it ef you was to kill me. Now, when I swap, and can't quite come ter terms on a bargain, I think hit's a mighty mean man that won't split the difference. What d'ye say, Yank? Shall we fight, or split the difference?"

"Less split the difference," said Jack. And they both rode away.

Thus was won the important victory of Nashville, that saved the North from its last threatened invasion. It was another Gettysburg. While Sherman and his host were marching through Georgia with terror in their front and ashes in their rear, making a desert sixty miles in width from Atlanta to the sea, Hood's army was shattered in his rear. Sherman's success on that march, though multiplied by a score, would have been more than counterbalanced by a failure to conquer Hood. It would have been as pleasant for Hood to march from Cincinnati to the lakes, as for Sherman to march from Atlanta to the sea, and the march would have been quite as picturesque, and the cities quite as combustible.

General Logan heard the news at Louisville, and buttoned in his pocket the orders to relieve Thomas. General Grant heard the news in Washington, and went back to his fighting on the line that had taken all summer, and was to take the winter. And the wreck of Hood's splendid army drifted south, and came north again no more.

XXXI

How Jack Met the Enemy

IMMEDIATELY after the battle of Nashville Jack's command was hurried back into East Tennessee, and his company was attached to one of the regiments of the "Governor's Guard," then under command of General Alvan C. Gillem. This guard was not responsible to the military authorities, but received its orders from self-willed Andrew Johnson, who, besides being Military Governor, held also the rank of General. His troops had just suffered a severe defeat at the hands of General Breckinridge, who made a raid through the mountains while Thomas was fighting at Franklin, and defeated Gillem. Thomas believed the defeat to have been caused by Johnson's assumption of authority over this brigade, and the time was gladly looked forward to when Johnson, having been elected Vice President, would be in Washington, and the military affairs of the State could be managed without so much interference. General Gillem proved an able officer, and the ability which he displayed after the Rebellion, in fighting the desperate Indian murderer, "Captain Jack," and his band of bloodthirsty Modocs in the lava beds of California, he acquired in part in East Tennessee; for a part of the force which he there opposed consisted of North Carolina Indians employed by the Confederate government.

Before Jack arrived, Gillem had retrieved himself
by a raid upon the salt works in western Virginia,
had broken the kettles, filled the drilled wells, one
hundred and sixty feet deep, with twelve-pound
shells and railroad iron, and so devastated the
country as to make himself secure against further
raids from that quarter.

Since the battle of Nashville Jack had gone by
his brevet rank of captain.   He enjoyed leadership,
and his men respected him.   But his heart ached
when he reflected to what the war had degenerated.
The marks of its wicked work were plain in the lives
of many of his men.   There was much necessity of
sending out small bands to kill or capture desperate
men, and for this work men were often selected who
knew the ones they pursued.   Thus it sometimes
happened that soldiers would lie concealed near the
homes of their old neighbors who had become guerillas, and shoot them on their own door-steps as they
attempted to enter their homes.   It was war, no
doubt, but to Jack it seemed like murder.   Already
there was apparent the spirit which continues to this
day in some mountain counties, and manifests itself
in the deadly feuds that now and again break forth.
All these, and many other evils, did the war
bequeath to these communities; for while the war
settled one problem, it precipitated twenty.

Jack had not seen his mother or Jennie or Cub
for many months; but he saw his old home now
and then, and several times called on the Hansons
and the Marshalls.   He had a frank talk with Bessie and told her what she did not already know of
his story, including his love for Jennie.   Bessie ex-

pressed great interest in Jack's sweetheart, of whom she had already heard from Sam, and was sure that she and Jennie would be good friends. Jack hoped so, but he had a feeling of discomfort which he was ashamed to confess. He wondered how Jennie would appear in the eyes of Bessie, nay, though this he never admitted even to himself, he wondered how she would appear to him after having known Bessie. He could not bear that Jennie should suffer by comparison, or seem uncouth in Bessie's sight or presence.

One day while Jack was pursuing a small band of guerillas beyond Bull's Gap, at the head of a score of men, they suddenly found themselves surrounded by a superior force of Confederate cavalry belonging to the force of General Martin, then stationed near Asheville, in the mountains of North Carolina. There was a short, sharp fight. Two of Jack's men were killed and five were wounded. Jack was knocked from his horse by a partly parried sabre-stroke, and when he recovered consciousness, five minutes later, half his command were prisoners with himself and the rest had fled.

Jack's wound did not prove serious, though the blood flowed freely and his head ached severely. He was soon mounted again and disarmed. Two of his most badly wounded men were left at the nearest house, and the remaining seven, of whom three were slightly wounded, were placed on their horses and started on.

It was hazardous, indeed, for so small a body of men to be on a raid so far from home, but both armies had come to take desperate chances, which the roughness of the country favored. Martin's army by this time had in it many companies which rode afar and did a considerable amount of their fighting half on their own account. They were in no haste to turn back till toward night, but bore northward and toward the Holston. Jack knew the way well. A few miles further, and they would pass Sam Marshall's. Six miles across the river, still beyond, was his own home. It was a bitter thought that he would be marched, a prisoner, past the houses of his friends, and perhaps past the door of the house where he had been born, but the thought had in it a gleam of hope.

"Captain," he said to the commander of the rebels, as they rode on, "the second house on the left they's a doctor that's treated some o' my men. He uster be a Confederate surgeon. I wisht you'd stop there a minute and let him tie up my head. It aches fit to kill. Some o' these other men, too, needs lookin' after a little."

The suggestion was accepted by the captain, who had two wounded men of his own ; so they stopped at the door of Dr. Marshall.

"Doctor," said Jack, hastening to forestall any sign of more intimate relation between them, "I reckon you remember me. You've doctored some o' my men."

Sam started so that Jack was alarmed, but recovering himself said, "'Pears like I remember you. Captain — ? "

"Casey," said Jack. "I'm wounded, and so's some o' these other men, and we'd sorter like to have you patch us up so's we can ride on."

"An' don't ye be long about it, nuther," said the Confederate captain. "Hit'll be night right soon now."

"Fetch your wounded men in," said Sam. "I'll do the best I can for 'em."

Sam stepped into the other room to get his instruments. Calling Bessie aside he whispered hastily, "Jack Casey's a prisoner. They'll ride across an' back towards V'ginny. I'll keep 'em here as long's I can. You hurry ahead an' warn his friends to find some way to capture him back come night."

No other word of recognition passed between Jack and Sam. There was no opportunity for conference, no chance of escape that suggested itself. But, unknown to Jack, while Sam was binding up his head, Bessie was saddling a horse in the barn and riding by a roundabout way toward the Hansons'. She tried to think what to do, whom to tell. There were so few men. There was so little that could be done. She did not want to cause a fight. She knew that her husband could not fight on either side. What was done must be done by strategy. It was hardly worth while to tell any one here. The soldiers, if they crossed the river, as they were about to do, would pass the Hanson house a half dozen miles away, and it would be toward night when they arrived there. She would hasten on there and together they would form a plan. But before she came to the Hanson house she passed Jack's old home. It was closed now, and had been for two years, and things looked desolate enough about it. But stay, there was smoke issuing from the chimney. The door was open. What could it mean? She gathered her reins to hasten by, but a sudden thought came, and she turned toward the house.

An hour later the Confederate soldiers with their prisoners came down the road. Jack's head was bound up with needless care, and the doctor had given him many words of caution in the hearing of the captain, making the wound seem fully as serious as it was, and had warned him against too hard riding. Jack looked out from beneath his bandages at the home of his childhood. Dreary as were its surroundings just then, its roof had never looked so inviting a shelter as it did that day. The short day was drawing to a close. They would ride, he felt sure, all night; for the captain well knew that the escaped soldiers would bring after him a much larger force by the break of day. It was hard lines riding past one's own door, wounded and a prisoner. And his mother, it would be long before she would know. Jack gave a yearning look at the house as he approached it. Then he rubbed his eyes and looked again. It could not be! And yet it was so! The smoke was curling lightly from the chimney, the door was ajar, and there at the fence, where she had stood the day he left for the war, was his mother! Before he had time to think twice, Jennie Whitley came from the house with a panful of hot corn pones.

"Howdy," said Mrs. Casey, addressing the captain. "Heerd you was comin', an' reckoned you'd think it was 'bout supper time."

"Howdy, mam," said the captain. "You're mighty good. I hain't had no sech kindness afore fur many's the day. You mus' be Confed'rate?"

"Don't ye ast me no questions an' I won't tell ye no lies. But I've fed more'n one rebel afore, an' more'n one Yank, too. Ef ye wanter talk politics, ye ken jes' go on. But ef ye want some good hot corn dodgers, thar they be, an' they's more in the oven bakin' an' some hoe cakes on the griddle."

"We hain't got time to stop fur them that hain't baked, but I'm mighty glad to take what you got baked."

"'Twon't be long till I'll have some more. I want 'em to go 'round ef I feed any on ye. Got some wounded men, hain't ye? Ye best let them git down an' rest while the balance on ye eat. Don' you alls want to go in an' lie down a spell while these men eats a snack?"

"I'd like it mighty well," said Jack. "My head aches right smart. I don't want nothin' to eat, but I'd like to rest."

"We cyan't stop long," said the captain; "but you men that's wounded mought go in an' lay down about a minute. I reckon we won't lose no time in the end ef you rest."

The men who had tasted the corn pones wanted more, and those who had had none were eager for a share. Elizabeth knew well that if she got them halted, they would not get away for a good half hour, and meantime it was growing dark. The two wounded Confederates went in with Jack, and one also of his own men. The others were less severely injured, and did not care to lie down. A half dozen soldiers carelessly guarded the doors, and ate the hoe cakes which the women gave them. The two wounded Confederates threw themselves across the bed in the living room, and the Union soldier sat in a chair by the fire. Jack entered the room, and there was Bessie at the bake-oven.

Jennie followed the wounded men into the house and said to Jack, "You'd best lie down on the bed in the loft. I'll go up an' see if everythin's ready."

Jack climbed to the loft and she followed him.

"Get off yer cloes," she whispered, "an' git inter bed. Be ready to put on yer mother's cloes when she comes. You'll hatter give her that bandage, too!"

She hastened down, and Jack quickly obeyed. He could hear his mother and the younger women below talking cheerfully with the soldiers, and foiling every suggestion that they must go on, with promises of more corn bread. And what with the Dutch oven baking pones, and the two griddles making hoe cakes, there were always some nearly done. The girls chatted and laughed with the soldiers about the door, and they were neither very vigilant nor in haste to go. And the dark came on apace. A half hour had passed, and all the men were fed. Then the captain called for the wounded men to come out. Bessie and Jennie helped the three below to mount, while Elizabeth ascended "to see how the pore feller above was gittin' on." A moment, and she had removed her dress, and in another she was dressed in Jack's trousers and coat, and was wrapping her face with the bloody bandage. Jack meantime had gotten into her dress, and was tying her sunbonnet over his face. Then they descended the ladder together. The girls at the door diverted the attention of the soldiers, starting toward the fence and drawing after them the already mounted guards, while Jack helped his mother to mount, and they rode away in the gathering dusk.

Jack stood with the girls at the door and watched the procession ride off. There was no suspicion of a ruse, and no investigation. The captain was in haste to gain a few miles before complete darkness fell. Soon they were out of sight, and Jack knew that if they could go a half dozen miles before they found their mistake, they would never think of returning. Then Jack turned to Jennie. "How did you come here?" he asked.

"We come yistiddy," said Jennie. "Your ma wanted to look atter some things she left here, an' she'd got anxious not hearin' from you in so long. So the corn was all husked an' the way was safe, we reckoned, an' we lef' Cub with the neighbors an' come over."

"And to her, young man, you owe your escape," said Bessie. "The plan was Jennie's. I couldn't think what to do, and she thought it all out. She offered to be the one to take the ride, but your mother insisted that it was best she should go instead. But the credit of it belongs to Jennie. You ought to love her with all your heart."

"I do," said Jack, fervently. "I do love you, Jennie! God bless ye!" Bessie had taken Jennie's hand, and now took Jack's and put them in each other's, and Jack drew Jennie to him.

A half hour later Dr. Sam Marshall came over in haste with a half dozen neighbors whom he had collected. He waited only long enough to applaud the scheme, and to command Jack to go to bed, and then he rode on with the men to meet Mrs. Casey. The rest waited in anxiety, but without much fear. It was toward morning when they returned, and Mrs. Casey was in high glee over her success. The exchange of prisoners had not been discovered, when, about midnight, the captain ordered a halt for rest. Then she rode up to him and said, " Cap'n, ef you don' mind, I b'lieve I'll go back now."

The captain was too much surprised to speak.

" That was my boy, Captain, that wounded officer. I reckon I kin keer fur him better'n you kin. An' you hain't got no use fur me. I'm only a pore ole woman."

The captain started to swear, and then changed his oath to a laugh. " You fooled us mighty nice," he said. " An' that hoe cake did taste mighty good. Your boy, was he? Wall, I don't blame ye. I only wish that I dast let some o' my men go back. I'd send ye under escort."

But her escort met her a few miles back, and conducted her home with triumph, and the dawn broke on a happy household.

The Marshalls waited till daylight and for breakfast before leaving.

" I got enough left fur breakfast," said Elizabeth, cheerfully. " I had jus' laid in a week's supply from the Hansons. I 'low I'll hatter go over agin afore dinner. I didn't look fur so much company."

" You always treat folks well, Mis' Casey," said Sam. " You've fed me here afore, you remember."

" Yes, I thought o' that first thing when you an' the men met me this mornin'. I reckon ye don' bear me no gredge fur talkin' about shootin' ye?"

"Nary bit. I'd druther not look inter the bar'l of a gun in your hands agin, though."

"To think," said Bessie, "that Sam should helped bring Mrs. Casey back, and Jennie and I should have shared in rescuing Jack. But Jennie deserves the credit of the plan."

"She deserves credit for a heap more," said Mrs. Casey. "Did ye hear, Jack, about her capturin' eleven men?"

"No," said Jack, "but I could believe it. I know she's made *one* prisoner — that's me. How was it?"

"You needn't never want to break away," said his mother. "It was when Kirby Smith was retreatin' from Kaintuck. We hadn't no warnin' the rebels was a-goin' no more'n we had that they was a-comin'. I was up at Galloway's, nussin' little Bill that had the fever, an' Jennie was alone. There come a squad o' eleven rebels down the road about an hour b' sun, an' come in an' tuck possession. They run down the chickens, an' killed seven on 'em, an' ordered her to cook 'em."

"You needn't tell about that, mother," said Jennie.

"Yes, tell it. We all want to hear," said Bessie.

"Sartin I'll tell it, fur it's Gospel truth. Jennie told 'em to go inter the room an' se' down, an' she'd cook 'em supper. While she was a-cookin', they ripped up the new hit-an'-miss carpet for horse blankets."

"That was what made me the maddest," interrupted Jennie. "Atter sewin' all them rags, an' mother a-weavin' of it — twenty-eight yards of it!"

"They'd stacked their guns by the door that leads inter the kitchen," continued Mrs. Casey, "an' when Jennie took them in their supper, an' got 'em all to eatin', she'd keep passin' through with somethin' or nother, an' as she went back every time she'd take a gun, an' putt it in the kitchen, till she'd packed all but two on 'em away. Then she tuck one gun, an' pinted it at 'em, an' ordered 'em all to surrender. One man jumped at her, an' she shot him through the shoulder, an' then grabbed the other gun. The rest didn't follow, but all kep' still, an' she gyarded 'em till I got home. Then we both stood gyard over 'em till mornin', an' then we marched 'em up to Cap'n Ben Bailey's, an' he an' some o' the home gyards tuck 'em to Cap'n Bright of the 23d Kaintucky that was campin' over towards Wild Cat. We kep' the horses in the Holler. We've got two of 'em — the two we rode here. The cap'n said she was the pluckiest girl in Kaintuck."

"So she is," said Jack. "And Sam, how does it feel to be on the side o' the Union?"

Sam's dark face flushed just a trifle. Then he said, "I b'lieve the South had a right to secede as much as ever I did. But I b'lieve we was fools for doin' it. I ain't a-goin' to fight ary side now, but the sooner it's over, the better."

"The end is a long time a-comin'," said Jack; "but they's just one way for it to end."

"You're right," said Sam, "we're outnumbered. We've got no show. The North has more men than we, without takin' a man from north o' Mason and Dixon's line."

"What d'ye mean?" asked Jack.

"I mean the furriners in the Yankee army, an' the Southern men, black an' white, make a bigger army than the hull rebel army. Man for man, the South has got the best army, an' we've showed the best generalship over an' over. But it's got to end sometime."

"I wisht it would hurry up and end," said Jennie.

"And so do I," said Bessie; "but it makes me sad to think of our poor Confederacy. But see, Sam, it is light, and we must go."

XXXII

The Last Fight

WE see some things more plainly at a distance. It is now apparent that the Confederacy was doomed from the day that Grant captured Vicksburg on the Mississippi, and Lee's heroic army fell back from Gettysburg; and that the 4th of July, 1863, gave the country a new and perpetual reason for the celebration of the national holiday. But that fact was not so plain at the time. To the end of 1864 it was uncertain to thousands how the war would terminate. The Knights of the Golden Circle were strong at the north. Two peace movements — one led by Horace Greeley, and one involving direct conference with Jefferson Davis, and between President Lincoln and Alexander H. Stephens — had but recently been concluded, with no readiness on the part of the South to concede the victory. A powerful political party affirmed that the war had been a failure, — a statement often quoted for partisan effect, but which deserves attention now for its historic value only. The repeated calls for troops had become burdensome. There was determined opposition to the draft. President Lincoln at one time shortly before the election expected to be defeated. Thousands of sore and weary hearts were praying for the war to cease before the plough to which the Government had put its hand, and from which it could not look back, should have driven its hot share deeper into the quivering, bleeding heart of the nation. To many, after four years of fighting, the end seemed much farther away than it did at the beginning, when ninety days' enlistments were considered ample.

This inability to discern the approaching end of the struggle was particularly true in the mountains. There was no outlook. There was only the grim reality, the poverty, the bloodshed, the march and countermarch, the interminable chess-play and see-saw of moving bodies of men, and the sorrow that reached in time its limit of suffering. Not till the very end of the war were these people relieved, for whom the first movement under Nelson was undertaken in 1861. When the armies went the bands of marauders were, if anything, worse, and when the Union army came it was a comfort, but also a sore trial.

Jack's wound proved not to be troublesome. He remained at his old home a fortnight with his mother and Jennie, and the Marshalls came over every day. There was genuine love-making now, between Jack and Jennie, and Sam and Bessie gave appreciated but needless aid and encouragement. Jack found that Jennie seemed more lovely and sweet, even beside Bessie Marshall; and Bessie and Jennie became the warmest friends from the start.

It was with a sinking of heart, then, that Jack went back to duty. The war had grown irksome. He hated the raiding and wanton destruction of property and life which had now become its main occupation. He longed to see the end of it and be with Jennie and his mother and Cub. So it was with little relish that he heard the call for "boots and saddles" one day in March, 1865. General Stoneman had ordered General Gillem to advance into Virginia and North Carolina. So, ride they must, and did. They rode to Morristown, where each man received five days' rations and four horse-shoes, and then they took the road.

Gillem advanced along the line of the railroad, tearing up the track, meeting only small bodies of Confederates and easily defeating them all. He met nearly as many deserters as soldiers, and the soldiers captured were paroled on the field. Up into Virginia, almost to Lynchburg, his men continued on their tour of destruction, then turned south into the Old North State.

On the 2d of April they crossed the Yadkin. From here on the camp was thronged with colored refugees. There are few negroes in the mountains, and it was a novel sight to most of the soldiers to see them in such swarms.

The colored men were jubilant over their new-found freedom. At night they would sing in camp:

> " Wake up, snakes, pelicans, and 'sesh'ners !
>   Don' yer hear 'um comin',
>   Comin' on de run ?
>   Wake up, I tell yer ! Sit up, Jefferson !
>   Bobolishion's comin',
>   Bob-o-lish-i-on ! "

The soldiers were cheered by the songs and contagious vivacity of the jubilant freedmen, but found them in their way when they came to march. They were a menace, also, in case of an attack, and the soldiers needed all their rations. So they sent the freedmen across the mountains, well guarded, into East Tennessee, where many of them were promptly enlisted in the Union army.

At Greensboro, to which place Jefferson Davis was following them, there to establish for a few days the ghost of the Confederate government, they met with little resistance, but destroyed large quantities of stores. It was pathetic to see the joy of the people at the sight of the flag. Even on such a crusade of destruction, they welcomed it, where Jefferson Davis, fleeing south just behind it, was received a few days later with cold indifference.

At Salisbury, Statesville, Mocksville, and Lenoir they repeated their programme — a resistless dash that bore down the faint opposition, and then the destruction of railroads, factories, and all public, besides not a little private, property.

At Charlotte, where the fugitive President of the Confederacy still was hard behind them, finding for himself and escort only one hospitable roof, they destroyed thousands of arms, $15,000,000 of Confederate money, and medical stores that had cost $100,000 in gold and were needed by both armies; and the pity of it was, that, had they known it, the war was already over. But they rode on, knowing only that there was still fighting and destruction before them, and turned to attack the force of General Martin at Asheville.

Martin was supposed to have three thousand men, but on March 10th he could find only one

thousand seven hundred and forty-five of them.
They had had no pay for nineteen months. They
were in rags, and, while just now they had food,
there were times when they had been near to starving. The Confederates saw more plainly than the
Union soldiers how near was the war to ending, and
now of Martin's force there were only five hundred
left. These had fortified Swannanoa Gap, and
with four cannon prepared for a vigorous defence.
Gillem saw that he could not take it without great
loss. Leaving one brigade before the Gap, he
started with the other, forty miles south. On
Sunday morning, April 23d, he captured Hender-
sonville with three hundred men, and turning north
again on the other side of the ridge, by three o'clock
in the afternoon he was in the rear of Martin's
position, in the valley of the Swannanoa, and between him and Asheville. The men were in high
spirits. They had ridden sixty-nine miles around,
and had turned the Confederate position. They
advanced to the attack with all the spirit of resistless
dash, which for a month had known but one issue.
It was a beautiful Sunday, and the earth was waking
to the life of Spring. And neither side knew how
two weeks before, on Palm Sunday, Lee had surrendered to Grant, nor yet how Good Friday had
seen the nation's crucifixion in the assassination of
Lincoln, and Easter the hope of a nation arising
from the tomb of four years of death. The war
was never more real, and never stretched out more
interminably into the future, than on that morning
when Gillem's cavalry formed to attack Martin in
the now famed " Land of the Sky."

The bugles blew the charge, the men struck their spurs deep. The jaded horses gathered themselves for a rush, and then was given the order to halt.

"The white flag! They surrender!" said General Gillem. "No, it is a flag of truce. Captain Casey, go forward and meet it."

Jack rode ahead, holding above his head a handkerchief that had once been white, and met in the road the captain who had captured him but a few weeks before. They exchanged friendly greetings, cut short by more important matters. Then Jack turned his horse suddenly and rode back at a gallop. He could hardly keep from cheering all the way.

"Johnston has surrendered to Sherman!" he cried. "They hain't got official news yet, but they'll know by mornin'. They want an armistice till then, and General Martin wants to meet General Gillem then in person."

"I will meet him in person to-morrow morning," said General Gillem, "and will accept his surrender on the same terms that General Sherman may have extended to General Johnston."

Jack rode back with the news, and the two armies settled down in sight of each other to spend the remainder of that Sabbath in peace: a peace, thank God, that never has been broken! There was visiting along the picket line, and agreement back and forth that this meant the end of the war. And they waited the confirmation of the news.

It came at eleven o'clock that night. Johnston had indeed surrendered. More than that, two weeks that very day, Lee had laid down his arms. The Confederacy was dead. The war was done. The word passed down the line and the men woke, rubbing their eyes, and heard the news and cheered. The rebels knew the meaning of the cheer that broke thus the silence of the midnight, and echoed it back again in the rebel yell. They, too, were glad that the war was done, and their yell was a glad one; but oh! there was sadness in it, too! And a few weeks before that yell had rung out so defiantly, so cheerily, so bravely!

There was no more sleeping that night. They kindled up the camp-fires. They shouted and danced. They hugged each other in their joy. The rebel fires were burning brightly, too. The Swannanoa valley was having a midnight illumination. After a while some one started to sing. The song started on the Union side, but the rebels took it up, "When Johnny comes marching home." It had been long since they had sung it, and it took on a new meaning there in the mountains about Asheville that Sunday night.

"Boys," said Jack, "they want to sing with us. Let's sing 'Dixie.' We're Southerners, too, the most on us, an' we can all sing 'Dixie's land is the land I was born in.'"

So back and forth between the armies echoed the song,

> "In Dixie's land I'll take my stand,
> To live and die in Dixie."

There was silence then for a little while, and then from the rebel side there came the strains of another song. The Union soldiers listened a moment with dim eyes and then caught up the air. And so at midnight, not far from where their ancestors had fought at King's Mountain under Shelby and Robertson and Sevier, they plighted their troth anew and sang their devotion to the united nation :

> " Land where my fathers died,
> Land of the Pilgrim's pride,
> From every mountain side,
> Let freedom ring ! "

Secretary Stanton repudiated the terms of Sherman's agreement with Johnston, and Johnston's surrender had to be made on other terms. But long before Gillem and Martin knew of the decision at Washington, their armies had separated in peace. The two armies met in friendship that Monday morning, and parted brothers. Martin gave Gillem three days' rations for his men, and Gillem rode back to East Tennessee, and let the rebels go home when they got ready. And they were ready very soon.

XXXIII

The Flag and the Fiddle

"MOTHER, mother! Have you heard the news? The war's over!"

Jennie Whitley rushed into the kitchen breathless on her return from the post-office.

Mrs. Casey stood with her hands in the mush, preparing the corn pone for the baker.

"Be ye right sure, Jennie? I can't bear to believe it an' be disappinted."

"They hain't no manner o' doubt of it. Lee's surrendered, and so's Johnston, and their armies is bein' paroled and sent home."

Mrs. Casey forgot that there was mush on her hands. She raised them to heaven with a cry of joy, and then threw them about Jennie, and the women wept; while Cub, who was now a boy of seven, and knew his spelling-book through, looked on with a sense of superior dignity at this distinctively feminine weakness.

Not a day passed after that without inquiry and anticipation of a return of friends. One by one the soldiers who had enlisted from the Holler began coming home, some well and happy, some with empty coat sleeves, some weak and maimed. Alas, some never came!

One bright day in summer, when the Holler was

all glorious with the many shades of green of the trees upon its slopes, and the soft gray of the rocks upon its mountain crests, and the corn was in tassel in its valley, and the creek was rippling in the sun, and the Sinks were humming a soft, low song, and the mocking-birds were busy in the apple trees, and the woodpecker was tapping on the tall pine stump in the deadening, a cavalcade came through Oxyoke Gap, and down the road, and over the bottom, and halted at the gate. Jennie and Elizabeth knew the riders from afar, and ran to meet them at the creek. The horses came splashing through the ford, and would have stopped to drink, but the riders urged them on, and the two men dismounted at the stile blocks; and none of them could speak for joy, but Elizabeth wept in the arms of her son, and Jennie Whitley was sobbing on her brother's neck, and Cub looked on in wonder.

"This hain't much like sojers," said Jack, wiping his eyes with the back of his hand; "an' say, Eph, you mighty nigh forgot Marthy."

Eph turned apologetically and helped Martha to dismount from the spotted steed which Steph Crowell had captured at the circus, and had loaned for this occasion.

"Why, Marthy Hanson," said Jennie, "I'm plumb ashamed o' myself. I'm right glad to see you. 'Light, an' come in."

"She ain't Marthy Hanson no more," said Eph, chuckling. "I've fetched ye a sister."

"I wouldn't ast fur no better sister," said Jennie. "I'm awful glad, Marthy. When did ye git married?"

"Last Sunday week," said Eph. "I was sorter triflin' an' in the hospital at Nashville fur a week, an' when I got out, the reg'maint had come back ter Kaintuck an' ben discharged. Jack had jes' ben mustered out at Knoxville, an' I went thar an' met him, an' Marthy come an' met us thar. Parson Brownlow — he's *Gov'nor* Brownlow now — was back in Knoxville spendin' Sunday, an' we jes' walked up an' got married."

"Jes' think of it, Marthy!" said Jennie. "Married by the Gov'nor o' Tennessy !"

"We'll soon have another weddin'," said Jack, "an' I ain't a-keerin' much whether it's a gov'nor does it, or just a common preacher; but I'm mighty p'tic'lar about the girl," and he took Jennie in his arms.

It was already decided that Jack and his mother should make their home on Roundstone, and Jack soon began preparations for the building of a new house just up the creek from the Whitley's. It was a merry time, the day of their raising, as the Holler well remembers, and the soldier boys came out, and neighbors gathered to honor the young couple who there were to begin life together. The logs had been hewed and hauled, the shingles had been split, and the puncheons had been shaved; and the house, as all the Holler knows, was raised and roofed and floored, all in a single day. There were friends from near, and friends from afar, and Joe and Becky Whitley came from Estill, and brought with them a pole, with one end carefully wrapped.

Steph Crowell was there with his fiddle, declaring that he felt so jealous of Jack that he wouldn't a

The Flag and the Fiddle.   Page 391.

come, but he 'lowed that was the only way to git his pied horse back, and being thar, he reckoned he mought as well make the best on it.

Sam and Bessie Marshall were there, and Sam was foremost in the work of the raising, and Bessie and Martha and Becky decorated the bare logs of the new house with festoons of ground pine and bunches of holly and flowers of early autumn. They made a bower where the fireplace stood, and Becky carefully undid Joe's long bundle, and draped above the bower the flag of the 8th Kentucky.

The work of raising was over. The supper was waiting in the yard. The bonfire was ready for the lighting. The men washed themselves in the spring-branch and prepared themselves for appearance in polite society by putting on their coats, and gathered in the house and about the door. Then Sam and Bessie and Mrs. Casey and Cub stood on one side, and Joe and Becky and Eph and Martha on the other, and Jack and Jennie took their places in the middle. The girls had planned it together, and the result was a very pretty one. Old Parson Nesbit stepped to the front, and Jack and Jennie were married beneath the folds of the flag that first ascended Lookout Mountain.

The service was simple, but impressive — every bit and grain as good, so Jack asserted, as if the Governor had performed it. There was a moment's pause after the prayer, and Jack and Jennie were still standing, hand in hand, when Bessie led Cub forward, and placed a hand of his in each of theirs, and so doubly were they united.

Then came the supper and the pine-knot illumination and the merry-making that lasted until midnight. They danced a Virginia reel by the light of the moon and the pine-knots, and Jack led with Bessie in the first set. They played "Skip t'-m'-loo," and Sam pronounced the bride to be " Pretty as a red-bird," as indeed she was. And the great sweet gum tree that grows before the door, lighted up by the flickering glare of the torches, was glorious in all the wealth of its autumnal foliage.

The minister stayed to supper, but left before the dancing, and thereby showed his discretion. As Jennie had insisted that no stronger drink be served than a delicious sarsaparilla beer of her own brewing, there was no drunkenness and no quarrelling. There was never a happier wedding on Roundstone than that of Captain Andrew Jackson Casey, in his faded suit of army blue and his shoulder-straps dingy with service, and Jennie Whitley in a dress of her own spinning, standing under the flag, where they both had earned the right to stand. And so the tale ends, as indeed it ought not, with the heroine, and not the hero, in homespun.

They went to work in the stony Holler, with its thin soil and its rocks and stumps, to dig an honest living from the grudging earth. The war had left all hearts sore. To whom did the war mean as much as to these people, whose whole horizon it covered, and whose calendar to this day begins with that portentous event, which has cast all preceding time into one prehistoric reminiscence? The cares of their daily life soon occupied their minds and hands. They split out new rails and made fences where the old ones had been used for fuel. They turned to the fields that had grown up to sedge and sassafras, and broke them anew with the hillside plough. They "made" annually their "little crap o' corn," cultivating it with the bull-tongue plough, and with hoes whose every stroke rang on the stones of the hillsides. They brought home with them a few horses to replace those that had been stolen by the armies, and little by little made good the numbers of their small herds of sheep and hogs and cattle and poultry. They lived over in each day the external features of the day preceding, with its common round of petty duties. They made their visits to mill or to meeting, and to neighbors up the creek or down. And that is all.

They are still there, living their commonplace lives. They are older, now, and have children and grandchildren, who listen almost with incredulity to the stories of a time that seems so remote and so strange. They seem to themselves, sometimes, to be talking about other people, when they describe those thrilling incidents in their own past. They have long since forgotten, if they ever suspected, that they once showed any elements that were heroic. They do not know, and the world has yet to learn, that in the days when our nation's fate hung trembling in the balance, the scale was in their hand, and they held it without faltering for the Union. They will never know that they were heroic; but their country ought to know that beneath many a coat of homespun in Roundstone Holler there beats the heart of a hero.